The Beginner's Quilt

The Beginner's Quilt

WANDA E. BRUNSTETTER

YOU are the reason we do what we do here at Barbour Publishing. We promise that we will always use our God-given talents to produce content with you in mind—and that we will remain biblically faithful, no matter what.

Thank you for being the heart of our business.

Print ISBN 979-8-89151-159-0
Adobe Digital Edition (.epub) 979-8-89151-160-6

Unless otherwise indicated, all scripture quotations are taken from the King James Version of the Bible.

All German-Dutch words are taken from the Revised Pennsylvania German Dictionary found in Lancaster County, Pennsylvania.

This book is a work of fiction. Names, characters, places, and incidents are either products of the author's imagination or used fictitiously. Any similarity to actual people, organizations, and/or events is purely coincidental.

No medical advice in this work of fiction is intended as a substitute for the medical advice of physicians. The reader should consult a physician in matters relating to their health, particularly with respect to any symptoms that may require diagnosis or medical attention.

For more information about Wanda E. Brunstetter, please access the author's website at the following internet address: www.wandabrunstetter.com

Cover Design: Kirk DouPonce, DogEared Design

Cover Model Photographer: Richard Brunstetter III

Published by Barbour Publishing, Inc., 1810 Barbour Drive, Uhrichsville, Ohio 44683, www.barbourbooks.com

Our mission is to inspire the world with the life-changing message of the Bible.

Printed in the United States of America.

Dedication

In loving memory of my grandmother Matilda Thiel,
whose special quilt remains in my family.

Every good gift and every perfect gift is from above,
and cometh down from the Father of lights,
with whom is no variableness, neither shadow of turning.

James 1:17

Prologue

1967
Shipshewana, Indiana

DIANNA BONTRAGER PACED FROM ONE end of the living room to the other, stopping only to glance out the window at the rain shower that had just begun.

"Oh no—not again," she muttered.

"What's wrong?" her husband, Philip, asked from across the room, where he sat reading the latest issue of *The Budget Newspaper*.

"Would you believe it's raining again? For goodness' sake, we've had more than our share of rain this spring, and it makes me long for the hot weather of summer."

Philip left the paper on the chair and came up behind her. "Is it really the rain bothering you, or is there something else on your mind that has you in a sour mood?"

Dianna folded her arms and groaned. "You know me too well, don't you, Husband?"

He chuckled and slipped his arm around her waist. "*Jah*, but then what do you expect after being married to me these last thirty-six years?"

She shrugged without giving a response.

Moving directly behind Dianna, Philip rubbed her slumped shoulders. "Come on now. . . Tell me what's really on your mind. It'll make you feel better to get it out, and you know you want to."

Dianna gave a sharp intake of breath. "You're right. Maybe I will feel better if I verbalize my thoughts." She turned to face him. "It's Emma. I'm worried about her."

"How come?"

"Do you really not know?"

He shook his head. "Why don't you enlighten me?"

"She's almost twenty years old and lacks the skills that she'll need for marriage."

"Such as?" Philip questioned.

"Do I need to remind you that our daughter can't cook or sew and that she doesn't show any interest in learning to do so?" Dianna heaved a sigh. "Emma wants to be outdoors all the time, either doing chores in the barn or helping you with various things in your woodworking shop." She glanced upward and shook her head. "I've tried so hard to pique our daughter's interest in the kitchen and sewing room, but with little or no success. I feel like a complete failure."

"You're not a failure, Dianna." He gave her a tender hug. "Apparently, Emma is simply not interested in those things. Sure wish I had an answer for you that might make things easier."

"Don't you understand, Philip? It's not for me that I want Emma to learn domestic chores. It's for her own sake."

They stood quietly together, staring out the window, until a brilliant idea popped into Dianna's head. "I think I know a solution to the problem." She clapped her hands as a ray of hope rose in her chest.

"What do you have in mind?"

"We can send Emma to Arthur, Illinois, to live with my parents for the entire summer."

"How's that gonna help?" Philip reached up and scratched behind his right ear.

Dianna's lips parted slightly as a smile formed. "As you know, my *mudder* is an excellent cook and can sew just about any item of clothing, and it all turns out well. She's also a patient woman. If anyone can teach our youngest daughter how to cook and sew, it's my dear mother."

Philip quirked an eyebrow and smirked at Dianna. "But even if your *mamm* is successful at teaching her those domestic skills, can she find Emma a husband?"

Chapter 1

Three weeks later
Arthur, Illinois

Emma Bontrager said goodbye to her female driver and stepped out of the vehicle. A lump formed in her throat when she gazed at the familiar farmhouse and spotted her grandparents seated upon a wooden bench on their front porch. Over the years, Emma had enjoyed spending time with Grandma and Grandpa whenever her family had come here for visits. But this time things would be different. At her mother's insistence and her father's agreement, Emma had been sent here to hone her domestic skills. Not that she really had any. Truthfully, from the time Emma was a little girl, she'd done everything she could think of to avoid helping her mother in the kitchen. Mom hadn't pressured Emma back then, because Emma's older sister Rachel loved everything about learning how to cook, and she'd taken to the sewing needle really well too.

Now Emma was about to embark on a new adventure that would tie up her entire summer, doing things that had no appeal to her whatsoever.

Emma started up the path leading to her grandparents' home, hauling her suitcase with one hand and an oversized canvas tote bag with the other. She wasn't one bit surprised when Grandpa stepped off the porch, and Grandma followed. "*Willkumm*, Emma!" they said in unison.

Grandpa gave Emma a firm hug before taking the suitcase from her. "I'll haul this inside for you."

Then it was Grandma's turn to wrap her arms around Emma's waist, giving her a tender squeeze. "Ever since your mamm wrote and said you were coming, we've been looking forward to your extended visit."

Emma wished she could say the same. It wasn't that she didn't like spending time with Grandma and Grandpa; she just didn't like the reason she'd been sent here for three whole months. Even so, Emma politely smiled and said, "You and Grandpa are looking well."

"We're both in pretty good health," Grandma responded. "And we're ever so thankful for that."

"For sure," Grandpa said as they all started into the house. "And I credit most of that to your *grossmammi's* healthy and hearty cooking." He glanced over his shoulder and winked at Emma. "In no time at all, you'll be cookin' up a storm and loving every minute of it."

Emma doubted that would ever happen, but she kept her opinion to herself. No point in upsetting the applecart, so to speak. If she was going to be here for the next three months, she planned to be as pleasant as possible and never say anything rude to either one of her grandparents.

"You're just in time to help me fix lunch," Grandma said when Grandpa disappeared up the stairs with Emma's suitcase and tote bag.

Emma cringed inwardly but kept a forced smile on her face. She was tired after the nearly five-hour drive from Shipshewana to Arthur, and the last thing she wanted to do was help her grandmother make anything in the kitchen, especially when she didn't feel the least bit hungry.

I hope it's nothing too difficult, she thought. *I just want to go upstairs to one of the guest rooms and unpack. After that, it would be real nice if I could lie down and take a little nap. But I suppose that's out of the question.*

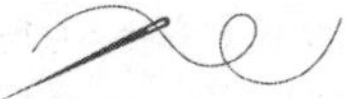

"What kind of sandwich would you like?" Grandma asked when she and Emma entered her spacious kitchen.

Emma shrugged. "I don't know. I'll eat whatever you and Grandpa are having."

"Do you like liverwurst with mayonnaise, mustard, and lots of lettuce?"

Emma struggled not to wrinkle her nose as she replied, "Uh. . .not particularly. My mamm likes it though," she quickly added.

"Jah, I am aware. It was one of her favorite sandwiches when she was a little girl," Grandma commented. "How about your *daed*? Does he also enjoy liverwurst?"

Emma shook her head. "He's never been fond of it, so guess I take after him—at least in that regard."

Grandma moved to the end of the counter and removed a loaf of bread from the bread box. "It's normal for most children to have likes and dislikes that either or both of their parents had. You could learn to acquire a taste for liverwurst, though. That's how it's been for me over the years when trying new foods that I had avoided eating in my younger years."

Emma made no comment, because she'd glanced out the window and spotted the old tree house Grandpa had built back when she was a young girl. He'd said it was for all his grandchildren to enjoy whenever they came to visit. But Emma had always assumed he'd built the sturdy structure just for her because he knew how much joy it would bring her, and he had been right. Emma's sister Rachel, who was four years older than her, had never shown much interest in the tree house. In fact, she'd often said that it was too dangerous to climb way up there just to sit on the wooden platform and stare down at the backyard. *"I'd rather be inside reading a book, or helping Grandma bake brownies, than be outside with all the bugs and dirt to mess up my dress,"* Rachel had often said. She did, however, help pull weeds in the garden and harvest the produce each year, but they weren't her favorite things to do.

Emma loved being outdoors. She enjoyed the scent of freshly mowed grass and even liked smelling the smoke from Grandpa's old firepit they sometimes used for roasting hot dogs on sticks.

Emma had never minded getting dirty, and she even enjoyed the prickly feeling of grass under her bare feet. The sound of grasshoppers and crickets was like music to her ears. Even listening to the chatter of squirrels and croaking frogs had brought a smile to her lips during childhood, and it still did.

"Emma, dear, did you hear what I said?"

At the sound of Grandma's voice, Emma's head jerked as she turned away from the window. "Uh. . .no. . .I guess not. Would you mind repeating it, Grandma?"

"I asked if you would rather have a peanut butter and jelly sandwich for lunch instead of what your grandfather and I are having."

"Oh jah, please. That sounds good to me."

Grandma pushed the loaf of bread to the other end of the counter, closer to where Emma stood. "Here you go. You'll find the peanut butter and some strawberry preserves in the pantry." She pointed in that direction.

Emma remembered all the times that she'd come here as a child. Not once had Grandma asked Emma or any of her siblings to make their own sandwich. She'd always graciously done it for them and had looked quite content when they'd all taken seats at the kitchen table. What had changed? Well, at least Emma would be fixing something she liked that wasn't the least bit difficult to make. It was a comfort. Of course, nothing would be as comforting or comfortable as lying on the guest bed and sleeping for a few hours. But that wasn't to be.

Emma removed two slices of bread and placed them on a plate. *Or better yet, I wonder if Grandpa would mind if I went outside for a while and took a nap in his hammock.* She sucked in her bottom lip. *Guess I won't know till I ask him, which I plan to do while we're eating our noon meal.*

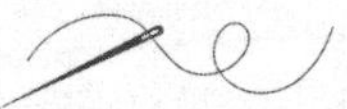

When Grandpa took his place at the head of the table and bowed his head, Emma and Grandma did the same. Other than thanking God for the peanut butter and jelly sandwich on her plate, Emma wasn't sure what to pray about. She didn't feel thankful that she'd been sent here to become domesticated like her sister, who could cook and sew quite well, or any of her brothers' wives, who all seemed to enjoy their roles as homemakers. Benjamin's wife, Anna, was very competent in the kitchen and baked some of the best-tasting pies. Phoebe, who was married to Harvey, also loved to cook, and made a fine beef stew. Jacob's wife, Elizabeth, was noted for her country-style baked beans, which she often served at family gatherings.

And then there's me, Emma thought ruefully. *Sandwiches I can make, but not much of anything else to brag about. Of course,* she mentally added, *bragging about one's abilities—cooking, sewing, or otherwise—would be considered* hochmut, *so even if I was good at something, I would never boast about it.*

Emma's eyes snapped open when she heard Grandpa clear his throat. She noticed that both his and Grandma's eyes were open, and she wondered how long they'd sat waiting for her to finish praying.

Emma's face felt warmer than usual, and she quickly reached for her glass of lemonade. After taking a drink, she set the glass down and allowed her contemplations to resume as she stared across the room, where a ray of sunlight filtered in through the kitchen window above the sink. *I don't understand why my parents think I need to learn how to cook or sew. I've never had a boyfriend, and it's not likely that I'll ever get married, so what's the point in trying to teach me how to run a household? I will probably spend the rest of my life as an old maid, living alone and eating simple things like cold cereal and easy-to-make sandwiches.*

"Emma, didn't you hear what your grandmother said?"

Grandpa's deep voice pulled Emma's thoughts aside, and she blinked in rapid succession. "Uh, no." She turned to face her grandmother. "Sorry, Grandma. What did you say?"

Grandma reached over and placed her hand on Emma's arm. "I asked if you were going to write your parents a letter to let them know that you arrived safely."

"Oh, um, jah, I should do that as soon as we're done eating." Emma picked up the remainder of her sandwich and was about to take a bite, when another thought popped into her head. "It's probably not necessary, though. I'm sure when my driver, Helen, gets back to Shipshewana she'll let Mom and Dad know I made it here safely."

"Most likely you're right," Grandpa put in. "But it would still be nice if they heard the news directly from you. Don't you agree, Emma?"

She nodded. "Jah. I'll take care of that after I've helped Grandma do the lunch dishes."

"There are only a few," Grandma said, "so I can manage those by myself."

Emma smiled. "Okay, *danki*." She looked forward to going outdoors and walking to the mailbox, where the air was fresh and much cooler than here in Grandma's kitchen. Emma would write the letter while sitting outside too.

When the three of them had finished their lunch, Emma followed Grandma's instructions and got a notepad, envelope, and stamp from the old rolltop desk, and then she excused herself and scooted out the back door. Pausing on the porch and leaning her head back, she savored the fresh early-summer air. Emma remained in place for several minutes, breathing slowly in and out. It felt good to be out here. If only she could stay out of the suffocating air inside the house for the rest of the day.

Taking her time to absorb the fragrance of flowers growing in Grandma's yard, while listening to the chattering of birds swooping from tree to tree, Emma made her way around the side of the house. Upon entering the front yard, she spotted the extra-long wooden picnic table Grandpa had made several years ago. She remembered well the many times when her family had come to visit and gathered in the yard, sharing meals at this rustic table.

Emma took a seat on the same side she'd sat upon as a child. She'd always thought that food tasted better when eaten outdoors. *Maybe I'll suggest that we eat breakfast out here sometime*, Emma thought as she placed the notebook in front of her, in readiness to write her folks a letter. She really didn't have much to say. She clasped the pencil between her second and third finger and began to write a short message saying she'd arrived safely and that it was good to see her grandparents again.

A short time later, Emma had written enough to fill one page and figured that was enough. After placing the letter in the envelope, addressing it, and sealing it shut, Emma put a postage stamp on it and rose from her seat.

When she got to the mailbox and pulled the door open, she nearly got hit in the face by a cobweb. *Or maybe it's not a simple* schpinnenescht, she thought. *It could be a web spun by some lurking* schpinn *just waiting to get me.* Emma had an aversion to spiders, especially the big ones that ran fast when she tried to get them, and she didn't like the hopping kind of spider either. As far as she was concerned, God must have made a mistake when He'd created the creepy insects known as *spiders*. Emma wasn't sure why she had a fear of the crawling insects. She'd never been bitten by one, but there was always a first time.

Seeing no sign of a spider, Emma pushed the web aside, reached inside the mailbox, and was surprised that there was no mail inside. She remembered then that Grandpa had mentioned once that their mail was always delivered in the latter part of the day, but usually before suppertime. Emma placed the envelope inside, and after closing the door, she lifted the metal flag on the side of the box to let the letter carrier know there was mail to be picked up.

Emma was about to turn back toward the house when a well-groomed chestnut-colored horse pulling an open carriage approached. A young, beardless Amish man with reddish-brown hair was seated on the driver's side and lifted his hand to wave as he went by. Emma didn't recognize him and figured he must not live close by. Either that or he was new to the area since her last visit. She smiled and waved in response. It was the polite thing to do. Emma watched for a few seconds as the *clip-clop* sounds grew quieter and the horse and buggy continued down the road.

Emma turned and made her way up the driveway, hoping she could rest in the hammock for a little while. Even though she hadn't asked Grandpa's permission yet, she felt sure he wouldn't mind. She was almost to the hammock when she discovered a cluster of lovely daffodils in the flower bed bordering the front of the house. She decided to take a few minutes to admire their beauty, and for the first time in her adult life, Emma wished she had a camera and could snap a picture to capture the essence of the bright yellow blooms. After squatting down for a closer look, Emma almost let out a yelp when Grandma came out the front door and called to her.

"It's time for your first cooking lesson, Emma. Since it's almost the right hour to start supper preparations, you may as well begin now."

Emma sighed as she glanced up at the billowy white clouds floating overhead. *So much for taking a nap in Grandpa's hammock today.* She'd forgotten to ask him about it during their early lunch, and now it was too late to ask, since Grandma had decided it was time to start supper. Oh, how Emma wished she'd only come here for a short visit, and not to spend the entire summer learning how to cook and sew. She didn't want to leave all this wonderful fresh air and sunshine for the confines of the hot and stuffy kitchen.

"All right, Grandma, I'm coming," Emma called in return to her grandmother's request. What other choice did she have?

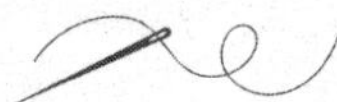

Grandma glanced at the battery-operated kitchen clock, and then she looked at Emma. "Are you ready to begin?"

"I—I guess so. What are we making?"

"Not we—you." Grandma pointed at Emma. "I'll give you the directions and show you how to do specific things if necessary, but you won't learn if I do it for you."

Emma's shoulders slumped. "Okay then—what will I be making?"

"I think a simple meat loaf would be a nice beginning, and it will be a hearty main dish for supper."

Emma grimaced. She'd never cared much for meat loaf—simple, fancy, or otherwise. Just the thought of having to learn how to make it, much less sit at the supper table and force herself to eat some of it, took away any appetite she may have had for eating the evening meal.

Why, oh why, did my parents have to send me here? Even if I were to learn the fine art of cooking, meat loaf would never be on my menu. Now it was Emma's turn to look at the clock. She hoped this lesson wouldn't take too long, because while the meat loaf was in the oven baking, she hoped to do something fun.

After Grandma instructed Emma about where she would find the necessary ingredients, Emma asked why she needed two pounds of ground beef instead of one.

"It's simple, dear one," Grandma responded. "If you make a big enough meat loaf, then we'll have leftovers for *kalt* meat loaf sandwiches."

"Oh, I see." Emma didn't voice her thoughts, but she didn't care for cold meat loaf sandwiches any more than she did when the meat loaf was warm.

As she began gathering the ingredients listed on the recipe card her grandmother had given her, Grandma took their conversation in another direction by asking Emma what type of sewing she'd learned to do.

"Well, uh, I've sewed buttons on a few of my daed's shirts."

"Is that all?"

"Pretty much."

"Well, for goodness' sake. Haven't you made any dresses for yourself?"

Emma shook her head. "All my dresses, capes, and aprons have been made by Mom or Rachel."

"How is your sister doing these days?" Grandma asked. "Is she still being courted by that Lambright fellow?"

Emma nodded. "Rachel and David have been seeing each other for nearly two years now, and my daed says if David doesn't ask Rachel to marry him soon, Dad's gonna tell her suitor that he either must propose or break things off with Rachel."

Grandma's mouth opened wider than normal. "Oh my. I can't imagine how that would make poor Rachel feel. I'm sure your daed isn't serious about his intentions."

Emma shrugged. "I don't know. He might be."

"Now that would be most embarrassing for both Rachel and David. How about you, Emma? Do you have a steady beau back home?"

"No way! I don't think I will ever get married."

"Never say never. You might be surprised what the future holds." Grandma wagged a finger in Emma's direction. "Now, changing the subject. . . We'll go to the fabric store in town tomorrow so you can pick out the material you would like, and when we get home, we'll start working on a new dress for you."

Emma's fingers clenched around the small glass measuring cup she held to beat the eggs. Although cooking a meal wasn't on her wish list, sewing a dress was definitely not something she wanted to do.

"With the exception of the dinner rolls I made today, Emma cooked all the main dishes for our evening meal." Grandma gestured to the oddly shaped meat loaf, and then the bowl of lumpy mashed potatoes. Emma hoped the food would taste better than it looked.

"That's terrific." Grandpa grinned at Emma. "I can't wait to try the meat loaf. It's one of my favorite things to have for supper."

Emma held her breath as Grandpa reached for the meat platter and cut two hefty pieces. After placing them on his plate, he picked up the bowl of potatoes and took several spoonfuls. He didn't mention the lumps, so Emma thought that was a positive thing. *I should have tasted everything before putting them on the table,* she thought. *But since I don't like meat loaf, I wouldn't have known if it was good or bad. Guess I could have suggested that Grandma give it the taste test, though.*

She blew out her breath and breathed in another one as Grandpa took his first bite of meat loaf.

He chewed, swallowed, and quickly grabbed for his glass of milk. After drinking most of it down, Grandpa looked right at Emma and said, "What in the world did you do to the meat loaf? It doesn't taste anything like what I'm used to."

"I—I just followed the recipe Grandma gave me when she left the kitchen to go outside and check the towels hanging on the line."

"Here, Marlin, let me try it." Grandma reached for the platter, but before she could pick it up, Grandpa forked another hunk off his plate, leaned forward, and popped it right into her mouth.

Grandma's dark eyes widened as she grabbed a napkin and spit the piece of meat loaf into the paper. "*Ach*, Emma, didn't you add any ketchup?"

"Well. . .umm. . .I thought I had."

"And why so many *brot grimmele*?" Grandpa questioned. "Using too many breadcrumbs makes for a dry, crumbly meat loaf."

Tears sprang to Emma's eyes and threatened to spill over. It was bad enough that she'd been expected to cook a dish she didn't like, but to find out that she had botched the job added insult to injury. Without asking to be excused, Emma pushed back her chair and fled the room.

Chapter 2

After a fitful night of tossing and turning, Emma awoke the following morning feeling like she had not slept at all. If only she hadn't messed up the meat loaf and lumpy potatoes. Her feeble attempt at cooking left a lot to be desired, but she felt like a failure in so many aspects of life. She knew Bible verses that referred to talents and gifts, but Emma was quite sure she had been left out in the talent department. Oh sure, she could catch and clean a fish, but cooking one was another story. Emma figured her biggest roadblock was that she had no reason to learn domestic skills other than to appease her mother and grandmother, who obviously thought cooking and sewing were necessary.

Maybe it would be necessary if I were planning to get married, Emma thought as she slid out of bed. *I just wish Mom and Grandma understood that.* Emma's lips compressed. *I wonder what will happen if, by the end of summer, I still haven't learned to cook or sew. Will I be allowed to go home, or will my parents insist that I remain here for the rest of the year or at least until I can prove that I've mastered the skills they expect me to?*

With a heavy sigh, Emma removed her nightgown and put on a clean dress. It was time to go downstairs and see what Grandma expected her to do to help with breakfast. No doubt Emma would be in for another cooking lesson. Maybe Grandma would expect her to fry Grandpa's eggs. Emma remembered from previous visits that he liked them over easy with the yolks intact. She had made decent scrambled eggs a time or two, but every time Emma had tried to cook eggs over easy, she'd ended up breaking the yolks. And one time while boiling some eggs, Emma had left the kitchen long enough to feed the cats, and when she'd returned, the kettle was dry. Every single egg had been overcooked.

Emma doubted that she would ever be proficient in the kitchen. There were too many things she'd rather do besides slave over a hot stove or get her hands sticky rolling out dough to make bread, rolls, or cutout cookies.

She heaved a sigh. *Guess I'd better get downstairs to the kitchen before someone comes looking for me.*

When Emma entered the kitchen, she was surprised to see that the table had been set and Grandma was at the stove flipping pancakes with an oversized spatula. "What do you need me to do?" Emma asked when she approached her grandmother.

"Nothing at all. I have it under control." Grandma paused what she'd been doing and turned to look at Emma. "I'm sorry that the comments your grandfather and I made last evening about your meat loaf sent you to your room in tears. We didn't mean to upset you."

"That's right," Grandpa spoke up from where he sat at the kitchen table with a cup of coffee in one hand. "We should have realized how insensitive we were being, and I'm sorry for my part in it too. Will you forgive us?"

"Jah, of course, and I'm sorry for running out of the room like a crybaby," Emma said. "Guess I'm too sensitive at times."

"You were upset because we'd hurt your feelings, and that's understandable," Grandma acknowledged. "So let's just put it behind us now, okay?"

Emma nodded and moved closer to the stove. "Will you be giving me another cooking lesson today?"

Grandma shrugged her shoulders. "We'll see what the day brings. Right now, though, please take a seat at the table so we can eat before the pancakes get cold."

Emma did as she was told, seating herself in the chair across from where her grandmother had sat yesterday. She still didn't understand why Grandma had fixed breakfast without her help and wondered if it really was because she felt guilty about her comment last night about Emma's meat loaf. *Or maybe,* Emma thought, *Grandma and Grandpa don't want their breakfast ruined, because, in true form, I'd probably make a mess of whatever I'd been asked to fix.*

Grandpa got the syrup and butter, and when Grandma set the platter of pancakes on the table, everyone bowed their heads for silent prayer. This time, Emma thanked God for the breakfast she knew would be delicious, for protection over her family in Indiana, and for loving grandparents who'd been willing to apologize for hurting her feelings.

Once they had all started eating, Grandpa made a few comments to Grandma about the exceptionally warm weather they'd been having, and then he looked over at Emma and said, "While you are here this summer, how would you like to go fishing with me sometime?"

She tilted her head in his direction. "Seriously?"

"Absolutely. Of course, that will be when you're not here in the kitchen with Grandma for lessons."

She smiled. "I'd like that a lot, Grandpa. I've enjoyed fishing since I was a young girl."

"I am well aware." He reached over and gave Emma's arm a tap. "You can't be cooped up in the house all the time, and it's always nice to get some exercise in the fresh air and sunshine."

"It would be fun," Emma admitted, "but it sounds like Grandma has other plans for me this summer."

"Not every single day," Grandma spoke up. "And certainly not every single hour of each day."

"If you are too busy during the week, then some Saturdays we could try out a few of the ponds in our area." Grandpa grinned, and his blue eyes held more sparkle than usual. "And who knows—you might strike up a friendship with one or more of the young people in our church district, and then you could end up going fishing with some of them while you're here too."

Emma shrugged. "Since I'll only be here a few months, it's doubtful that I will make any friends. And even if I did, with me living in Indiana, I would only see my new friends when I came for a visit."

"Don't close yourself off to the idea," Grandma interjected. "We all need friends, even if we live miles apart. Letter writing can hold the friendship together."

Emma's mind wandered as she ate the rest of her tasty buttermilk pancakes, oozing with fresh creamy butter and just enough mouth-watering syrup. She didn't think she'd ever be able to make pancakes or any other breakfast food that tasted this good.

Emma's thoughts changed direction. She had made friends with a few of the young women back home, but most of them were married now, and those who weren't had steady boyfriends. Emma didn't feel that she fit in with the group she'd hung out with during her teen years anymore, and she had concluded that she didn't need to have a close friend—or a boyfriend either. Accepting that fact was far better than sitting around feeling sorry for herself or wishing for something that would probably never happen.

"As soon as you've finished eating, Emma, we can get the breakfast dishes done and be on our way."

"Huh?" Emma pulled her thoughts aside to give her grandmother full attention.

Grandma repeated herself.

"Where are we going?" Emma asked.

"To the fabric store in town. Weren't you listening when I mentioned that previously?"

"I—I guess not. Sorry, Grandma."

"I bet she was enjoying your pancakes so much that her mind couldn't absorb what you were saying, Luellen." Grandpa chuckled. "That happens to me sometimes when I'm eating a good meal. I say something, eat a few bites, and then can't remember what I said because my thoughts are solely on the good food."

"Why are we going to the fabric store?" Emma asked, focusing on Grandma again.

"As I mentioned before, we're going to buy some material so you can begin your first sewing lesson when we return home." Grandma finished what was on her plate, pushed her chair aside, and stood. "So let's hurry and get the dishes done, and then we can be on our way."

Oh great," Emma thought. *A cooking lesson yesterday that turned out badly, and now Grandma expects me to learn how to sew. I wonder what kind of blunders I'll make this afternoon with a needle and thread in my hands. Or maybe she'll expect me to use her treadle sewing machine. Oh my! I wonder what kind of a mess I'd make with that. Probably end up sewing the sleeve of the dress I'm wearing to the material under the needle.*

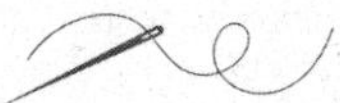

When Emma and her grandmother entered the quaint-looking store where fabric, quilt patterns, and even a few colorful quilts were sold, Emma felt a sense of foreboding. *What if, despite Grandma's teachings, I simply can't learn how to sew? If I go back home at the end of summer, and haven't learned what I came to Arthur for, how will it make my parents feel? I'm sure they won't blame Grandma for it. I'll be the one in the wrong because I refused to learn or was unteachable.* Emma swallowed around the constriction in her throat. *Too bad I wasn't born a boy—then the need to cook and sew wouldn't even be a problem.*

Emma stood off to one side while Grandma spoke to the Amish woman behind the front counter. They chatted for a bit, and from some of the conversation she heard, Emma figured her grandmother and the woman might be friends. When she got tired of standing still, Emma decided to wander around the building for a closer look at the fabric. Emma hoped Grandma would allow her to choose some burgundy or maybe a royal-blue material and not some boring brown or ghastly green fabric. Emma didn't care for dresses in either of those colors, and she'd had to plead with her mother many times over what color material to buy for her clothes.

Emma was about to approach a bolt of blue material when Grandma called out to her. "Emma, dear, please come over here to the counter."

Emma did as she'd been requested.

Grandma put one hand on Emma's arm and said, "Emma, I'd like you to meet my friend, Ida Mae Yoder. She and her family are part of our church district, and Ida Mae works here part-time."

"It's nice to meet you." Emma put on what she hoped was a pleasant smile and reached across the counter to shake the woman's hand.

"It's good to meet you too, Emma." Ida Mae gave Emma a firm handshake. "I understand that you'll be staying with your grandparents for the summer to learn how to cook and sew."

Emma gave a brief nod, feeling the heat of embarrassment cover her cheeks. She didn't understand why her grandmother had felt it necessary to tell her friend the reason she was here for the summer. Ida Mae probably wondered why a full-grown young woman needed to learn either of those things—especially when most women Emma's age not only had perfected those skills but were either happily married or at least being courted by an eligible young man.

Grandma looked at Emma, then gestured to the bolts of fabric stacked on a shelf along one wall. "Shall we choose a color for the making of your first *frack*?"

"Okay." Emma moved across the room and when Grandma approached, Emma pointed to the royal-blue material. "How about that one? That shade of blue is one of my favorite colors."

Grandma's brows furrowed a bit as she pressed her lips together. "I don't think so, Emma. How about this one." She picked up a bolt of boring brown.

Emma cringed. "How about this one?" Emma pointed to some burgundy material.

Grandma shook her head. "That's too bold of a color."

Then why's it being sold here in an Amish-owned store? Emma didn't voice her thoughts, but she sure wanted to. She figured it might be best not to make a fuss and just go with the brown material for her first self-made dress. "Okay, let's get the brown one," she murmured, keeping her gaze on the floor and not on her grandmother.

"Are you sure? We could make your dress from that material." Grandma touched the top of the bolt of khaki-green material.

Emma shook her head. "No, that's okay. I'm fine with the brown color."

Grandma smiled and hauled the bolt of material over to the counter where Ida Mae stood. Then she returned to Emma and said, "Now we need to get some matching thread."

"What do you think you're doing here in the back room, Son? Aren't you supposed to be up front waiting on customers?"

Ivan Yoder turned in his chair to look up at his tall, bearded father. "This is my lunch hour, Papa. Aaron's taking my place at the counter."

"Okay, that's fine, but you're not eating lunch." Papa gestured to the clock pieces lying on the table where Ivan sat.

"I'll get something soon. Just wanted to work awhile on this project the bishop brought to me."

"Puh!" Papa flapped his hand like he was trying to shoo away a bothersome fly. "In the first place, Bishop Dan shouldn't bring clockwork here to my shop for you to work on."

"He didn't, Papa. The bishop came by our house last week to deliver his broken clock, and it was my idea to bring it here today to work on during my lunch hour."

"Well, be that as it may, in case you've forgotten—this is a harness shop, where we repair and make new leather items. It's not a place to repair old clocks. When are you gonna realize that the money you earn comes from workin' here, not repairing clocks on the side?"

Ivan tapped his fingers along the edge of the tabletop to release some of his frustration. He was well aware that his dad didn't appreciate the desire he felt to repair clocks, but he enjoyed the work and didn't want to give it up. In fact, Ivan hoped that someday he could make a living doing what he loved best instead of working here in the harness shop, which he'd never enjoyed.

Papa tapped the toe of his right boot against the cement floor, loudly enough to get Ivan's attention. "Did you not hear my question?"

"Umm. . .jah, I did. I was just takin' a few seconds to answer." Ivan turned to face his father again. "I realize that you've provided a job here for me, and ever since I started working for you at the age of sixteen, I've always tried to do a good job. Even so. . ." Ivan's voice trailed off.

Papa's features tightened as he crossed his arms. "I suspect there's a *but* in there someplace. Am I right, Ivan?"

He nodded. "As I'm sure you already know, harness work is not the profession of my choice. That isn't to say that I don't appreciate the job, though," Ivan quickly added.

Papa pulled out a chair on the other side of the table and sat down. "Listen, Son, you're twenty-two years old now, and you'll probably be taking a *fraa* soon, so you need a good-paying job that will provide you with steady work—something that is in demand."

"I won't be taking a wife soon," Ivan said with a shake of his head, "because I don't even have a girlfriend."

"That'll change when the right girl comes along." With an open hand, Papa pounded his chest a few times. "Ask me. I was in no hurry to get married, and then your mama, being new to the area, showed up at one of our church services with her parents and siblings, and I said to myself, 'Eldon, that young woman with dark brown hair and eyes to match is gonna be my fraa someday.'" Papa chuckled and stood. "And now, just thirty-some years later, we are the parents of seven children. So you mark my words, Son. Your turn's a-comin', and when it does, you'll need to be prepared for it."

Ivan shrugged his shoulders. "We'll see about that, Papa. Jah, we'll just have to wait and see how it goes. Right now, though, there's no one special in my life."

Ivan's father looked down at him and shook his head. "The trouble with you, Ivan, is you're too particular. There's no perfect woman, ya know. Just like us men, we all have our flaws, so you can't be too picky."

"I'm fully aware, and I'm not looking for perfection," Ivan responded. "If and when I decide to seek a wife, it'll be because I've met a charming woman and fallen in love. But since that hasn't happened yet, there's not much point in talking about it."

"Guess you're right. If you are meant to take a wife, it'll be in God's time, not yours, mine, or your mamm's." With that said, Papa turned and walked out of the room.

Ivan heaved a sigh of relief. It was bad enough that his dad had scolded him for working on the bishop's clock during lunchtime. But did he also have to bring up the topic of Ivan needing a wife? Just because two of his brothers were married didn't mean he should be too. *Maybe I'll stay single for the rest of my life. Would that really be so bad? I mean, I can cook and clean, so who needs a fraa?*

Chapter 3

SOMEONE KNOCKED ON EMMA'S BEDROOM door, and she jumped at the sound.

"Emma, are you awake?" Grandpa's resonating voice could be heard easily through the door.

"Jah, Grandpa, I'm up," she called. "But I don't have my stockings and shoes on."

"Okay, well, I'll let your grandma know that you're not ready for breakfast yet."

"I promise I'll be ready soon."

"That's good," he said, "because we don't want to be late for church."

When Emma heard her grandfather's heavy footsteps move down the hall and descend the stairs, she plunked down on the cedar chest at the end of her bed to put on her stockings and shoes. Although Emma had always enjoyed attending church, she felt some apprehension about going to the service this morning. There would be many people there she didn't know, and she'd be expected to socialize during the simple meal following the service.

What if someone questions me about why I'm visiting my grandparents for the summer? Emma asked herself. *What would they think if I told them I came here to learn how to cook and sew?* Her shoulders curled over her chest. *Oh, how humiliating that would be. They would probably think there was something wrong with me. I might even be asked why my own mother didn't teach me those things. Would I have to explain that my mamm had tried, but I'd simply refused to listen because I wanted to do other things?*

Emma worked her stockings up both legs and slipped into her shoes. Forcing her shoulders back and moving toward the door, she made a decision. *If anyone does ask the questions I'm dreading, I'll simply smile and change the subject.*

Emma sat quietly and reverently on a backless wooden bench positioned on the women's side of the room. Although a few people had greeted her when she and her grandparents first arrived, Emma was glad that no one had asked any questions of her before she'd come into the building. The service they were attending today was being held in one of their church member's buggy sheds that had been cleared out and cleaned thoroughly for today's three-hour service.

Singing from the *Ausbund*, the church hymnal, was over, as well as reading Scripture passages. Now one of the church ministers, an elderly man with a long white beard, stood before the people, about to preach a message in German. He had no notes—only a Bible in his hands, which Emma knew he would be quoting from frequently. At least that's how it was in her family's church district back home.

I bet my parents and sister are sitting in church right now too, Emma thought. *I wonder if they miss me not being with them today.* It had only been three days since Emma's arrival at her grandparents' house, so Mom and Dad wouldn't have received her letter yet. She looked forward to hearing from them, and hoped it would be soon. It was probably silly for her to miss home so much, but Emma was already homesick, longing for her own bed and everything that was familiar to her. Emma cared about her grandparents, of course, but she didn't know them nearly as well as she did Mom, Dad, and Rachel. Besides, expectations were being placed on her now that she hadn't had to deal with at home—like the cooking and sewing she disliked.

The meat loaf I made the other night was terrible, and yesterday's sewing lesson didn't go well either. Emma glanced down at her hands, clasped in her lap. Pins and needles—needles and pains. Emma had lost track of how many times she'd stuck herself. The use of Grandma's treadle sewing machine hadn't helped any either.

I couldn't even sew a straight line on the pieces Grandma had cut out for me after I'd proved to her that I couldn't cut the material that we'd brought home from the fabric store without making a mess of things. Emma sighed. *Guess I'm a hopeless case when it comes to cooking or sewing. Grandma oughta send me home tomorrow instead of trying to make me into something I'm not.*

Emma pushed her thoughts aside and focused on the minister standing between the men's side of the room and the women's. She didn't know why she'd let her thoughts wander down a negative path. After all, she enjoyed going to church and hearing God's Word preached. But she hadn't enjoyed it as a young girl. Back then it had been hard for her to sit for three hours and listen to someone speaking in a language she hadn't fully learned. Of course, once she'd started going to school, German had been taught along with the English language. Up until first grade, the only language spoken in Emma's home was the traditional Pennsylvania Dutch. Out shopping, at the bank, or when they were around their English neighbors who didn't speak or understand their Amish language, Emma's parents had always spoken English. For that reason, before her school days, Emma had picked up a few words but couldn't speak English fluently until she'd learned it well in school. She was glad that she'd been taught German too, since it was spoken in all Amish church services.

There I go, thinking too much again when I should be listening. Giving the minister her full attention, Emma reflected on the verse the man had just quoted. He said it was verse 17 of James 1: "*Every good gift and every perfect gift is from above, and cometh down from the Father of lights, with whom is no variableness, neither shadow of turning.*"

"We can use this passage of scripture as the basis for a prayer of gratitude and being able to recognize God's blessings," the minister stated. "Our prayers should express thankfulness for all the good things in life, acknowledging that they come from God and not man. It can also be a prayer for discernment, seeking God's guidance in recognizing and appreciating every one of His gifts."

Emma sucked in her lower lip as she thought more about what the white-haired man had said. *Do I express my thankfulness for all the good things God has given me?* she asked herself. *Probably not. Like many others here today, I often take all the good things for granted and forget to thank the Lord for His gifts. I need to do better in that regard and stop feeling sorry for myself because I was sent here to learn how to be a good homemaker. I need to be more appreciative of Grandma's efforts. I'm sure that she and Grandpa, as well as my folks, only want what's best for me.*

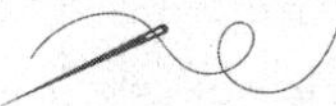

After the church service concluded, a light meal was served. Ivan wished there had been more food to eat, since he hadn't eaten much breakfast this morning, due to the number of chores that had to be done in the barn before it was time to leave for church.

Ivan glanced over at the tables where all the women sat eating their meal, and he noticed a newcomer—a young, petite woman with light brown hair, sitting next to Luellen Herschberger. She looked familiar to him, but he couldn't figure out where he'd seen her before. Ivan tried not to stare, in case she might look this way and see him watching her. And then there was his brother Aaron sitting across the table from him, who could easily say something if he noticed Ivan looking at the women's tables. Oh yes, Ivan could almost hear Aaron embarrassing him with an unnecessary comment or question. Aaron was newly married, and sometimes he teased Ivan about not having a serious relationship with anyone yet. He liked to remind Ivan that at the age of twenty-two, he should have found someone by now. Well, Ivan was in no hurry to get married and raise a family, but if and when he did decide to seek a wife, it would have to be a young lady who had common interests with him. He knew too many couples, like his parents and older brothers, Peter and Delbert, who seemed to love each other but didn't have a lot of similar interests. It seemed odd to Ivan, and he wondered sometimes how they made it work.

I've heard it said that opposites attract, but I'm more inclined to seek a woman whose likes and dislikes are more like mine, he told himself, pulling his gaze away from the young woman he'd spotted, and looking back at the slice of bread on his plate that had been covered with ham and cheese spread, which he'd chosen rather than the traditional Amish peanut butter spread. There were also some pickles and slices of red beets to choose from, and Ivan had taken some of both, along with a cup of coffee and a few shortbread cookies to dunk in the warm brew. At least that's what Ivan liked to do whenever he'd been served any kind of cookie with hot coffee.

Ivan chanced a peek at the young woman again, and it dawned on him. Although he'd only seen her briefly, just long enough to wave, he was quite sure that she was the one he'd seen standing by the Herschbergers' mailbox the other day, when he'd been on his way back to his father's harness shop after running a few errands in town. He'd offered her a friendly wave, and she had waved back.

Ivan wondered if the young woman might be a relative of Marlin or Luellen and was visiting them for the weekend. He wished he had the courage to go over to the women's section and ask. But that would be too forward, and it might embarrass her. *Me too,* Ivan thought, glancing at Aaron again. *No doubt he'd have something to say about it. If not here, then the next time he and his bride visit our home.*

Ivan grabbed another cookie and dunked it in his coffee. *No, I'd best just sit here and mind my own business. After all, if she is visiting the Herschbergers, she'll likely be going back to wherever she is from within the next day or so, and I may never see her again.* Ivan ate the cookie and washed it down with a swallow of coffee. *And why do I care anyhow? For all I know, she could be married. Even if she's not, it makes no difference to me.*

Ivan refocused on what was left on his plate and started a conversation with his brother Peter, who sat to the left of him.

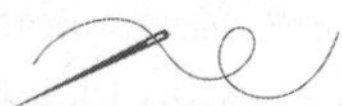

When Emma and her grandparents got home from church, Grandma announced that they had been invited to her friend Ida Mae Yoder's house for a light supper. "We want you to go along too," she said, gesturing to Emma.

"Well, I'm kind of tired and thought I might take a *gelegge*," Emma responded, dropping her gaze.

"We won't be leaving for a couple of hours, so you have plenty of time for a nap," Grandma said. "The Yoders are nice people, and some of the children still live at home, so there will be young people to talk to." She gave Emma's shoulder a gentle pat. "I'm sure you'll have a good time."

To be compliant, Emma looked at Grandma and managed a smile of her own. "All right, I'll go with you." What else could Emma say? She didn't want to upset her grandmother by refusing to go.

"Good to hear. I'll wake you about thirty minutes before we're ready to leave."

"Okay." Emma headed up the stairs and entered her room. After removing her church clothes and shoes, including her head covering, she slipped on a lightweight robe and collapsed onto the bed. With the concern she felt about going to someone's home she didn't really know, Emma wasn't sure she could even fall asleep. She closed her eyes and tried to relax, but all kinds of jumbled thoughts rolled around in her head. What if she didn't fit in? What if the young people who lived there weren't even home? Worse yet—what if they were at home but weren't interested in talking to her? Maybe she should have spoken up and told her grandmother that she really did not want to go.

Emma shifted her body, trying to find a comfortable position. When that didn't help her relax, she rubbed her arms as if they were cold, which made no sense considering that the room was hot and stuffy, even with the window slightly ajar.

Emma engaged in self-talk, hoping to encourage positive thinking and optimism. *Going to visit Grandma and Grandpa's friends probably won't be nearly as bad as I'm making it out to be. I'm just second-guessing what might happen while we are there, and it makes no sense at all. When I met Mrs. Yoder at the fabric store yesterday, she seemed nice enough, and I'm sure the rest of her family will be too. I just need to set my insecurities aside and go there expecting the best.*

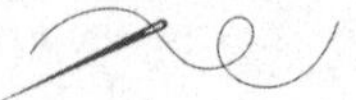

"Oh, look, there's a group of young people playing baseball in that open field," Grandma said when Grandpa directed their horse and buggy into the Yoders' yard and up to the hitching rack.

Emma looked toward where her grandmother was pointing. Despite the warm late-afternoon sun, the whoops and hollers coming from the field was a good indication that everyone was having a great time and didn't seem to mind the heat. She longed to hop down from the buggy and join them, but without an invitation it would be too bold. Instead, when Emma got out, she went around to the front of the horse and secured him to the rail. Grandma got out too and suggested that Emma come with her to meet some of the women who had gathered on the lawn. Before Emma could respond, Grandpa moved toward Emma and said, "I'm going over to watch the game for a while. Would ya like to join me?"

Emma didn't hesitate to bob her head. Even though she wasn't brave enough to ask if she could join the game, it would be fun to at least watch the goings-on. It would be much more exciting than sitting around trying to make conversation with a bunch of older women she didn't know.

As Grandma wandered into the yard, carrying a basket of cookies she'd brought along, Emma followed Grandpa over to the fence line dividing the Yoders' yard from the field.

"I sure do miss the days when I was young and spry enough to hit the ball and run around the bases," Grandpa commented as he leaned on the wooden fence rail. "Now the best I can do is watch and cheer the players on."

Emma wasn't sure what to say in response, so she simply put her hand on his arm and gave it a few pats. Seeing the slump of his shoulders and hearing the regret in his tone made her feel kind of gloomy. A person might be wiser when they reached their senior years, but it was sad to think about all the things they could no longer do. She wondered how things might be for her when she was Grandpa and Grandma's age.

As long as my health holds out, maybe when my hair turns gray and my face is full of wrinkles, I won't care that I can't do all the physical things, like playing ball, Emma reasoned.

They stood quietly watching for several minutes, and then Grandpa turned to Emma and said, "Guess I'll go on over and visit with some of the menfolk for a while. You wanna go be with your grandma or stay here and continue watching the baseball get hit around?"

"Think I'll keep watching until the game is over," she replied. "I'd like to see which team wins."

"Okay." Grandpa turned and walked away, and Emma's attention went back to the game.

The young man up to bat had reddish-brown hair and a determined look on his face as he waited for the pitcher to throw the ball. She'd seen him today after church during the simple meal and had thought he might be looking at her. *I probably imagined it,* Emma told herself. *He was most likely looking past me, at someone else.*

She kept watching until the ball came hard and fast, and then—*whack*! The young man hit it with such force, it sailed way over the pitcher's head and clear past center field. Two players went after the ball and almost collided. Meanwhile, the hitter made his way around the bases at lightning speed.

Emma was impressed. She'd never seen anyone who could hit a ball like that and run with such ease. As a woman, with a skirt to contend with, there was no way she could have run even half that well, nor hit the ball with such force. She stood watching in awe as the man's team members cheered when his feet hit home plate. The game was obviously over, and he followed the others as they left the field and headed for the picnic tables that had been set up on the front lawn.

As the young man made a detour and approached Emma, he paused and flashed her a dimpled smile. "I saw you after church today. Are you new to the area, or just visiting?" he questioned.

Emma opened her mouth to respond, but the only sound that came out was a little squeak. She leaned heavily against the fence board, fighting the desire to turn and run.

Chapter 4

Shipshewana

I wonder how things are going for Emma," Dianna Bontrager said after she'd removed her shoes and taken a seat on the sofa next to her daughter Rachel. "I hope we hear something from her soon."

"Emma's driver said she made it to your parents' house, so there's no need for you to fret," her husband responded from across the room, where he sat in one of their comfortable overstuffed chairs.

"I am not fretting, Philip. I'm just eager to get a letter from Emma so I know how things are going."

Rachel crossed her arms and gave a little huff. "I still don't understand why my sister had to go all the way to Arthur, Illinois, to learn how to cook and sew. You taught me how—right, Mom? Surely Emma could have learned from you too."

"First of all"—Dianna held up one finger—"Arthur is not that far away." A second finger sprang up. "And I did try to teach Emma the skills she would need to run a household of her own, but I couldn't keep her attention long enough for anything I showed her to sink in."

"Emma's not *dumm*," Rachel said. "I think she's just stubborn because she'd rather be outside doing something she likes better than spending time indoors."

"Rachel has a point," Philip interjected. "With Emma being our youngest child, you've been inclined to spoil her a bit and given in to her wishes too often."

Dianna blinked rapidly, feeling the thrum of her pulse on her inner wrists. Her attention latched on to the monotonous ticking of the clock over the entryway, which was the only sound to break the stillness of the room. What her husband had stated was true, but it was difficult to admit. She should have tried harder and been firmer with Emma, but there was no going back. All she could do was hope and pray that somehow her mother could get through to Emma and teach her the necessary skills to prepare for marriage and running a home of her own someday. Hopefully, when Emma returned home at the end of summer, she would be skilled at sewing and cooking, or at least be able to function in the kitchen well enough to make a decent meal. If for some reason Emma's grandma couldn't teach Emma to sew, she could always buy her dresses and other clothing items from some other Amish woman who sewed well and needed the extra money.

*Clippity-clop...clippity-clop...*the sound of a horse and buggy coming into the yard brought Rachel to her feet and over to the front window. "David's here to pick me up for a ride over to his parents' house for a light supper, so I better not keep him waiting."

"I hope you have a good time," Dianna called as Rachel hurried to the front door.

"I will, and don't feel that you need to wait up for me, although I shouldn't be too late."

Dianna heard the door shut, and a few minutes later the *clippity-clop* of the horse's hooves resumed along the gravel, which let her know that David's carriage was heading for the road. She looked over at Philip and asked, "Do you think that young man will ever propose to Rachel?"

Philip shrugged. "If I were a betting man, I'd say jah, but then who knows? As long as the two of them have been courting, he should have asked her by now."

"It does seem so," she agreed, "but then I'm sure he must have his reasons."

"Whatever those reasons are, David better not be giving our daughter the impression that he will propose when he really isn't all that interested in her." Philip grunted like a grizzly bear. "At this rate it doesn't look like either of our daughters will ever get married."

Dianna pursed her lips as she thought about their oldest daughter, Betty, who had left home before Emma was born. She was a headstrong young woman with a mind of her own, and she'd made it clear that she wanted nothing to do with her family or the Amish way of life. Dianna sniffed, hoping she wouldn't give in to the tears pricking the back of her eyes. In all the years since Betty had left home, they'd never heard a single word from her.

Is it any wonder I've spoiled Emma and even Rachel? Dianna asked herself. *I'd die a thousand deaths if either of my two youngest girls left home for good and made a new life for themselves that didn't involve their Amish family. Emma's time with her grandmother this summer may be the last chance to shape her into the woman she's destined to become, so I hope things work out while she's there with my mom and dad.*

Arthur

"Are you all right? Have you got something stuck in your throat? Is that why you can't talk?"

Emma shook her head. *For goodness' sake. Why is this man asking so many questions? This is so embarrassing.*

"Do you need some water to drink?" The young ballplayer stared deeply into her eyes as he leaned closer to Emma, clearly concerned.

"No, I–I'm fine." Emma felt the heat of embarrassment flood her cheeks. "For a few seconds there, I just couldn't find my voice."

"Does it happen often?" the youthful man asked.

"No, not really." *Just when I'm nervous and tongue-tied.*

"Well, good." He held out his hand, and when Emma shook it, she was surprised by his gentle, yet firm, grip. "I'm Ivan Yoder, and I believe we met a few days ago."

Emma tilted her head to one side. "Oh, I don't think so. Surely I would have remembered meeting you."

"We didn't meet face-to-face," he said with a grin. "You were standing in front of the Hershbergers' mailbox, and I was driving by with my horse and buggy. I waved, and you waved back."

Emma moved her head slowly up and down. "Jah, I do remember now that you've mentioned it."

"*Was is dei name?*" he questioned.

"My name is Emma Bontrager."

"Are you new to the area?"

"Not quite. I'm from Shipshewana, Indiana, and I came to Arthur to visit my grandparents for the summer," she replied. Emma hoped he wouldn't ask why, because it would be awkward to explain that she came here to learn how to cook and sew. Emma had always tried to be honest and upright, so she wasn't about to tell him an out-and-out lie.

"So you're here through the month of September?"

"I—I guess so," she stammered. Emma wasn't sure why, but looking into this man's piercing blue eyes made her feel giddy and unable to think or speak clearly. Even so, she couldn't turn her head away. It was as though his gaze held her captive.

"Do you have any special plans for while you're here?"

Emma moistened her lips. *He's very direct. Now I have to come up with a sensible answer that won't be a lie.* "I'll probably be helping my grandmother in the kitchen, and—"

"Oh, so you like to cook?"

"Well, I—"

"Ivan, the food's been set out. Are you coming to join us?"

Ivan turned his head in the direction of the voice that had beckoned him, and Emma looked that way too. A young, slender woman stood near one of the picnic tables, waving her hand. Emma had seen her out on the ball field and wondered if she might be Ivan's girlfriend. If that was the case, Emma figured the woman probably wouldn't appreciate her boyfriend talking to a stranger.

"That's my sister Norma, and she likes to boss me around sometimes. I often choose to ignore her, but other times I do what she says just so she'll think she's in control." Ivan laughed and offered Emma a quick wink. Then he gestured to the group of people on the lawn. "Why don't you come with me, and we'll get something to eat. I'll introduce you to my family and some of my friends who are here."

Emma hesitated. It had always made her uncomfortable to meet new people, especially when there was a large group of them. When Grandma had said they'd been invited to go over to Ida Mae's place this afternoon, she hadn't realized there would be a crowd gathered on the lawn.

"Come on, Emma," Ivan encouraged. "I'm sure you must be *hungerich*, and there's bound to be lots of good food."

Emma had to admit that she was hungry, so she nodded and walked beside Ivan onto the thick green lawn where the people were already seated at tables and some on the grass. Emma cringed when she realized that many heads had turned in her direction. It felt like all eyes were on her. Like a bird with its wings clipped, Emma longed to escape and avoid having to speak to anyone. She wished she had stayed in her room at Grandma and Grandpa's and gone to bed early tonight.

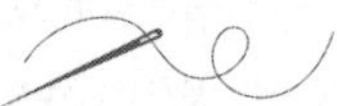

Ivan led Emma over to one of the tables, where his parents and two of his siblings sat. Emma's grandparents were there as well. "Why don't we sit here?" he said to Emma, motioning for the young woman to sit on the wooden bench. "I'll introduce you to some of my family members, and then we can eat and get better acquainted."

Without giving Emma a chance to respond, Ivan proceeded with the introductions. "This is my daed, Eldon; my mamm, Ida Mae; and my two *schweschdere,* Jane and Norma." He then gestured to Emma. "And this young lady is Emma Bontrager. She's Marlin and Luellen Herschbergers' granddaughter."

Emma extended a hand to each of them before sitting at the table, stating that she'd met Ivan's mother at the fabric store in town and that it was nice to meet everyone else. They greeted her warmly, and Ivan's mother said she was pleased to see Emma again.

"I have four more siblings too," Ivan remarked as he slid on a bench beside Emma. "My three *brieder*, Aaron, Peter, and Delbert, are all married and live in a different church district, so they're not with us today. Oh, and my youngest sister, Bertha, who recently turned fifteen, is sitting at another table with some of her friends." He looked over his shoulder and pointed.

Emma gave a brief nod, and then she, along with everyone else at the table, bowed her head for a silent prayer. Each of the four tables held platters piled high with slices of meat and cheese. Oblong baskets were filled with white and wheat bread, and other plates held layers of lettuce and tomatoes. Mayo, mustard, and glass jars filled with homemade dill pickles completed the fixings for everyone's sandwiches. Macaroni and potato salad were also provided, ensuring no one would go hungry.

"Everyone, eat yourselves full," Ivan's father said with a gleam in his eyes. "But be sure to save some room for homemade vanilla ice cream to go with two kinds of pie."

Ivan looked over at Emma to gauge her reaction to his father's dessert announcement, but she remained quiet. He wondered if she might be bashful among people she didn't know. Perhaps it was a mistake on his behalf to introduce Emma to his family and invite her to share a meal when they hardly knew each other. He waited until the food had been passed around before he continued their conversation, hoping it would make her feel at ease.

"What do you like to do for fun?" Ivan asked, leaning a bit closer to Emma. "You mentioned cooking before, but is there anything else you enjoy doing during your spare time?"

She set down the sandwich that she'd just picked up and nibbled, then said in a soft-spoken voice, "I enjoy fishing, hiking, and playing most outdoor games."

"Like baseball?"

"Jah."

He offered her a wide grin. "I enjoy all of those things too, and since you like to play ball, you should have joined our game. We would've been happy to have you out there with us."

Emma wiped at the breadcrumbs stuck to the corners of her mouth. "I didn't want to interrupt. The game had already started with the right amount of players, and it would have been impolite if I'd asked to play."

"Not at all. I would have been fine with it, and I'm sure someone would have voluntarily stepped out for a while so you could have a go at it. I would've willingly stepped aside if I'd known you wanted to play."

"Well, it didn't happen, and I'm fine with it, really." Emma took a bite of her sandwich.

Ivan figured he'd better drop the subject and find something else to talk about. Dwelling on something that never happened was pointless. He did, however, want to learn more about Emma and hoped he would have another chance to get to know her better, beyond whatever time they would get today. One thing was certain: They shared interests, and Ivan was excited to find out more details about the young woman he'd just met.

After the meal, Emma excused herself to help several other women clear things off the tables. She'd enjoyed talking with Ivan as she ate. He appeared to be a nice enough fellow, and they seemed to have a few things in common, but it wouldn't be appropriate to take up all his time this afternoon. No doubt there were people here he would like to visit with, and she didn't want him feeling obligated to keep her entertained.

When Emma entered the house, following Ida Mae, the first thing she spotted was a lovely quilt draped over the back of the sofa in the living room. Since it had been folded, she couldn't tell what the measurements were, but she figured it might be the size of a lap robe, which would be a perfect covering on a chilly winter evening. The small squares of fabric had been arranged by color to form rings of brightly colored diamonds, which were framed by a wide border. Emma couldn't help but stare at the sections where she could see most of the quilt.

"I see you have noticed my mother's old quilt," Ida Mae said to Emma. "It's a beautiful pattern, don't you think?"

"Jah, it's very appealing. Does the quilt have a name?" Emma questioned.

"It's called the Sunshine and Shadows pattern," Ida Mae replied.

"Before we had the option of using a sewing machine to assemble a quilt, my mother stitched this together by hand. My father gave it to me when she passed on." With a faraway look, Ida Mae sighed. "After receiving this quilt, I became interested in quilting. When I found a good teacher, I spent many hours, and still do, either quilting by hand or doing some of the work on my treadle sewing machine."

"If I was ever going to make a quilt, I think I'd want to stitch it by hand."

"Would you be interested in learning?"

Emma nodded. "I would be, but there isn't time for that, since my grandmother is trying to teach me how to sew my own dresses and cook a decent meal. I imagine it'll take me the whole summer to be able to do either one adequately, if at all."

"Don't lose heart, Emma. My dear friend Luellen is skilled at both sewing and cooking, so I'm quite sure she's a good teacher." Ida Mae patted Emma's shoulder with her free hand. "In your free time, you might be interested in coming by the fabric store on a Friday or Saturday, which is when I normally work there. If you like, we can look at some quilt patterns together. After you find one you like, I'd be happy to give you some lessons here at the house on any of the days I have off. I'm sure you'll have some free time to do other things besides sew and cook."

Emma thought about Ida Mae's offer a few seconds before responding. "I would surely like that, but I'll have to wait and see what Grandma has to say about the idea. She might feel that learning to quilt would take up too much of my time."

"Would you like me to speak with her about it?"

Emma shook her head. "I appreciate your willingness, but if I feel that the time is right, I'll bring up the topic to Grandma."

Ida Mae's lips curled upward. "All right then, and I guess for now, we'd better take the empty plates we're holding into the kitchen."

Emma allowed Ida Mae to lead the way, and as they headed down the hall, Emma's thoughts were overtaken by the idea of learning how to quilt. She hoped when she had the courage to bring up the topic, Grandma would be in favor of letting her take some quilting lessons.

Her sentiments on the intricate design of the Sunshine and Shadows quilt lingered. She had been enthralled by its design and the heritage tied to the old quilt, and it reminded Emma of the first quilt she'd been given. Wouldn't she want to pass on those memories to her children someday? Emma considered that learning to quilt might make her time here in Arthur more interesting and give her a good reason to get up every morning.

Chapter 5

"It's sure nice that you could join us today," Ivan's sister Jane said when Emma entered the kitchen with Ida Mae.

Emma smiled. "*Danki* for the meal. The food was *appeditlich*."

"Oh, it was nothing special," Ida Mae commented.

"You're being too modest," her daughter Norma protested. "Everything our mamm makes is delicious. She's a great cook, and I'm glad we have her to teach us, so that when we get married someday, our husbands won't be disappointed."

"What about you, Emma? Do you enjoy cooking?" Jane questioned.

"My granddaughter will be learning to cook in my kitchen while she's staying at our home this summer," Grandma piped up from across the room, where she was packing leftovers into a plastic container. "Fortunately, Emma hasn't charred any kettles or frying pans yet."

Emma's eyes burned, and her cheeks felt as if they were engulfed in their own kitchen fire. She quickly dropped her gaze to the floor. It was all she could do to keep from dashing out the kitchen door. *How could Grandma embarrass me like that? I can only imagine what these ladies must think of me. Most women my age know how to cook and are fully prepared for marriage. I should have listened when Mom tried to hold my attention and teach me how to follow recipes so I could bake and cook with ease. If I had done that, I wouldn't have been sent to Grandma's house and wouldn't be standing here filled with humiliation.*

As though she was keenly aware of Emma's embarrassment, Ida Mae stepped up to her and slipped an arm around her waist. "I didn't always cook well," she said in a soothing tone. "It took time and patience on my mother's part to teach me, not to mention a willingness on my part, which didn't come easy."

Emma's shoulders relaxed a little, feeling a bit better after hearing those words of encouragement. Dabbing at the corners of her eyes, she immediately set to work helping to put away all the leftovers, then offered to help Jane wash the empty serving dishes.

"I appreciate your help," Jane said, handing Emma a dish towel. "It'll give us a chance to talk and get better acquainted."

Emma wasn't sure what they had to talk about. Other than her grandmother, she didn't know Ivan's sister or anyone else in the kitchen, for that matter. On the way to church this morning, Grandma had mentioned that a little over a year ago, the Yoder family had moved here from the town of Sullivan, which was southwest of Arthur. Emma and her family hadn't been to Arthur to visit her grandparents for two years, well before the Yoders had moved to the town. Grandma and Grandpa had come to Shipshewana to see Emma's family a couple of times during that two-year period, but there had been no mention of a new family moving to the area and becoming a part of their church district.

I sure hope Jane doesn't say anything to anyone else about me not knowing how to cook, Emma thought as she began to dry one of the serving dishes. *I wish Grandma had never blurted that out, and I don't understand what caused her to do so. Didn't she realize how embarrassed I would be with that announcement being made in front of the women who had come to the kitchen to help with the cleanup? If only I could say something to her about it, but would it really do any good? She'd probably tell me that I was making a big deal out of nothing.*

"What do you enjoy doing for fun?" Jane asked, bringing Emma's thoughts to a halt.

"I like fishing, hiking, and baseball," Emma replied. "Not much else that I can think of."

"So you're the outdoorsy sort. You'd probably like spending time with my brother. Ivan enjoys those pastimes too."

"He mentioned that while we were eating our meal."

"That doesn't surprise me. Doing what he loves does make him feel truly happy." Jane handed Emma another dish to dry. "I do feel sorry for Ivan at times."

"How come?"

"He's been pressured to work in our daed's harness shop, but he doesn't enjoy working there at all." Jane lifted her shoulders and gave a huff. "I don't understand why some parents think their children have to follow in their footsteps. Don't they realize everyone has their own dreams and hopes for the future?"

Emma paused for a moment before peering over at Jane, her hands twisting the damp dish towel. She was about to ask Ivan's sister what her hopes and dreams were, but Emma never got the words out because Ivan bounded into the room, grinning from ear to ear as he rubbed his hands together.

"Wanted to let you ladies know that the ice cream's done now, but it has to set awhile until it's nice and firm. Sure will be glad when Papa announces that it's ready to dish up."

Seeing the look of exuberance on Ivan's face, Emma couldn't help but smile. He reminded her of a child eager to open his presents on Christmas Day. There was something about this young man that made Emma long to know him better. There didn't seem to be a shy bone in Ivan's body, and she yearned to have some of that enthusiasm spill out on her. It wasn't that Emma was depressed, but she hadn't found anything that excited her enough to become all fired up about it. Maybe that was because she kept too many of her feelings bottled up and wasn't even sure what she wanted or what would make her feel complete. It sure wasn't sewing or cooking—Emma knew that much. But one way or the other, she needed to learn both, or Grandma would probably feel like a failure. Mom wouldn't be happy either if Emma returned home knowing nothing more than she had when she left. It was pretty much a no-win situation, and Emma was the loser.

Emma put her musings aside and concentrated on the job at hand.

The kitchen was overly warm and stuffy, and the sooner she and Jane got the dishes done, the quicker she could go outside, where the early-evening air was bound to be more tolerable than being cooped up in here.

Half an hour later, Emma wandered out of the house and paused on the porch to take a few welcoming deep breaths. She'd been right—the air was better outdoors, and a slight breeze had picked up, cooling the yard to a tolerable temperature. One thing about summer that Emma appreciated was that when the sun went down, cooler temperatures normally made the evening hours more bearable.

"You ready for a bowl of ice cream, Emma?" Ivan called to her from the front yard.

She gave a hearty nod. "Jah, that would be nice and refreshing."

"Okay then, why don't you have a seat at one of the tables, and I'll bring you a bowl?"

"Oh, you don't have to wait on me," Emma was quick to say. "I can walk over to wherever the ice-cream maker is located and dish some up myself."

"I don't mind bringing it to you. Besides, you're a guest here, and you shouldn't have to do anything." Ivan stepped onto the porch and came over to stand beside her. The nearness of him caused goose bumps to erupt on Emma's arms. At least she thought that was the cause. Maybe it was simply the evening breeze that had given her a chill.

"Since you won't let me serve you, I'll walk with you over to where my daed has the big canister of ice cream." Ivan bumped shoulders with her. "You coming, Emma?"

"Jah, of course." After Emma and Ivan left the porch, they both picked up a clean bowl from the end of one of the tables, where a variety of cookies had been set out. Feeling kind of giddy suddenly, Emma walked with him across the yard to where his father knelt by the oversized ice-cream freezer. Her lips quivered in anticipation of what was to come.

"One scoop or two?" Ivan's father asked, grinning up at Emma and scooping the frozen dessert from the gallon-sized mixing canister.

"I think just one," she responded.

"Better give her two, Papa. Your ice cream is always so good, and one scoop is never enough."

Ivan was very persuasive, so Emma didn't argue. She simply handed her bowl to Ivan's dad, waited for the two scoops, and said, "Danki."

"Let's get some *kichlin* now and find a place to sit, Emma. There should be plenty of empty places, since several of our friends have gone home already."

"Okay." Emma couldn't help wondering if Ivan enjoyed her company or was only being polite. Surely there were other people here whom he would rather spend time with, like the young people he'd been playing ball with earlier. Whatever the reason, he'd invited her to join him to eat their ice cream and cookies, so she wasn't about to turn down the offer. Truth was, Emma felt comfortable with Ivan, and she appreciated his kindness and willingness to spend time with her. Although most of the young people had introduced themselves during their earlier meal, none of them had shown an interest in her the way Ivan had.

Emma noticed the lawn and the lush foliage were bathed in a golden color, courtesy of the setting sun. They found a table where Ivan's sisters, Norma and Jane, were enjoying their dessert, and seated themselves across from the young women.

Emma took a cautious bite of ice cream, hoping the cold treat wouldn't give her a brain freeze, and then she followed it with one of Grandma's peanut butter cookies.

Yum! Tasty as always, Emma thought as she took another bite of the homemade treat. *I do wish I could learn to at least bake cookies that taste half this good.*

"Next Sunday evening we've been invited to attend a young people's singing," Jane said, glancing at Emma. "I hope you'll be able to join us."

Before Emma could form a response, Norma spoke up. "Jah, you should come, Emma. It's gonna be held at my friend Mary Sue Lehman's house." Norma paused to brush a few cookie crumbs off the front of her dress. "Actually, it's Mary Sue's parents' home. They live in a different church district from ours, but their place is only a few miles from here."

Emma wasn't sure how to respond. She loved to sing, and had always enjoyed the singings held back home. The problem was, she wouldn't know the majority of young people in Arthur, and it would be hard to socialize with people she wasn't acquainted with. "Umm. . .well, I'll have to wait and see how it goes. Grandpa would have to drive me there, and my grandparents would need to give me their approval to go."

"No, he wouldn't have to bother hitching a horse to his carriage to drive you," Ivan interjected. "I'd be happy to come get you. I'll be taking my sisters anyway, so one more person in the buggy won't be a problem at all."

"My brother's right," Jane chimed in, scooping up what was left of the ice cream in her bowl. "The more the merrier, and we'd love to have you at the singing."

Emma looked over at Ivan and couldn't help but notice his broad grin. He rubbed one side of his reddish-brown hair, exposing a small mole on his upper neck. How could Emma say no to the enthusiasm that these three siblings shared? She licked the last of her vanilla ice cream from her spoon. "All right, as long as my grandparents have no objections, I'd be happy to accompany you all to the singing."

On the way home that evening, Luellen noticed how quiet their granddaughter was in the back seat of the buggy. *Is Emma tired, or could she be upset with me for blurting out earlier that she didn't know how to cook and had come here to learn under my tutorage?* Luellen's stomach knotted as soon as she considered such a possibility.

Once they arrived home and Marlin had unhitched the horse and taken him to the barn, Luellen stopped walking. She turned to face Emma and said, "About what I said earlier, I'm truly sorry for blurting out this afternoon that you'd come here to learn how to cook and sew." She took a deep breath. "It was not my intent to embarrass you. The words just came flying out of my mouth before I had a chance to think about what I was saying."

Emma stepped onto the porch before replying. "What you said did upset me, Grandma, but I'm not mad and I accept your apology. I do embarrass easily, and I know I need to have thicker skin."

Luellen nodded and followed Emma onto the porch. "Sometimes people say things without thinking, and unfortunately, I tend to be one of them. It's an area in my life that still needs to be worked on, and I will try to do better from now on so I don't embarrass you again."

They entered the house, and before it became too dark to see in the dimly lit space, Luellen began lighting the gas lamps overhead in the living room, noticing how the shadows of her granddaughter's body in the light from the lamp snaked along the wall of the entryway. "Much better. We don't need anyone tripping over anything in here. Would you like something cold to drink, Emma, or maybe a bite to eat?"

"No thanks, Grandma. After all I ate today, I'm really not hungerich. Also, the ice cream and cookies we had filled me up real good."

Luellen nodded. "Me too."

Emma yawned, lifting her arms above her head covering. "I am feeling *mied*, though, so I think I'll head on up to bed."

Luellen placed the empty basket she held, that had once been filled with cookies, on the accent table by her favorite chair. "I'm tired too, so as soon as your grandpa comes in, we'll probably both call it a night."

"All right, I'll see you in the morning."

"Hope you sleep well, Emma."

Her granddaughter stroked the tip of her upturned nose and said, "You too."

Luellen watched as Emma left the room and headed up the stairs. Overall, today was a good day, and it had been pleasant to visit with friends at the Yoders' house. It had also been nice to see Ivan visiting with Emma, which Luellen felt sure had helped to make her granddaughter feel welcomed. She wondered if the young man was just being polite or if he had taken a personal interest in Emma.

Now wouldn't it be something if Ivan and Emma began courting, and she ended up staying here in Arthur permanently?

Ivan reclined on his bed and settled in against the pillow with both hands behind his head. Today was good, and he'd enjoyed visiting with Emma even more than eating his fill of ice cream and cookies. A smile tugged on Ivan's lips as he stared up at the ceiling. There was a sweetness about her, and he looked forward to getting to know Emma even better this summer.

Ivan was glad his sisters had invited Emma to go with them to the singing next Sunday. When the invitation was given, he'd noted Emma's reaction. Her cheeks deepened in a rosy shade yet still retained those prominent dimples, a fine mix of meekness interwoven with excitement. Although Emma hadn't committed to going, she had said she would ask her grandparents' permission. He really hoped that neither of them would object to him picking Emma up and taking her to the event. After all, it wasn't like they would be alone. Jane and Norma would be along as chaperones, so to speak. Ivan had considered asking Emma himself, but Norma had beaten him to it.

If Ivan had a chance to find some free time away from work this week, he might go over to the Herschbergers' place and ask Emma's grandparents if they would mind if he and his sisters gave Emma a ride to the singing. Then he'd know for sure if Emma could go, and he wouldn't have to worry about it anymore. He sure didn't want to wait until the evening of the singing and show up at the Herschbergers, expecting to give Emma a ride, and then be told by Marlin or Luellen that Emma did not have their permission to go.

That's what I'm gonna do, all right, Ivan told himself. *The first chance I get this week, I'm going to head over to their house and ask the question myself.* Now that the problem was settled, Ivan's eyes became heavier and the remembrance of what had taken place a few hours before lulled him to sleep.

Chapter 6

THE FOLLOWING MORNING, WHEN EMMA entered the kitchen, she found Grandpa sitting at the table, munching on a bowl of cold cereal. There were no delicious smells wafting in the room, no coffee perking on the stove, and no heat radiating from the oven. Emma thought it was strange, and she asked Grandpa where Grandma was this morning.

"She's still in bed," he replied.

Emma rubbed underneath her brow. "How come? Is she *grank*?"

"I don't believe she's sick—just tired is all."

"Did she stay up too late last night?" Emma questioned.

"Not really. We were both in bed before ten." Grandpa finished his bowl of cereal and brought it over to the sink. "She hasn't been sleeping well lately, and I'm thinking it might be our *matratz*."

"What could be wrong with your mattress?"

"Nothing specific, but it's old. We've had it almost thirty years, and it's probably time for a new one. Almost every morning when your grandmother wakes up, she complains of her back hurting. I've been sleeping on the old thing with no trouble, though." Grandpa opened the shade at the window above the sink, which brought a welcoming ray of light into the room. "That's probably why she tosses and turns most every night. My poor fraa can't seem to find a comfortable position. She also sleeps with a pillow under her knees, but it doesn't seem to help much either."

Emma was tempted to question her grandfather as to why they hadn't purchased a new mattress in the span of thirty years, but he'd probably tell her they were too expensive or they had been sleeping on it well up to this point, so there had been no need to spend money on a new one.

"That's too bad," Emma said. "No wonder I've seen her rubbing her back several times."

He drummed his fingers along the counter with a nod. "Think I'm gonna hire a driver soon and visit one of the furniture stores in Champaign. It's about the largest town near Arthur. But since it's forty-one miles north of here, it's too far to go by horse and buggy. Of course," he added, "I'll have to wait until your grandma is available to go with me. She might not like me picking out a matratz without her having the opportunity to try it out in the store."

"That makes good sense," Emma agreed. "You need a mattress that you're both comfortable sleeping on."

"For sure." Grandpa grabbed his straw hat from a wall peg near the back door and slapped it on his head. "I'd best get on out to the barn now and take care of the chores."

"Don't you want more to eat than just cereal? I could probably boil you some *oier*," Emma offered. She figured she wasn't likely to mess that up, unless she boiled the eggs too long or not long enough. As she recalled, her mother always set a timer for ten minutes, and the eggs came out fine.

"No thanks, Emma," he said with a tip of his head. "Once your grandma gets up and fixes her breakfast, I might have a little of whatever she's prepared. Right now, I need to get out to the barn."

"Okay. I'll see you later."

When Grandpa went out the back door, Emma stood with her arms folded as she debated what to prepare for her own breakfast. It would be nice if she could fix something substantial and serve it to Grandma when she got up, but knowing her lack of cooking skills she'd most likely mess up whatever she made.

Maybe I'll just settle for cold cereal too, Emma told herself as she opened the pantry door. *Besides, it could be a while before Grandma gets up, and if I did fix her something and it flopped, I'm sure she wouldn't appreciate the taste, texture, or anything else.*

Rays of light spilling into the room from the window shade drawn up halfway greeted Luellen as she opened her eyes. A quick glance at the alarm clock by her bed let Luellen know immediately that she'd overslept.

"Oh no," she murmured as she sat up in bed. "I should have been up two hours ago." She pulled the sheet and lightweight blanket aside and sat on the edge of the bed. A sharp pain shot through her lower back when she stood.

If I hadn't slept in and gotten up when I should have, maybe my back wouldn't hurt so much. Luellen reached around to rub the tight muscles and winced. *Too many hours lying on a mattress that's no longer firm isn't good for me or Marlin.*

Luellen managed to get dressed without too much pain, and then she started for the kitchen, wondering if her husband had fended for himself. *Or perhaps*, she thought, *maybe Emma managed to fix something for both to eat.*

When she entered the kitchen, Luellen discovered her granddaughter sitting at the table with what appeared to be a letter in her hands. She moved slowly across the room with care before coming to a stop next to her granddaughter. "Good morning, Emma. Did you write a letter to somebody, or is that one you received?"

"It's a letter from my mamm, letting me know that she'd heard from my driver that I arrived here safely."

"Well, that's good." Luellen scooted out a chair and joined Emma at the table. She hoped sitting might ease the pain in her back. "I apologize for not getting up on time and neglecting to fix breakfast this morning."

"It's okay, Grandma. Everyone deserves to sleep in once in a while."

"I suppose. Did you manage to fix something for you and your *grossdaddi* to eat?"

"Actually, by the time I got up, Grandpa had already fixed himself a bowl of cold cereal. In fact, he was almost finished when I came into the kitchen."

"That's good to know. My dear husband was very thoughtful to allow me to sleep in." Luellen reached over and placed a hand on Emma's slender arm. "What about your breakfast? Did you have some cereal too?"

"Jah, and after I finished eating, I washed and dried the dishes. Then, I walked down to the mailbox. That's when I found the letter from home." Emma pointed to the desk across the room. "I put yours and Grandpa's mail over there."

"Danki, Emma." Luellen pushed back her chair and stood. "Guess I'd better get busy and fix myself something to eat." Holding her right hand against the small of her back, she made her way across the room to the pantry. "Think I'll have some cereal too."

"I can get it for you," Emma was quick to offer. "It looks like you might have a *buckelweh*."

"You're right, I do have a backache, but it isn't so bad that I can't fix my own breakfast. I appreciate your offer though." Luellen grabbed a box of cereal, took a bowl from the cupboard, and poured the cereal in. The only thing left to do now was get out the milk from their propane-operated refrigerator.

"Did your mother have any interesting news to share?" Luellen asked after she'd taken a seat at the table again.

"Not really. Mom just said she was glad I made it here safely and that she hoped my training was going well." Emma gave a quick shake of her head. "The only thing I've made was that horrible meat loaf, and as you know, my first sewing lesson didn't go well either." She leaned forward with both elbows on the table and released a sigh. "What if I'm not teachable, Grandma? How can I return home at the end of summer and face my parents if I don't learn a thing?"

Luellen felt bad for her granddaughter. Emma's wounded expression and tone of defeat pulled at her heartstrings. "It'll be okay, Emma," she assured. "As you stated, you've only had one cooking and one sewing lesson. Things like that take some time, so don't give up hope. When

I've finished eating breakfast, we'll go to the treadle sewing machine, and you can work more on your dress. Then later this afternoon, I'll teach you how to make fried chicken for supper."

Emma folded her mother's letter and slipped it into its envelope. "Okay. Hopefully I won't mess things up too much, here in the kitchen or at the sewing machine."

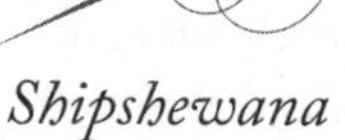

Shipshewana

"How was your day?" Dianna asked when Rachel arrived home from her job, where she cleaned house and did a few additional chores for one of their elderly widowed neighbors.

"It went okay." Rachel swiped a hand across her forehead. "But I'm tired, hot, and sweaty. I need a breather before I can even think of doing anything else today."

"Come into the kitchen, and I'll give you something cold to drink. How's that sound?"

"It would be appreciated." With slumped shoulders, Rachel shuffled into the kitchen.

Dianna followed, and when Rachel lowered herself into a chair, Dianna got out the lemonade she'd made earlier and filled a glass. "Here you go." She handed it to her daughter.

Rachel took a long drink and set the glass down. "Ah, that hit the spot. Danki, Mom."

"You're welcome." Dianna poured a glass for herself and sat across from Rachel. "I didn't get a chance to ask you this morning, but how did things go at the singing last night? Did you have a good time with your steady boyfriend?"

"The singing itself went all right, I guess." Rachel dropped her gaze to the table. "But I'm not sure how steady David and I are anymore."

Dianna raised her brows. "What makes you think that?"

"For one thing, he wasn't very talkative, at least not with me." Her chin quivered slightly as she looked up at Dianna. "He talked with some of his pals before the singing started, though. I even saw him speaking to my friend Alice, and it wasn't the first time I've spotted them together." Tears welled in Rachel's eyes. "I believe David may be interested in her, and I have to wonder if he might be on the verge of breaking up with me."

Dianna leaned forward and clasped her daughter's hand. "I hope that's not the case. I can't imagine after going out with you these past two years that David would suddenly take an interest in someone else—and especially not your best friend."

Rachel drew back and slouched in her chair. "Two years with no proposal in sight, which to me means he doesn't really love me."

"Has David said as much?"

"Well, no, but. . ."

"Then perhaps you're worried about nothing. You may be reading too much into it."

"It's not that simple, Mom. Something has changed between us, and I need to face up to that fact. I can't talk about this anymore. It's too painful." Rachel pushed her chair back and stood. "I'm going up to my room and rest for a while until it's time to help you make supper. Maybe resting in the privacy of my room will do me some good."

Dianna wanted to say something more, but Rachel darted out of the room too quickly for her to get any words out. As she remained seated at the table, her hands resting on its aged surface, Dianna reflected on her three daughters and their ongoing struggles. She believed that her unwavering faith in God and unrelenting trust would help her girls withstand their trials and persevere through their hardships.

With folded hands and her head bowed, Dianna said a silent prayer. *Heavenly Father, I'm concerned about all three of my girls. The daughter who left home and may never return; the one who is hurting because she believes her boyfriend doesn't love her; and my youngest girl, who is struggling to find her way while she learns the skills of sewing and cooking under the teachings of my mamm. Please be with them all, and may Your will be done in each of their lives.*

Arthur

With the encouragement of her grandmother, Emma settled into a chair in front of the treadle sewing machine for her second sewing lesson. Nothing about learning to sew came easy to her—especially not the use of the pedals on this machine that Grandma had used a good many years.

"Now remember, Emma," Grandma said, "When using a treadle machine, don't place your feet side by side. You need to have one foot higher than the other on the treadle plate. Let's have you practice for a while without the use of fabric or thread until you get a good feel for it. Treadle machines sew very well, and once you get the hang of it, you'll do a fine job of stitching your fabric to create an acceptable dress."

"I hope you're right, Grandma." Emma struggled to keep her feet in the correct position as she pushed against the treadle plate, which moved the threadless needle up and down.

"Practice makes perfect, dear one, which is why I suggested you use the machine for a while before sewing any seams on the dress we cut out the other day. The pieces are all pinned, so as soon as you feel confident using the machine, you'll be ready to start sewing some seams."

Emma gulped against the lump that had formed in her throat. She wasn't sure she could even sew a straight seam, much less complete a dress.

"Oh, there are a few more things you should know," Grandma added. "This sewing machine is very reliable and sews the straightest stitches. However, the backward stitching can sometimes be a bit annoying when you lift the pressure foot, flip the project around, lift again, and flip it back around."

"You said there were a few things. What else do I need to know about?" Emma questioned.

"Be sure you pull the flywheel toward you to start stitching. Otherwise, it won't work."

Oh great, Emma thought with a grimace. *Now I have even more to worry about. This is hopeless.*

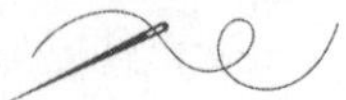

When Emma took a break from practicing, she brought up Ida Mae's suggestion about teaching her how to quilt. Since she had first laid eyes on Ida Mae's quilt, Emma remained curious about what it would be like to quilt. She didn't want to pass up the opportunity to learn something and perhaps even make her own quilt by hand, because this might be her only chance before she returned home.

"I'd really like to try it, Grandma," Emma said. "Do you think there would be time for me to do something like that?"

A smile spread across her grandmother's face. "We'll make time. You won't be spending every hour in a day learning to cook and sew, and it would be nice if you had the opportunity to learn the art of quilting."

Emma rolled her neck from side to side. "Quilting looks hard, though, and I might be too dumm to learn."

"You're not dumb, Emma. You're an intelligent young woman, and if you wish to learn something badly enough, then you'll catch on quickly." Grandma gestured to the material they'd bought last week. "We can talk about that later, though, because right now you need to get busy and start stitching on that frack."

Emma sighed, pinching the thin steel of a sewing needle between her fingers. *Well, at least Grandma didn't say no to my request to learn how to quilt. I hope she gives me an answer soon so I can let Ida Mae know whether I can take lessons from her or not.*

That afternoon, once the sewing project had been stowed away for another day, Grandma presented Emma with a freshly plucked and cleaned chicken. Then, before Emma could comment, Grandma said, "Remember now, we will be having fried chicken for supper this evening."

Emma had a feeling about what was coming next, and she braced herself for it.

"I'm going to cut up the chicken for you into proper pieces," Grandma stated. "And then it will be your job to fry each piece so that they all come out crispy on the outside and juicy inside."

Emma didn't figure it would be that hard to handle the frying part, but she wasn't sure where to begin. She gripped her hands together, awaiting further instructions.

Several minutes later, after her grandmother had cut up the chicken, she turned to face Emma and rattled off the recipe instructions quicker than Emma could blink. No recipe book; no 3x5 recipe card—Grandma obviously knew the fried chicken recipe by heart.

"You got all that, Emma?"

"Not all of it. I—I think I may have missed a few things that you said. Would you mind repeating the instructions for me?"

Grandma began again, stating that Emma should use a cup of buttermilk, two cups of all-purpose flour, salt and pepper to taste, and one teaspoon of paprika. Then she went on to tell Emma how to dip the chicken pieces in the buttermilk, then put them in a bag with the flour and dry ingredients. Next, she explained what to do with the coated chicken, and said something about the consistency and that it was crucial.

By this time, Emma felt like her head was swimming with information that she might not remember once she began the process of preparing the chicken for frying.

A loud knock sounded on the front door, at which time Grandma looked at Emma and said, "Go ahead and do what I told you, while I see who's at the door." She whirled around and scurried out of the kitchen.

One by one, Emma took all the ingredients out of the cupboard and set them on the counter. She couldn't help but notice as Grandma left the room that she wasn't holding or rubbing her back, the way she'd done this morning. Emma figured that maybe after Grandma had been out of bed for a few hours, the pain lessened. Perhaps Grandpa had been right when he'd said they needed a new mattress. That would probably be all it would take to fix Grandma's back.

Emma pushed her thoughts aside and tried to concentrate on the job at hand. She was about to reach for a cast-iron skillet when Grandma returned to the kitchen with Ivan Yoder at her side.

"Look who came by to see us." Grandma fairly beamed as she

gestured to Ivan. "He was out in the barn talking to your grossdaddi, and then he came up to the house to speak with me."

"Oh?" Emma's single word came out in a squeak.

"Jah." Ivan bobbed his auburn head. "I asked your grandparents if they had objections to me comin' by here this Sunday evening to give you a ride to the singing my sisters and I will be going to." His prominent cheekbones seemed to expand as he looked over at Emma. "They both said it was fine, so I'll come by Sunday around four thirty to pick you up. That is, if you're okay with it."

Emma was afraid to respond verbally, for fear of losing her voice again, so she merely nodded. Her fingers, covered in flour, curled into the palms of her hands as waves of heat rushed over Emma's body.

"That's great," he said, rubbing one hand down the side of his trousers.

"Okay, I'll see you then," Emma said, glad that she'd been able to get the words out.

"You definitely will," he responded with a wink. "But you'll see me this evening too, 'cause your grandma invited me to stay for supper."

Emma almost dropped the chicken wing she'd just picked up. *This is not good,* she thought, attempting to concentrate on coating the chicken pieces in the mixture. *If I mess up this meal, Ivan will truly know that I can't cook.*

Chapter 7

Ivan stood quietly for a few minutes, trying to analyze the expression he saw on Emma's face. Was she disappointed that he'd been invited to stay for supper, or had she been caught off guard and merely surprised? Would it be rude to ask? He couldn't decide.

Although Ivan had come here to ask Emma's grandparents if he could give her a ride to the singing this coming Sunday evening, the thought of eating supper with Emma and her grandparents was too appealing, and he couldn't say no.

Marlin sauntered into the kitchen just then and put his hand on Ivan's shoulder. "I bet my fraa invited you to stay for supper. Am I right?"

Ivan bobbed his head. "And I accepted gratefully." He glanced at Emma again, hoping she might give him some sign that she was glad he was staying, but she'd turned her back to him. Emma appeared to be busy doing something to the chicken Ivan had seen lying on a baking sheet on the counter.

"Do you think your folks will mind you not being there to eat with them tonight?" Marlin asked, tapping Ivan's arm.

"Huh?"

Emma's grandfather repeated what he'd said.

"Uh, no, I don't think my folks will mind. Although I have no way of letting my mamm know about your invitation, I'm sure she won't be surprised when I don't show up for supper. Mom knew I was coming here to seek your approval to take Emma to the singing, so she'll probably assume that I stayed here to eat supper with you."

"That's real good then. Glad to have you here with us." Marlin started moving toward the kitchen door, then turned and gestured for Ivan to follow. "Let's go in the living room and rest awhile, until the ladies get supper on the table. I had a busy day butchering several chickens, and I'm sure you must be tired from working in the harness shop today."

"You got that right. There's always a lot of work in my daed's shop," Ivan said as he followed Marlin out the door. He'd been tempted to volunteer his services in the kitchen, but with the strange way Emma had looked at him, he figured his presence probably wouldn't be wanted.

And maybe, Ivan thought, *she's not pleased about me being here for supper. When we were together last time, I thought we were bonding a bit. I enjoyed talking with Emma, but perhaps she doesn't share my sentiments. I may have made her feel uncomfortable.*

After Luellen got some iced tea made and poured in glasses for the men, she turned to Emma and said, "You go ahead and finish getting the *hinkel* ready to fry, while I take these cold beverages into the men."

Emma repeated Luellen's instruction as a question.

"Jah, and if you run into any trouble or have a question about something, just give me a holler." Luellen picked up the glasses and left the room.

When she entered the living room, she found her husband and Ivan engaged in conversation as they sat beside each other on the sofa. "I brought you both some iced tea." Luellen handed each man a glass.

"Danki," they said in unison. They even took a drink at the same time.

Luellen couldn't help smiling. She started to leave the room, but Marlin called out to her. "Do you know where I put the old clock that was my grandfather's?"

She tipped her head from side to side. "Hmm. . .I believe it might be up in the attic with a bunch of other things we rarely look at."

"You may be right. Think I'll go up there and see if I can find it."

"Right now?"

"Jah. I want to show it to Ivan. See if he can get it running again." Marlin drank some of his tea, set the glass down on the small table beside the sofa, and stood.

"Would you like me to go with you?" Ivan asked.

"No, probably better not. It might take me some time to find it. Why don't you just sit here and relax while I'm gone?"

"Oh, okay." Ivan sagged against the back of the sofa as Marlin left the room.

Luellen figured the young man was probably disappointed that he hadn't been invited to investigate the attic. If Ivan was interested in seeing an antiquated clock, he may have enjoyed looking at some of the other old things up there too. Rather than leaving Ivan here all alone, she took a seat on one of the straight-backed chairs and struck up a conversation with him.

"Your mamm mentioned to me that you enjoy repairing clocks." Luellen laced her fingers together.

Ivan nodded and sat up straight. "Jah, it's my dream someday to own my own clock shop, where I can not only repair timepieces, but also build them from scratch, and of course, sell them as well."

"So it's much more than a hobby for you?"

"Definitely. I first became interested in clocks and watches when I was given my grandfather's old pocket watch after he passed away. I was honored to receive it, and since the watch had quit running, I was determined to get it working again."

"And did you?"

"Jah. I opened up the back and kept fooling with the mechanism till it started running again." His chest puffed out a bit. "I wasn't proud, but I'll have to admit, I felt pretty good about it."

"And rightly so," Luellen commented. "Not everyone has the ability to do what you did."

"That's what my mamm said too. In fact, she encourages me to follow my dream, although we both know I'm not ready to quit workin' for my daed at the harness shop and open up a clock store of my own."

"Perhaps it will happen sooner than you expect."

He smiled. "I hope so. No doubt I'd wake up every day with a big grin on my face."

"That's how Marlin used to feel when he was farming full-time. Those days weren't that long ago either."

The objects in the room faded as Luellen's thoughts took her back to the years when her husband was busy in the fields most of the day and came into the house every evening with a smile on his bearded face. He'd worked hard and put in long hours, but Marlin loved what he did, so he'd never seemed to mind the daunting tasks.

"Well, I found it!"

Marlin's booming voice scattered Luellen's thoughts, and she looked up to see him enter the room with the clock in his hands.

"I'm glad you were able to locate it." She left her seat and came over to stand beside him.

"Jah, but it wasn't easy." His brows furrowed. "Had to look in every nook and cranny, till I finally spotted it under a pile of old trousers that I'll never wear again. Don't know why you're even keeping 'em, Luellen."

She shrugged her shoulders. "You never know. I might need the material to patch the knees in a pair of your trousers. You do spend quite a bit of time on your *gnie*."

Curious to get a closer look at the clock, Ivan got up and approached them. He was also curious as to why Marlin spent a lot of time on his knees but figured he shouldn't ask, since it was none of his business. Maybe the man did a lot of praying and preferred to do it on bended knee.

One glance at the clock and Ivan knew it was an antique German Eastlake Victorian mantle clock. It was made of walnut wood, and he estimated it to have been made around 1890. The beautiful intricacies and carvings along the casing left him in awe, and he was excited to inspect it.

"Let's say we go over to the sofa again, Ivan," Marlin suggested.

"You can get a better look-see if we're both sitting down."

"Sounds good to me."

Ivan ambled back across the room and sank onto the sofa cushions. When Marlin joined him, he handed the clock to Ivan, while Luellen seated herself on the chair again. Ivan figured she might return to the kitchen to help Emma with supper preparations, but apparently, she thought her granddaughter could handle things on her own.

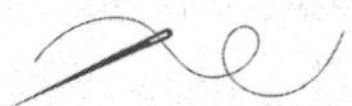

Emma had prepared the chicken, but she wasn't sure what to do next. Grandma had left the room with iced tea for the men a while ago and hadn't left further instructions for her. Here was Emma alone in the kitchen, overly warm and feeling frustrated, not sure if she was doing anything right, and wishing Grandma hadn't invited Ivan to stay for supper.

By the time her grandmother returned to the kitchen, Emma had the chicken in the frying pan with a lid. Seeming pleased, Grandma said, "Well, it certainly looks like you have everything under control."

I wish. My nerves are on edge and I can barely think straight. Emma didn't voice her thoughts. Instead, she turned to Grandma and said, "I hope so, but I'm not sure what else needs to be done while the chicken is cooking."

"You could set the table, while I cut up some potatoes and get them boiling on the stove. Once those are done, you can mash them and then make some chicken gravy."

"Will you be here to give me instructions?" Emma felt moisture on her forehead and above her upper lip. There wasn't a single thing about cooking that she enjoyed. She dreaded the outcome of everything she made.

"Yes, I'll be here in the kitchen with you, Emma," Grandma assured. "You'll do fine, so there's nothing to worry about."

That's easy for you to say, because cooking comes easy for you, Emma thought as she went to the cupboard and took out the plates. She wished once more that Ivan Yoder wasn't joining them for supper.

I need to stop stressing over this, she told herself. *The fact is he's here, and I can't do anything about it.*

"I need to go down to the cellar to get a few things," Grandma said after she'd finished peeling the potatoes.

"If you'll tell me what you need, I can go there for you," Emma volunteered. She would be happy to do most anything that would get her out of the kitchen for a while. And maybe if she was gone long enough, Grandma would take over the job of cooking the rest of the meal.

"I appreciate the offer, but it'll be easier if I go because I know where everything is." Grandma gestured to the potatoes she'd placed on the counter. "Besides, the makings of this meal are supposed to be all yours." On that note, she hustled out of the room. One would never know that her back had been hurting this morning.

Emma turned to the task of cutting the potatoes and sighed. She'd helped with this chore at home many times, but because Mom or Rachel always took care of this chore, she had never been responsible for cooking the potatoes or mashing them.

"Guess it can't be that hard," Emma murmured.

At Luellen's call, Ivan and Marlin came into the dining room, slid their chairs out, and took a seat while the two women carried out the supper dishes and set it all in the middle of the table. Once they prayed together in silence, Emma's grandfather was quick to dish up a heaping spoonful of mashed potatoes, and Luellen offered Ivan the chicken.

I don't think chicken is supposed to taste like that, Ivan thought as he drank water from his glass past his lips to moisten the piece of chicken in his mouth. He chewed on the meat as though it were a stick of bubble gum. *Tastes better watered down at least, but it's definitely overdone. I think Emma must have left it in the frying pan too long.*

Ivan gulped it down, then set the glass near his napkin and rubbed the condensation from his hand on his pant leg. Taking a breather from gnawing on the dried-up meat, Ivan picked up his fork, preparing to sample the mashed potatoes drizzled with the gravy he'd poured out of the gravy boat. Unfortunately, the chicken wasn't the only thing on Ivan's plate that hadn't been cooked well. The potatoes resting on his tongue were lumpy, while the gravy was overly floury and kind of bitter. Ivan realized he hadn't been masking how he responded to Emma's cooking very well when his gaze met hers across the table. Emma's glance fell on her plate, and judging by the looks of it, she hadn't even touched a thing.

"It isn't good." With a pensive expression, Emma's shoulders curled as she twisted the corner of her napkin. "I'm sorry. I messed up, didn't I?"

Before Ivan could swallow his mouthful of food and respond to her, Emma's grandfather cut in and said, "I'll say! What happened while you were in the kitchen, Emma? I would've thought you'd at least know how to make something as simple as chicken and mashed potatoes."

I thought Emma had said that cooking was one of her pastimes, but it seems more like she's a beginner, trying to learn how. I'll bet that's what she meant by being in the kitchen with her grandmother while she's here. It makes sense why Emma didn't seem thrilled that I was invited here tonight. Ivan bit down on his bottom lip. *Poor Emma must've tried her hardest to make all of this for us. She must be devastated that supper did not turn out well, and I sure don't want to discourage her from attempting to make anything else.*

"The chicken is nicely seasoned, Emma," Ivan commented. "And I can't get enough of the mashed potatoes you made." He stuffed another heap of the potatoes into his mouth, then another, and another, to prove his case. Ivan gave it a thumbs-up after chewing and swallowing, and then said, "I love having lumps in my spuds. It's great exercise for my mouth."

"What are you saying, Ivan?" Marlin grimaced. "Mashed potatoes aren't supposed to have lumps—"

A thump resounded from underneath the table, and Marlin let out a yelp. His neck twisted toward his wife. "Hey! What'd ya do that for?"

"Shh," Luellen whispered with her finger pressed to her lips. "I believe you've said enough, Marlin. Now please, eat the rest of your supper."

Ivan continued to scoop up the remainder of the lumpy potatoes that rested on his plate. Though the gravy was the least appealing part of the meal and covered the mounds of potato, Ivan felt confident that he could finish devouring it efficiently, unlike the chicken. Ivan took the last bite of his mashed potatoes and looked around the table, then right at Emma, offering her a reassuring smile. Unfortunately, she barely met his gaze as she began to cut into the chicken on her plate.

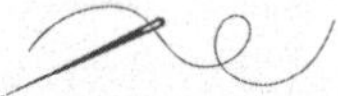

"Say, I have an idea," Emma's grandpa announced after the supper dishes had been cleared and put in the pan that had been placed inside the kitchen sink to soak.

"What idea is that, Marlin?" Grandma asked.

"Well now, as I'm sure you all know, it's still pretty hot in the house, so I was thinking it might be nice if I go outside, build a *feier*, and. . ."

"A fire?" Grandma's thin brows shot up. "You want us to sit around a hot bonfire?"

"Don't look so concerned, Luellen," he responded. "I'm not planning to make a big roaring fire. I'll make sure it's just enough so we can roast marshmallows. It'll be our dessert." His gaze swept over everyone in the room. "How's that sound?"

"Sounds good to me," Ivan was quick to say.

Emma nodded, and so did Grandma. Letting out a sigh, Emma pushed aside the lingering embarrassment of tonight's supper mishap to the back of her mind. After all, they might need a firepit gathering under the stars to forget about the dried chicken and lumpy potatoes she had served.

Grandpa rubbed his hands together and offered them a wide grin. "All right then. I'm gonna head outside." He looked at Ivan. "You comin'?"

"Sure, I'll help you get the fire started." Ivan glanced at Emma over his shoulder before following her grandfather out the back door.

"I feel terrible about messing up our supper," Emma told her grandmother. "I can only imagine what Ivan must think of me and my cooking skills." She frowned. "Or it might be better to say—the lack of them."

"Don't be so hard on yourself. It really wasn't that bad." Grandma patted Emma gently on the back. "You're still learning, remember?"

"Jah, learning to mess up everything." Emma lifted her hands, and then she touched her sweltering cheeks. "I'm sure Ivan must realize that I can't cook. He was just being polite by eating his meal and not agreeing with the things Grandpa said."

"Humph!" Grandma's features tightened as she folded her arms. "That husband of mine deserved the kick I gave him under the table. Sometimes he's entirely too blunt, and he doesn't even think about whether he will hurt someone's feelings or embarrass them, which I'm sure he succeeded in doing. Right, Emma?"

Emma lowered her gaze, fighting back tears of frustration. "I was embarrassed, but what he said was the truth. There was nothing good about the meal I cooked for us this evening."

"You'll get the hang of it soon, just wait and see. Practice makes. . ."

"I know—perfect."

"That's right. And now, my dear granddaughter, it's time for the two of us to join the menfolk outside."

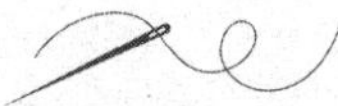

"I'm sorry about the way supper turned out," Emma said when she took a seat on a bench beside Ivan.

"Wh–what do you mean?" he questioned.

Emma scrunched up her nose. "My grandpa was right. The gravy was awful, the potatoes were chunky, and the chicken was way too dry. I think you were just being polite by eating the food and not agreeing with him."

"Well, I—"

"I saw the way you cringed when you took your first bite of those lumpy, bumpy potatoes. And of course, the gravy was just as bad, not to mention the chewy pieces of hinkel."

Ivan squirmed on the bench. He couldn't lie, but at the same time, he wasn't about to tell Emma the truth and hurt her feelings. Even though she was well aware of his reaction to the food she had prepared, it wouldn't be right to agree with her.

"Things happen sometimes in the kitchen," he said. "Mistakes can be made by anyone, don't ya know? Least that's what my mamm always says."

"Yes, I do know," Emma stated with a firm nod. "And for me, things always go bad when I'm in the kitchen, and would you like to know why?"

"Umm. . .I guess so." Ivan felt concerned when he saw Emma's hunched posture and drooping head. Whatever she was about to say, he had a feeling she really didn't want to say it, but he would listen nonetheless.

"You may as well hear this from me," Emma said in a near whisper. "Because I'm sure the truth will come out sooner or later, and everyone in the town of Arthur, and possibly other towns in this area, will hear it too."

"What truth is that?" he dared to ask.

Emma raised her head and looked right at him with a trembling chin. "I can't cook or sew. I'm good at outdoor things but not in the house." Her shoulders lifted as she heaved a big sigh. "I came here to live with my grandparents for the summer so Grandma could teach me those skills. But I think I'm a lost cause."

Ivan took a few seconds to formulate his response. Then, impulsively, he reached out, clasped her hand, and said, "Well, don't give up trying, and even if you never learn the fine art of cooking, it's not the end of the world."

"You don't think so?"

He gave a vigorous shake of his head. "All you have to do is find a man who can cook, get married, and there you go. Problem solved."

Emma gave him a blank stare at first, and then she broke out in laughter. When Ivan saw her facial features relax, he gave a loud chuckle too.

"You know what, Ivan?" Emma nudged his shoulder. "That might be the most helpful advice I've ever received."

"Glad I can help ya out with your dilemma." Ivan grinned, and they both continued to laugh.

Chapter 8

Champaign, Illinois

"WELL, HERE WE ARE," THEIR driver Tom Jenkins said to Emma's grandfather as he parked his vehicle in front of the mattress store two days later. "I'll be here in the vehicle waiting, but you folks take your time looking. You'll want to make sure you get just the right mattress."

"You got that right," Grandpa replied. "And it might take us a while to find one that we both think is comfortable." He slid out of the front passenger seat and opened the back door where Emma sat with her grandmother. "Emma, you may as well come in with us, because we might need some help choosing the right one."

Emma didn't think her opinion should matter that much, but she agreed to go in and got out of the vehicle behind Grandma. If she had stated what she really preferred, Emma would have said that she would rather wait in Tom's station wagon so she could take a nap. She hadn't slept well the night before, lying awake till well past midnight, thinking about Ivan and how kind he'd been to her Monday evening. He'd been especially gracious about the meal she had ruined, and Ivan hadn't judged her when she'd revealed to him that she couldn't cook and had come to her grandparents' house to learn how to cook and sew. Although Ivan had been too polite to say so, he probably thought there was something wrong with Emma. After all, the young women Emma knew, including her sister and her best friend, Arlene Lehman, had already honed their cooking skills, and most likely they could sew without issues. Ivan's sisters and any other women he knew who were around Emma's age probably had cooking and sewing skills mastered as well.

When Grandma nudged Emma's arm, her thoughts dissolved, and she responded, "Okay, jah, I'll offer my opinion if you need it."

As soon as the three of them entered the building, a middle-aged man rushed over to them and greeted her grandparents. "Good morning, folks. Welcome to the Mattress Shop. What can I do to help you?"

Grandpa gave the man a hearty handshake. "We came to see about getting a new mattress for our bed."

"Well, you're in the right place. What size is your bed?"

"It's a queen. We used to have a double bed, but the older we got, the more crowded it seemed." Grandpa chuckled. "Guess when a person gets to be our age, they flop around more and take up the space."

"I should be able to help you, because we have several queen styles." He looked at Grandma and smiled. "Did you know that queen-sized beds have been available since the mid-1940s?"

Grandma shook her head. "I hadn't heard that."

"Yes indeed," he said. "They were actually introduced here in the United States in 1925 but didn't become popular until later. By the 1950s and into the '60s, more and more people were purchasing queen-sized beds."

Emma stifled a yawn. All this talk about beds was making her sleepy. She wished the salesman would stop talking and just show her grandparents the mattresses they'd come to see.

"How long have you had your current mattress?" the man asked, looking first at Grandpa and then turning to face Grandma.

"Too long," she said with furrowed brows. "My back's been hurting lately, and I'm sure it's the fault of our bed, because the mattress feels saggy to me."

"We've had the bed a good many years, all right," Grandpa spoke up. His gaze shifted to Grandma. "Wouldn't you say so, Luellen?"

She nodded. "I can't remember the exact date that we purchased it, because the time has gone so quickly. All I know is we need a new one, which is why we are here."

The salesman rubbed his hands briskly together. "Yes, indeed. If you'll follow me, I'll show you what we have."

The three of them headed off to another part of the store, and Emma, not knowing what else to do, trailed behind. Looking at mattresses wasn't very exciting, but this morning at breakfast, Grandma had promised Emma that when they returned to Arthur, they would stop by Ida Mae's house to talk about her teaching Emma how to quilt. Emma was glad she wouldn't have to wait until a day when Ida Mae was working at the fabric store again, although she had enjoyed going there and seeing the hand-stitched quilts on display.

"Now this one is an innerspring mattress," Emma heard the salesman say as she approached one of the beds on sale. "A mattress like this uses a system of coiled springs for support, with a layer of foam added on top for comfort." He gestured to Grandpa. "Feel free to lie on the bed so you can get a feel for the mattress and see if it's comfortable enough for you."

"I think my wife oughta go first, since she's the one complaining of a backache every morning."

"That's all right," Grandma said. "I'll wait till you've tried it out." Her cheeks were a little flushed, and Emma wondered if the thought of lying on a bed here in the store, for anyone who might be shopping to stare at her, made Grandma feel uncomfortable.

It would me, Emma thought as she stood beside Grandma, watching as Grandpa reclined on the mattress.

"Ahh. . .this is not bad. Not too bad at all." He stretched his arms out to the sides, then held his hand up to his mouth and yawned. "Oh boy. . .just lying here's enough to make me feel tired. Sure wish I could take a little snooze."

Grandma flapped a hand in his direction. "Don't be silly, Marlin. You know you can't take a nap here in the store."

"Guess you're right." He propped himself up and got off the bed. "It's your turn now, because we can't buy a new mattress without you trying it first."

"Okay." Grandma handed Emma her purse. "Would you mind holding this for me?"

"I don't mind at all," Emma responded, clasping the handbag by the handles. She watched as Grandma got up on the bed and stretched out on the mattress, holding the sides of her skirt.

"This isn't bad," Grandma said. "I'm not sinking into it like our current mattress, but maybe we should try a few others so we have something to compare it with."

"That's a good idea," the man who'd been helping them agreed. "It's always smart to try more than one mattress."

When Grandma got off the bed, he led them to one with a different kind of mattress. Emma's grandparents tried out several mattresses, while the salesman described the comforts and structural support of each one. He was obviously quite eager for a sale.

Emma's grandparents spent the better part of an hour considering their options, while Emma stood quietly holding her grandmother's purse. She wished this process would go quicker and they could be on their way back to Arthur. Knowing that they would soon be going to Ida Mae's, Emma decided to remain in the moment without complaint, though her mind kept straying to whether she'd be able to learn the technical aspects of quilting.

Guess I'm being selfish, Emma told herself. *Choosing the right mattress is important, so I need to be patient.*

Arthur

It was lunchtime for Ivan, and his turn to eat in the back room, so he figured his dad wouldn't mind if he worked on the old clock he'd come home with Monday night. Before Ivan had departed the Herschbergers' home, Marlin had asked Ivan to take the clock with him and see if he could get it running again. The kindly man had offered to pay Ivan for his time, even if it ended up that he couldn't fix the antiquated item. Of course, Ivan had said he wouldn't charge anything if he was unable to get the clock working again, and if he did manage to fix it, the fee would be small.

Sure hope I can repair this cherished clock, Ivan thought as he held a magnifying glass in one hand while examining the inside of the clock. After a brief check, Ivan realized that several places were gummed up, a good indicator the mechanism had been oiled too much. It would have to be taken out, cleaned, and relubricated, but the first step was to remove the movement. He'd just begun inspecting it when his father wandered into the room.

"You about done with lunch yet?" Papa eyed the object on the table. "Guess not. Doesn't look like you even have your lunch box out." His lips flattened for a few seconds, and then he opened his mouth and spoke again. "Whose clock is it this time, and why is it more important than eating your *middaagesse*?"

"I did eat part of my lunch, but it was before I began working on this clock. It belongs to Marlin Herschberger."

"Jah, well, I think you oughta work on this relic on your own time. I am not paying you to fix people's junk."

"I thought my lunch break was my own time, Papa. You said before that it was okay for me to work on clocks at the harness shop as long as it didn't interfere with my working hours."

Papa squinted while rubbing his forehead. "You're right, I did say that, but I've changed my mind. I think it's best if you find a place in your bedroom to do that kind of thing."

"Whatever you say." Ivan picked up the clock, set it back in the box he'd brought it in, and put it in the closet where he kept his personal things. He set aside his father's increasing demands for the moment and redirected his attention to his work, for there would be plenty of time later to find a solution for the vintage clock's repair. Ivan wasn't thrilled that his dad had gone back on his word, but for now at least, he needed this job and wasn't about to ruffle his father's feathers any more than he already had. Someday, he planned to open his own clock shop and become self-sufficient. Until that day, however, Ivan needed to cooperate with whatever his father said.

His thoughts turned to Marlin's granddaughter and the conversation they'd had after supper Monday evening. Ivan had enjoyed the time he'd spent with Emma, sitting around the fire. She was a likable young woman, and he felt comfortable with her. The mere thought of seeing her again set Ivan's mind at ease. Emma had been more reserved during the gathering with his family, but at her grandparents' house, Emma's personality had shone like the brilliant rays of a sunset. Ivan still found himself wanting to get to know her better.

He'd felt sorry for Emma when she admitted that she couldn't cook. She'd clearly been embarrassed by it, but the fact that she'd been able to talk to him about it had let Ivan know that Emma felt comfortable with him. The feeling was mutual, and Ivan looked forward to seeing her again Sunday evening when he would escort her to the singing. They wouldn't be able to visit as much as he'd like, though, since his sisters would be with them, but the arrangement would be better than not seeing Emma at all.

"Son, are you coming? It's time to get back to work."

His father's commanding voice shouting from the other room ended Ivan's contemplations, and he called in return, "Jah, Papa, I'm on my way!"

Emma sat in the back of their driver's vehicle, hoping they would find Ida Mae at home. They'd stopped a while ago at a restaurant the salesman had recommended for a bite of lunch before heading back to Arthur.

Grandma sat beside Emma with her eyes closed and head drooping to one side against the window. Emma figured she was likely asleep.

All that trying out of different mattresses probably tuckered her out, Emma reasoned as she fiddled with the ties of her head covering. *It made me feel sleepy just standing around waiting for Grandma and Grandpa to get done and put their order in for the mattress they'd finally chosen. Hopefully, it will be delivered to their home soon so Grandma can get a good night's sleep and wake up with no back pain.*

Soon, their driver was pulling up the Yoders' driveway, and Emma gingerly patted her grandmother's shoulder. "Grandma, we're here at Ida Mae's house."

Grandma straightened her posture, then reached under her glasses and rubbed her eyelids. "Already? Seems like we just left the restaurant in Champaign. Guess I must have dozed off for a bit."

"I'd say it was a lot longer than a bit, Luellen," Grandpa called from the front seat. "Soon after we got on the road, I looked over my shoulder and saw you nodding off."

Grandma giggled a little and yawned. "I believe that all the mattress shopping we did this morning about did me in."

"Same here," Grandpa replied. "I'm ready to go home and take a nap."

"Not yet," Grandma said with a vigorous shake of her head. "I promised Emma we would stop by to see Ida Mae about teaching her to quilt, and I will not go back on my word."

"Okay," he responded. "Once we get home, we can all nap if we want to."

Emma pressed a palm to her chest as she felt a flood of relief. "We probably won't be here very long," she assured him.

A few minutes later, Emma and her grandmother were on the Yoders' front porch and Grandma knocked on the front door. Grandpa had opted to stay in the station wagon with their driver while the ladies went inside.

Ida Mae answered the door with a welcoming smile and invited them into the house. "How nice of you to stop by," she said after suggesting they all take a seat at the kitchen table where they could have a cup of tea and sample the chocolate chip cookies she'd made earlier.

Emma was glad when Grandma said, "That would be real nice."

As Grandma made small talk with Ida Mae on their way to the kitchen, Emma fixated on how her grandmother appeared to be less heavy-eyed and had resumed her usual zesty demeanor. Once they were seated at the table and the refreshments had been served, Grandma brought up the topic they'd come here to talk about.

"If your offer to teach my granddaughter how to quilt is still open," she said, "then Emma has my permission to accept."

Ida Mae reached over and placed a gentle hand on Emma's arm. "That's *wunderbaar.* When can you start?"

Unsure of how to respond, Emma looked over at Grandma.

"She can begin tomorrow, if you're available, but it will have to be after her morning cooking lesson."

"That's fine," Ida Mae said, her laugh lines prevalent. "My schedule is wide open, and I'll be here all day."

After taking a sip of her herbal tea, Grandma turned toward Emma. "We'll put the sewing project aside for a day and get back to it on Friday. Since sewing isn't very forgiving on the hands, I don't want you to get too overwhelmed by it."

"I understand," Emma said with a nod. She looked back at Ida Mae. "How much would the lessons cost?"

"Nothing at all," the woman was quick to say. "I would count it a privilege to teach an eager young woman like you how to quilt. My daughters have shown no interest in quilting whatsoever, so it will be a blessing for me to teach my good friend's granddaughter the fine art of making a quilt."

Emma's pulse quickened. Quilting would be a challenge, to be sure, but the idea of making her own quilt was exciting. She could hardly wait until tomorrow and hoped the cooking lesson wouldn't take too long. The enthusiasm Emma felt brought a smile, but after a few seconds, it vanished like the warm vapor rising from her teacup.

I suppose I shouldn't get too excited over this, Emma thought as she nibbled on a cookie. *I didn't do well with the instructions Grandma gave me in the kitchen the other night, and look how that turned out. I botched up an otherwise straightforward supper. What if I fail at quilting too? If I can't learn something that most women my age can do with ease, what else is there for me?* Biting the inside of her cheek, Emma thought back to what Ivan had joked about the night before. *I guess I would need to find a husband who can cook. But that's not likely.*

Chapter 9

THURSDAY MORNING, WHEN EMMA REACHED the last step at the bottom of the staircase, the aromatic odor of coffee brewing filled her senses. She entered the kitchen and found her grandmother holding the small of her back with one hand while she bent over to check something in the oven.

"*Guder mariye*," Emma greeted as she approached.

Standing upright, Grandma turned and winced before offering Emma a smile. "Good morning, Emma. Did you sleep well?"

"I slept okay, but I should be asking you that question. Is your back hurting again?"

"Jah, and I will surely be glad when our new mattress arrives."

"Hopefully it won't be too long." Emma pointed to the oven door, still hanging open. "Were you getting ready to put something in there?"

"I was just going to warm up some of the banana muffins I made yesterday after we got back from Ida Mae's." Grandma gestured to the baking pan on the counter, covered with aluminum foil. "I thought they would be good with the oatmeal you'll be cooking for our breakfast this morning."

Emma pointed to herself. "Me?"

"Jah. You're the only other person in the room besides me. It's part of your cooking lesson today, and it won't be hard at all," Grandma said. "I'll walk you through it, step-by-step."

"Oh, I thought we'd be doing the lesson after breakfast. I—I mean, closer to lunchtime."

Grandma shook her head. "There's no time like the present, and by getting it done now, once we've had our noon meal, Grandpa can drive you over to Ida Mae's for your first lesson with her."

"Oh yes—I'm really looking forward to that, and I hope I do well and don't mess up." Emma's words were rushed. She was eager to see Ida Mae, but at the same time, she couldn't help creating a mental tally of what could go wrong. She couldn't help wondering if it was in her nature to mess things up.

Emma reached up and rubbed the back of her neck. *Maybe some people aren't meant to have a talent, and I could be one of them.*

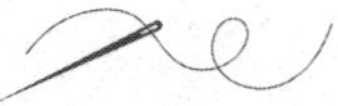

Luellen heard the back door open, and she hurried out to the utility room to speak to her husband before he came into the kitchen for breakfast.

"I need to talk to you," she whispered.

"Can it wait till after breakfast?" Marlin patted his belly. "I'm hungerich."

She gave a quick shake of her head. "No, I need to say this now."

The wrinkles in his forehead deepened. "You look so serious. Has something bad happened that I should know about?"

"It's not bad. At least, I hope it's not." Luellen guided her husband to the far end of the narrow room and kept her voice low in case their granddaughter was in earshot. "I wanted you to know ahead of time that Emma made the oatmeal this morning."

He lifted his gaze to the ceiling. "Oh, great. Sure hope it's not sticky or tasteless." He tapped his fist against his lips and mumbled, "That girl sure doesn't know much about cooking."

"That's why she's here, remember?"

"Of course I do. My taste buds just don't like her practicing on me."

Luellen held back the groan threatening to escape her lips. "I know," she said in a continued hushed tone. "We just need to be patient and encouraging as she strives to learn and do her best. In time, I feel sure she'll get the hang of it." She squeezed his forearm. "In the meantime, though, we must try not to hurt Emma's feelings. Even if we don't particularly care for something she makes in my kitchen, we must not say unkind things. You do understand that, don't you, Marlin?"

"Jah, and I'll do my best to bite my tongue if it becomes necessary." He paused a few seconds. "But I can't promise I'll eat the oatmeal if it's not to my liking, so I hope there'll be something else on the table. Otherwise, I'll be as hungerich when I leave the table as I was when I sat down."

Luellen reached up and gave her husband's beard a little tug. "You're incorrigible, you know that?"

"I'm not sure what that means, but if you say so then I guess I must be."

"It means, dear Marlin, that you're hopeless."

"Is that so? Well tell me this, dear wife of mine. How'd ya learn such a big, fancy word like that?"

"I saw it in the dictionary one evening when I was looking for the right word to fill in on a crossword puzzle." She patted his arm and grinned. "Now let's get on in to breakfast, shall we?"

Marlin leaned down and kissed Luellen's cheek. "You're right, I am hopeless—hopelessly in love with you."

"I love you too," she responded.

He motioned to the kitchen door. "Lead the way, and I shall follow."

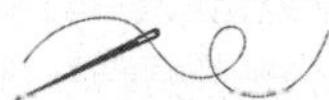

Emma held her breath as she watched Grandpa take his first bite of oatmeal. Grandma was right—it really wasn't that difficult to make. She hoped the consistency was okay and it wasn't over- or undercooked.

Grandpa's nose wrinkled for a brief moment, and then he swallowed and gave Emma a wavering smile.

"How's it taste?" Emma dared to ask. "Is the texture all right?" She hadn't even tasted it herself, which was probably a mistake.

"Umm. . .yeah. . .it's fine. My only complaint is that I don't taste any cinnamon. Did you forget to include that?"

Emma's head snapped in Grandma's direction. "Did you tell me to add cinnamon to the oatmeal?"

Grandma rubbed the middle of her nose, pushing her glasses back into place. "Well, I thought I did, but maybe I forgot. That happens sometimes when I get busy doing something else."

"It's okay," Grandpa said with a wave of his hand. "I'll get the cinnamon and add it to my bowl."

"Yes, yes. . .we can all do that," Grandma was quick to say. "And don't bother getting up, Marlin. Since this is my kitchen, I know exactly where to find it." She was up on her feet before either Grandpa or Emma could comment.

Emma watched as her grandmother hobbled across the room like a lame duck, holding the small of her back and limping a bit. *Poor thing, she's still hurting. I should have been the one to get the cinnamon,* she thought. *I'm the person who didn't sprinkle some in the oatmeal while it was cooking.*

It was too late to do anything about that now, since Grandma was already heading back to the table with the cinnamon. She handed Grandpa the jar, then lowered herself into her chair.

"Danki," he said, seemingly unaware of her pain. Grandpa sprinkled a fair amount of the spice on his oatmeal, then handed the bottle to Emma. "Want some?"

"I guess so." Emma dusted some on and passed it to Grandma. Meanwhile, Grandpa had added several scoops of brown sugar, stirred it around, and poured milk over the top.

With the churning of her empty stomach, Emma decided it was time to take her first bite. The hot cereal was kind of dry, and it wasn't sweet at all, so she followed Grandpa's lead. Since he was eating his without complaint, Emma picked up her spoon and dug right in.

Hmm. . .not too bad, I guess. Better than the chicken and mashed potatoes I messed up earlier this week, Emma mused.

Grandma's muffins were passed around next, and after Grandpa slathered the two he chose with creamy butter, Emma took one and handed the basket to Grandma.

Grandma seemed unusually quiet during the rest of the meal, and

Emma wondered if it had to do with the pain she felt in her back, or could something else be wrong?

As Emma stood at the sink, washing their dishes from lunch, she spotted Grandpa heading for the barn. No doubt he was on the way to get his horse so he could hitch it to the buggy that would take Emma to her first quilting lesson. Emma's gaze rested on the empty hammock. She wished she was in the hammock right now instead of helping Grandma do the dishes. Of course, if she had been able to lie in the hammock, she'd have probably dozed off and would have missed her quilting lesson.

Another thought popped into Emma's head. *If I do poorly today, it could be my first and last quilting lesson.*

Soon Grandpa came inside and informed Emma that he was ready to take her over to Ida Mae's. He said he would come back for her around four o'clock.

"Okay," she replied. "I'll finish the last few dishes, and then I'll head right out to the buggy."

"That's all right, Emma." Grandma interjected. "I can finish them for you."

Emma shook her head. "You have enough to do just drying the dishes and putting them away. I can finish off the dishes so you can go rest."

"Rest?" Grandpa chuckled. "You oughta know by now that your grossmammi likes to keep busy."

Emma was about to comment, but Grandpa was already out the door. She turned to her grandmother and said, "I really don't mind washing the dishes."

Grandma gave Emma's shoulder a tender pat. "There's no need for that. Now you dry your hands and go along with your grandpa. I'm sure the horse is eager to head out, and you should be as well."

"I am," Emma admitted. "Just a little *naerfich* is all."

"There's no need to be nervous, dear one. Ida Mae is a kind person, and she'll be patient with you."

Emma hoped her grandmother was right, because even though she was quite excited to learn quilting, her mind continued to be filled with doubts about how well she would do.

Guess I won't know till I try, Emma told herself as she finished the last dish and handed it to Grandma to dry. *I just need to keep a positive attitude and do my best.*

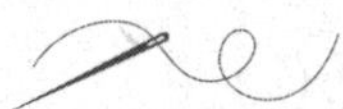

Feeling nervous again now that she was here, Emma rapped on the Yoders' front door. A few minutes passed, and then the door opened and Ida Mae greeted Emma with a smile and a hug.

"I'm so glad you could make it," Ida Mae said. "I have everything laid out and ready for your first lesson. But before we start, can I get you something cold to drink, or perhaps a few peanut butter kichlin?"

"Maybe a glass of *wasser*, but I don't need any cookies. We just ate our noon meal not long ago, and I'm still full from that." Emma glanced around, wondering if anyone else was at home, or if she and Ida Mae were here alone.

She didn't see or hear anyone and figured the rest of the family must be at their jobs or someplace else in the house. Ivan would no doubt be at the harness shop with his dad, but Emma was not sure about his sisters. She didn't know if Jane or Norma had jobs outside the home, and Bertha, the youngest sister, didn't appear to be here either.

"Feel free to take a seat while I get us both some water." Ida Mae gestured to the living room.

Emma went inside and sat on the sofa. Although she had been here before, she'd never taken it all in. Now her gaze traveled about the room, resting on the grandfather clock positioned against the left wall. It was a beautiful piece of furniture, and she enjoyed listening to its rhythmic ticking. Emma thought the tall frame with such intricate woodwork was fascinating, and she wondered why she hadn't noticed it before.

Ida Mae came into the room and handed Emma a glass of water. "If you'll come with me, we'll go to the room where I do all my quilting and sewing," she said.

Emma got up and followed Ida Mae down the hall and into a

spacious room filled with sewing supplies, a quilting frame, and several quilt racks where a variety of beautiful quilts had been displayed.

"Oh my! These quilts are amazing!" Emma made her way around the room, studying each one but being careful not to touch any of them. She spun around to face Ida Mae. "I had no idea you had made so many quilted bed coverings. Are they all for sale?"

Ida Mae nodded. "Some I sell from my home, but others I take to the fabric store and put on display, like the ones you saw last week."

"Even if I do learn how to quilt," Emma said, "I'd never be able to make anything as beautiful as these. You obviously have been blessed with a talent for quilting, Ida Mae."

Ida Mae shrugged her slim shoulders. "I suppose some would call it a talent, but I simply enjoy making quilts, and I'm sure there are a lot of other quilters who do better work than me."

Emma found that hard to believe. She'd never seen quilts so beautiful and with such interesting patterns. Emma began asking questions, particularly about the name of each design.

Ida Mae obliged her, but then she said, "All right now, Emma, it's time to begin your first lesson."

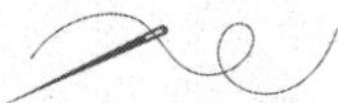

Ivan got off work a little earlier than usual, so he looked forward to going home and working on Marlin's old clock—especially without his father interfering. Upon entering the house, Ivan opted to follow the voices he heard from down the hallway. To his astonishment, Emma and his mother were in the sewing room. The young woman seemed as equally surprised to see him, and explained that she had just finished a quilting lesson. Leaving Ivan and Emma alone for the moment, his mother excused herself from the room.

"If anyone can teach you, it's my mamm," Ivan commented as he leaned against the doorframe. "She makes the most beautiful quilts."

"That's true," Emma agreed. "Making one at least half as good as hers would be a distant dream of mine. I haven't decided on a special quilt pattern of my own yet, but your mother showed me how to cut out some simple, basic squares and had me practice sewing them together by hand."

After several minutes of conversation, Emma's eyes flitted to the wall clock adjacent to Ida Mae's treadle sewing machine.

"It's getting pretty late," she said. "I figured I'd be back at my grandparents' home by now. My grandpa was supposed to pick me up almost an hour ago."

"Why don't I take you home?" Ivan offered. "If we see your grandpa's horse and buggy on the road, I can stop so you can go on home with him."

Emma sat up straighter, pursed her lips for a second, and nodded. "That's very kind of you, Ivan. Danki."

Emma said goodbye to Ida Mae, then accompanied Ivan out into the yard and waited while he secured his horse to the buggy beside the hitching post. Soon after they'd climbed into the interior of the carriage and began their journey, Ivan's horse hastened his stride as the buggy wheels rolled beneath them. Emma's attention seemed to be fixed on the road ahead, no doubt on the lookout for signs of her grandfather's rig.

As they traveled along, the galloping of Ivan's horse filled the silence. The sun's rays faded in his line of sight, reducing the vivid green of the branches with its ember glow along the path.

"Are you excited about the singing this Sunday evening?" Ivan asked.

Emma glanced sideways at him. "I suppose. I don't mind singing, but being in a group with strangers can be nerve-racking for me."

"I sort of had that figured out the evening when we formally introduced ourselves." Ivan tightened his grip on the reins. "I really hope I didn't make you uncomfortable that night."

She shrugged. "It's just the way that I am. I hope I will eventually feel more at ease in such situations."

The conversation between them fell silent again, and Ivan looked to the side of his buggy, where its silhouette clung to the pavement.

"Say, I have been wanting to do a fishing trip pretty soon. I know that's more of your kind of pastime, so if you want, I wouldn't mind it if you tagged along. I—I mean, I would enjoy your company."

"Are you sure, Ivan? I don't want to intrude, and besides, my grandmother might be having me do another cooking or sewing lesson whatever day you end up going out to fish."

"It's all right with me either way. If you're too busy, I will understand." Ivan quirked an eyebrow at her in a deliberate manner. "Though part of me wants to know how skilled you are at fishing, since you claim to be into outdoorsy things."

Emma blinked. "You don't believe that I know how to fish, do you?"

"I mean, I could take your word for it, but I'd rather see what you're capable of with my own two eyes." He grinned at her and winked.

As they rounded the next bend, the Herschbergers' house came into view, and Ivan could see Marlin dozing in a hammock in the front yard. Ivan brought the buggy to a standstill.

"I wouldn't be surprised if my grandma might be napping in the house too," Emma said. "Surely if she was awake, she would have woken Grandpa and reminded him to go pick me up." Emma tucked a flyaway strand of hair behind her ear before dismounting from the carriage. "Thank you for bringing me home, Ivan."

"My pleasure." He tipped his straw hat. "But you still haven't given me an answer about going fishing."

"I'll let you know what day I might be free Sunday evening when you pick me up for the singing. With you working during the week, it would probably have to be on a Saturday, though."

He tipped his straw hat and nodded. "Good thinking, Emma."

Chapter 10

THE FOLLOWING DAY, IN ADDITION to another brief cooking lesson, Grandma instructed Emma on how to finish the dress they had started for her last week. Not only did she still struggle with having full control of the treadle machine, Emma also lacked confidence in everything Grandma asked her to do.

Emma's fingers trembled as she attempted to pin the sleeve of her dress in place, and she felt relief when Grandma stepped in and did it for her. Emma figured if she hadn't done so, they'd probably be here in the sewing room all day.

Emma heaved an audible sigh. There were so many other things she'd rather be doing on this beautiful Friday in June. She still hadn't been given the chance to relax in Grandpa's hammock, and since he was in town running an errand, this would have been the perfect time. But no—she was stuck here in the stuffy house, trying to do the impossible. At least that's the way Emma saw it.

Grandma, on the other hand, kept encouraging Emma, saying things like, "You can do this. Try to relax and take your time."

If there was one thing Emma did not feel, it was relaxed. She'd been ever so glad during her time with Ida Mae yesterday that she hadn't been expected to use the treadle machine. Cutting out squares for the patchwork quilt and pinning them together in readiness to stitch by hand had seemed so easy compared to making a dress.

"Emma, your shoulders are tense. Please try to relax and stop frowning."

Grandma's comment and gentle touch scattered Emma's thoughts, and she responded with a groan. "This isn't easy, and I don't think I'll ever get the hang of it."

"Yes you will, if you give yourself time and try to be patient." Grandma pulled up a chair and took a seat so she was closer to where Emma sat in front of the machine. "Take a few deep breaths, start again, and remember to guide the material slowly as your foot moves up and down on the pedal in the correct position."

Emma was almost sure she'd done a better job baking cookies earlier today than she was doing now with the drab-colored material beneath her fingers. At least stirring the batter and adding the ingredients to the bowl hadn't put her nerves on edge. Emma wished she could be honest and just tell her grandmother that she'd rather be outdoors in the sun than cooped up in here, trying to do something she was sure she would never be good at. But she held her tongue and continued with her attempt at finishing this dress that she probably might not be able to wear. The hem would probably be uneven, one sleeve could be shorter than the other, and when all was said and done, she might not even be able to slip it on over her head. If that turned out to be the case, Emma would have the perfect excuse to hang the dress in the closet and never wear it anywhere.

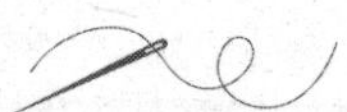

"How was your day?" Ivan's mother asked when he stepped onto the front porch, where she sat shelling peas into a container on her lap.

"It went okay, I guess. Papa had some paperwork to do, and he told me to tell you that he might be another hour or so."

"That's fine. We won't be eating supper for a while yet." She smiled up at him. "There's a jar of kichlin on the table, if you'd like a snack."

"Danki, Mama. I'll take a few cookies to enjoy while I'm upstairs workin' on Marlin's old clock."

"Are you getting anywhere with it?" she questioned.

"I think so. It's keeping time now, but I've still got some work to do to get it to chime." Ivan felt energized just talking about the challenge of repairing the clock. He could hardly wait to get back to it.

"You really enjoy that tedious work, don't you, Ivan? I can tell by the certainty I hear in your voice that you are determined to repair the clock—not just as a favor to Marlin, but because you love the challenge."

Ivan bobbed his head. "You're right, Mama. Just wish I could drum up enough business to do clock repairing full-time. Wouldn't that be something?"

"Maybe someday you will, Son. Just don't give up your dream. Keep your eyes on the goal, and remember to pray about your future. God has a plan for each of us, and we need to make sure that whatever we do, it's within His will."

"I'll try to remember that. Right now, though, there are some cookies and a clock waiting for my attention."

Leaning forward at the workstation he'd set up in his room, Ivan toiled over Marlin's antique clock, drawing in a breath of the metallic aroma of the lubricant. Little by little, he'd been figuring out the steps he needed to take in order to get the vintage timepiece to sound its hourly chime. Ivan was aware that it was a deep-seated problem with the antique's mechanism rather than a reset issue. To get the clock to function again, the internal components needed to be upheld, which required much patience and steady hands. Although immersed in his work, the sound of approaching footsteps behind him caught his attention.

"Have you figured out what the problem is?" Ivan's mother questioned.

"Sure hope so. It had been gummed up because the mechanism had been oiled too much, but that wasn't the only thing, unfortunately." It's difficult to know whether I'll get this chiming after all these years because the springs can be a little awkward to deal with." His shoulders lifted, and then he lowered them in a more relaxed position. But maybe if I'm diligent enough, I can get it done without causing further damage."

"I don't know how you do it, Ivan. I am sure that if I were the one messing with the clock, it probably would end up in worse shape than before."

"We all have something we're good at. I know I wouldn't be able to quilt like you do, Mama."

"In some ways, the project you're carrying out is similar to quilting, in that it takes great patience. Maybe you should try quilting sometime, Ivan. You could even join in on a lesson with Emma when she comes over here again." Ivan's mother smiled while gently patting his shoulder.

"I think I'll leave the quilting to you and Emma," he said, feeling heat creeping along the bridge of his nose. "Speaking of Emma, how do you think it went with you teaching her yesterday?"

"What I've noticed the most about Emma is that she isn't particularly kind to herself," his mother responded. "Anytime Emma makes a slipup, she says she'll never get the hang of it. But as I reminded her, that's exactly how you learn. You cannot hone your skills if you don't allow room for mistakes. When putting effort into learning something new and experiencing countless instances of trial and error, it's important to have faith that something wonderful will eventually emerge."

"Very true, Mama. I know I've made plenty of mistakes over the years, fiddling with clocks, and I hope not to do the same with this one." Grasping the pliers, Ivan narrowed his eyes while adjusting the spring gradually.

"All right, I'll leave you to it. Keep up the good work."

For a brief period, Ivan's mother lingered in the room, and he was certain that she was observing him as he continued working on his project. When Ivan finally heard her footsteps fade away, he wiped the perspiration from his forehead and went back to work on the clock's internal mechanisms. Holding down the arbor, he snapped the spring into its proper position. Ivan twisted off the lid of the oil canister and applied a little drop into the bearing after hooking the spring onto the arbor and ensuring it was in place.

"I think that oughta do it," Ivan muttered to himself. "If not, I'll just have to take it apart and start over."

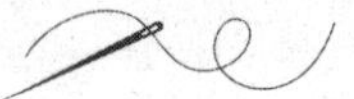

"What do you think now that your frack is finished?" Luellen asked, holding Emma's dress in front of her.

"It looks okay, but that's only because you fixed all my mistakes." Emma pursed her lips. "I doubt that I'll ever be able to sew anything as well as you do, Grandma."

"Sure you will. It's just going to take more practice and determination." Luellen handed Emma the dress. "While you're hanging this up in your room, I'm going to get out those speedy brownies you made earlier and fix us both a glass of cold milk. Then I think it would be nice if the two of us went outside with our treats and enjoyed some time on the front porch. Would you like that, Emma?"

"I sure would, Grandma." Emma grinned so wide that her teeth showed. It was the first smile Luellen had seen from her granddaughter all day.

"All right then. I'll get the snacks while you put your dress away, and then we'll meet on the front porch."

Emma nodded and hurried off with the dress in her hands.

Luellen ambled into the kitchen. Her back still hurt, but not as bad as it had when she'd first gotten out of bed this morning. *Maybe I should try sleeping on the sofa tonight and see if that's any better for my back than our old mattress.* Luellen shook her head almost as soon as the thought entered her mind. *If I slept on the sofa, I don't think Marlin would like it. He likes the feel of my cold feet when his body gets overheated under the covers, especially during the warmer months of the year.*

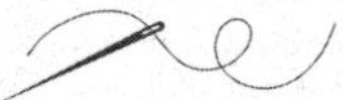

Luellen had no sooner set the milk and brownies on the small table between two chairs on the porch when Emma showed up.

"Take a seat and relax awhile." Luellen gestured to the other chair.

Emma sat down, removed her shoes and socks, and wiggled her bare toes. Ignoring the brownies and milk, she stared out into the yard with a wistful expression.

"What are you thinking about, Emma? Are you missing your family at home? Is it hard being away from them?"

"I do miss my family," Emma admitted. "But I enjoy being here with you and Grandpa too."

"I'm glad, because we love having you." Luellen picked up a brownie and took a bite. "You know, Emma, these turned out quite well. This brownie is moist and flavorful, just as it should be."

"Danki. I'm glad it's at least edible." Emma grabbed one and bit a piece off. "Yum. . . This isn't half bad."

"It's not bad at all," Luellen said. "And you know what, Emma?"

Emma shook her head.

"If you can bake a batch of brownies that tastes this good, then I can't help but believe you will soon be making all kinds of tasty treats and even good-tasting full-fledged meals."

"I—I hope so, but success with those quick and easy brownies could be a one-time thing for me. The next thing I make might turn into a disaster."

"You must have positive thoughts, Emma dear, and always keep trying." Luellen reached over and patted Emma's knee. "It's never good to give up."

Emma nodded. "I know, Grandma, and I will keep trying."

Shipshewana

Dianna stood at the kitchen counter, looking through some of her favorite recipes. Today had been so hot and humid, and she needed to fix something for supper that wouldn't heat up the kitchen.

After finally deciding on a fresh fruit salad to go with meat and cheese slices for sandwiches, Dianna poured herself a glass of lemonade and took a seat at the table to look through today's mail. She'd hoped to find a letter from Emma, or even a postcard, but all there was were several catalogs and a few bills.

Dianna released a deep sigh. "Sure wish I'd hear something from Emma," she murmured.

"Who are you talking to, Mom?"

Dianna swiveled her head to the right. "Oh, Rachel, I didn't hear you come in. How was work today? Did everything go okay?"

"About the same as usual." Rachel sat in a chair across from Dianna and hunched forward with both elbows on the table. After a few seconds of sitting in that position, she began stroking her forehead.

"Do you have a *koppweh*?" Dianna questioned.

Rachel pulled her hands away and gave a slow shake of her head. "I don't have a headache. I'm just tired and worried."

"About what?"

"David hasn't asked me to go with him to the young people's singing this Sunday." She drew in some air and blew it out quickly. "I have this horrible feeling that he's planning to go with someone else."

"Oh, Rachel, no—you must not think such a thought. As long as you and David have been going out, I'm almost certain that he wouldn't get involved with anyone else."

"I want to believe that, Mom, I really do. But remember, I did see him talking to my friend Alice at the last singing, and..." Rachel's chin trembled as tears filled her eyes. "It hurts me to think that he would break things off with me after all this time, but I can't shake the feeling that he doesn't love me. I mean, if he did, wouldn't he have asked me to marry him by now?" She paused a moment and drummed her knuckles on the tabletop. "I'm not getting any younger, Mom. I bet most people already see me as an old *maad*." She sniffed. "At the rate things are going, Emma will be married long before me. If I get married at all, that is."

"You're not an old maid, Rachel. And as far as your sister goes, Emma doesn't even have a boyfriend, much less have been proposed to."

"Maybe not now, but I'm sure it's not in the distant future." Rachel rose from her chair. "I really don't want to talk about this anymore. I'm going upstairs to change my clothes, and then I'll be back to help you with supper preparations."

"Take all the time you want," Dianna said. "I'm just planning on sandwiches and a fruit salad for supper this evening. It's too hot to heat up the kitchen by turning on the stove."

"Jah, okay. I'll still help in any way I can when I return to the kitchen."

Rachel hurried from the room.

Dianna sipped some of her lemonade and then set the glass down. *I would very much like to see Emma happily married, but not before Rachel receives a proposal. This isn't fair for my second-eldest daughter to have her relationship ruined by a man who can't seem to commit to her.*

Arthur

"The radishes should be ready to harvest from the garden very soon."

Emma knelt beside her grandmother, sweeping her gaze over the rows of vegetable plants. "How can you tell? I mean, all you can see are the leaves poking out of the soil, so how do you know for sure when they're ready to harvest?"

"With just that, Emma. The leaves. It's likely that not much is occurring beneath the soil if there isn't much growth above where they sprout from the ground. Though, even when I did see leaves not long after I first started growing them, I wound up plucking them out of the ground when they weren't ready. Seeing the shoulder of the radishes emerge out of the soil is the best way to determine when to harvest them. No shoulder means more time getting a dirt bath."

When the tranquil June air was disturbed by the distant rattle of buggy wheels, Emma rose up and turned to face the graveled path that led to the house. Emma's grandmother followed suit, wiping the filth of the earth onto her apron, and they wandered to the spot where Grandpa arrived near the hitching post. To Emma's amazement, there was a puppy beside him. She rushed over to the side of her grandfather's rig and picked the dog up.

"Aren't you the most adorable puppy ever?" Emma giggled as she cradled the pup in her arms. After she elicited a little bark, the dog licked the tip of Emma's fingers.

"Marlin, where in the world did you find that *hund*?" Grandma asked, crossing her arms.

"I discovered the little critter by the side of the road, whimpering. At first, I thought the pup had been injured, but then after checking her over, I realized that the poor thing was just scared. I couldn't leave her there and ride off, knowing she could get hit by a car or worse, so I brought the dog home."

Grandma wagged her finger at him and said, "Now, Marlin—really? Just what are we supposed to do with that hund? You know I don't like dogs, much less a scraggly little puppy to care for. And you also know that I'll be the one stuck caring for it, right?"

"Not just you." Grandpa grinned from ear to ear. "You have Emma, and it looks like she's already taken a liking to the pup."

"That's what I mean. Emma won't be around our home forever, Marlin, and I doubt Dianna would appreciate her daughter taking a puppy back home with her at the end of the summer."

Emma's grandparents continued to bicker, while Emma peered down at the timid little baby. Wondering what breed the pup was, she ran her fingers through the matted fur close to its teddy bear muzzle. She was clearly not a purebred, but rather a cross between a terrier and something else Emma couldn't discern. Regardless, Emma acknowledged that having a puppy around would keep things interesting, and she looked forward to helping care for the cute pup. Hopefully, the rightful owner of the dog wouldn't show up.

Chapter 11

As Emma stood in front of her bedroom window Sunday morning, charcoal-colored clouds could be seen on the horizon. *I bet it's going to rain today. Sure hope Grandpa doesn't plan to take his open buggy to church.* She grimaced. *It would not be good for us to end up soaking wet and have to sit through a three-hour service in soggy, damp clothes thanks to the rain.*

Emma smiled, thankful that Grandpa had gotten his way concerning the puppy he'd found a few days ago. Even though Grandma had made it clear that she didn't want the dog, things had worked out in the pup's favor. The thing that had made Grandma accept the idea was when Emma volunteered to take care of the pup. Grandpa said he would do his part to help with the puppy too, so Grandma had shrugged and said, "Okay, you two, have it your way. Just don't expect me to lift a finger to help with that hund. She's your responsibility until someone comes along and claims the mutt as their own."

Emma hoped that wouldn't happen. The dog had only been with them a few days, and already Emma had bonded with little Fawn. Grandpa had given the pup that name, saying that the puppy's big brown eyes reminded him of a baby deer.

With an upturned face, Emma hummed a little tune she'd learned as a child. She liked the name Grandpa had chosen and enjoyed being able to help with the pup. She'd also given the dog a bath and brushed her tangled hair, and when she wasn't busy doing other things, Emma had made sure little Fawn got plenty of attention.

Emma pushed her musings aside and focused on putting on her shoes so she could go down to help with breakfast. She'd already gotten dressed for church, and she would cover her dress with a work apron during their breakfast hour. If she spilled something on her clothes, it would mean taking the time to change into another dress, and there might not be enough time for that.

This was their off-Sunday from attending church in their own district, but Grandpa had informed Emma last evening that they would be visiting another church district this morning. Emma knew that was customary for most Amish, so the news hadn't taken her by surprise. She couldn't say she looked forward to going, however. Since this wasn't their usual group of people to worship with, it was unlikely that she would know anyone at the service today.

Emma heard her name being called, and she turned away from the window. It was Grandma's voice, and Emma figured her help was probably needed in the kitchen. Since this was Sunday, it wasn't likely that there'd be another cooking lesson, but no doubt the table needed to be set, or perhaps there was some other task, like pouring fresh orange juice into their glasses. She would also need to feed the puppy and take her outside to do her business. Emma was still surprised that Grandma had allowed Fawn to sleep in the house. Of course, the pup had been barricaded in the utility room. Emma wished it didn't have to be that way. Maybe once Fawn was housebroken, Grandma would agree to let the dog have free roam of the house—or at least when Emma could be there to keep a watch on things.

When Grandma called Emma's name again, Emma refocused her thoughts once more and opened the bedroom door. "Be right there!" she called.

Once Emma entered the kitchen, Grandma looked at her with furrowed brows. "How come you're not wearing the dress you made? You worked hard on it, and I figured you'd want to wear it to church today."

"Well, I, uh, didn't think it was suitable for church," Emma replied.

Grandma tipped her head from side to side, as if contemplating what her next words should be. Finally, she shrugged and said, "It's your choice, Emma. You can wear whatever you like."

Emma couldn't miss the displeasure she'd seen on her grandmother's face. She really didn't want to disappoint Grandma, and since they'd be going to a church district she'd never been to before, it would be a little easier to wear a dress she didn't really care for. "I'll feed the puppy and take her outside for a few minutes, and then I'll run back upstairs and change my dress."

Grandma gave a quick shake of her head. "There's no need for you to bother with the hund this morning, Emma. Your grandpa already gave her food, and he's outside with Fawn right now." She gestured to Emma's dress. "And if you feel more comfortable in the frack you're wearing, then there's no need for you to change clothes either."

"Are you sure? I mean, if you'd prefer that I wear the other dress, I suppose. . ."

"No, it's okay. You can wear the dress some other time—maybe tonight for the singing."

Emma felt an ache at the back of her throat, and she swallowed a couple of times. The last thing she wanted to do this evening was wear the dress she'd struggled so hard to make to the singing. Ivan would see her in it, and his sisters would too. No doubt they were both good at sewing. The girls might even talk about Emma to others, criticizing her sewing skills. Although Grandma had helped with the dress in many ways, in Emma's opinion it still appeared to be a beginner's dress.

No, I can't wear it tonight, Emma told herself. *I will have to come up with some way to get out of putting on that dress. It's either that, or I'll need to stay home.*

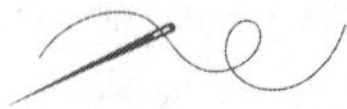

They had just sat down to breakfast and said their prayers when a clap of thunder sounded so loud, it nearly catapulted Emma out of her seat. She'd never liked storms, especially the ones that occurred during the hotter months. Summer storms always seemed so much more intense.

A downpour came next, with rain pounding hard against the house and obscuring their view out the windows. From time to time, Emma took a glimpse at the windowpanes streaked with rain, observing the immense drops trailing down the glass. She hoped and prayed that the storm would end soon and wouldn't cause any damage to people's property or do harm to anyone who might be outside.

"It's a bad one, jah?" Grandpa gazed at Emma, then focused on Grandma. "I managed to get the horse and buggy ready before the bad weather hit, but since it's storming so harshly right now, after we're done eating, we may have to wait a bit to leave for church until the weather improves." He reached for the salt and pepper and sprinkled some on his eggs. "It wouldn't be wise to travel the roads in hazardous conditions. Besides, with the crazy, unpredictable weather going on, my *gaul* would likely spook, creating a bigger problem for me as the carriage driver."

Another rumbling boom proclaimed itself, and the poor little dog, all alone in the utility room, let out several high-pitched howls.

With no hesitation, Emma got up and rushed into the utility room. She found the trembling pup hunched down between Grandpa's work boots and Grandma's galvanized washtub, now whimpering. The puppy looked up at Emma with wide eyes.

"It's okay, little Fawn. I'm here with you now." She spoke softly, hoping to calm the frightened puppy, and then Emma bent down and scooped Fawn into her arms. "It's okay, little one," she murmured again, nuzzling the dog with her nose.

"Emma, your scrambled eggs are getting cold," Grandma called from the kitchen.

Still holding the pup, Emma poked her head into the adjoining room. "The pup's really scared. Is it all right if I bring her into the kitchen? She could sit under the table by my feet."

Emma saw Grandma exchange glances with Grandpa, and when he gave a nod, she said, "All right, but the dog must remain on the floor. And no feeding the hund any table scraps."

Emma stroked Fawn's head. "You'll be safe in the kitchen with us, little one. There's no reason to be afraid now."

The puppy licked Emma's hand, and she giggled. Fawn seemed more relaxed now, which made her feel better as well. *We're two fraidy-cats who don't like storms,* Emma thought, stroking one of the pup's soft ears. She wished she could hold the puppy on her lap at the table, but knowing Grandma would never tolerate that, she took her seat again and placed Fawn beneath the table, making sure the dog was close to her feet. Apparently that was sufficient, because the cute little terrier-mix settled right down and was soon fast asleep. Emma heaved a sigh of relief. At least one problem was solved.

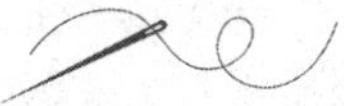

When they stepped outside and headed for Grandpa's closed-in family buggy, Emma noticed that a light rain drizzling down from the overcast sky was all that was left of the storm. Sheets of rainwater from earlier had soaked the ground so well that the soil appeared quite dark. Emma had also noticed several birds hiding in the foliage of bushes and trees. Some were darting toward the ground to feast on the worms. They had to avoid several puddles while making their way to the horse and buggy at the hitching rail.

After the three of them climbed into the buggy and Grandpa backed the horse away from the rail, Emma leaned against the seat back and tried to relax. She figured the heat of the day would soon take over, and then it would be warm and muggy. Something else to deal with, but at least it wasn't frightening.

As they headed down the road in Grandpa's carriage, toward the home where they'd be attending church, Emma thought about Fawn and wondered how she was doing. When Grandpa had announced that it was time to leave, Emma felt sad having to put the puppy back in the utility room. Fortunately, with the storm abating, the nervous terrier had calmed down and seemed settled in the wooden crate Grandpa had put together as a dog bed the day he'd brought Fawn home.

Emma was thankful that no one had come by her grandparents' house looking for a lost dog, but shortly before they'd finished eating breakfast this morning, Grandpa had stated that he and Grandma planned to do some grocery and bulk food shopping in town this coming week, and while they were there, he would put a notice on the stores' bulletin boards about the puppy he'd found.

As selfish as it seemed, Emma hoped with all her heart that no one would come forward to claim little Fawn. She really wanted to keep the dog and hopefully be allowed to take Fawn with her when she returned to her parents' home in Shipshewana.

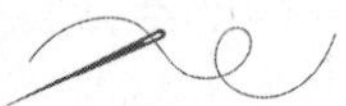

After Emma took her seat on a wooden bench within the women's side of the workshop where the worship service was being held, she glanced around and saw Ivan and his family enter the building. That was a relief. At least she knew a few people here, and that helped her feel like less of a stranger in this new church district.

As several others came inside, she realized it wouldn't take long for this already-warm building to heat up and cause discomfort for most everyone in the room. Two windows on each side of the shop had been opened, but there wasn't much of a breeze blowing in. It was hard to believe that just a few hours ago there'd been an abundance of rain and wind.

Despite the heat, the time went quicker than Emma expected, as she sang a few songs from the Ausbund hymnbook in German, along with the rest of the congregation. One of the younger ministers preached a short sermon on the topic of helping others. Following that, the congregation stood for scripture reading and silent prayer. Once everyone was seated again, one of the older ministers took his place in an area between the men's and women's sides of the room to deliver a longer sermon.

Emma squirmed on her bench when he stated that he would be preaching on the topic of envy. *Oh boy. . .maybe the Lord knows I need this sermon today.* Although Emma didn't want to admit it, not even to herself, she often struggled with envy toward other women—especially those who were close to her age—when she knew they were excellent cooks or very capable at the sewing machine. Emma felt like a failure at most things and didn't consider her ability to reel in a fish as anything important. And for sure, she didn't believe something as simple as that could be considered a talent.

Fanning her face with a piece of paper she'd taken from her pocketbook, Emma listened as Preacher Miller quoted several verses relating to his topic. The first one was Romans 13:13: "Let us walk honestly, as in the day; not in rioting and drunkenness, not in chambering and wantonness, not in strife and envying."

I do try to walk honestly, Emma told herself as she folded the upper corner of the paper. *I don't do any of the other things, except I'm envious. I am guilty of that, and I need to do better. But I have to wonder, if I never find something that would make me a more suitable wife for a godly man, will I forever continue to be envious of others, especially if Rachel happens to get married to David soon?*

Emma listened to the rest of the minister's message, as he quoted from James 3:16, Proverbs 14:30, and 1 Corinthians 13:4. The weight of the minister's words and the scriptures that touched Emma's heart caused her to ponder her attitudes as the sermon went on.

By the time the message ended, Emma was fully convicted and determined to learn to be happy for others who could do things well and not feel jealous because she couldn't. Of course, she couldn't change an old habit by sheer willpower. Rather, she needed the Lord's help with this issue. Emma also realized that she had to stop feeling sorry for herself and simply do the best she could. While she might never excel in cooking or sewing, under her grandmother's teaching Emma felt sure she could learn the two important domestic chores well enough to get by should she ever marry and move out of her parents' home.

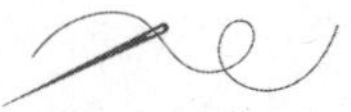

Ivan had noticed Emma and her grandparents as soon as he and his family had arrived at the service. He desperately wanted to talk to Emma and make sure she was still okay with him and his sisters picking her up this evening for the young people's singing. Church was over now, and everyone was just finishing up with the modest lunch that had been prepared for them, so he sat in silence, glancing periodically at the women's tables, awaiting his chance.

The opportunity arose when Ivan noticed Emma leave the table where she'd been sitting and head out across the field where most of the buggies had been parked. He looked back at the men's tables and saw Marlin still seated, talking to Ivan's father. That was a good indication that Emma's grandfather wasn't leaving just yet, so this might be his best and only opportunity to speak with Emma.

Ivan had also wanted to talk to Marlin about his clock, but he guessed that could wait until he came to pick up Emma this evening. *If she still plans to go to the singing, that is,* he told himself. *Otherwise, I'll just have to make a special trip over to talk about the old clock.*

Ivan hoped no one was watching him following Emma, and even though he was tempted to take off in a sprint, he slowed his steps and walked nonchalantly through the field. He picked up speed again when he was safely away from the people still in the yard visiting, and he approached Emma as she was about to get in the buggy.

"Will you be leaving soon?" he asked.

She whirled around, her cheeks red as ripe cherries. "Oh, Ivan, you startled me."

"Sorry. I didn't mean to. Just wanted to speak with you for a few minutes before you and your grandparents head for home." Ivan looked over his shoulder to make sure no one had followed him or was within earshot. "I wanted to make sure you were still planning to go to the singing with me, Jane, and Norma."

The color in Emma's cheeks deepened. "Jah, if that's still okay with you."

"Of course. I've been looking forward to it, and I. . ." Ivan peered down at the ground and prodded a clod of mud with the toe of his shoe. "And I'm sure my sisters are too," he said without looking up.

"What time shall I be ready?" she questioned.

"If my trusty horse cooperates, I should be there by four thirty." Ivan lifted his head, and when he looked at Emma, a sense of warmth radiated throughout his body. He knew it wasn't from the warm June sun that had broken through the clouds a few hours ago.

"I'll make sure to be ready by then," Emma said with a dimpled smile.

"Okay, good. I'll see you soon, Emma." As Ivan took his leave, the excitement he felt seemed to heighten his senses, because the grass looked greener, the birds chirped louder, and his heart raced like a runaway horse.

What's happening to me? Ivan asked himself as he drew in a massive breath of the murky countryside air from the earlier downpour. *Could I be developing strong feelings for a young woman I've only known less than two weeks? If it's true, then what am I gonna do about it?*

Chapter 12

Sunday evening, shortly before four thirty, Emma entered the living room where her grandparents were settled in their favorite chairs. Grandpa's eyes were closed, so she figured he was snoozing, and Grandma was reading a book. She looked up when Emma approached and tilted her head. "I see you're wearing a different dress than what you wore to church this morning, but it's not the dress you made."

"I know, Grandma, but I wanted to wear this frack instead." Emma touched the sides of her navy-blue dress.

"It shouldn't matter what you wear, as long as you like it," Grandpa spoke up from his chair across the room. Apparently, he hadn't been sleeping at all. Either that, or Emma's and Grandma's voices had awakened him.

"You're right, Marlin," Grandma agreed. "I just thought... Oh, never mind." She reached for Emma's hand and gave it a tender squeeze. "I hope you have a good time at the singing."

Emma smiled. "Danki, Grandma. I hope so too."

Although she kept it to herself, Emma was a bit nervous about going, but she also enjoyed Ivan's company and looked forward to spending the evening with him and his sisters.

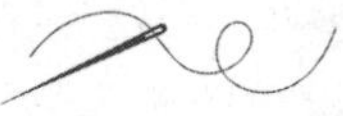

Ivan guided his horse, King, up the driveway leading to the Herschbergers' home and then over to the hitching rail. Before getting out, he handed the reins to Jane and said, "After I secure King to the rail, I'll go up to the house to get Emma. When we come out to the buggy, would you mind getting in the back seat with Norma?"

"How come?" she asked, eyeing him with a smirk.

Ivan's cheeks warmed. "Um. . .so Emma can sit up front with me."

Jane gave Ivan's arm a poke. "I figured as much. Just wanted to hear you say it."

"You like Emma, don't you?" Norma questioned from the rear seat.

"It's none of your business, but jah, I do. She's nice, and we have a few things in common."

"You gonna start courting her?"

Ivan looked over his shoulder at Norma. "I might, but you'd better not say anything to Emma about it." He turned face-front again and peered at Jane. "That goes for you too. If I should decide to ask Emma if I can see her again, I don't need either of you saying anything to her about it. Okay? Do I have your word?"

"Of course, Ivan. We would never say anything to Emma or anyone else. Right, Norma?" Jane glanced back at their sister.

"That's correct," Norma responded. "But we might be able to pave the way for you, Ivan. We can point out all your best qualities to Emma."

Ivan rolled his eyes while shrugging his shoulders. "Please, don't bother. If there's any paving of the way, it'll be done by me. Is that understood?"

"Of course, dear brother Ivan," the girls said in unison. Then they both snickered.

Ivan got out and sidestepped a few mud puddles as he made his way to the house. He knew his sisters were just funning with him, and he wasn't really worried about them saying anything out of line to Emma. Norma and Jane just enjoyed trying to get under his skin.

Once at the front door, Ivan gave three good knocks. He was pleased when the door opened and Emma greeted him with a welcoming smile. "I'm ready to go," she said. "But would you like to come inside and say hello to my grandparents?"

He bobbed his head. "Good idea, Emma. I'd be pleased to do that."

Ivan stepped in and followed Emma down the hall and into the living room. He shook Luellen's hand first, then Marlin's.

"Are your sisters with you?" Marlin asked.

"Jah, they're waiting for us in my carriage."

"That's good."

Is that a look of relief I see on Marlin's face? Ivan wondered. *Could he be worried about the possibility of me being alone with his granddaughter? I said I would bring Jane and Norma. Did he not believe me?*

"So how are you coming with that clock of mine?" Marlin questioned.

"I'm glad you brought it up." Ivan fanned his face with the brim of the hat he held in his hand. "The clock is running pretty well now, but so far I haven't been able to get it to chime. If you're not in a hurry to get it back, I'd like to keep working on it for a while."

"Nope, I'm not in a hurry. Take all the time you need. If you can't get the chimes working, though, I'll understand."

"I believe I can. It's just a matter of spending a little more time on it."

"Husband," Luellen spoke up. "You are taking up these young folks' time. I'm sure they would like to be on their way to the singing now."

Marlin's ears reddened. "Jah, of course. We can talk about the clock some other time." He motioned to Emma, who stood off to one side with her arms folded. "You two go on now and have a good time."

"Goodbye, Grandpa and Grandma," Emma said. "I don't know how long the singing will last, so if you two get tired feel free to head for bed. When I get home, I can let myself in."

"Not a problem," Luellen was quick to say. "I'm going to fix us a batch of popcorn and get out a board game to play, so I'm pretty sure we'll be awake when you get here."

"All right then, guess we'd best be on our way." Ivan swiveled around and followed Emma out the door.

When they got to the buggy and Jane climbed down, Emma smiled and said hello. But after the brief hug they shared, Jane climbed into the back of the carriage. Emma glanced around, as if looking for answers.

"Our *bruder* wants you to sit up front by him," Norma stated, leaning close to the open buggy door.

Emma blinked several times, and Ivan reached around to rub the back of his sweaty neck. He forced himself to meet Emma's steady gaze and mumbled, "Figured we could talk to each other without shouting if you rode up front."

"Guess you're right about that." Emma got into the left side of the carriage and took the passenger's seat. Ivan guided King down the driveway and out onto the road. He was glad Emma had agreed to sit up front but wished Norma had not blurted out what she did. Now Emma knew it was his idea for her to sit up front with him. He couldn't help wondering if she'd wanted that too.

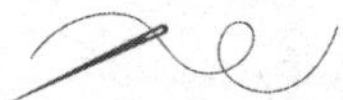

As they headed down the road toward the home where the singing would take place, Ivan tried to make conversation with Emma, but one or the other of his sisters kept butting in with questions of their own to ask Emma. Ivan was getting irritated and wished he could tell them to be quiet without being rude. What was the point in asking Jane to sit in the back with Norma if they were going to take up all of his time with Emma? Were they doing it on purpose to aggravate him, or could they be that interested in getting to know Emma better?

Ivan ground his teeth together as he held tight to the reins, making sure King didn't do anything stupid. Normally he was a cooperative horse, but occasionally, King decided to do something unexpected, like take off on a gallop when Ivan wanted to keep him at a slower pace.

Sure wish Emma and I were alone in the buggy, Ivan thought with regret. *Of course, I'm equally sure that her grandparents would object to that, since Emma and I are not officially courting and have only known each other a short time.*

Ivan glanced over his shoulder at Norma, who seemed to be doing the most talking, hoping she would look at him and he could give some kind of signal to let her know that he didn't appreciate her not giving him a chance to visit with Emma.

Norma didn't glance his way, however. She kept jabbering on and on, talking about the weather and asking Emma about her siblings and what kind of things she liked to do for fun.

At this rate, I'll never get the chance to say a single thing to Emma, and it'll probably be just as bad on the way back to her grandparents' house after the singing, Ivan fumed. *Jane, Norma, or both will most likely be jabbering like magpies about what they had enjoyed during the singing and asking Emma more questions that I had wanted to ask.*

Attempting to focus on something positive, Ivan realized that even though he hadn't been able to get a word in edgewise, through listening to the answers Emma was giving his sisters, he was learning some things about her that he hadn't known before—like the fact that she had an older sister named Rachel, not married and still living at home, and three older brothers, Benjamin, Harvey, and Jacob, who were all married with children.

So Emma is the youngest child in her family, Ivan thought. *I wonder how she feels about that.* He was about to ask, when Jane chimed in with another question.

"How do you like it here in Illinois? Is it quite different from your home in Indiana?"

"Not too much. We live in the country, like you do, and it's flatland, same as here," Emma replied. She glanced over at Ivan and opened her mouth, like she might say something else, but Norma was ready with her next question.

"So how do you like quilting, Emma?"

"I'm fascinated with it," she responded. "Someday, I hope to be able to make a really nice quilt for my bed at home."

"Our mamm says you have a knack for it, so I wouldn't be surprised if you succeed at quilting." Norma made a little grunting sound. "I think Mama was hoping either me or Jane would take an interest in quilting, but we both have other interests, so even though we've learned the basics, we've never done much with that knowledge."

"Norma's right," Jane interjected. "Quilting's really not my thing, but maybe our younger sister, Bertha, might show an interest when she gets a little older. I think Mama would be real pleased about that."

At this point, Ivan decided to give up on even trying to talk to

Emma. He would wait, hoping he might have a better chance when they arrived at the singing. If that didn't work, his last hope would be on the trip home. Maybe by then Jane and Norma would be all talked out.

By the time they got to the home hosting the singing, Emma was exhausted from answering so many questions. She had hoped for a chance to talk with Ivan and wondered if he felt the same way she did about his sisters talking so much during the entire ride.

Emma looked around at all the young people standing outside the home, apparently waiting for the signal to go inside. There were lots of young men and women, and she didn't know a single one of them. Emma hoped for a few minutes to speak with Ivan, but Jane took it upon herself to take Emma around to meet some of the young women, who Jane clearly knew. At the moment, Emma wished she hadn't agreed to come to this event. She felt like a fish out of water and wasn't fond of meeting so many new people. Even so, she was glad Ivan's sisters were there, because at least she'd met them before and knew a little bit about them.

Emma was also relieved that Grandma hadn't pressed her to wear the newly made dress, and she hadn't felt the need to make some excuse not to wear it this evening.

When someone announced that it was time for them to go inside, Emma went along with the other young women. The boys filed in first, followed by the girls. Several older adults were seated in the building, and all the young people filed past and shook the adults' hands. The young men sat together at tables in one part of the building, and Emma, along with Ivan's sisters, sat in another section with the other young women in attendance.

A light meal was served, and with the men on the opposite side of the room, Emma accepted the fact that there was no chance of her talking to Ivan now or during the singing portion of the evening that would no doubt follow soon.

After the meal and once everyone had been seated on benches or chairs, one member of the men's group took the lead by singing the first few notes of the first song. Everyone joined in, and soon all their voices blended and seemed to rise clear to the ceiling.

After a while, one of the girls led off with some songs. They sang from one of the songbooks the first hour, and later switched to another that contained some faster tunes for the final hour of singing.

The heat of the gas lamps hanging overhead made the room quite warm, but Emma enjoyed singing so much the heat didn't bother her. She felt more at ease. Maybe this evening wasn't so bad after all. Perhaps on the way home, she and Ivan would have a chance to talk.

Shipshewana

It was getting to be time to wind down for the evening, so Dianna had prepared some herbal tea for herself. To her astonishment, Philip wanted to have a cup of tea with her, so they stood side by side in the kitchen, mugs in hand. It had been quite a while since they'd had such a moment's peace together, and part of her wondered if this was a glimpse of what life would be like after their two daughters moved out of the house. They would be able to spend more time together like this every night, encompassed by the comfort of each other's companionship, after attending to their daily responsibilities.

The front door suddenly opened, yanking Dianna out of her fleeting thoughts. Her daughter barreled through the entrance, mumbling something as she slammed it shut.

"Rachel, you're home early." Dianna's eyes followed her daughter as she proceeded hastily to slip off her shoes. "Rachel, what's the matter? Did something happen at the singing to upset you?"

"We broke up!" Rachel stepped briskly into the kitchen, her words falling from her lips like stones tumbling down a hillside. "I was right about David. I caught him speaking with Alice again."

Philip grunted as he set his mug on the counter. "You broke up because you weren't happy that he was talking to your friend?"

With her face defined by the gas lamp's glow, Rachel shook her head, her eyes puffy and red, and tears gleaming. "I confronted him. David admitted that he'd planned to end things with me weeks ago. He said that we had 'drifted apart,' but I was always there for him. This isn't fair. I don't ever want to see David's face again, or any other guy's face, for that matter. I'm done with dating, once and for all!" She stormed out of the kitchen and clomped up the stairs, no doubt headed for her bedroom.

Sighing, Dianna turned back to her husband and said, "Now I'm concerned about both of our girls. Where did we go wrong, Philip?"

"We should've had only boys. They're much easier to handle," came her husband's response.

"You're saying that as if I could've changed the sex of our youngest *kinner*, Philip." She rubbed her upper right arm. "Besides, considering what David did to our daughter, I don't think having more boys would've made much difference."

His mouth twisting upward, Philip tilted his head slightly.

During all this, Dianna began to wonder if there was hope for her daughters to find any semblance of love in their lives. All she could do for Rachel was speak with her after her frustration had subsided from the heat of the moment and ask God to give her the right words that would encourage Rachel not to give up hope in finding the man she was meant to marry someday.

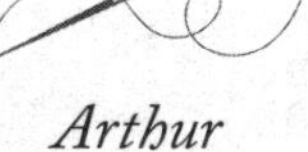

Arthur

Emma sat beside Ivan as he brought her home without his sisters in the back of the buggy. They had both been invited by two young fellows to take them home after the singing. Emma didn't mind much, especially since this wasn't the first time she'd ridden alone with Ivan. Though stillness hung in the air between them, Emma was certain the young man next to her was as exhausted from the singing as she was.

Emma's eyes grew weary from the lulling of the coarse surface of the road, and she glanced over at Ivan, wishing she could rest her head comfortably on his shoulder.

I can't believe I'm even thinking about this. Emma thought. *I don't know how Ivan feels about me, and besides, I doubt that he would ever ask to court someone like me. He probably sees me only as a friend.*

"I was gonna mention this to you earlier, but remember when I brought up the idea of going fishing sometime soon?" Ivan's question broke the silence, and Emma sat up straight.

"Jah, I remember."

Ivan rubbed the back of his head. "I'm planning to do a little fishing this coming Saturday, and I was wondering if you'd like to go with me."

"It would be nice to get out and do something just for fun, but I'll have to check with my grandparents first to see if it's okay."

"All right, but would it be okay if I ask them for you when I walk you up to the house? Otherwise, since we don't have a phone to call, I won't have an answer right now."

"That's true," she admitted. "Okay, if you want to do the asking, I'm fine with it, Ivan."

When they got there, Emma climbed out of the carriage, and after he'd secured his horse, she accompanied Ivan up to the porch.

She paused a moment to enjoy the fireflies emerging from the grass and scattering throughout the lawn in small clusters. Right when Emma's fingers curled around the cold metal surface of the doorknob, it opened, and there stood Grandpa.

"There you two are." Grandpa raised his right eyebrow. "Hope you weren't having too much fun."

"N–no, Sir," Ivan stammered. "I actually wanted to ask you for permission to take Emma fishing this Saturday."

"I suppose I can allow that, but I'll be going with you. I haven't done much fishing myself these days, but I'm pretty good at it, so I could help reel in a few to make the trip worthwhile."

"That's perfectly reasonable. It would be great to have you join us on this trip," Ivan stated.

"Good. Now, say your goodbyes, because it's getting late. I'm sure you don't want to keep your sisters waiting in the carriage." Grandpa vanished into the living room before Emma or Ivan could explain about Norma and Jane accepting rides home from two young men who had been at the singing.

Maybe it's a good thing we didn't say anything, Emma reasoned. She stepped into the house and turned to face Ivan.

"I suppose I oughta head on back home and get some shut-eye," Ivan said, leaving the porch with a wave. "*Gut nacht*, Emma."

"Good night, Ivan. See you this Saturday, if not sooner."

Emma observed from the porch as Ivan went to the hitching post and unfastened King. As she continued to watch as he drove his carriage off the property, an inkling of warmth sprang into her chest.

Chapter 13

"YOU'RE UP BRIGHT AND EARLY this morning," Luellen commented when she entered the kitchen and found Emma bent over the oven, removing a pan full of what appeared to be cupcakes.

Emma smiled as she placed the pan on a cooling rack. "I got up an hour ago so I could make some chocolate cupcakes to take on our fishing trip and wanted to make sure they had plenty of time to cool before Ivan picks me and Grandpa up." Turning to face Luellen, Emma added, "I used a recipe I found in your recipe box. I hope that was okay."

"Of course it is." Luellen squeezed Emma's shoulder. "I'm proud of you for taking the initiative to try something on your own. That's a good indication that you're feeling more *aagenehm* with baking."

"I'm not sure how comfortable I am, but I do plan to try harder, and maybe one of these days, I'll be able to cook well enough to at least get by."

Arf! Arf!

Luellen cringed. *There goes that puppy again. No doubt after a night of being cooped up in the utility room, she needs to go out.*

"I'll take care of Fawn," Emma was quick to say. "When I come back inside, I'll help you get breakfast started so we can be done eating before Ivan arrives." She started for the other room but swiveled back around. "Are you sure you don't want to join us at the pond today? It's a beautiful day, and I was thinking that you might enjoy a little fishing trip too, Grandma."

Luellen shook her head. "I appreciate the offer, but I'm not as interested in fishing as my husband is, and there are lots of things for me to do here." She didn't admit it, but the other reason Luellen chose not to go was because her back was bothering her again. *Still no new mattress,* she thought. *I wonder what could be taking so long for that delivery.*

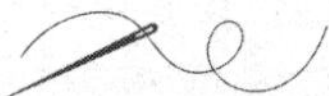

"Come on, little Fawn." Emma bent down and picked up the pup. "It's time for you to go outside for a bit."

She opened the back door and stepped onto the porch, feeling the vibration of the puppy's little tail against her arm.

"I know. I know. I just wanna get you somewhere away from the nice green lawn that Grandpa mowed yesterday."

Holding firmly to Fawn, Emma went down the stairs and headed for a patch of dirt toward the back of the garden shed. The puppy had behaved well about doing her business there, so Emma set her down.

While Fawn sniffed around, searching for a good spot, Emma eyed the dandelions, already popping up from the grass along the side of the house. It didn't take long for the persistent little plants to make their appearance after the lawn had been mowed.

As the morning wind carried hints of freshly mowed grass, Emma's mind strayed to the fishing excursion and the cupcakes she had made for the occasion. She regretted not tasting the batter in the bowl, but it was an afterthought, and Emma hadn't considered it until the bowl was already soaking in the sink.

Maybe I'll try a cupcake before I leave just to make sure, Emma thought. *Ivan won't be here for a while yet, so I might have time to start again if they don't taste good enough.*

After a few minutes, she looked over her shoulder at Fawn and saw that the dog was done with her business. "Come here, Fawn," she called. "You can chase me around the front yard for a bit." Emma clapped her hands, and within seconds, the pup came running and barking, her ears perked up and tail wagging.

Fawn trailed closely at Emma's heels, having no trouble keeping up with her as they rounded the garden shed. A few times around the yard left Emma panting for breath. *I'm out of shape,* she told herself, gulping down a few more breaths. *No thanks to all the lessons I've been having, keeping me mostly in the house. This fishing trip is a blessing. I need to spend more time outdoors doing things that exercise my body.*

When a horse and buggy pulled into the yard, the pup stopped barking, ran over to Emma, and nestled her little body against Emma's leg. Emma recognized the horse and buggy and was a smidgen flustered when Ivan clambered out of his carriage after bringing his rig to the hitching rail and securing his horse.

He's here early. Maybe Ivan's clock wasn't working this morning, Emma reasoned. She remembered distinctly that Ivan had told her last Sunday that he'd come by for her and Grandpa sometime between eight and nine this morning. Shortly before Emma came outside with Fawn, the clock in the kitchen had said seven o'clock.

After gathering up the puppy and giving her a good scratch behind the ears, Emma made her way over to where Ivan was securing his horse. "I'm surprised to see you so early," she said. "I didn't think you would be here for another hour or two."

Ivan rubbed his brows. "Didn't your grandfather tell you I was coming for breakfast?"

She gave a slight headshake.

Ivan leaned against the wooden rail. "Your grandpa came by the harness shop earlier this week, and while he was there, he invited me to join the three of you for breakfast this morning."

"Oh, I see. That was nice of him." Emma wondered if her grandmother knew about the invitation. If so, why hadn't she said anything?

"Who's your little friend, Emma?" Ivan pointed to Fawn and reached out to pet the top of the pup's head. "I didn't know your grandparents had a puppy."

"They didn't until Grandpa found this cute little pup by the side of the road and brought her home. He's tried to find her owner, but no one has come forward to claim the hund." Emma couldn't hold back a broad smile. "I'm the one who mostly takes care of her, so it almost feels like she's mine."

"Well, she's sure a cute little thing. Does she have a *naame*?"

"Jah. Grandpa named her 'Fawn,' because she has big brown eyes like a baby deer."

"Makes sense. That was a good choice." Ivan gestured toward the house. "Not to invite myself in, but shall we go inside in case your grandma has breakfast waiting for us?"

When they entered the house, Emma peeked into the living room. Upon seeing her grandfather holding the newspaper as he sat in his favorite chair, she suggested that Ivan join him while she helped her grandmother get breakfast on the table.

Ivan obliged and went right on in.

When Emma entered the kitchen, she rushed over to the stove where Grandma stood, pouring pancake batter onto a hot griddle. "Did you know that Grandpa had invited Ivan to join us for breakfast?" Emma questioned, speaking quietly so her voice wouldn't carry over to the room across the hall.

"Not until a few minutes ago," Grandma replied. "When you went out to take care of the hund, my dear husband informed me that Ivan would be joining us."

"I hope you're okay with it," Emma was quick to say. "It was a surprise to me when Ivan showed up early and stated that Grandpa had stopped by the harness shop earlier this week and invited him to come early today to eat breakfast with us." Her words rushed together. She wondered why her grandfather had kept Ivan's breakfast invitation a secret, or had he just forgotten to mention it previously?

"It's all right," Grandma said, as if sensing Emma's concerns. "I made enough buttermilk pancake mix to have plenty of flapjacks for all of us. Fortunately, during his last trip to the store, your grandfather brought home more baking ingredients for me to stash away."

"Okay, good to know it isn't an issue." Emma tugged at the neckline of her dress. "What would you like me to do in order to help?"

"You can set the table and get out the maple syrup and apple butter. You can also fill our glasses with milk and check on the sausage links I have warming in the oven."

"Sure, I can do all of that." Emma peeked in the oven and scurried off to the cupboard to fetch the plates and glasses and put them on the table.

Next came the silverware, apple butter, and syrup, as well as a slab of creamy, fresh-churned butter. Lastly, she poured milk into each glass at the table.

When Grandma had a good-sized stack of pancakes on a platter, she took out the sausage and asked Emma to let the men know that breakfast was ready.

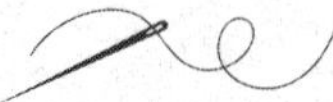

When Emma called Ivan and her grandfather to the table, Ivan followed Marlin to the kitchen. Once they were seated, all heads bowed for silent prayer.

After they began eating breakfast, Ivan commented on how tasty the pancakes were and asked if Emma had made them.

"No," she said with a quick shake of her head. "Grandma did all the cooking this morning, but I made some chocolate cupcakes earlier to take on our fishing trip."

Ivan smacked his lips. "Yum. I can't wait to try one. Chocolate is one of my favorite flavors."

"Mine too," said Emma, as she passed Ivan the sausage.

Turning his head, Ivan heard faint whining coming from the room adjacent to the kitchen. "Sounds like the pup I met when I first got here isn't happy about something."

"She wants in the kitchen," Luellen spoke up. "But if we let her, she'll just sit and beg. Besides, the hund's been shedding a lot, and I don't think any of us want to be eating fur-coated pancakes."

Ivan chuckled as he cut into the sausage. "She's sure a cute little thing. I'd be happy to have a dog like Fawn."

"You want to take her off our hands?" Emma's grandma asked in a most serious tone.

Before Ivan could form a response, Emma blurted, "No way! Fawn is my dog." A flush of pink crept across Emma's cheeks. "Well, she's mine to care for while I'm living here."

"Jah, that's true," Grandpa interjected. "I don't want to let go of little Fawn either."

The thought of Emma going back to her home in Shipshewana caused Ivan's shoulders to curl forward. He would miss her, but what could he do to stop Emma from going? And who was to say how she felt about leaving Arthur at the end of summer? Maybe Emma was eager to return home, although Ivan hoped that wasn't the case.

After breakfast, Emma and Marlin had loaded their fishing gear, and the lunch Luellen had fixed for them also went into Ivan's buggy. Then the three of them headed for the pond Ivan had chosen for them to try their hand at fishing.

Luellen saw this as a good time to get a few things done in the house and yard, although she wasn't sure how much she would accomplish with that whining dog in the utility room while she worked indoors. Fawn would also end up making a nuisance of herself when Luellen was outdoors cleaning the chicken coop and pulling a few weeds in the garden. It would be easier not to let the pup outside, but it wouldn't be fair to leave Fawn inside all day either. So Luellen put up with the dog's antics, thankful that so far, Fawn hadn't done anything worse than dig a few holes in a patch of ground near the coop, which Luellen had just finished cleaning.

I wonder if we should let Emma take the mutt with her when she goes home in August or maybe September, she mused. *Guess it will all depend on whether Dianna and Philip would be in favor of that. I sure don't want to keep the pooch after Emma leaves, but I know it'll be hard to convince my husband to drop it off at the shelter. Maybe the owners will turn up, and we won't have to worry about deciding on what to do.* She sighed. *One can only hope.*

Luellen took a seat at the picnic table her husband had made many years ago and watched as the puppy rolled in the grass. At this rate, the hund's fur would be interspersed with grass clippings from the freshly mowed yard.

What if my efforts to teach Emma the skills she needs to cook and sew have failed by the time summer is over? Luellen asked herself as her thoughts went in another direction. *I'm sure my daughter wouldn't be too happy if her decision to send Emma here to learn domestic skills was for nothing.*

While Emma had shown a bit of promise with some things, she was still a long way from perfecting her skills as a cook or seamstress.

"She would rather go fishing than spend the day sewing," Luellen said aloud. She shuffled her bare feet against the cool grass blades beneath the picnic table and pursed her parched lips. *If only I could convince Dianna to allow Emma to stay here longer. Not just to have more time to continue teaching her, but because she's been quite helpful for me as well. I will certainly miss my granddaughter when she goes home, and I'm sure Marlin will too. Well, the time for Emma to leave is still a few months off, so I'll try not to worry about it.*

Luellen heard the rumble of a vehicle coming down the road, and she watched to see if she recognized the driver, knowing it was not an Amish buggy approaching. As it came into view, Luellen realized it was a delivery truck. She forgot all about her dry mouth when she saw the words painted on the truck: Mattress Shop. Their new mattress was obviously being delivered, but they'd had no way of knowing that ahead of time, because they had no phone for the store to call and notify them.

Luellen stood and called for Fawn to come. She was thankful when the dog listened, and she quickly scooped the pup up before the driver got out of the truck. *I wish Marlin was here, and Ivan too, for that matter,* she thought. *If Marlin and I had known the mattress would be coming today, we could have removed our old mattress in readiness for the new one to take its place. I hope there are two men in that delivery truck and that they'll be willing to take the old mattress off the bed and haul it away.*

"Looks like our chaperone is having a great time, doesn't it?" Ivan scooted closer to Emma and pointed in the direction of where her grandfather leaned against the trunk of a tree with his eyes closed and his fishing pole lying across both knees.

She covered her mouth to keep from laughing out loud, which would no doubt wake Grandpa. "If he gets a bite, he'll probably never know it."

Ivan snickered. "That's for sure."

"If it should happen, guess one of us could grab his pole and reel the fish in without him even knowing it."

"Or," Ivan said with raised brows, "he could wake up in the middle of it all and start shouting because we've taken his pole."

"I doubt that would happen," Emma replied. "I've never heard my grandpa raise his voice—I mean, not in an angry sort of way. His tone of voice does raise a bit when he gets excited about something though."

"Well, you know what they say—there's a first time for everything."

Emma giggled. She figured Ivan might be right about that.

Around noon, with the sun beating down on them, Emma peeked at Grandpa and was surprised that, although he still slouched against the tree, he had one eye open as though looking through the lens of a telescope.

"How come you're lookin' at me so strangely?" he asked. "Have ya never seen a man half asleep and half awake?"

Ivan slapped a hand against his thigh. "Ha! That was a good one, Marlin."

Grandpa sat up and leaned forward with both eyes open, peering at his pole, devoid of any fish.

"What are you looking at, Grandpa?" Emma questioned.

"Nothin', but I'd rather hoped that, when I woke up from my nap, there'd be a big fish on my line." He pointed at Ivan. "Figured you might reel it in for this tired old man."

Emma wanted to refute that statement, but the truth was, Grandpa's seventy-nine years did qualify him as being old, especially compared to her and Ivan's youthfulness. Even so, for the most part, her grandfather didn't act old, and he certainly wasn't crippled like some folks his age. As far as Emma knew, both of her grandparents were healthy and still got around fairly well. Grandpa and Grandma were like that, except for Grandma's sore back, which Emma hoped would be remedied once their new mattress came and they'd slept on it a few nights.

"You two catch anything?" Grandpa directed his question to Ivan.

Ivan shook his head. "Naw, but it's been nice to sit out here and enjoy the warm sun and fresh air." He gestured to his horse, hobbled under a leafy tree and nibbling on some wild-growing grass. "I think King's enjoyed the day so far too."

"I bet that's true." Grandpa turned his head toward Emma. "I'm hungerich. Isn't it about time for lunch?"

"Jah, Grandpa. I'll go to the buggy and get the basket Grandma and I packed for our noon meal. Be right back!" Emma was on her feet before her grandfather could comment.

Chapter 14

While Emma was gone, Ivan scooted closer to Marlin. "I. . .uh. . .have a question I need to ask you."

Marlin quirked an eyebrow. "What might that be?"

Ivan cleared his throat a couple of times. He had to get this question out before Emma returned, but it felt like he had a wad of cotton in his throat. What if Marlin's answer was no?

Ivan looked toward his carriage, and seeing Emma pull the basket out of the back, he leaned in toward Marlin's ear and asked the question that had been on his mind all morning: "I enjoy your granddaughter's company very much, and I was wondering. . ."

"If you could begin courting Emma?"

"Jah. How'd you know?"

"Call it a hunch, but I've been through it myself when I was a young man and wanted to court a woman. I'm not so old that I can't remember the day I asked Luellen's father for permission to court her. I was a nervous wreck, and after I got up the nerve to ask, her daed looked me right in the eye and said, 'Marlin, you've got that look.' Then I asked, 'What look is that?'" Marlin paused a minute and threaded his fingers through the ends of his lengthy beard. "Luellen's father responded, 'The look of a young man who likes my daughter very much and wants to court her.'"

"Do I have that look?" Ivan questioned, already knowing the answer.

"You sure do, and I can also tell that you're a fine young man with good morals, who I feel certain has the utmost respect for my granddaughter. So my answer is yes, you have permission to ask Emma, and then, of course, the decision will be hers."

In one sense, Ivan felt relief. On the other hand, he still had to drum up the nerve to ask Emma. Maybe she didn't care for him the way he did her. Maybe the fact that she'd be going home in a few months might stand in the way, since they wouldn't see each other frequently after Emma returned to Indiana.

Or maybe, Ivan thought, *if our relationship develops into something serious, Emma will decide to stay here in Arthur and eventually become my wife.*

But Ivan couldn't worry about her leaving or make any real plans for the future. He simply needed to take one day at a time.

Emma was approaching them now, and it was time to eat. When the time was right, Ivan would ask Emma if she was willing to be courted by him. He sincerely hoped her answer would be yes. Ivan had never met a girl he enjoyed being with as much as Emma, and he wanted the chance to see if their relationship could develop into something permanent.

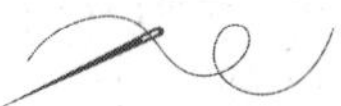

Luellen hummed as she put fresh sheets on the new mattress that had been delivered a while ago. She hadn't laid down on the bed yet, but would do so as soon as it was fully made.

When the top sheet was in place, Luellen straightened to her full height and arched her back, hoping to remove the muscle spasm she felt. She had been relieved when she'd seen two men get out of the delivery truck, because there was simply no way she would have been able to help with the removal of the old mattress, much less get the new one put in place.

Woof! Woof! Woof!

Luellen groaned. *There goes that puppy again. Does she need to go out, or is she simply seeking my attention? Well, whatever it is, she can wait till I'm finished making this bed.*

Luellen grabbed the lightweight blanket, spread it out on the bed, and then walked around each side of the bed to smooth the edges.

Fawn had quit barking, so she figured the dog had merely been trying to gain her attention, hoping she could be let out to roam around the kitchen for a while, sniffing for any morsels that might be on the floor. The puppy had done that a few times when Emma had let her roam, but fortunately, Luellen always made sure any food particles that had landed on the floor were swept up every morning after breakfast.

Of course, Luellen reasoned, *I'll be fixing my lunch soon, and then, unless I'm really careful, there could wind up being more crumbs on the floor.* She pursed her lips. *The answer to that is, I just won't let Fawn into the kitchen.*

Luellen paused from her musings and reached for the quilt folded neatly on the cedar chest at the end of the bed. Once it was in place and she added both her and Marlin's pillows, she decided to test the mattress.

She removed her eyeglasses and placed them on the nightstand. Then, settling onto the bed, with her head pressed into the comfort of her pillow, she noticed that the new mattress felt different beneath her body than the one that had been on display at the store. It was also a whole lot different than their old, worn-out mattress. But Luellen figured it was just a matter of getting used to the firmness of the new one, and once it was broken in a bit, everything would be fine.

Luellen had only been lying there a few minutes, listening to the leaves rustling from the parted window in the bedroom, when the dog started carrying on again. She grunted and sat up, attempting to straighten out the slight kink in her back as she swung her legs to the edge of the mattress. "All right. . .all right. . .I'm coming!"

When she headed toward the utility room a few minutes later, Luellen was greeted with a sight that put her teeth on edge. In addition to the fact that the pup had piddled on the floor instead of the newspaper that had been placed there for the dog's benefit, Fawn had something in her mouth and was shaking it back and forth like a rag doll. Luellen had forgotten to put her glasses back on when she'd gotten off the bed, so she couldn't make out what the dog had.

Avoiding the mess on the floor, Luellen leaned down to see what the object was and jumped back when she realized that it was a mouse. With no hesitation whatsoever, she quickly opened the back door and ordered the dog out. Their barn cats were all good mousers, but she'd never expected this small terrier to catch one.

Fortunately, Fawn obeyed and bounded out the door, which Luellen quickly shut. "Maybe I should have gone fishing after all," she declared, thinking about the mess she now had to clean up. First, however, she would return to the bedroom for her glasses so she could see better and make sure every inch of that puppy's wet spot was mopped up. *Guess I should have responded when the dog barked the first time. Fawn was most likely trying to tell me that she needed to go outside, so I suppose the mess she made is my fault.*

Luellen plodded down the hall to her and Marlin's bedroom. *I don't have the energy or the patience to deal with the puppy today. I really do hope Dianna will let Emma bring Fawn with her when she returns home. Of course, when Emma goes, I won't miss the hund, but I'll sure miss the company of my sweet granddaughter. After I clean up the mess Fawn made, think I'll sit down and write my daughter a letter while I eat whatever I decide to fix for lunch.*

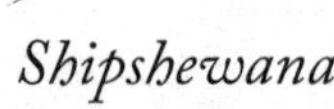

Shipshewana

Diana entered her husband's shop and handed him a tuna fish sandwich from the basket she'd carried from the house. "Here you go, Philip. I bet you must be hungry."

"You're right on time," Philip said with a wink. "My belly had begun to growl, so I knew it must be lunchtime."

"I'm out of lunch meat and cheese," she said apologetically, "so I'm afraid you're stuck with tuna fish today. Hope you don't mind too much."

He gave a quick shake of his head. "Not at all. In fact, tuna is a nice change once in a while."

"Danki for being so understanding." She pulled out a chair at the desk where he did paperwork and suggested that he take a seat while she poured him a cup of coffee from the thermos she'd also brought along.

"I will take a seat if you'll sit here with me and share my sandwich," Philip responded. "It's never fun to eat alone."

She smiled. "I appreciate the offer, but I don't need to eat the other half of your sandwich, because I brought one for myself, in case you wanted me to join you."

He leaned over and kissed her cheek. "Of course I want you to join me. That's a given, my dear fraa."

Dianna teared up, and she dabbed at the corner of her eyes, but it didn't prevent them from seeping out.

"What's wrong, my love?" he asked, swiping at the tears rolling down her cheek.

"You're such a kind, considerate man. I feel blessed to have found such a loving husband. I can only hope that our daughters are that fortunate."

"I'm sure they will be when they find the right mates." Philip pulled a second chair up to the table, and they both sat down. "Shall we pray so we can eat?"

"Jah." Dianna bowed her head and thanked the Lord for the man she had married. Then she asked God to send the right men for Rachel and Emma, and that they would both feel as blessed as she did right now.

When their prayer time ended and they began to eat their sandwiches, Dianna asked Philip a question that had been nagging at her most of the morning. "Is there anything we can do to help Rachel? When she's not working, she's been moping around here all week over the loss of the young man she'd hoped to marry."

"Give her some more time, Dianna," Philip said as he opened the lid on his thermos. "A broken heart takes a while to heal."

"I understand that, because my heart was broken once too."

His eyes widened. "Really? When was that?"

"I was fifteen years old and had the biggest crush on a young man in our church district. He was almost twenty."

Philip's brows rose as he tipped his head. "Seriously?"

"That's right, but Samuel didn't see me as anyone special, and I heard him tell his older brother once that I was just a kid." Dianna paused and took a bite of her sandwich. After chewing it thoroughly and swallowing, she continued. "Not long after that, Samuel met someone from another community and married her. I was brokenhearted when I heard the news."

"But Dianna, you had to realize you weren't old enough for love, much less marriage." Philip's tender expression caused Dianna's tears to flow again.

"You're right about that. However, my story doesn't end there," she stated after dabbing at her damp cheeks with the handkerchief she withdrew from the band of her apron.

"Oh, so there's more?"

Dianna bobbed her head. "My story ended when your folks moved to Arthur and I met you. I was older and more mature by then, and after we'd been courting awhile, I realized what true love really is." A few more tears fell, landing on her lap. "That's what I want for our girls. But what if it doesn't happen for them, Philip?"

"It will happen," he said with assurance. "But it will be in God's time, not ours, so it's best if we stop worrying about Rachel, and even Emma, and leave it all in the Lord's capable hands."

"You're right," she agreed. "But I may need to be reminded from time to time."

Philip grinned and lifted Dianna's chin with his thumb. "I can do that, Dianna. I'm good at reminding—and I'll be here to do that anytime you ever doubt."

Arthur

Emma brought the lunch basket she'd taken from Ivan's carriage over to the blanket that Ivan had spread on the ground and set it down. After the three of them prayed, she opened the basket, took out the ham and cheese sandwiches Grandma had made, and offered Grandpa and Ivan each one.

"Danki," the men both said.

Emma opened the plastic container the third sandwich had been put in and took a bite. It was good, and so was the conversation. Emma smiled when she heard Grandpa reminiscing about the biggest fish he'd ever caught back when he was a boy.

"Yes indeed," Grandpa said in an upbeat tone. "Why, that ole fish must have been two feet long." He looked over at Ivan and offered him a broad smile. "I'm not braggin' though—it's just a fact."

"That's a good memory," Ivan said. "Sure wish we were having better luck today. The fish in this pond don't seem to be biting—or maybe they don't like our bait."

"Could be either or both, I guess." Grandpa finished his sandwich and patted his stomach. "That took the edge off. Jah, it sure did, but now I'm ready for dessert." He looked at Emma. "Didn't you say you'd made some cupcakes to bring along today?"

"Yes, I did." Emma opened the basket again and withdrew the container. She lifted the lid and gave Ivan and Grandpa each a cupcake.

They both tore the paper lining off and bit into their cupcakes at the same time.

Emma held her breath, hoping for confirmation that the little chocolate cakes tasted all right. She watched as Ivan and Grandpa looked at each other with wrinkled noses, and both turned their heads and spit what they'd put in their mouths out on the ground. The heaps of gnawed cupcake mingled seamlessly with the dirt beyond the blanket.

"For goodness' sake, Emma, how much *salse* did you put in those cupcakes?"

"Only half a teaspoon. Does it taste too salty?"

"Like an ocean!" Grandpa bobbed his head and grabbed his thermos of water. "Was your grandmother in the kitchen when you made these cupcakes?"

"No, I made them early this morning, when you two were still in bed." Emma grabbed a cupcake and took a bite, which she promptly discarded inside a paper towel she pulled from the picnic basket. "Ew, you're right, Grandpa. The cupcakes are very salty, but I don't understand why." Her gaze went to Ivan to see his reaction. He had opened his thermos and was taking a drink.

"Well, apparently you didn't follow the directions very well," Grandpa said after he'd consumed some water and set his thermos cup down.

Emma's chin trembled, and she hoped she wouldn't give in to the tears threatening to spill over. "But. . .but, I'm sure I did everything that was written on the recipe card." She went over it in her mind, then gave an account of each ingredient she'd added to the batter. "Let's see. . .there was 1 cup of flour, 1 cup sugar, 1 teaspoon unsweetened cocoa, 1 teaspoon of baking soda, ½ teaspoon salt, one large egg, half a cup of milk, half cup of vegetable oil, ¾ teaspoon vanilla extract, and ½ cup of hot water."

"Maybe you mixed up the sugar and salt and put one cup salt and ½ teaspoon of sugar in the batter you were mixing," Grandpa suggested. "Jah, I'll bet that's what happened."

Emma shook her head vigorously. "No, I didn't. I followed the directions exactly the way they were listed. I'm sure of it."

"All that salt didn't get there by itself, Emma." Grandpa scooped up what was left of his cupcake and tossed it in the paper sack that the fishing bait had been in. "You had to have messed up somewhere—that's all there is to it. Better check the recipe again when we get home today because you must have read it wrong."

Grandpa's last words were Emma's undoing. She leaped to her feet, and tears blinded her vision as she ran through the tall grass along the edge of the pond. She'd never been so humiliated in all her life.

What must Ivan think of me? Emma thought, her heart pounding as she sprinted through the pond's surrounding greenery and away from her embarrassment. *Given how many times I've messed up, Ivan will probably never trust any food I offer him again. He probably believes I'm the world's worst cook.*

When Ivan saw Emma run off, he scrambled to his feet and ran after her, knowing she could probably use some cheering up right now. Emma pushed on toward the water's edge, despite his calls for her to slow down.

Ivan was gaining on Emma, but before he could reach her, she tripped on something and tumbled, headfirst, into the pond with a splash and a yelp. Emma's head disappeared under the water, then bobbed up again long enough for her to holler, "Help me! I can't swim!"

Barely giving it a thought, and ignoring any concerns for his own safety, Ivan's reflexes took over, and he plunged into the water. As the pond's surface rippled with each hacking stroke through the murky water, frantically he tried to reach Emma in time. Ivan's swirling thoughts were *I need to get to her before it's too late. Dear God, please help me save Emma from drowning.*

Chapter 15

The cold shock of the water caused Ivan to gasp and breathe rapidly. Refusing to let the pond's frigid hold deter him, Ivan plunged forward through the water, laden with leaves and algae. He needed to get to Emma. And he needed to get there quickly.

Ivan's adrenaline surged as he approached Emma from behind to avoid being grabbed. The last thing he needed was to be pulled under, leaving them both in a precarious position where they might drown.

It's important to stay composed, he reminded himself. *If I'm able to remain calm, hopefully Emma will relax and stop panicking.*

Emma had surfaced again and was frantically flailing her arms and whimpering, as though she'd been wounded.

"Calm down, Emma. It's okay. I'm here. Try to relax. I've got you." Ivan instantly put both hands beneath Emma's arms in a firm grip and brought her to safety as quickly as possible.

When they set foot on dry land, Emma's grandfather was there with the blanket they had previously sat upon. He had Emma sit down and wasted no time in wrapping it around her trembling body.

"Did she swallow much wasser?" Marlin asked, turning his head to look at Ivan.

"I don't think so, but her head was under the water a few seconds, so..."

"We should have her checked out." Marlin's brows drew together in the process of his deep frown. "Even if Emma only took in a small amount of water, it could irritate her lungs and cause complications. I want to get her to the hospital as soon as possible."

"But we're miles from the hospital, and. . ."

"I realize that, Ivan, but there's an English family living down the road a ways, so we can get in your buggy and drive over there. If they're willing to let me use their phone, I'll call one of my drivers to pick us up for a ride to the hospital."

Ivan bobbed his head. "You're right, Marlin. That is what we should do. If you don't mind gathering up our fishing gear and the lunch basket, I'll carry Emma to the buggy."

"Jah, okay." Marlin placed his hand on his granddaughter's wet, matted hair. "You doing okay, Emma?"

Emma's eyes flickered up at him with apparent confusion, but at least she wasn't coughing or wheezing. Her *kapp* had come off and was floating in the pond somewhere, but that didn't matter right now.

Ivan bent down, scooped Emma into his arms, and headed straight for his buggy. He could only hope and pray that this sweet young woman would be okay.

Ivan waved when he saw Abe, the driver he'd called, pull in front of the Yoders' house and turn off the ignition. "I'll just sit out here and wait until you've had a chance to change, and then we can head on over to the Herschbergers' place," Abe called through his open window.

"Okay. Thanks, Abe. I shouldn't be too long."

"It's all right. Take your time."

Ivan appreciated Abe's patience, but he wasn't about to take his time. He was worried about Emma and wanted to go to the hospital as soon as possible.

Ivan barged into the house and found Jane carrying a laundry basket in her hands. "Is Mom home?" he asked.

"No, she's working at the fabric store today, remember?"

"Oh yeah, I forgot."

Jane looked at him with an incredulous stare. "What in the world happened to you?"

Before Ivan could form a response, his sister said, "I thought you were going fishing with Emma and her grandfather today."

"I did, but. . ."

She pointed at him. "You're wet from head to toe, Ivan. What did you do—go swimming instead of fishing? Or did you fall in the wasser trying to reel in a fish?"

"I did end up in the water," he said, "but that was after Emma fell in."

Jane touched a finger to her lips. "Oh dear. How did that happen?"

Ivan gave a quick explanation and informed Jane that he'd stopped by their English neighbors on the way home and called for one of their drivers to pick him up here. "Abe is here right now, in fact. He pulled in a few minutes after I put King in the barn."

"Oh, I see. Can you fill me in on a bit more information so I can tell Mama and Papa when they get get home from work?"

Ivan shook his head. "I don't have time to go into any more details. I'm only here to change into dry clothes, and Abe and I will be heading over to pick up Emma's grandmother so both of us can go to the hospital in Champaign, where Emma was taken."

"This is all so *baremlich.* I hope Emma will be okay."

"I do too," Ivan responded. "I'm worried about her, which is why I need to go to the hospital with Luellen to see for myself." He paused for a breath. "And you're right, Jane, what happened to Emma was, and is, terrible." Ivan swallowed against the thickening lump that had lodged in his throat. "It scared me so bad when she fell in, and I didn't even think twice about jumping into the pond to save her."

"You were very brave, Ivan." Jane positioned the basket against her hip, holding it there with one hand while extending her other hand to rest on Ivan's shoulder.

"I just did what I needed to do." He turned toward the porch stairs. "I'd better go change now. Don't forget to tell our folks what happened to Emma today, okay?"

"Of course."

As Ivan hustled up the stairs, Jane called up to him, "I'll be praying for Emma."

"Thanks, Jane," he hollered back. "And believe me, I've been praying too."

Luellen sat at the kitchen table eating a tossed green salad for lunch. She had planned to fix a sandwich but decided the salad would be healthier, and it was a good chance to use the radishes, leafy lettuce, and spring onions that were thriving in her garden.

She glanced at the battery-operated clock on the kitchen wall near the stove. It was getting close to two o'clock, and Luellen would have eaten more than an hour ago if she hadn't taken a nap on the new mattress.

Well, what does it matter? she thought. *Marlin, Emma, and Ivan aren't home from their fishing excursion yet, so I can pretty well do whatever I want this afternoon.* Luellen figured they must be reeling in the fish today—otherwise they would have been back early. She hoped they had enjoyed the lunch she'd prepared for them and that Emma's cupcakes had turned out well.

It pleased Luellen that her granddaughter had taken the initiative to bake something on her own. She took it as a good sign that Emma wanted to improve her baking skills.

Luellen's deliberations shifted as she thought about the new mattress that had been delivered this morning. She was looking forward to Marlin returning home soon so she could show it to him.

Luellen had only eaten half of her salad when Fawn started barking, and she heard someone pounding on the front door. Knowing it wasn't likely to be her husband, she pushed her chair aside and went to see who it was.

When Luellen opened the front door, she was surprised to see Ivan on the porch, but she saw no sign of Marlin or Emma. She also noticed a station wagon sitting in the front yard. *Now, that's sure strange.*

"Ivan, where's your horse and buggy, and where are my husband and granddaughter?"

"They're at the hospital in Champaign."

"What? Why?" Fearful thoughts took over, and Luellen's legs felt so weak she could barely remain standing. "W–what happened while you were all out there fishing?"

Ivan extended a hand and steadied her. "Everything's all right, Luellen. Emma fell in the pond this afternoon and almost drowned, but she's gonna be okay."

"Then why is she at the hospital?" Luellen's lips quivered. All of this was really difficult to process.

"Just to be examined, mostly to make sure the water she took in doesn't cause any lung complications. I'm sure she's gonna be fine," Ivan quickly added. "I came here to get you, because I thought you'd want to go to the hospital with me to check on Emma."

"Jah, of course I want to go. I'll just need to make sure there's newspaper down for the puppy, and that she's secured in the utility room while I'm gone." Luellen fanned her hot cheeks with both hands. "Oh dear, I'm feeling so rattled by all of this, I can barely think straight."

"Let me take care of Fawn while you do whatever you need to get ready to go," Ivan offered.

She heaved a sigh of gratitude. "Danki, Ivan. I so appreciate you coming here to tell me what happened, and for securing a ride for us to get to the hospital."

"Not a problem, Luellen. I'm just glad it worked out that Abe was available."

"Jah, me too."

Luellen didn't bother to clear her dishes from the table. She just hurried down the hall to get her pocketbook and make sure her kapp was on straight, with no unruly hairs sticking out. She paused long enough to whisper a prayer before leaving her room. "Heavenly Father, please give us a safe trip to the hospital." Tears stung the back of her eyes. "And I beg of You—please let my precious granddaughter be all right."

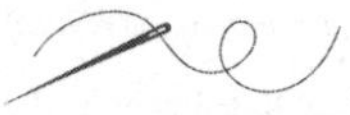

Emma sat in the back seat of their driver's station wagon, staring out the side window as they rolled on into the countryside. They had kept her at the hospital for four hours, running tests and poking and prodding to make sure she was okay. The truth was, she wasn't okay—at least not emotionally. She'd been confused and disoriented when Ivan first pulled her out of the water, but that part had disappeared by the time they'd arrived at the hospital. Replacing her confusion was a feeling of guilt for running off when Grandpa had made an issue of her terrible-tasting cupcakes. She didn't blame him, because they had tasted bad, but Emma's pride had been hurt, and she'd felt like a failure for messing up what she'd hoped would be some tasty chocolate cupcakes. Not only that, but Emma had been embarrassed that this had happened when Ivan was present.

What must he think of me? she thought. *It was bad enough that I messed up the cupcakes. Did I have to run off like a child unable to face the truth?* Emma rubbed a spot between her eyes. *It's obvious to me, and I'm sure it is to Ivan, that I'll never have the skills needed to be a good wife. I wouldn't be surprised if Ivan never wanted to see me again.*

Emma didn't know why that part even mattered. She and Ivan didn't know each other well enough to even be thinking about the topic of marriage. They weren't even a courting couple, so it was silly for her to be worried about what Ivan might think about the potential of her being anyone's wife, let alone his. Emma did, however, acknowledge how much they had gotten to know about one another in such a short period of time. What if Ivan had been interested in her, and now any remnant of that interest was swept away from what occurred today?

Emma turned her attention to Grandma, sitting quietly beside her, while Grandpa chatted with their driver up front. At the hospital, he'd apologized for the things he'd said about the cupcakes, and she'd forgiven him, but it still hurt to know she'd messed up the recipe so badly.

A short time before Emma was released from the hospital, Ivan had gone home, saying he would see Emma later. She wondered if "later" would be before this day was out, or if he would drop by sometime tomorrow after church. Part of her wished she didn't have to face Ivan again or at least could have time to regain her composure before she saw him.

The thought of getting up in the morning and going to church seemed overwhelming. Emma wasn't sure she would even have the strength to get out of bed, much less get dressed and sit through a three-hour service in a hot, stuffy building.

Maybe I won't have to go, she determined. *The doctor did say I should rest for at least twenty-four hours and then take it easy for as long as I needed to. I'll bring this topic up to Grandma after we get home.*

When they arrived at the house, while Grandpa paid their driver, Grandma got Emma settled on the sofa, and then she asked if Emma wanted something to eat or drink.

Emma shook her head. "No thanks, Grandma. Not right now, at least. I just want to rest. Even the ride home wore me out."

Grandma sat next to Emma and gently patted her hand. "I expected you would be exhausted. I'd be drained too if I'd gone through all of that, and honestly, I am worn out from worrying about you. I don't think we should go to church tomorrow, either. You need to stay home and rest."

"I agree," she said with a nod. "I don't think I could make it through the three-hour service."

"And there's no need for you to worry about that. All you should be doing is resting and concentrating on feeling better."

Emma mustered a weak smile. "Danki, Grandma, for your understanding."

"No problem. I'll let you rest now while I go speak with your grandfather. I want to tell him about the new mattress that was delivered today." Grandma gave Emma's hand another soft tap, rose from the sofa, and left the room.

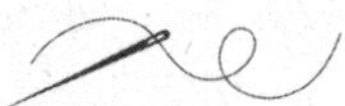

Luellen found her husband outside with Fawn. The dog was sniffing around the yard, while Marlin sat on the front porch. Above him, the wind chimes clunked slightly in the mellow evening breeze.

Luellen took a seat in the wooden chair next to his. "Emma's resting, so I came out here to talk to you about something."

He tilted his head toward her. "Is it about Emma, and the reason she ended up falling in the pond?"

"No, it has nothing to do with Emma's close call. Besides, I already know the reason she was running and fell into the water. You told me when we were at the hospital, waiting to hear how Emma was doing."

Marlin smacked the right side of his head. "That's right. I forgot. Sorry, Luellen. My mind's been whirling ever since the accident occurred."

"I can imagine. No doubt it was very frightening."

"You got that right. We could have lost our dear granddaughter if Ivan hadn't taken action so quickly and jumped into the pond to save her."

Luellen nodded. "I'm very appreciative too. We owe that young man our gratitude."

"For sure." Marlin looked at Luellen with a steady gaze. "So what did you want to talk to me about?"

"Our new mattress was delivered this morning," she replied. "It's on the bed right now, in fact."

His eyes widened a bit. "Now that's a surprise. I wish we would have had some advanced notice so I could have taken the old mattress off and found a place to take it."

"It would have been nice, but it's too late for that," Luellen responded. "The two men who delivered the mattress took the old one off, and at my request, they propped it against the back wall in the barn. I figured that once you came home, we would figure out how and where to discard the old one."

Marlin rubbed his forehead as though deep in thought, and then he gave his left earlobe a tug. "Say, I have an idea."

"What did you have in mind?"

"Rather than getting rid of the unwanted mattress, I can lay it on the floor someplace in the barn where there's enough room for it."

Luellen touched the base of her neck. "What would be the reason for doing that?"

"To let the cats use it as a bed."

Luellen blinked in succession, wondering if her husband had lost his sense of reasoning. "Why would they need our old, worn-out mattress for a bed?"

"Well, think about all the times you've said that you wished there was a warm, comfortable place for all of the mama *katze* to have their babies," he replied. "Problem solved."

Although Luellen thought it would not be practical to let the cats sleep on the mattress, she merely shrugged and said, "Do whatever you like, Marlin. However, my back's still acting up, so I won't be able to help you put the mattress in position."

"Oh, I'm not worried about it," Marlin said with a carefree tone of voice. "I'll ask Ivan to help me as soon as he gets here."

"Ivan is coming over? But I thought his driver was taking him home."

"That's right, but he's planning to get his horse and buggy and come over here to check on Emma." Marlin leaned closer and said in a near whisper, "Ivan is planning to ask Emma if he can court her. He asked my permission today, and I said it was fine with me." He clasped Luellen's hand. "I figured you'd feel the same way."

Luellen hitched a breath, unsure how to respond. Although Ivan Yoder seemed to have a good head on his shoulders, she couldn't help wondering, and worrying a bit too, about what would happen to the young couple's relationship once Emma went home.

Chapter 16

Luellen and Marlin were still sitting in their chairs on the porch when Ivan came up the lane with his horse and buggy. Once he had King secured at the hitching rail, he paused long enough to pet Fawn, since the dog had darted over and begun pawing at Ivan's trousers, begging for his attention. A few minutes later, after Ivan obliged the dog, he joined Luellen and Marlin on the porch.

"I came over as quick as I could," Ivan stated, while rubbing the perspiration off his forehead. "How's Emma doing? Is she up for some company?"

"Right now, she's resting on the sofa in the living room," Luellen was quick to say. "She might be sleeping, though, so let me go in and check for you."

"Danki, I'd appreciate that."

Luellen stood and motioned to her seat. "Here, Ivan, you can have my chair."

"Okay. Much appreciated." He sat down with a groan, then slipped off his straw hat and fanned his face with the brim. "Sure is hot and muggy this evening," he said, turning toward Marlin.

Luellen opened the screen door and stepped inside.

When she entered the living room, Luellen saw that Emma's eyes were shut, so she figured she was asleep and decided not to disturb her. Although Luellen was sure that Emma would be glad to see Ivan, rest was what her granddaughter needed right now.

Luellen draped a lightweight throw blanket over the lower half of Emma's body and tiptoed out of the room. She would go to the kitchen and fix a light snack to take out to the men, along with some iced tea she'd made earlier today.

When Luellen went back outside carrying a tray full of goodies, she was surprised to see that the men were gone. Figuring Marlin may have asked Ivan to help him move the old mattress to a better spot in the barn and lay it flat, Luellen returned to the kitchen with the tray. It was all just finger food that needed no refrigeration, so she placed it on the table and went back outside to sit on the porch.

May as well enjoy the solitude for a while, Luellen told herself. *I'll just sit here and listen to the crickets while watching hummingbirds flit from feeder to feeder.*

"Danki for helping me with this chore," Marlin said as Ivan grabbed one end of the mattress leaning against the wall. "This would have been a little cumbersome for a man my age to handle on his own."

"Not a problem. Glad I can help," Ivan replied. "Where would you like the mattress put?"

"How about right over there?" Marlin pointed toward the back wall. Except for the concrete flooring and the pieces of hay strewn over it, the area was essentially barren.

"Okay, sure. Are you ready with your end?" Ivan asked, adjusting his straw hat.

"Ready as I'm gonna be."

Ivan lifted on Marlin's command, maneuvering the mattress to the other side of the barn. After they dropped it in place, Ivan stood back with his arms folded as he sniffed in the sweet fragrance of hay. "If you ever need to move it again or get rid of the mattress altogether, let me know and I'll help you with it."

Marlin grinned at him. "I'll sure keep that in mind."

Woof! Woof! Woof! Fawn came out of nowhere and leaped onto the mattress. Then she plopped down and rolled over onto her back with all four legs in the air.

Marlin rolled his eyes. "Fawn does that when she wants her belly rubbed, and from the looks of it, she's claimed this mattress as her own. I'll bet the cats never get the chance to use it."

"That could be." Ivan chuckled and leaned over to stroke the pup's stomach. "She may be kind of hyper, but Fawn sure is a cute dog."

"Jah," Marlin agreed, "but my fraa isn't too fond of Fawn and her rowdiness. I think she's still hoping someone will show up and claim the puppy."

"I bet Emma would be disappointed if that happened."

"You're right. My granddaughter and that hund have made a real connection."

"I can see why." Ivan started to walk toward the barn's entrance, but when Marlin called out to him, he turned around. "What is it? Did you need me to do something else?"

Marlin shook his head. "I just wanted to offer you an apology for what happened today, which was completely my fault."

"You weren't to blame for Emma falling in the pond," Ivan stated.

"That might be true, but it was my fault she ran off in the first place." Marlin's shoulders curled forward as his head lowered. "If I hadn't said all those negative things about the cupcakes Emma made, she never would have gotten upset and run off in tears. I had told my wife I wouldn't do that anymore, but I got caught up in the moment."

Ivan stepped up to Marlin and placed a hand on his shoulder. "I may only be a young adult, but I've already concluded that it does no good to beat yourself up over something that's already happened. Emma didn't have to run off, you know. She could have stayed and defended herself."

"She tried that, and I wouldn't listen."

"I was in on it too, you know. Although I didn't make all the comments that you made, I am sure Emma could tell by my reaction to the bite of cupcake I spit out that I wasn't thrilled with what she'd served us."

"Guess you're right," Marlin agreed. "Those cupcakes were so salty that it was hard for me to hold back a reaction. But I still feel bad for the things I said."

"Have you apologized to her?" Ivan asked.

"Jah. More than once, in fact."

"Just as soon as I get the chance to talk to Emma, I'll apologize too. Then we should both put it behind us and try to be more considerate of her feelings, if there's a next time."

Marlin thumped Ivan's back a few times. "You're pretty *schmaert*, ya know that?"

Ivan's face warmed, and he swung the barn door open and held it for Marlin. Truth was, he didn't always feel so smart.

Emma opened her eyes and blinked. For a minute, she didn't know where she was. Her head felt full—like it had been stuffed with a wad of cotton batting, and she struggled to breathe. She remembered being underwater and how difficult it was to hold her breath.

She shivered and rubbed her arms briskly. Although it wasn't cold in the living room, the remembrance of her near drowning brought out goose bumps on her arms. *If I'd only known how to swim,* she thought, *I could have stayed afloat and gotten myself out of the pond. Why, oh why, didn't I let my daed teach me when he'd wanted to? Guess I was just a big chicken, afraid he wouldn't catch me if I started to go under.*

"Oh good, you're awake."

Emma jerked her head, realizing that her grandmother had entered the room. "Jah. Guess I must have dozed off for a bit." Emma sat up and scooted over so Grandma could sit beside her.

"Ivan's here," Grandma said after seating herself on the sofa. "He and your grandpa are out in the barn right now, but I'm sure they'll be in soon."

"Okay."

They sat quietly for a few minutes, and then Emma asked a question she'd been wondering about. "Did Grandpa tell you about the salty cupcakes I made?"

"He did."

"I was pretty sure I'd grabbed the right container, but then maybe I messed up," Emma said.

Grandma rubbed the bridge of her nose. "You know, I think I'll go to the kitchen and check the plastic containers I replenished a few days ago with sugar and salt. Maybe I'm the one at fault, Emma." Grandma rose from the couch. "I'll be right back."

While she waited for her grandmother's return, Emma tried to focus on something positive so she wouldn't think about her near drowning. Hearing the steady *tick-tock* of the grandfather clock in the room, she thought about some of the things Ivan had told her as they'd traveled to the pond earlier today. He'd said that tall, stately clocks had long symbolized tradition and craftsmanship and had initially become celebrated designs in the seventeenth century for their appearance and their accurate timekeeping. Their elegant cases and chiming movements added character to formal living spaces. In early American homes, however, grandfather clocks were practical and served as the main timekeeping piece, in addition to being a finely crafted furniture item. Their solid wood construction and mechanical precision made them ideal heirlooms passed from one generation to another. Ivan had also mentioned that an Amish-made grandfather clock could suit every style of room, whether it was practically bare or crowded with furniture. He hoped to make one himself someday when he had more time to pursue such a project.

Grandma wandered into the room again. "I'm terribly sorry, Emma," she said. "I just discovered that I mixed up the lids on the containers I poured salt and sugar into, so when you reached for what you thought was sugar, you ended up with salt by mistake. So you see, dear granddaughter, you were not at fault for the cupcakes tasting salty." She sank to the sofa with a groan. "So if anyone is to blame for your accident today, it's me."

"No, Grandma," Emma said sincerely. "It was a mistake, plain and simple, and I do not hold you responsible. I should have been grown up enough to accept the criticism I got from Grandpa and not run off like a crybaby."

Grandma gave Emma a hug. "You believed you messed up those cupcakes, even though you were so sure that you'd followed the recipe. It was understandable why you were upset, Emma. But now you know that you have gotten better at baking, so please don't give up. I think we all have something to be sorry for, and each of us has learned a lesson today."

Emma nodded. "Jah, we sure did."

When Ivan entered the house with Marlin, he looked toward the living room, where Luellen had said Emma was resting. He was disappointed to discover that she wasn't there and figured she may have gone to bed. Emma had been through a lot today.

Guess I should probably head for home and check on Emma tomorrow after church. Ivan was about to ask Marlin to give his granddaughter a message, when he heard Emma's voice in the kitchen talking to her grandmother.

Ivan positioned himself like a statue outside the doorway, struggling with the desire to barge into the kitchen but not wanting to be so bold.

Marlin was there with him, and he gave Ivan a nudge. "Go on in. I'm sure Emma will be happy to see you. I'll be right behind you, so don't hold back."

Ivan hoped Marlin was right, and desperate to see Emma, he pushed the kitchen door open and stepped inside. His eyes feasted upon Emma, who sat at the table, cutting pieces of cheese and arranging the slices on a silver tray. Luellen stood at the counter near the sink, with three ripe apples, which she appeared ready to cut.

Emma turned to face Ivan, and he felt relief when she offered him a smile.

"How'd things go with the mattress?" Luellen asked, turning toward her husband. "Were you able to find a good place to lay it out for the cats?"

"I did, but that crazy hund laid claim to it before any of the cats could even check out the mattress," Marlin responded.

She gave a quick shake of her head. "Silly pup. Maybe she'd prefer to sleep out there at night, instead of in our utility room."

"That's not a good idea, Grandma," Emma chimed in. "Fawn would be lonely out there all night. Besides, it could be unsafe for her if some wild animal were to get into the barn." She looked at Ivan, hoping he would agree with her, but he stood with arms folded and said nothing in the dog's defense. Emma figured he either didn't agree with her or had chosen not to take sides.

Emma was glad when Grandma told the men to fill their plates with snacks and take them outside to the picnic table. "It's too warm in the house to eat in the kitchen," she added.

"It's plenty warm outdoors too," Grandpa spoke up. "But it's probably hotter in the house." He gestured to Ivan. "You can go first."

Ivan hesitated a few seconds, but then he took one of the plates on the table and picked out some cheese, lunch meat, cut-up veggies, and a handful of pretzels.

Grandpa followed behind him, and then at Grandma's insistence, Emma went next. Before the men went out the back door, Grandma asked Grandpa if he would bring some of his homemade root beer out to the picnic table.

"Oh, sure, I can do that." He set his plate on the counter, told Ivan to go ahead, and went down the cellar steps where the root beer and other bottled and canned items were kept.

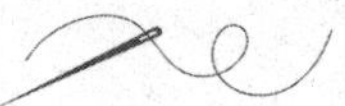

While the four of them sat at the picnic table, Fawn came running up, looking for a handout.

"Mind if I feed her something?" Ivan directed his question to Emma's grandfather.

"Suit yourself," Marlin replied, "but be ready to be pestered, 'cause the more you feed her, the more she'll keep begging."

Ivan laughed. "I figured as much." He picked up a piece of bologna, tore off a small piece, and then leaned down and let the pup take it from him.

Fawn gobbled it right down and slurped the top of Ivan's hand.

"That hund is disgusting." Luellen wrinkled her nose. "I bet you feel like you ought to go wash your hand now."

Ivan shook his head. "Naw, I've been eating with my fingers, not the top side of my hand."

Luellen shrugged and picked up her glass of root beer, guzzling what was left of it.

Ivan glanced over at Emma, who had barely touched the food on her plate. He figured she either wasn't hungry or had no desire to eat. Ivan had also noticed the way Emma's hands repeatedly rose to touch her face. It was clear that she wasn't herself this evening. Her darting gaze and frequent swallowing were good indications that she was dealing with anxiety, no doubt from all that had happened to her today.

Hoping to distract Emma and take her thoughts in another direction, Ivan leaned closer and said, "I was wondering if you would like to join me and my family for supper tomorrow evening—if you feel up to it, that is."

Without speaking, Emma's mouth opened and closed. She swiftly reached for her glass and took a drink.

Ivan wasn't sure what to make of her lack of response. If Emma didn't want to join his family for Sunday supper, he certainly wouldn't press the issue.

"Actually, Ivan," Luellen interjected, "Emma won't be going anywhere tomorrow, because she needs to rest for a few days."

"Oh, jah—guess that makes sense." Although Ivan understood, he couldn't help feeling disappointed. He'd really wanted to confess his feelings to Emma today, but the events that unfolded had stymied Ivan's plans to do so.

"I'll tell you what," Marlin spoke up. "Why don't you come over here Sunday evening? I'll make a batch of homemade ice cream, and we can all sit out here and watch the sun go down. Does that sound good to you two?"

Ivan looked at Emma before responding. He wanted to be sure she would be okay with her grandpa's suggestion before he gave a reply.

Emma offered him a smile that didn't quite reach her eyes and nodded.

"Okay, jah," Ivan said, feeling a little better about things. "What time would you like me to come over?"

"Six o'clock, if that works for you," Marlin replied.

"That'll be fine." Ivan finished the rest of his beverage, gave Fawn what was left on his plate, and stood. "Guess I'd better be heading for home now." His muscles tightened in readiness to go, but before he turned away from the table, he looked at Emma and said, "I hope you sleep well tonight and wake up feeling rested in the morning."

"Danki."

Ivan told her grandparents goodbye and then sprinted for his horse and buggy. He hoped when he returned tomorrow evening that Emma would be more talkative and looking more relaxed. It concerned him to see her like this, and he wondered if it was from the fatigue she felt or if something else could be wrong.

Chapter 17

Sunday evening, right on schedule, Ivan arrived at Marlin and Luellen's house for the ice cream Marlin had promised to make. The thought of dipping into the cold, creamy dessert caused Ivan's mouth to water, but he was more excited to be able to see Emma. In the short time they'd known each other, Ivan had developed strong feelings for her, and he hoped she felt the same.

Once Ivan had his horse and buggy situated, he meandered into the yard, where he was greeted by an overly eager pup. Fawn kept yipping and jumping up and down, until Ivan finally bent over to pet the rambunctious dog.

"You're a determined one, aren't ya, girl?"

Ivan was rewarded with a few swipes of the dog's pink tongue on his hand.

"Better not get your face too close or she'll lick you right on the mouth." Marlin's voice carried throughout the yard as he announced himself. He then approached Ivan after stepping down from the front porch. "I speak from experience too," he added with a wrinkled nose.

Ivan couldn't help laughing. He could almost visualize the look of disgust on Marlin's face when the little dog slurped his lips. *That won't happen to me, 'cause I will make sure not to get my head that close,* Ivan told himself, giving Fawn a final scratch between the ears.

"You ready for some homemade ice cream?" Marlin asked as the two of them went up the porch steps.

"Sure am." *I'm also more than ready to see how Emma's doing this evening.* He kept that thought to himself. His mind stayed set on Emma as he followed Marlin through the open front door. Ivan hoped that this evening, he could muster the courage to tell Emma how he felt about her.

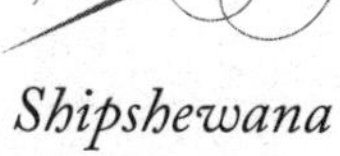

Shipshewana

Rachel sniffed and blew her nose on the handkerchief her grandmother had sent with a birthday card a few months ago. In addition to the hankie, a $10 bill had been included.

Rachel envied Emma and wished she could also be at Grandpa and Grandma's house in Arthur right now, instead of sitting up here in her room feeling sorry for herself.

She'd spent the last half hour crying and trying to figure out what had caused David's sudden attraction to Alice. Or had it been there all along, and she'd been too blind to see it?

If David lost all feelings for me, then why didn't he have the courage and decency to come right out and say so? Rachel asked herself. *And why did he let our relationship go on so long, leading me to believe he really cared for me and would likely propose marriage soon?* More tears trickled down Rachel's cheeks, and she swiped them away with the back of her hand. *How could David have broken things off with me after two full years of courting?*

Rachel's thoughts turned to Alice then, her supposed best friend. *Doesn't she care how her betrayal has hurt me?*

She got up from the end of the bed and strolled over to the window to look out, hoping the green grass and chirping birds in the yard might soothe her aching soul. But the serene view below and the birds' song on the verge of dusk did nothing to dry up Rachel's tears. She felt like a clock that had been wound up too tight and wondered if her heart would break and she'd never be the same again. The laughter that used to pour forth from Rachel so easily was gone.

How could my mamm even suggest that I go to the singing this evening? Rachel's fingers tightened as they curled into the palms of her hands.

Doesn't Mom realize how difficult it would be for me to see David and Alice together? I don't understand it, because Mom's usually so sensitive and caring.

An unexpected thought popped into Rachel's head. *What if I were to take some time off from my job and go visit Grandma and Grandpa Herschberger? I'm sure they would welcome me the way they did Emma, and it would give me some time to heal from this horrible hurt that I feel so deep in my heart.*

Rachel pushed her shoulders back as she made a decision. *I'm going to pray about this, and if I feel the same way I do now in the morning, I'll speak with Mom and Dad about the idea of me going to stay with Grandpa and Grandma for a while. It would be nice to spend some time with my sister too.*

Arthur

While Emma sat at the picnic table with her grandfather and Ivan, her thoughts took her back to the day before, when she'd fallen into the pond.

Emma remembered the concern she'd seen on both Grandpa's and Ivan's faces after she'd been rescued and was safely on dry land. She also recalled the sensation of being carried in Ivan's arms to the buggy. Despite her body being cold, she had felt secure and safe.

"This ice cream is sure appeditlich, isn't it, Emma?"

Ivan's comment drove Emma's thoughts aside, and she nodded. "I'm glad Grandpa made vanilla ice cream, so we could choose our own toppings to put on."

"That's how I like it too." Ivan reached for the bowl of fresh sliced, lightly sweetened strawberries and added a few spoonfuls to the ice cream in his bowl. Following that, he drizzled a little chocolate syrup on top and took a bite. "Yum! Homemade ice cream is so much better than store bought."

Emma added the same toppings and passed the bowl of strawberries to Grandpa.

"No thanks. Think I'll just enjoy the full flavor of vanilla this time." Grandpa looked toward the house. "I wonder what's taking your gross-mammi so long to bring out a few kichlin. Maybe she needs some help."

"I'll go see." Emma was on the verge of getting up when she spotted her grandmother coming out of the house carrying a plastic container.

Grandma ambled toward them, moving at the pace of a snail, and with a pinched expression on her face. Ivan must have seen it too, for he was quickly on his feet and racing across the yard before either Emma or Grandpa could react.

Emma watched as Ivan took the container, and Grandma, with one hand behind her back, inched forward until she was at the picnic table. Emma compared Ivan's quick reaction to Grandma's evident pain to his act of kindness when he dove into the water after her. Ivan's nature to be attentive and help those in need without hesitation was evident.

"What's the matter, Luellen? Your back still bothering you?" Grandpa asked.

"A little bit," she replied with a frown.

"Well, sit on the bench and get off your feet for a while." He motioned to the spot beside him.

"Did your back bother you this morning?" Emma questioned.

"Some. I figured that new mattress we bought would take care of the problem, but guess I was wrong." Grandma eased herself onto the seat beside Grandpa, and Ivan placed the container on the table.

"I slept fine." Grandpa pulled the lid off and reached in to grab two chocolate chip cookies.

"Grandma, maybe you should make an appointment to see the doctor about your back," Emma suggested.

Grandma gave a vigorous shake of her head. "That'd be a waste of time. He'd probably say that aches and pains come with old age, and the only thing he would likely offer would be pills I wouldn't want to take."

"Maybe it won't go that way," Ivan chimed in. "The doctor might have some helpful suggestions for you, or suggest that you have an X-ray taken."

"Ivan's right," Emma agreed. "You can't keep living in misery. I really think you should see a doctor about your back."

"Maybe these two young people are right, Luellen." Grandpa reached for another cookie and dipped it in his ice cream. "A trip to see the doctor might be exactly what you need."

"I'll think about it," Grandma replied. "If I'm not feeling better by tomorrow, I might end up going over to our English neighbors' place and asking if I can borrow their phone to make the call."

Emma smiled and passed Grandma the cookies.

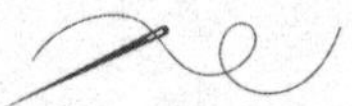

When they'd finished their refreshing cold treat, Grandma and Grandma went back to the house, taking the empty ice cream container with them but leaving the cookies on the table. Emma was too full for anything else. She'd eaten three of them, in addition to a full bowl of ice cream, and that was more than enough.

"How are you feeling this evening?" Ivan asked, leaning close enough to Emma that she felt his breath blowing against her left cheek.

"I'm okay. Just tired, and I've been trying not to dwell on what happened yesterday."

"I know what you mean," Ivan said. "It's been on my mind as well. When you fell in the water, Emma, it really scared me. I was afraid I might lose you."

"I'm fine now, thanks to you." Emma traced her fingers along the table's wooden surface, turning her head to look directly at Ivan, while offering him what she hoped was a reassuring smile.

Ivan scraped a hand through the back of his Dutch-bobbed hair. "There's a question I've been wanting to ask you, Emma."

"What is it?"

Ivan exhaled through his nose and reached for her hand before he spoke. "I would like to court you, Emma. Would that be all right with you?"

Ivan's pupils appeared to be dilated as he sat waiting for her answer. How could she say no to Ivan, especially since his presence provided her such comfort and joy? After what had transpired at the pond, Emma felt sure that Ivan truly cared for her. There was no doubt about it—Emma cared for him too.

Emma didn't make Ivan wait long to give her response. "Jah, Ivan,

I would be pleased to have you court me."

"I'm so glad. I was afraid you might say no, or that you're not interested in me as a boyfriend."

I'm very interested, Emma wanted to say. Thinking that might be too forward, she murmured, "I enjoy being with you, Ivan, so there would be no reason for me to say no."

They sat quietly for several minutes, as the sun began to set in the west, bringing a glorious sunset of pink and red hues. The lawn was enveloped in lengthy shadows from the waning daylight, and the evening breeze cooled Emma's arms.

"I have another question to ask, if you don't mind," Ivan said, breaking the silence between them.

"Oh?"

"I was wondering if you would have any objections to us going in the house to tell your grandparents that I asked, and you agreed, to become a courting couple. Or maybe you would prefer to tell them after I leave."

"I have no objection at all," Emma responded. "In fact, I think we should do it together."

Ivan nodded. "I'm fine with that, and then I really need to get home so you can get some sleep. I'm sure this day has been a long one for you."

"It was, but I did take a nap this afternoon."

"You probably needed it."

"Jah, that's true." With regret, Emma let go of Ivan's hand and stood. "Guess I'd better take what's left of the cookies inside. Unless, you want to finish eating them."

Ivan held his stomach and groaned. "I ate too many as it was."

"Same here."

As Emma walked beside Ivan up to the house, she felt a sense of weightlessness. *Could this be happening to me? Did Ivan really ask to court me? Am I falling in love with Ivan Yoder, or is it too soon for that?*

Chapter 18

Monday morning, while eating breakfast, Ivan decided to tell his parents and siblings that he'd asked Emma if he could court her and she'd said yes. He waited for a lull in the conversation, then jumped right in at the opportune moment with what had occurred last night when he'd asked Emma.

"That's wunderbarr!" Jane, who sat beside Ivan, reached over and patted his arm.

His other siblings and father all nodded in agreement. Ivan looked over at his mother, surprised that she hadn't said anything. He was about to ask what she thought, when she spoke up.

"I understand why you'd be happy about courting a sweet girl like Emma," Mama said. "In fact, my mother's intuition told me this might be coming. However, I am a little worried about how things will go when Emma returns home."

"It's a valid concern, Ida Mae," Ivan's father interjected. "But our son isn't a child anymore, and if he's comfortable courting Emma, knowing she will be returning home in a few months, then we shouldn't worry about how it will turn out."

Ivan bit his lip to keep from smiling, thankful that his dad had stuck up for him. It didn't happen very often, especially during work hours at the harness shop.

"I agree with Papa," Jane chimed in. "Ivan is old enough and has the right to make his own decisions."

Ivan appreciated his sister's approval, but he was bothered by the fact that their mother had thrown cold water on the joy he'd felt in telling his family the good news. Did Mama believe there might be someone better for Ivan, or was she worried that he would be hurt if Emma broke up with him when she returned to Shipshewana?

I'm willing to take that chance, Ivan thought as he forked a piece of egg into his mouth. *Besides, maybe Emma will decide to remain in Arthur permanently, and I won't have to worry about anything.*

Luellen had taken a seat at the kitchen table to write Dianna another letter, when Emma entered the room.

"Good morning, Grandma," Emma said. "How did you sleep, and how's your back feeling?"

"I slept well," Luellen replied. "And my back doesn't hurt as much as it did last evening."

"That's good to hear." Emma inched closer to the corner of the table. "Looks like you're writing a letter. Is it to my mamm?"

"Jah. I like to keep her up to date on how things are going here so she doesn't worry about us."

"Please don't say anything to her about me falling in the pond when I went fishing with Grandpa and Ivan."

"Don't you think your folks have the right to know?"

Emma shook her head. "Reading about the mishap would only cause them to worry—especially my mamm. Besides, I'm all right and no harm was done, so I don't see any reason for my parents to know."

"Well, I—"

"Please, Grandma, don't say anything to my mamm about what happened on Saturday."

"All right, since everything turned out fine, but if it had been something more serious, I would have definitely let your parents know."

"I understand." Emma pushed back her chair and stood. "What did you have in mind for breakfast this morning? I'll get started on it while you finish the letter."

"That's very thoughtful of you," Luellen responded. "Why don't you try making buttermilk pancakes this morning? The recipe's written out on a 3x5 card in my recipe box, filed under Breakfast Items. Since you will be having another quilting lesson with Ida Mae this afternoon, making pancakes will count as your cooking lesson for the day."

"Okay. I'll do my best, and since you're here in the kitchen with me, I can ask questions if I need to, right?"

"Absolutely."

Emma kept busy mixing the ingredients for the pancake batter. She made an effort to concentrate and tried not to mess up. She wanted the pancakes to turn out well.

By the time Emma had the griddle heated and was ready to begin pouring the batter out to cook the individual pancakes, Grandma had finished her letter and slid it in an envelope.

"How's it going?" Grandma asked, coming alongside Emma.

"Pretty good, I think. At least mixing the batter went okay. Now I just have to keep from burning the pancakes or not cooking them enough." Emma wrinkled her nose. "I just hope I'm able to flip them without making a mess."

"It's not really that difficult," Grandma said. "As the pancakes cook on one side, watch for bubbles to form on the surface. Wait until the bubbles pop and leave small holes that stay open. The edges of the pancakes should also start to look set and slightly dry." She went to the desk for a stamp, which she licked and stuck on the envelope. "Now where was I?"

"You were telling me what to look for before flipping the pancakes over."

"Right." Grandma's pointy finger went up. "Then, once you feel confident that the pancakes are ready to turn over, gently slide a spatula under each one to check the underside. If it's a golden-brown color, flip the pancakes with the spatula and cook the other side of each one."

Her grandmother's instructions seemed simple enough, but Emma couldn't ignore the quiver in her stomach. She had a tendency to mess things up, and this morning's breakfast might be no exception.

With pursed lips, Emma turned toward Grandma. "Maybe it would help if you stood next to me to make sure I'm doing it right."

"I'll watch you cook and flip one pancake, and then you'll be on your own while I set the table. Your grandfather will be in soon from doing chores in the barn, and it would be nice if breakfast is ready when he comes in so we can all eat together."

"Okay." Emma spooned the batter for the first pancake onto the hot griddle, and then she squeezed in two more. Watching carefully, she waited until bubbles had formed. "Are they ready to turn now?" she asked, glancing at Grandma.

"Not yet, Emma. You must wait for the bubbles to pop."

"Oh yes, that's right." Emma waited for several more seconds, and then when the bubbles popped, she carefully checked the underside, then flipped each pancake over. *Maybe this isn't so hard after all.*

Grandma gave Emma's shoulder a tender squeeze. "Keep doing what you're doing, and you'll be fine." She handed Emma an ovenproof pan. "I will turn the oven on low, and when you take the pancakes off the griddle, place them in here and then put the container in the oven so they will stay nice and warm."

"All right, Grandma." Emma drew in a few quick breaths, hoping to steady her nerves. The last thing she wanted to do was ruin this breakfast.

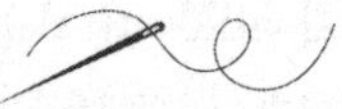

"These *pennekuche* are sure appeditlich," Grandpa declared as he forked another pancake onto his plate. "You did well, Emma, and I think we've got ourselves a chef in the making."

Emma brightened. "I'm so glad they turned out okay."

"They're more than okay," Grandma interjected. "Everything about them is just right."

"Your grandmother is correct," Grandpa agreed. "You've got the makings of a fine cook, Emma."

It wasn't the warmth in the kitchen that caused Emma's face to heat up. "Danki. This is the first thing I've made that really turned out fine, and I couldn't have done it without Grandma's instructions. Which I won't have once I go home," Emma added.

"By that time you'll be all set," he responded, "and ready to become someone's fraa. Maybe Ivan's, in fact."

The heat Emma felt in her face generated to the rest of her body.

"You shouldn't tease the girl like that." Grandma poked his arm. "She and Ivan have just begun their courtship, so if and when a marriage proposal should occur, it won't happen tomorrow."

Grandpa shrugged. "Well, you never know—some things happen sooner than later."

Emma's chin dipped, and she felt a trickle of sweat roll off her forehead and onto her cheeks. This discussion was unnecessary and embarrassing.

As though sensing Emma's discomfort, Grandma changed the subject and mentioned a work frolic that would be coming up soon to spruce up the schoolhouse and the grounds the building sat upon. Grandpa quickly joined in, and Emma felt better having a discussion focused on something other than her.

Shipshewana

Dianna hadn't been in the kitchen very long when Rachel showed up, offering to help fix breakfast. She appeared tired, with dark creases beneath her eyes.

"I thought we'd have scrambled oier this morning," Dianna replied. "So if you feel up to it, you can help with fixing those, or if you'd rather set the table, I'll scramble the eggs."

"If you don't mind, I'll set the table."

"No, that's fine."

Rachel went to the cupboard and took down three plates, which she promptly placed on the table. "Has Dad come in yet?" she asked, glancing toward the back door.

"No, but I'm sure he will be here soon."

"When he comes in, I'd like to talk to you both about something."

Dianna noticed her daughter's fluttery hand movements. Rachel was obviously nervous. She was tempted to ask why but decided to let it go.

Dianna mixed the eggs with a whisk and got busy at the stove. The eggs were well cooked by the time Philip entered the kitchen.

"I'm hungerich. Is breakfast ready?" he asked.

"Yes indeed," Dianna said. "As soon as you wash up, we can eat."

A short time later, they were seated at the table. After silent prayer, Dianna passed her husband the platter of scrambled eggs and some sausage links she'd heated in another pan.

After taking some of each, he handed the platter to Rachel. She took a small amount and passed it on to Dianna.

"You didn't put much on your plate, Rachel," Philip commented. "No appetite this morning?"

"I. . .uh. . .have a question to ask you and Mom."

Dianna gave Rachel her full attention. "What is it?"

"I've been thinking it would be nice if I could stay with Grandpa and Grandpa Herschberger for a while."

Dianna's head jerked slightly, and Philip gave an unexpected bark of laughter. "You're kidding, right?"

"No, Dad," Rachel said with a shake of her head. "I need to get away for a while. I've been missing Emma too and would enjoy some time away where I wouldn't have to see David or even think about him."

"What about your cleaning job?" Dianna questioned.

"I'll ask for a few weeks off." Rachel fiddled with her fork. "Or maybe even longer."

Dianna was about to say that she didn't think it was a good idea, when Philip blurted out, "I think that's a fine idea, Rachel. A little time away will be good for you, and it'll give you a chance to gain a new perspective on things."

Dianna's eyes narrowed. She wished her husband sat closer to her, because if he were, she might have kicked him under the table. With both of their daughters staying at their grandparents' house, it could mean that one or both of them might decide to stay in Arthur permanently. Then Dianna and Philip would have no children living close to them. Hadn't he thought about that?

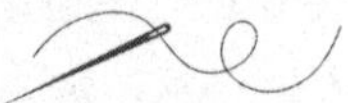

Shortly after noon, Emma arrived at the Yoders' home for another quilting lesson. There was a spring in Emma's step as she approached the porch stairs. Her pancakes had turned out well this morning, she had a steady boyfriend for the first time, and Emma felt hopeful about her ability to do something well today.

Emma only knocked once before the door opened and Ivan's mother invited her in.

"Good afternoon, Emma." Ida Mae gave her a hug. "Let's go into my sewing room and get started, shall we?"

Emma smiled and nodded. She could hardly wait. There was so much she wanted to learn about quilting—not just becoming an expert quilter, but learning the different patterns and even discovering some information about the history of Amish quilting.

Following Ida Mae down the hall, Emma noticed a stack of pot holders on a narrow table. She wanted to stop and take a closer look at them, but Ida Mae moved along quickly, and Emma didn't want to hold her up by taking the time to sort through the stack. So she hurried her footsteps and entered the sewing room behind her quilting instructor.

For the next several hours, Ida Mae guided Emma through the process of sewing more basic patchwork squares, reminding her to keep her stitches small and even. This held the seams together tightly and neatly.

"I hope someday I'll be experienced enough to make an unusual quilt," Emma commented. "I'd like it to be something different that most people don't have or even know about."

Ida Mae grinned. "You're thinking like a true quilt designer."

Without taking her eyes off her quilting project, Emma said, "Thinking is one thing, and doing is another."

"That is true," Ida Mae agreed. "But in order to do something, one must first think about it."

"I see your point." Emma looked up. "Are the pot holders that I saw in the hallway for sale? I assume you must have made them."

"They will be once I take them to the fabric store later this week."

"Would it be possible for me to buy one? I'd like to give it to my grandma."

"I have a better idea," Ida Mae said. "Why don't I show you how to make one yourself? If you don't get it done today, you can finish the next time you come for a lesson."

Emma bobbed her head. "I like that idea. And once I learn how to make a pot holder, I can do more and give them to other family members, like my mamm, and my sister Rachel, who will probably be getting married soon."

"That's a good idea, Emma. Pot holders make nice gifts." Ida Mae cleared her throat a couple of times. "Umm...there's something I'd like to talk to you about."

"What would that be?"

"This morning during breakfast, Ivan told us that he'd asked if he could begin courting you."

Emma's cheeks grew warm. It wasn't really a surprise that he'd told them, since her grandparents had been informed last evening, but she was surprised that Ida Mae had brought it up and had said she wanted to talk about it.

Does Ivan's mother disapprove of her son going out with me? Emma wondered.

As if sensing Emma's discomfort, Ida Mae placed a hand on Emma's shoulder and gave a few gentle pats. "You're a very sweet girl, Emma, and Ivan obviously cares for you, or he wouldn't have asked if he could court you."

Emma sat quietly and waited, for she felt certain Ivan's mother had more to say.

"Ivan's father and I have no objections to you and Ivan seeing each other socially, but I do have a concern about what will happen to your relationship when you return to your home in Shipshewana."

Emma shifted uneasily on her chair. She'd been thinking about this herself, and she hadn't come up with anything she could feel good about. Breaking things off with Ivan, when the time came for her to return home, was not a good option. The mere thought of it caused Emma heartache.

Emma felt sure that Ida Mae was waiting for her response, so she swallowed past the lump in her throat and said, "I guess when the time comes for me to leave Arthur and return to my parents' home, Ivan and I will have to work things out so that we can still see each other from time to time. And of course, we would keep in touch through letter writing."

Ida Mae's lips parted like she was about to say something more, when Ivan bounded into the room.

"Oh good, you're still here." He grinned at Emma. "I was hoping I'd get home before you left, because there's something I want to ask you."

"Well, before you get into that," his mother said, "I'm going to the kitchen for something cold to drink. Would either of you appreciate a glass of root beer?"

"I would," Ivan was quick to reply. "It would surely hit the spot on this hot, muggy day."

Emma nodded. "That does sound good, Ida Mae. Would you like my help serving it?"

"No, that's okay," she replied with a shake of her head. "You two stay here and talk about whatever my son wants to say." Ivan's mother turned and skirted out of the room.

He pulled up a chair close to Emma, glancing at the quilting project in her lap. "Looks like you've had a busy day here with my mamm."

"Jah."

"So now it's time for you to relax awhile."

"I guess so."

Ivan struggled with the desire to take hold of Emma's hand, but he didn't want to embarrass her in case Mama came back sooner than expected. So instead, Ivan leaned a little closer and said, "How would you like to go on a picnic with me, Norma, and her boyfriend, Timothy, this coming Saturday?"

"That sounds nice," she said, "but I'll need to check with Grandma first, to make sure she doesn't need me for anything that day. It won't involve swimming, will it?" she asked with furrowed brows.

"No, the place we were thinking of going doesn't have a body of water, not even a stream running through."

Her facial features relaxed. "That's good to hear. A picnic does sound like fun. Maybe I can make those chocolate cupcakes again, only this time, I'll make sure that I'm using sugar and not salt."

Ivan chuckled. "Before I went home last night, your grandma told me what had happened and how she'd been to blame for putting the wrong lids on the containers."

"True, but I should have been able to tell the difference between sugar and salt."

"You're too hard on yourself, you know that, Emma?" Ivan asked.

She merely shrugged in response.

Ivan figured she wasn't willing to admit it. That didn't matter. Since he and Emma enjoyed doing many of the same things, Ivan had decided that whenever he wasn't working and Emma wasn't busy learning to cook, sew, or quilt, he would come up with a plan for them to get together. Ivan wanted to make the best use of their time before Emma returned to her parents' home.

Chapter 19

"Look what came in the mail," Luellen called as she trudged up the driveway, waving the envelope she'd taken from the mailbox.

When she approached the hammock where her husband lay, he groaned and opened his eyes. "Why did ya wake me, Luellen?" he asked. "I was nappin' in peace."

"We got a letter from Dianna, and I thought you'd be interested in hearing what she had to say. You don't need to snap at me for telling you that."

Marlin yawned and pulled himself to a sitting position. "You're right, Luellen. Sorry for snapping at you. I am definitely interested in knowing what our daughter's letter says."

"Should I read it to you, or would you rather read it yourself?"

He slipped off the hammock and stood. "Let's go up to the shaded porch, and you can read it out loud."

"Are you sure? I wouldn't want to come between you and your nap more than I already have."

Marlin shook his head. "Truthfully, I slept long enough." He extended his hand in her direction. "Come on, Luellen. . .please don't keep me in suspense."

They ascended the porch stairs hand in hand, and once they were both seated, she opened the letter and read it to him:

Dear Mom and Dad,

I'm writing to ask if you would be okay with Rachel coming to Arthur to stay with you a few weeks. She and her boyfriend, David, recently broke up, because he ended things with her and is now pursuing Rachel's best friend. Poor Rachel has been moping around here ever since.

It was her idea to come there for a visit. She believes a few weeks away might help her come to grips with the breakup, and the time spent with you and Dad might help to heal her broken heart. Rachel also mentioned that she misses Emma and would like to spend some time with her too.

Luellen paused and looked over at Marlin to check his reaction.

He sat with his head lowered, while rubbing his forehead.

"Marlin, did you hear what I said?"

He lifted his chin and sat up straight. "Jah, I heard. Just thinking is all."

"About Rachel?"

"Jah. That was not a nice thing her boyfriend did to her."

"I agree. I'm sure she's brokenhearted."

Luellen waited to see if he would say anything further, but Marlin just rested in his chair, staring out into the yard. Finally, when she was on the verge of asking if her husband thought they should tell Dianna to hire a driver to bring Rachel here for a two-week visit, Marlin spoke again.

"Won't having Rachel here cut into your time of teaching Emma how to cook and sew?"

"I don't believe so. I'm sure Rachel will find some things to do on her own."

"Maybe," he said, "but if Emma's sister is here, Emma will want to hang out with Rachel instead of paying attention to the instructions you give her in the kitchen and sewing room."

Luellen tapped her foot against the wooden floorboards beneath her chair and frowned. "I suppose that could be a problem. Should I tell Dianna that when I write back to let her know we received the letter she sent?"

Marlin swiped a hand across his forehead. "I guess not. She might take it wrong and think we don't want Rachel to visit us."

Luellen turned the letter over. "Exactly. So I think the best thing to do is allow Rachel to come. It'll only be for a few weeks, so even if having Rachel here distracts Emma from cooking and sewing lessons, I can get back in a routine of teaching her once Rachel goes home."

"All right then. Go ahead and write Dianna a letter and tell her that we're fine with Rachel staying here for two weeks."

"Never mind, Marlin. I don't need to do that," Luellen replied as she pointed at what was written by her daughter on the other side of the page. "Dianna has asked me to see about using our English neighbor's phone to call Dianna's neighbor and let her know if it's all right for Rachel to come. Dianna included her neighbor's phone number in the letter too."

"Oh, I see. Then I guess you'd better take care of that right away."

"This is such a nice park," Emma commented as she and Ivan, along with Norma and her boyfriend, began walking toward a vacant, grassy spot. As Emma strode alongside Ivan, she glanced up at the clear sky above, thankful for the lovely weather. Her ankles were cooled by the morning dew–covered grass, but the rest of her body was plenty warm from the sun pouring down its warmth.

"I thought you might like it," Ivan said. "The park, here at the southwest edge of the village, was established in 1951 through a donation of nine acres from the Eberhardt family. It's mostly used for picnicking. Some people eat their meal while sitting on the grass, like we're going to do, but there are three large pavilions and playground equipment available for gatherings."

"The park is also transformed into a winter wonderland during the Christmas season, with festive lights and decorations," Norma put in. "Since you'll be leaving at the end of summer, it's a shame you won't get the chance to see how beautiful it is here at Christmastime."

A deep sense of sadness set in, and Emma had to fight the urge to allow the tears she felt pushing the back of her eyes to spill over. Now that she and Ivan had begun courting, she was filled with doubts over whether she and Ivan could remain a couple once she returned to Shipshewana. Emma shook the thought aside and told herself to concentrate on having a fun relaxing day, instead of focusing on something she could do nothing about and that was still a few months away.

When they reached a certain spot beneath some trees providing much-needed shade, Timothy pointed to it and said, "Let's spread the old quilt Ivan brought along right here."

Everyone agreed, and while Norma and Timothy took care of that, Emma stood beside Ivan, who held a wicker basket that had been filled with their picnic foods.

Once the quilt was in place, they all took seats. Emma hated to see any quilt thrown on the damp grass, but she kept quiet about it since Ivan had explained that his mother had given it to him for the picnic, stating that it was an old one, not fit to be placed on a bed any longer.

Norma opened the picnic basket lid and announced in a boisterous voice that, with the exception of the cupcakes Emma had made, she had put the rest of the lunch items together to share with everyone.

"Sounds like you're filled with a bit of hochmut today, Sister." Ivan nudged Norma's arm.

She brushed his hand aside. "I'm not filled with pride. I was merely stating a fact."

"Before this brother-to-sister conversation goes from banter to bicker, I suggest that we pray," Timothy spoke up.

"Good idea." Ivan lowered his head, along with the others. When they'd all finished praying, the food was removed from the basket and set on a towel in the middle of the quilt, where it could be reached by everyone.

Emma's eyes widened as she surveyed the array of items to choose from. In addition to the ham and sliced pineapple sandwiches Norma had provided, there were pickles, baked beans, cold fried chicken, pretzels, cut-up veggies, and slices of angel food cake, as well as Emma's chocolate cupcakes. Grandpa had eaten one for breakfast this morning and declared that they were delicious, so Emma felt confident in serving them as a dessert.

"I brought the beverages," Timothy exclaimed, grabbing a small ice chest, while Norma and Emma passed out the paper plates, napkins, and silverware.

"Have you got any soda pop in there?" Ivan asked.

"Sure do. In fact, that's all I brought to drink." Timothy looked at his date and flashed her a big grin. "I have grape soda, orange, lemon-lime, and everyone's favorite, root beer." He pulled a bottle of orange soda out of the cooler and held it up. "Believe it or not, this is my favorite flavor."

"Eww. . ." Norma wrinkled her nose. "I have an aversion to anything orange."

"Even the color orange?" Timothy bumped Norma's arm. "I thought you enjoyed watching sunsets."

She rolled her eyes at him. "No, silly. I just don't eat or drink anything with an orange flavor, so I'll have a lemon-lime, please. Oh, and I do like to watch the sun set."

He reached in and withdrew a bottle at her request. "Here you go, and just so you know, I was only teasing you. We all have our likes and dislikes."

"True," Ivan interjected. "It's all right to not like certain things as long as there's mostly common ground." Ivan looked at Emma and winked.

She smiled in return and asked Timothy for a bottle of grape soda. Ivan did the same.

"See, that's one more thing we have in common," he whispered. "We both like the same soda pop flavor."

She gave a brief nod and proceeded to help herself to the food, taking a small amount of each item. Picnics were fun, especially when shared with friends.

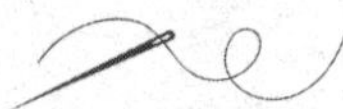

When they finished eating and had stowed everything back in Ivan's buggy, he suggested that the four of them take a walk and enjoy the scenic surroundings within the park.

Everyone was agreeable, and as Ivan and Emma strolled along behind Norma and Timothy, he decided to be bold and reached for her hand.

And why not, he thought, glancing ahead at the younger couple. *My sister and her boyfriend are holding hands, and they haven't known each other as long as Emma and I have.*

"I don't know about you, Emma, but this relaxing day is just what I needed," Ivan commented.

"It's been a peaceful time for me as well. The meal we all shared was delicious too," Emma added.

"You're right about that," Ivan agreed. "I especially enjoyed your tasty cupcakes. Way better than the ones you'd brought on our fishing trip."

"Danki, Ivan. I'm glad you liked them. Though, I don't want to ever think about that afternoon again if I can help it."

"That's understandable. I'm sorry for bringing it up."

They walked a little farther, and Emma spoke again. "I made pancakes for breakfast Monday morning, and they turned out pretty well. At least, my grandparents said so." Emma slowed her footsteps. "In fact, Grandpa even said I had the makings of a fine cook."

"I believe he's right." Ivan walked slower as well. After all, there was no hurry, and moving along at an easy pace meant he could hold Emma's hand a little longer.

After their walk, Ivan and Timothy spent some time tossing a Frisbee around, while Emma and Norma sat on the quilt and visited. Emma watched the two men fling the saucer-looking toy back and forth. Ivan had invited Emma to join them in the game, but she'd declined, wanting to let her stomach settle from all the food they'd consumed not long ago.

"I'm curious about something," Norma said. "What do you like about my bruder?"

Emma blinked. She hadn't expected such a direct question. Was Ivan's sister simply curious, or had Ivan put Norma up to asking Emma what she liked about him?

"Your brother is kind and helpful," Emma replied. "We also have several things in common."

"Like what?"

"Hiking, fishing, and playing ball."

"Guess that makes sense," Norma said. "Ivan has always liked doing things outdoors. He also enjoys fiddling around with old clocks."

Emma nodded. "He has a clock my grandfather owns and is trying to fix it so the chimes work again. I do like to listen to your brother describe how he tinkers with the inner workings of clocks, even though I don't know much about it. The history and how they work is fascinating, and Ivan seems to love sharing his interest in them."

"Trouble is, he doesn't get to mess with clocks as often as he'd like." Norma swatted a fly buzzing overhead. "Our daed doesn't understand Ivan's fascination with clocks and pocket watches. He thinks Ivan ought to be satisfied with working at the harness shop and forget about his dreams to do clock repairing for a living."

"What kinds of things do you enjoy doing?" Emma asked Norma.

"I like reading, baking, and putting puzzles together." Norma glanced at the area where Ivan and Timothy were playing with the Frisbee. "And I enjoy being around people who make me laugh the way Timothy does." She yawned and stretched both arms over her head. "The warm sun is making me sleepy. In fact, I could lie down right now and take a nap."

Before Emma could respond to that comment, Ivan and Timothy ran back to the quilt and plopped down. They were both huffing and pulling back their damp hair.

"We need a break. I'm gonna get my mouth harp out of Ivan's buggy and some water for us all too," Timothy said. "Then we can sit here and sing for a while. How's that sound to you girls?"

"I'm all for it if you're not too tired, Timothy." Norma turned to face Emma. "How about you?"

Emma liked to sing, so she didn't take long to respond. "As long as we're not disturbing anyone else in the park, I think singing is a nice idea."

"I don't think that'll be a problem," Timothy said. "There's no one but the four of us in this area right now. Be right back." He jumped up and took off for the buggy, and Ivan went with him.

When the young men returned, everyone drank some water, and while Timothy played his mouth harp, Emma, Ivan, and Norma sang several of their favorite songs.

Before Timothy packed his mouth harp away, the four of them remained on the quilt for a bit, taking in the afternoon's golden rays. Finally, they collected the rest of their possessions, and when Emma helped Norma fold up the quilt, she glanced at Ivan, and an inkling of warmth entered her chest when she saw his tender expression. How she wished this pleasant day didn't have to end. Emma was sure she would remember it for a good many years to come.

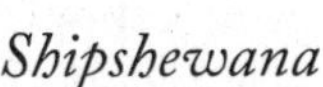

Shipshewana

Dianna was about to get her laundry basket and go outside to check the clothesline when a knock sounded on the front door.

When she answered it, she discovered their closest English neighbor, Linda Carlson, on the porch.

Dianna smiled and invited Linda in.

"I can't stay, but I came over to give you a message from your mother." Linda tugged at the floral collar of her dress. "She wanted you to know that it's fine with her and her husband if your daughter Rachel comes to visit them for a few weeks. She also stated that they would appreciate knowing when they can expect her to arrive."

"Thank you for letting me know," Dianna replied. "As soon as we know the date, would it be all right if I come over to your place and use the phone to call my folks' neighbor so she can give them the message?"

"Of course," Linda said with a nod. "As long as either I or my husband is at home, you're welcome to use the phone."

"I appreciate that and will be over as soon as we have things set for Rachel's travel to Arthur."

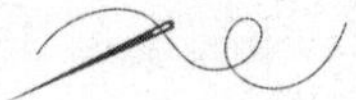

Rachel had entered her room to clean the windows and sweep the floor, when her mother came in. "Linda Carlson came by a few minutes ago," Mom announced. "She'd received a phone call from my folks' neighbor, stating that my mamm had asked her to call and let Linda know that it's okay for you to visit your grandparents for a few weeks. They just need to know when you're coming."

Rachel sagged against the bedpost with relief. "I'm so glad to hear that, Mom. I feel sure that getting away for a few weeks will help to heal my emotional wounds."

Rachel's mother gave her a hug. "I hope so too, but it might take longer than two weeks to heal your broken heart. My concern is whether you will be able to face David when you return home and see him with Alice again."

Rachel dropped her gaze to the floor. "I hope so, Mom, but if two weeks with Grandpa and Grandma isn't enough, then I'll have to either stay longer or come up with something else that will help me forget about David."

Chapter 20

Shipshewana

MONDAY MORNING, AFTER BIDDING FAREWELL to Rachel and her driver, Dianna ventured out to the mailbox, and while thumbing through the handful of envelopes, she discovered a letter from Emma. Eager to see what her daughter had written and fighting the urge to tear open the envelope right then, Dianna hurried into the house, set the rest of the mail on the kitchen table, and took a seat in the living room to read Emma's letter.

Upon reading the part where Emma said she had made some cupcakes and pancakes that turned out well, Dianna smiled. Emma had also mentioned that she was still taking quilt lessons and enjoyed them very much.

"That is so good to hear," Dianna spoke aloud. "I think there might be some hope for my daughter's domestic skills after all. My mamm must have a special way of teaching her that I don't possess. Then again, Mom did teach me most of what I know, so I guess that explains why Emma is picking up on it."

Dianna read on and nearly dropped the piece of paper when she read the next paragraph, announcing that Emma and Ivan Yoder had become a courting couple.

"Oh my, that's sure unexpected." Although happy for her daughter, she couldn't help wondering how Rachel would take this news once she heard about it. Poor Rachel. Her younger sister had a boyfriend, and Rachel was filled with heartache because the man she loved and had hoped to marry had fallen in love with someone else.

Dianna's other concern was how things would go between Emma and her boyfriend after Emma came home and they couldn't see each other regularly. Surely that would have an impact on the couple's relationship and could even lead to a breakup.

"Life is full of ups and downs," Dianna murmured as she slipped Emma's letter back into the envelope and rose to her feet. *Guess I should go out to Philip's workshop and give him the news that Emma is being courted by a young man from Arthur, Illinois.*

Another thought sprang into her head. *What if Emma and Ivan's relationship becomes serious and he eventually proposes marriage? Would Emma decide to move to Arthur, or is it possible that Ivan might be the one to relocate? Even though I've encouraged my daughter to figure out what she wants in life, it seems as though it's happening all at once, and it's a little unsettling for me.*

Arthur

Rachel fiddled with the straps on her pocketbook. After the five-hour drive from Shipshewana, she was eager to get out of the car and stretch her legs. Even more than that, Rachel looked forward to seeing her grandparents again. It had been nearly a year since they'd visited Shipshewana, and even more time than that since Rachel had visited their home here in the small town of Arthur.

Rachel's senses heightened as her driver, Karen, headed the vehicle ever closer to Grandpa and Grandma's two-story home. To settle the flutter that stirred within her stomach, Rachel inhaled deeply.

She still couldn't believe the woman she worked for had given her two weeks off, or that her parents had agreed coming here might help to erase her depression over the breakup with David. Perhaps a change of scenery would give her the perspective she needed before her return to Shipshewana.

I haven't even stepped foot into the house, yet I already feel better, Rachel told herself after she'd said goodbye to her driver and exited the car with suitcase and tote bag in hand. *And I can't wait to see the look on Emma's face when she sees me walk in the door.*

After stepping onto the front porch, Rachel set her suitcase down and rapped on the door. It didn't take long before the door swung open and Grandpa greeted her with a hug.

"Ah, Rachel, it's so good to see you. Glad you made it safely. How was your trip?"

Hearing the enthusiasm in her grandfather's voice and seeing his raised cheekbones all rosy caused Rachel to smile. "The trip went well, and there were no problems along the way."

"Good to hear." Grandpa glanced out toward the driveway. "I see your driver is gone already. Did you think to invite her in to join us for the noon meal?"

"Well, I wasn't sure if you had already eaten or not, and besides, Karen was eager to be on her way."

"We haven't had lunch yet. Emma and your grandma are in the kitchen preparing it right now." Grandpa leaned over and picked up Rachel's suitcase. "Let's go inside. It's too hot to stand out here on the porch and visit anyway."

Rachel followed him into the house. After he'd set her suitcase in the hall and she'd placed her tote bag beside it, they headed straight for the kitchen. The familiarity of this home and the experiences from childhood lingered in Rachel's mind. A lot of memories had been built here, and she missed those carefree days when her parents had brought the family here to visit Grandma and Grandpa.

"Look who's here," Grandpa announced after they'd fully entered the room where Grandma and Emma stood with their backs to them near the sink.

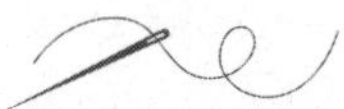

Emma turned to see who had come into the room with her grandfather, and her eyes opened wide at the sight of her older sister standing next to him.

"Rachel, what are you doing here?" The question came out almost as a squeak.

"I came to see you, as well as Grandpa and Grandpa." Rachel rushed forward and wrapped her arms around Emma, and then she embraced Grandma.

Touching the base of her overly warm neck, Emma spoke again—this time with more clarity. "I didn't know you were coming. Was it meant to be a surprise for us?"

"Just you," Rachel responded. "Grandma and Grandpa knew, but when Mom wrote the letter asking if I could come and stay for a few weeks, I asked them not to tell you, because I thought it would be fun to catch you unaware."

"You did that, all right." Although Emma was happy to see her sister, she felt a bit intimidated because Rachel could cook so well, and that was bound to make it more difficult for Emma when they were both in the kitchen helping with a meal. Worse yet would be if Emma made something and it didn't turn out well, and then when Rachel went back home, she told their mother about it.

Well, at least, Emma thought, *since Grandpa and Grandma have a second guest room, I won't have to share a room or a bed with my sister while she's here.*

Grandma placed her hand on Emma's shoulder. "Would you mind setting an extra plate on the table and finishing the sandwiches for our noon meal while I get Rachel set up in the guest room? It will give her a chance to freshen up before we eat too."

"Sure, I can do that," Emma replied. "By the time you two come back, lunch should be on the table."

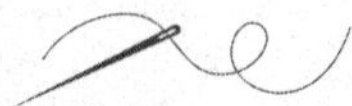

"This is a yummy-tasting egg salad sandwich," Rachel remarked, pointing to the sandwich she held, while directing her comment to Emma. "There's just the right amount of mayonnaise, salt, and pepper mixed in with the egg."

"I'm glad you like it," Emma said. "Grandma's a good teacher, and

I think I'm finally getting the hang of fixing a meal that doesn't taste baremlich."

"That's true," Grandpa interjected. "Some of the earlier things you fixed tasted pretty terrible, but you're doing much better these days, Emma."

Leave it to Grandpa to say something like that, Emma thought as she swallowed what was left of her sandwich. *He doesn't think twice about embarrassing me. Grandpa may as well bring up how I fell in the pond while he's at it.*

Although slightly agitated by his remark about her cooking skills, Emma felt sure that her grandfather didn't blurt things out to be mean. He was blunt, for sure, but also a helpful, kindly man, and she loved him very much.

"How's the weather in Shipshewana been lately, Rachel?" Grandma asked, shifting their conversation in another direction.

"Hot and muggy, like it seems to be here," came the reply.

"I'll be glad when the cooler days of fall replace the summer heat," Grandpa stated. "I like to take naps in my hammock, but it's not as comfortable as I'd like it when the humidity is so thick you could cut it with a knife."

Both grandparents plied Rachel with a few more questions, and when the meal wound down and the table had been cleared, Grandma announced that she was going over to their English neighbor's house to call their mother's neighbor and leave a message that Rachel had made it there okay.

"That is, if you two don't mind doing the dishes without my help," she added, looking at Emma and then Rachel.

They both shook their heads and assured her that they didn't mind, and then Grandpa said, "While you two are taking care of the dishes, I'll be in the living room napping in my favorite chair."

After Grandma left for the neighbor's, Emma prepared the dishpan, and Rachel got out the drying towel, while Grandpa retired to the living room. Silence hung in the room for a while, with only the clanking of dishes being cleaned and dried by the sisters.

Following a long exhale, Rachel was the first to break the silence between them. "I guess you probably heard that David broke up with me."

Emma nodded as she sloshed the sponge around in the sudsy dishpan full of warm water. "I was sorry to hear about that, and it certainly came as a surprise. I really expected you two would be getting married soon since you've been together for so long."

Rachel's eyes quickly filled with tears. "I had hoped for that, but I guess it was not meant to be. David obviously prefers my best friend over me."

"What does Alice have to say about this situation?" Emma questioned. "Has she apologized to you or tried to explain how it all happened?"

"No, but then I've tried to avoid both her and David. I don't really want to hear the excuses Alice would give me for what she did." Rachel sniffed deeply. "That's why I came here, Emma. I couldn't deal with seeing Alice and David at church or any other function. I was desperate to get away from Shipshewana and hoped that a few weeks away might help the ache in my heart go away and give me an opportunity to come to grips with their betrayal."

"I understand, and I hope your time here will help." Emma's heart went out to her sister. Given Rachel's recent heartbreak with David, she was hesitant to tell her about Ivan. Emma figured there was a good chance that her sister might be envious, and she didn't want to cause Rachel any more hurt than she'd already dealt with.

"Anything new with you, Emma?"

Emma jolted, and her hand dropped a glass into the sink, splashing some water on her face. Fortunately, it didn't break. "Not much, other than learning to cook and sew."

"There has to be more than that. We haven't spoken in weeks, so I would think you'd have more to share that has happened since you left home."

"Well, uh. . ." Emma scrubbed harder than she should on the glass she'd scooped up from the sink, trying to come up with something else she could share with her sister.

Fortunately, the sound of scampering little feet treading on the tile floor was enough to break Rachel's attention and turn it toward Fawn, who ran up to her with a tongue hanging out and her tail wagging.

Rachel's lips curved upward as she wiped her hands on the rag and then knelt down next to Fawn. "Whose adorable hund is this? This cute little fellow can't belong to our grandparents since Grandma isn't keen on dogs."

"Fawn's a girl. Grandpa found her on the side of the road one day, and we've been taking care of her ever since."

"Fawn, huh?" Rachel stroked her fingers beneath the puppy's chin. "What a cute name. She definitely has the eyes for it, doesn't she?"

Emma was appreciative of Fawn's prompt interruption as she wiped the water droplets from her cheek. On her hind legs, Fawn attempted to jump high enough to lick Rachel, but Emma's sister was too smart and tilted her head away from the enthusiastic pup. Knowing she would eventually need to address her newfound relationship with Ivan, Emma pondered when to do so as she wrung out the sponge and laid it by the sink's edge.

So maybe, Emma told herself, *at least for now, I won't say anything to my sister about Ivan or the fact that we've begun courting. Jah, for my sister's sake, that would be the best thing to do. In fact, I hope neither Grandma nor Grandpa mentions Ivan's name while Rachel is here. Of course,* she reasoned, *I'm bound to see Ivan at church this coming Sunday, and since we are courting, it's quite possible that he will come by to see me sometime during the two weeks my sister is here. So that leaves me with a decision to make. Do I tell Rachel about my relationship with Ivan or hope the news doesn't get out?*

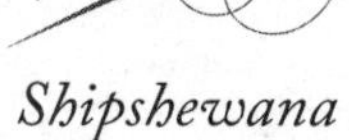

Shipshewana

Dianna swept a stray hair off her forehead and stayed on the porch for a while, allowing the breeze to cool her skin as she relished in the peace and quiet of the late afternoon. She enjoyed having time to herself but also missed the company her girls had provided while helping with chores.

So far today, Dianna had accomplished a lot, both indoors and outdoors.

She was about to bring in some throw rugs she'd hung over the porch railing earlier, when her English neighbor came up the driveway, holding a basket in one hand and waving with the other.

Dianna waved in response and waited until Linda made her way up the porch steps. "It's nice to see you," she said.

"Same here." Linda nodded. "I hurried over to let you know that your mother called to say that Rachel made it safely to your parents' home in Arthur."

"I'm glad to hear that. Thank you for taking the message and coming over here to let me know."

"You're welcome." Linda reached into the basket and handed Dianna a jar of what appeared to be raspberry jam. The color of the contents inside matched the deep scarlet shade of the woman's fingernails. "I picked an abundance of raspberries this morning and decided to make some jam. Thought you might like to have a jar."

"I certainly would. Thank you so much, Linda."

The older woman smiled and said, "Guess I should be on my way now. Frank might wake from his nap and wonder where I am. That man of mine takes more catnaps than our cats in the barn. The biggest problem is he stays up late at night, watching TV." She scrunched up her face. "Worst part is, he's also hard of hearing, so that means the television is always turned up too loud."

Dianna was about to comment, when her neighbor spoke again. "You Amish don't know how lucky you are. No TV or loud stereo blasting means peace and quiet in the house." Linda pointed to herself. "Me, I'd be happy if we didn't have so many noisy distractions in our home." She gave Dianna a brief one-arm hug, her floral perfume flooding Dianna's nostrils. "Have a good rest of your day." With that, Linda turned and stepped off the porch.

Dianna watched as her kindly neighbor made her way down the driveway and disappeared behind the blue and pink hues of the hydrangea bushes that grew along the side of the road. She felt thankful for such a nice neighbor and even more thankful that she wasn't married to a man who liked fancy gadgets or loud noises in the house. Her neighbor was right: Dianna was fortunate to be Amish and not have to cope with the latest innovations that were being offered to the general public.

Dianna put the jar of jam in the kitchen and gathered up the rugs she'd been about to take in before Linda arrived. Once the rugs were in place and the jam had been stowed inside one of the kitchen cupboards, she headed on out to Philip's shop to give him the news that Rachel had made it safely to Arthur. At least that was one thing Dianna no longer had to worry about.

Chapter 21

Arthur

A LIGHT DRIZZLE OF RAIN CAME down early Tuesday morning, but by eleven o'clock there was no sign of rain, and the warm sun had quickly dried the freshly mowed grass in Grandpa and Grandma's yard. Rachel had volunteered to do the mowing, while Emma had another cooking lesson with Grandma. Today, she was in the process of making cream of mushroom soup, which they would have for lunch, along with slices of sourdough bread and some cut-up veggies from the garden.

"Yum. . .that *supp* sure smells good," Grandma said, moving closer to the stove, where Emma stood with a metal spoon, stirring the kettle of soup.

"I'm letting it simmer awhile longer, and I hope it tastes as good as it smells," Emma responded after inhaling the rich aroma of garlic and mushrooms rising from the kettle.

Grandma patted Emma's back. "I'm sure it will."

"Maybe you should sample it," Emma suggested. "Just in case I didn't put in enough salt or beef soup base. The sourdough bread might not be any good either."

"I will test both if you want me to, but I don't think it's necessary," Grandma replied. "I can tell by the aroma that the bread and soup are just right. You've come a long way, Emma, so try not to be so hard on yourself."

Emma shrugged her shoulders and emitted a sigh. "Okay." She couldn't help feeling nervous about serving the bread and soup, knowing Rachel would be eating lunch with them. She'd no doubt compare it to anything she'd ever made. Although Emma would not admit it to Grandma, and especially not her sister, she secretly wished Rachel hadn't felt the need to come here. It wasn't that Emma disliked her sister. But she couldn't help feeling intimidated by Rachel's ability to cook and sew without any apparent problems. Emma thought it almost seemed like her sister had been born with the ability to cook. Of course, that was ridiculous, since Emma was certain that Rachel didn't start cooking when she was a little girl. One thing was for sure: Emma had always been aware that her sister knew her way around the kitchen a lot better than she ever did.

Emma turned the gas burner to low and moved over to the sink to look out the window. She stood watching as Rachel went past, pushing the lawn mower through the thick grass on this side of the house. *My sister is a hard worker, there's no doubt about it. She would have made a good wife to David.* Emma shook her head. *I can't believe what he did to her.*

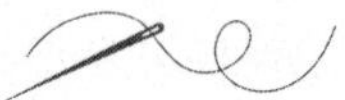

The frisky little dog that Rachel had met yesterday ran alongside the mower, barking all the way. Rachel wasn't sure if the mutt liked to play, was trying to keep up with her, or didn't like the push mower—hence the rowdy barking.

Rachel paused from her mowing long enough to reach under the band of her apron, pull out a handkerchief, and wipe the perspiration from her forehead. The day seemed to be growing hotter by the minute, and she was glad this chore was nearly finished. Just a few more passes on this side of the house, and then she could put the lawn mower away and go into the house, which she hoped would be cooler than the temperature out here in the yard.

Woof! Woof! Woof! Fawn pawed at Rachel's leg.

"What do you want from me?" she asked. "Why do you keep barking like that?"

The dog persisted, and choosing to ignore Fawn's continual yapping, Rachel began pushing the mower again, wondering the whole time how Grandpa managed this job in the heat—especially at his age. She couldn't figure out why her grandparents continued to live here in this big old house by themselves. Shouldn't they be living in a *daadihaus* connected to one of their children's homes—or at least on the same property? Was it by their own choice that they continued to live alone, or could it be for some other reason? If so, what was it?

Maybe I should ask them one of these days, Rachel reasoned after she'd finished mowing and pushed the lawn mower back in the garden shed. *The worst thing they could say is that it's none of my business.*

When Rachel entered the kitchen a short time later, Grandma informed her that Emma had made lunch, and all that needed to be done was for one of them to let Grandpa know the noon meal was ready to eat.

"I'll go tell him," Rachel volunteered. "Is he still where he was when I went out to mow?"

Grandma nodded. "Jah, and I wouldn't be one bit surprised if he hasn't fallen asleep by now."

Emma, who had been pouring iced tea into their glasses across the room, interjected. "If that's the case, then I can't blame Grandpa for taking a nap, because it's such a warm day." She grimaced. "I hope the cream of mushroom soup I made won't cause our bodies to feel even warmer."

"I don't think it will, Emma," Grandma was quick to say. "For me at least, sometimes eating or drinking a hot beverage, or even food, makes me feel cooler on the outside."

"That's how it is when our mamm drinks coffee or a cup of hot tea," Rachel chimed in.

Grandma smiled. "Exactly."

"Well, I'm really hungry, and eager to try Emma's soup, so I'd better let Grandpa know that it's time to eat." Rachel whirled around and rushed out of the kitchen.

Emma watched Rachel's expression as she took her first bite of soup. She really hoped it would meet with her sister's approval. Otherwise, Emma would feel deflated.

All I need to do is have faith in what Grandma taught me, Emma thought as she clasped her hands together underneath the table. *I've learned so much from her. When I first came here, I wasn't comfortable preparing anything in the kitchen on my own, but now I can cook several things and not be embarrassed by how they turn out. I think before, I mostly lacked the confidence to try.*

Rachel's brows rose a bit, and then she smacked her lips. "Good job, Sister," she said, reaching over to place her hand on Emma's shoulder. "Your creamy mushroom soup is just right."

"I completely agree." Grandpa picked up a piece of bread, slathered it with butter, and took a bite. "And your sourdough bread is equally tasty." He grinned at Emma from where he sat at his end of the table. "You're turning into quite the cook. Once your sewing skills improve a bit more, you'll be ready for marriage."

"Grandpa, Emma would need to have a suitor before marriage is a consideration," Rachel stated.

"She already does," Grandma spoke up. "I figured Emma would have told you that she's being courted by a nice young man whose name is Ivan Yoder. Ivan's mother is the one who is teaching Emma how to quilt."

Emma wished she could crawl under the table with Fawn and stay there. Of course, the dog wasn't supposed to be underneath the table, but she'd snuck under there anyway, as she so often did without Grandma's knowledge. Well, the truth was out about her and Ivan now, so Emma prepared herself mentally for whatever questions her sister might ask.

Rachel leaned forward with one elbow on the table, looking directly at Emma. "How long ago did this happen, and why didn't you mention it in any of your letters?"

Grandma's mouth parted, like she might say something, but Emma spoke first. The question was, after all, directed at her.

"It's only been a few weeks since Ivan and I started courting, and I did write to Mom and tell her about it."

"It's strange that Mom's never said a word about it to me." Rachel's stiff posture and pursed lips let Emma know her sister felt frustrated and probably left out.

"Maybe your mamm hasn't received Emma's letter yet," Grandpa spoke up.

"Or perhaps she didn't mention it to you because she thought it would be upsetting," Grandma interjected.

"Why would it upset me?"

"Because you and David broke up, and I'm sure it's still very painful for you," Grandma replied in a gentle tone of voice.

Rachel shrugged and mumbled, "There's nothing I can do about it, and if my little sister has a boyfriend, I'm happy for her."

Emma couldn't tell by Rachel's placid expression whether she meant it or not, but she hoped that was the case. Even if it wasn't, Emma knew her sister still grieved for the love she'd thought she had with the man who'd ended up betraying her. She couldn't imagine how she would feel if something like that happened to her. Emma hoped that if she and Ivan ever broke up, she'd be able to deal with it and not let bitterness set in.

"Grandma and Grandpa, there's something I've been wondering about," Rachel said, looking at each of their grandparents.

"What might that be?" Grandpa questioned.

Grandma leaned forward like she was eager to hear what Rachel wanted to say.

Rachel tapped her knuckles against the tabletop a few times before speaking. "Well, Grandpa and Grandma, I hope you won't take this the wrong way, but I was wondering if the two of you had ever considered moving closer to one of your children and living in a daadihaus."

Grandpa stroked his densely coiled beard a few times, shifted his gaze toward Grandma, and then looked back at Rachel. "With the exception of your grandma's back bothering her sometimes, we are both in pretty good shape and are getting along on our own just fine."

Grandma nodded. "Also, we don't want to be a burden to anyone in our family. As much help as your sister has been around here, she has her own life to return to, and we know that. You don't have to worry about us, Rachel."

"I guess that's understandable," Rachel responded. "Even so..."

She stopped talking when a knock sounded on the front door, which caused Fawn to start barking from under the table. A few seconds later, the dog bounded out and dashed out of the room with her tail wagging.

Emma quickly pushed her chair aside and stood. "I'll go see who is knocking and causing Fawn to bark."

Grandma frowned. "That hund should not be under the table, Emma. In fact, she shouldn't be in the kitchen at all while we're eating."

"I know, Grandma. She must have snuck in when I wasn't looking." Emma hurried out of the room.

When Emma opened the door, she was surprised to see Ivan on the porch, holding a cardboard box in his hands.

"Hello, Emma. It's good to see you," Ivan announced when she answered the door.

"It's nice to see you too. Please come in," she responded.

After Ivan entered the house, he bent over and set the box on the floor. Then he stooped down and scratched Fawn between her silky ears. The dog had stopped yapping, but her tail swished exuberantly to the point that it nearly hit Ivan's face. He didn't mind, though, as he remained firmly in place, enjoying the attention he was getting from the dog. Emma, on the other hand, didn't seem as pleased to see him as she normally did, which he thought was a bit odd. Maybe she was preoccupied or had been having a difficult day with cooking or sewing lessons.

"My daed had an appointment in town this afternoon, and since he closed the harness shop early today, I decided to come by here to give your grandpa the clock I've had these past several weeks." Ivan grinned up at Emma as he continued to pet Fawn. "I finally figured out what was wrong with the chiming mechanism and fixed it. I think the clock is almost as good as new now."

"I'm sure Grandpa will be pleased to hear that. He's in the kitchen right now. Let's go there, and you can give the clock to him."

"Okay, sure." Ivan stood, then leaned forward and reached for the box, while Emma let Fawn out into the yard.

"Right this way," Emma said, glancing over her shoulder at Ivan. She then started walking down the hall in the direction of the kitchen.

When Ivan caught up to her with his long strides, he stopped, sniffed, and asked, "What's that heavenly smell coming from the kitchen?"

"That must be the creamy mushroom soup I made for lunch," Emma replied.

"Oh, sorry. I didn't realize you were in the middle of eating your noon meal."

"It's okay. We're almost done." Emma stepped into the kitchen, and after announcing to her grandfather that Ivan was there and had come to give him the clock he'd repaired, she took a seat at the table.

"Oh, that's sure good to hear. Let me see what you accomplished." Rising from the table, Marlin approached Ivan.

Ivan suggested they move to the counter, where he set the box down. Then, lifting the lid, he withdrew the antique clock. "See here," he said, pushing a button. "The chimes are working again. Good as new."

Marlin's grin stretched from ear to ear. "That's great, Ivan. Thanks for all your hard work. How much do I owe you for the repairs?"

Ivan shook his head. "No, that's okay. Working on the clock was good practice for me."

"I appreciate that," Marlin said, "but I still want to pay for your time. I'll get you some money as soon as we finish our lunch. Speaking of which, there's still plenty of soup left, so why don't you join us?"

"It does smell pretty good." Ivan glanced over at the table, which he'd barely taken notice of upon entering the room. That's when he became aware that in addition to Luellen and Emma, a young woman he didn't recognize sat at the table. "Oh, sorry. I didn't realize you had company. I probably should go."

"Don't be silly, Ivan. You're more than welcome to join us," Marlin said. "In fact, we were rude not to introduce you when you first entered the room. This is our granddaughter Rachel. She's Emma's older sister." He looked at Rachel while gesturing to Ivan. "This is Ivan Yoder. He's the young man who recently began courting Emma."

Rachel got up from the table and moved across the room. Ivan met her halfway. They both extended their hands at the same time. "It's nice to meet you," they said in unison.

"Rachel came for a two-week visit," Emma explained from her seat at the table. She pointed to the empty chair across from her. "You can sit right there, Ivan."

He hesitated, but only for a moment, and put the clock back in the box before taking the offered seat.

Luellen dished up a bowl of soup for Ivan and offered him some bread and cut-up vegetables.

"Danki," he said, taking some of each after he'd prayed.

"So did you make all this?" Ivan directed his comment to Emma.

She nodded.

He spooned some soup into his mouth and smacked his lips. "This has a real good flavor, Emma. And the texture is just right too."

Patches of red erupted on Emma's cheeks. "You really think so?"

"Very much. If I didn't know any better, I'd assume you've been cooking like this for a long time."

"I'm glad you like it," she said in a near whisper.

As Ivan munched on a piece of bread, he grinned at Emma from across the table. "This is also quite tasty."

She made no reply this time, but the color on her cheeks deepened.

"Emma's turning into a fine cook," Luellen remarked.

"I can see that." Ivan chuckled. "Actually, guess I should have said, 'I can taste that.'"

Ivan swallowed another spoonful of Emma's soup, delighting in the flavors as they bloomed in his mouth. Even though the soup was still warm, it was cool enough to keep from burning his tongue. Ivan eyed the bread, tore off another piece, and dipped it into his bowl, allowing it to absorb the soup broth like a sponge before he brought it to his lips.

When Ivan paused from eating long enough to speak again, he smiled at Emma and said, "Are you still planning to attend the young peoples' singing with me this Sunday evening?"

She offered a brief nod and glanced at her sister.

Pretty sure he knew what she was thinking, Ivan gestured to Rachel and said, "There's plenty of room in my buggy, so you're welcome to come along and ride with me and Emma. My younger sister Norma has a boyfriend, so I'm pretty sure she'll be going to the event with him."

"I appreciate the offer," Rachel said. "But I don't want to impose. I could stay here Sunday evening and spend a pleasant evening with my grandparents."

Ivan's gaze wandered to Emma again, hoping she would say something. But she just sat there, staring at her barren plate.

Emma didn't seem to be herself this afternoon, and Ivan had a feeling that either she wasn't pleased to see him or she wasn't comfortable with the idea of her sister going to the singing with them. Either way, it concerned him. He couldn't deal with the idea that there might be something wrong between the two of them. He wanted to ask, but that wouldn't be a good idea with her grandparents and sister sitting here with them. He'd have to talk to her about it some other time. Right now, Ivan decided to simply enjoy this delicious meal Emma had prepared and put all negative doubts and thoughts aside.

Chapter 22

RACHEL PUSHED THE BEDSHEET ASIDE, rolled over, and stood up. After padding in her bare feet to the window to raise the shade, she yawned and stretched both arms over her head. For the past two days, since Emma's boyfriend had stopped by, Rachel had been thinking about his invitation for her to join him and Emma at the singing this coming Sunday. With this being Thursday, it meant there were only a few days left in the week to decide if she should accept Ivan's invitation or stay home that evening with Grandma and Grandpa. In the two years Rachel and David had been courting, they'd never suggested that Emma go anywhere with them, so it wouldn't seem right for her to tag along on Ivan and Emma's ride to and from the singing. It was a dilemma, and she didn't know what to do.

If I went with them, I'd probably feel like a fifth wheel on a buggy, and Emma might not appreciate having her big sister along for the ride, Rachel told herself.

Her gaze came to rest on Grandma's garden below, and she tried to focus on that. Last evening, Grandma had mentioned that some of the bush beans were ready for harvesting. Rachel figured that would probably be on her grandmother's agenda for the day, and picking beans would involve both her and Emma.

She turned away from the window and went to open her suitcase, which she had placed on the cedar chest at the foot of the bed. Her dresses were hung on wall pegs in the room, but she'd left stockings and undergarments in the suitcase. There was no point in unpacking everything since she would be here for such a short time.

"Sure wish it could be longer, though," Rachel murmured. "Emma doesn't know how lucky she is to be able to spend the whole summer with our grandparents."

Rachel hated feeling sorry for herself, but it seemed like nothing good was happening in her life right now, and everything was going so well for Emma.

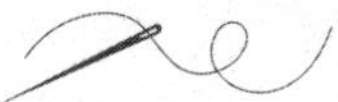

During their breakfast of pancakes and bacon, which Emma had made, Grandma talked about the garden and what she thought might be ready to pick, while between bites, Grandpa read the local newspaper.

"Will it be just the bush beans like you had mentioned previously?" Emma asked while cutting a knife into her pancake. "Or are you wanting us to pick something else as well?"

With a thoughtful expression, Grandma rubbed her chin. "Let's see now. . .when I went out to the garden last evening to check on things, I discovered that the zucchini and yellow crookneck squash are doing well, and I believe some of those are big enough to be picked."

"Anything else?" Rachel asked, slathering a side of her pancake in raspberry fruit spread.

"It's all that caught my attention," Grandma replied. "But maybe you and Emma, who are more agile than I and don't have bad backs, will be able to get down low and find more things that are ripe enough to pick."

"How is your back feeling this morning?" Emma questioned after swallowing a bite of her buttery pancake. "You haven't complained much about it lately."

"It still bothers her some," Grandpa spoke up for the first time. "She just hasn't said anything about it."

"I'm sorry to hear that," Emma said, while gently patting her grandmother's arm. "How bad is it?"

Grandma picked up her cup of tea and took a sip. "I have a few twinges sometimes, but it's nothing to worry about." She lifted her shoulders in a brief shrug. "It's probably just old age setting in. It might not be long before I'll need to walk around here with a cane in hand."

Grandpa rolled his eyes. "Jah, right. Just admit it, Luellen, you need to see a doctor about your back."

She looked at him and wrinkled her nose. "I'll see a doctor when I need to, but not until then."

"Okay then, suit yourself." Grandpa flipped open the newspaper and started reading again, and Grandma continued to talk more about the garden.

Emma, on the other hand, had switched her thoughts and was thinking about the quilt lesson she would have this afternoon with Ivan's mother. She hoped they could move on to something more challenging today than the simple patchwork pattern.

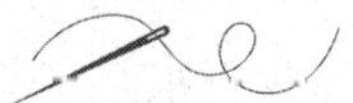

Once they had finished breakfast and cleaned the dishes, Emma ventured outside along with her older sister to their grandmother's garden. The sun's intense heat rested on Emma's shoulders as she wandered the rows with the basket handle dangling from her wrist.

"I'd say the bush beans are definitely ready to harvest," Rachel commented as she bent forward, snapping off a lengthy pod from the plant. "Emma, look at how many sprouts there are. Without a doubt, our baskets will be filled in no time, and maybe there will be room for the squash and zucchini without making a second trip to the house."

With her fingers sweeping the leaves away to uncover groupings of bush beans on the branches, Emma crouched next to her sister. "This will certainly keep us busy for a while."

"I'll say. We better get a move on before it gets too hot out here." Rachel dropped several beans into the basket and began to gather more.

Following suit, Emma proceeded to pick the bush beans and plop them in her basket. Except for the typical small talk, not much conversation was exchanged between the sisters. Emma was scooping up a bush bean that had slipped from her grasp when she saw a ladybug scuttling on the ground, its wings as vibrant as the raspberries growing near the blueberry shrubs.

Over time, Emma's basket grew heavier, as did the humidity from the summer heat. She continued down the row to where her sister had gone, which was among the zucchini and squash.

"This is a lot of work," Emma said as she set her basket down. "I'm glad we're almost done since I need some time to freshen up before leaving."

"Where are you running off to?" Rachel questioned. "Are you going somewhere with Ivan today?"

"No. I'm planning to go to Ivan's house, though, for another quilting lesson with his mother."

"A quilting lesson? That sounds like fun. Do you mind if I tag along, Emma?"

Emma whipped around to face her sister just as she was raising her arm to grab for a ripened squash. "Why? I—I mean, why would you want to? You already know how to quilt."

"I do, but I'm not an expert and could use some pointers. Grandma told me that Ida Mae's very talented, and I could maybe learn a thing or two from her." Rachel smiled. "Besides, wouldn't you like to have your sister's company?"

Emma's gaze fell on her basket, weighing her options along with her harvest of bush beans. *It's not like I can really say she can't go with,* she thought. *I'm not exactly thrilled with the idea, but it's easier to go along with it to keep the peace.*

"I guess it would be all right if you went," Emma said as she snapped off a squash and dropped it in her basket.

Rachel nodded. "I could give you some insight too, if that's okay. I have plenty I'd like to share with you, and now that you've learned some of the basics, you should be able to understand what I'm talking about."

Emma compressed her lips. *I can't wait.*

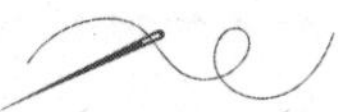

"It's nice to have you here with us today, Rachel," Ida Mae greeted as they entered the Yoders' home.

Rachel shook her hand. "I'm excited to be here and see some of your quilts."

After guiding her and Emma to the sewing room, Ida Mae invited them to take a seat wherever they were most comfortable. Although the space was small, Rachel could see that Ida Mae made do with it, keeping all her supplies neatly tucked away and some on display.

"For today's lesson, I believe we should begin with something a bit more advanced now." Ida Mae spoke to Emma, but then she turned to face Rachel. "I'm assuming that you're already familiar with quilting?"

Rachel nodded. "Of course. So what did you have in mind for us to do?"

"Let me think about it." Glancing over her arranged display cases, Ida Mae smoothed her fingers on a quilt that hung on the wall. "This pattern right here is the Double Wedding Ring. Do you know that one?" she questioned.

"Oh yes. Our mother has a quilt with that pattern, which our grandmother gifted her for her wedding," Rachel said.

"I wouldn't be surprised if your mother gives each of you young women a Double Wedding Ring quilt when you get married."

"It'll probably be Emma first before me." Rachel frowned. "I thought I'd marry David, but now I'm not sure if it's worth finding someone else and risking having my heart broken again." Rachel bit the inside of her cheek. *I don't know what made me blurt that out. I'm sure Ida Mae doesn't know anything about me and David or our breakup.*

"True love doesn't always happen on the first try." Ida Mae laced her fingers together. "But for most, first loves are not everlasting, and many people experience plenty of heartbreaks before they end up finding the right person to spend the rest of their life with."

"All I know is, I'm not getting any younger, and having to start all over with someone new isn't what I was hoping for."

"You never know, Rachel. You might meet someone new while you're here in Arthur."

"I'm not sure about that. A long-distance relationship could make matters even more complicated. Besides, I'll be returning to my parents' home in Shipshewana soon." Rachel's gaze shifted to her younger sister, who sat by the window quietly fiddling with a sewing needle. She hadn't said a word since they'd arrived. "Sorry, Emma. I didn't mean anything by that. Simply put, I don't think I'd ever fall for a man from outside our community."

"You never know unless you give one of them a chance. My son mentioned that you might be joining him and Emma for the singing this weekend, so if you go, you may take a liking to one of the young fellows while you're there." Ida Mae's gaze darted back to the Double Wedding Ring quilt hanging from the wall. "As for the quilt, we won't be tackling that kind of project today, given that it's a bit more involved. However, I do want to change things up for this afternoon. Rachel, do you have any thoughts on what we might do today?"

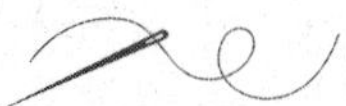

Emma shifted in her chair, tapping her right foot against the floor as she followed the interconnecting circles of the quilt on the wall with her gaze. With its curving edges and abundance of vibrant fabrics creating the rings against the ivory background, it was undoubtedly a gorgeous pattern. How many months would it take to complete the entirety of a quilt so beautifully made?

Would it even be possible for me to stitch together something so intricate? Emma wondered. *Here I wanted to do more than just a patchwork pattern, yet I don't even know if my hands would be steady enough for a quilting project like the beautiful Double Wedding Ring pattern.*

Her attention lingered over to the pincushion casting shadows that threatened to cover the display shelf's surface. Emma found herself pondering over her sister's words. Rachel was correct that Ivan residing so far away from her would make it difficult for them to be together when she left, and this had been weighing on Emma's mind even before Ivan had made their relationship official.

"Emma? Are you listening?"

She tilted her head to look at her sister and Ida Mae, who were both staring at her. "I'm sorry. What were you saying, Rachel?"

"I was asking if you'd be okay with trying to stitch together a Center Diamond?"

Leaning over the table, Emma drew in a breath and said, "I'm up to trying something different, Rachel, but that sounds a bit too much for a beginner like me."

Rachel shook her head. "It's actually one of the most straightforward patterns, so you should have no trouble understanding how to put it together."

"Your sister's right," Ida Mae agreed. "This quilt pattern is comprised of a large square tilted on its side, which appears like a diamond in the center. Emma, I set out everything for you both while you were deep in thought. Your sister knows how to put this quilt together, so I'll have her walk you through how to get started while I make us some tea."

Excusing herself, Ida Mae left the room, leaving the two sisters to themselves.

"It's all right if you don't want to, Emma," Rachel said. "We could relax and wait for Ida Mae to come back with our beverage, and she could have us do something else."

Sighing, Emma tugged on the ties of her kapp. "Since you said that the pattern is simple to follow, I might as well try my hand at it."

"Good to hear." With a grin, Rachel sifted through the fabric swatches Ida Mae had laid out for them on the table. "Might as well get started. Stitching together this pattern will help prepare you to make a quilt like the one hanging on the wall."

"Do you really think I could make a quilt like that?" Emma questioned.

"Absolutely, and that's not just me saying it because I'm your sister. I mean, look at how much you've improved your cooking skills. If I didn't know any better, I'd think you've been cooking and baking tasty treats for some time."

"Ivan said almost the exact same thing to me."

"If it's not just me who believes it, then you know I must be speaking the truth. I also think you have been keeping a lot of your skills hidden from us," Rachel stated.

"I've been keeping them from myself too, apparently." Emma chuckled, allowing herself to pick up a square of blue from the pile as the tension in her shoulders slacked. "Do you think this would work for the center of the quilt?"

Rachel inspected the fabric, her eyes brightening as she nodded. "Good choice, Emma. That dark shade of blue will make the diamond stand out beautifully. Now we need to figure out the fabrics to use for the border."

"I have the tea for you girls," Ida Mae announced as she came into the room with cups in both hands. "How's it going in here?"

"We're making progress." Rachel held up the material she was currently stitching. "We chose our fabrics, measured and cut them, and are now sewing together our blocks. Emma's having no trouble following my instructions. She's a natural."

A flush of pink crept along the bridge of Emma's nose. "I'm not as good as Rachel by any means, but I'm doing what I can."

"Don't be so hard on yourself, Sister. You're doing just fine."

Ida Mae bobbed her head. "I suppose it's time to take a break and give you young women some time to rest your hands. A warm cup between your fingers should do the trick."

As Ida Mae handed Rachel her tea, steam rose from the rim and came to rest on her face, which was still warm from the time spent in their grandmother's garden.

As she sipped the chamomile tea, Rachel's mind drifted to how things might be going with her folks back home. She figured they probably missed having her and Emma around to help with the responsibilities in the home and around the property, but they probably were enjoying some well-earned time to themselves too.

Coming here and having time away from home is already doing me some good, Rachel thought as she lowered her cup, gripping the handle as she looked at the open window shade on the sewing-room window.

I wonder if Ida Mae's right about me possibly finding someone while I'm here. I guess it wouldn't hurt to go to the singing, but am I really ready to do that right now? I wouldn't have to seek out a serious relationship with a man. Or maybe love will await me when I return home and least expect it.

Chapter 23

Luellen arched her back and reached around to rub a kink that had formed since she'd been sitting during the first hour and a half of church. It was getting more difficult to remain on the backless wooden bench during their three-hour worship service, but she would make every effort not to let on. Even at home, Luellen either made light of her back troubles or did everything she could to hide the pain that she felt. There was no point in worrying Marlin or either of her granddaughters, and she didn't want to be thought of as an invalid, either. As far as Luellen was concerned, it was simply best to bear the pain and make the best of her situation without making a fuss or complaining. It certainly would not change the fact that things weren't right with her back. She'd hoped the new mattress might make a difference, but in all honesty, it hadn't helped much at all.

Luellen drew in a breath and tried to relax, hoping it would ease the pain in the middle of her back. She knew from experience that concentrating on the sermon one of their ministers preached was the best medicine right now. This morning's message was a good one too. It revolved around the importance of learning to trust God in all things.

The first verse of scripture the minister quoted was Proverbs 16:3: "Commit thy works unto the Lord, and thy thoughts shall be established."

I need to remind myself daily to do that, Luellen told herself. *I wish that for my grandchildren too. Each of them need to remember to rely on God to give them strength and guidance, now more than ever.*

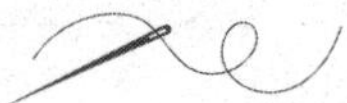

"Granddaughters, your ride to the singing is here," Grandpa announced when he entered the living room where Emma and Rachel sat beside Grandma on the sofa. "You better get a move on and not keep your boyfriend waiting, Emma."

She jumped up and peered out the living room window. Sure enough, Ivan's horse and buggy had pulled up to the hitching rail.

Emma gripped the backrest of the couch as her heart skipped a beat. The more time she spent with Ivan, the deeper her feelings grew for him. It was selfish, but Emma wished her sister wasn't going with them to the singing. More than likely, Rachel would monopolize the conversation going to and from this evening's event.

Emma pushed her negative thoughts aside and went to open the front door. If she didn't do it now, Rachel might get there first.

Emma bit the inside of her cheek. *There I go again. . .thinking undesirable thoughts.* She glanced over her shoulder and saw that her sister was still sitting on the sofa with Grandma. *Is Rachel giving me a chance to go out and talk to Ivan for a bit? Or does she simply have more to say to our grandmother on the topic of quilts, which is what we have been talking about for the last hour?*

"I'm heading out to Ivan's buggy," Emma called.

"Okay, I'll be there soon," Rachel responded.

Emma grabbed her black outer bonnet and headed out the door.

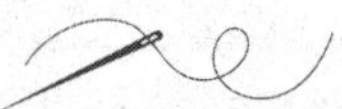

Ivan smiled when Emma approached the buggy, where he was still seated but on the verge of stepping down. "You didn't have to come out. I was gonna walk up to the house."

"That's okay," she responded. "I just came out to tell you that I'm ready to go, but Rachel's still talking to Grandma."

"No problem," he said. "It'll give the two of us a chance to spend a few minutes alone."

Emma nodded. "Jah. The rest of the evening, other young people will be around us, and my sister will be here in your buggy too, so there won't be any chance to talk privately."

Ivan patted the seat beside him. "Why don't you get in and we'll take advantage of the time we have right now."

Emma did as he suggested, and once she was seated next to him, he took hold of her hand. It was soft and warm, and Ivan wished he could sit like this with her hand in his for the rest of the evening. But it was not meant to be, for Rachel had left the house and was swiftly heading in their direction.

"Sorry for holding you up," Rachel said as she slid into the back seat. "I had a few more things I wanted to say to Grandma before coming outside."

"No problem," Ivan assured her. "The host of tonight's singing doesn't live far from here, so unless my horse decides to move along at a snail's pace, we won't be late."

They arrived at the singing, just as a group of young Amish people from the Arthur community began congregating on the lawn, outside of the host's home. As Ivan led his horse to where the other buggies were situated, Rachel craned her neck to get a better view.

I see some guys congregating over there by the fenced-in pasture. I wouldn't be surprised if they're wanting to play baseball. Rachel shifted on the buggy seat. *Why am I so nervous about attending this event? Usually, I'm all for the idea of wandering up to people I don't know and starting a conversation. This evening, however, the thought of talking to strangers—especially when it comes to any of the nice-looking young fellows—makes me break out in a cold sweat. It's been a while since I've even talked to any of the young men I know back home, since I was with David for so long. But he was so quick to move on from me, so shouldn't I be able to do the same?*

Following her sister, Rachel stepped out of the buggy and trailed behind Emma and her tall boyfriend, feeling a wave of envy when she noticed their hands entwined like thread binding together two pieces of fabric. As they made their way over to the group, Rachel's heart ached, even though she was pleased to see Emma in a loving relationship.

At the threshold of the gathering, Rachel halted her steps, her eyes straying to the group of young men who were still engaged in conversation. Rachel then noticed Emma turn halfway around and look back at her. Emma and Ivan's fingers were still intertwined. *My sister is so fortunate,* Rachel thought.

"What do you want to do before we go in for the meal, Rachel?" Emma asked.

Rachel's gaze flickered to the young men again. "I'm not sure. I could leave you and Ivan alone and—"

"Do you want to go visit with some of the other young people?" Emma gestured to the group standing nearby. "It's okay if you do."

"I'm not really sure, Emma. It feels strange to be here with so many people I don't know."

"You're welcome to come join us to play baseball, Rachel." Ivan said. "The more the merrier."

Rachel pressed her lips together. "No thanks. I'm not really into any of that outdoor stuff like Emma is. I think I'd rather find a place to sit and watch."

"Oh, okay." Ivan looked at Emma. "If you want to play ball with us, I'll meet you out there in the field." After letting go of Emma's hand, Ivan slipped off his straw hat and handed it to her. Then he sprinted to the field, along with the others who were getting ready to start a game, leaving the sisters alone.

Emma lingered at Rachel's side, holding onto the brim of her boyfriend's hat. "Are you sure you don't want to do anything besides sit and watch the game, Rachel? Not even just mingle with the other young women here?"

Rachel shook her head. "Guess I'm more tired than I thought I'd be. I'm sorry. I probably should've stayed home tonight."

"Well, don't worry about it. I can stay right here and keep you company."

"You don't need to worry about me, Emma." Rachel lowered herself and settled down on the grass as she stared up at her sister. "You seem eager to go, so feel free to play ball with your boyfriend and the others. Enjoy yourself. I'll be fine here on my own. You can go ahead and have fun."

"I don't mind sitting here with you, and you don't have to talk to anyone else if you're not up for it. You don't know any of the young people here, so I understand."

Emma seated herself beside Rachel on the lawn as the first pitch was thrown and the sound of the bat cracking resounded.

Giving her sister's arm a tender squeeze, Rachel expressed gratitude to Emma for staying there to keep her company. But she also felt terrible for preventing Emma from having a good time with Ivan. Part of her had suspected this would happen, and perhaps if her breakup with David wasn't weighing heavy on her heart, she could've let loose and had fun this evening. She tried not to think about it and opted to concentrate on the game that was being played in direct view of them.

One of the young men who was up to bat hit the ball far from home plate, but not far enough to qualify as a home run, and Emma clapped for Ivan as he ran to the next base.

Although Rachel rarely partook in playing baseball, she remembered well how David had enjoyed the game, and he'd explained the rules to her many times during their dates.

Maybe if I had played ball with David back home, he wouldn't have lost interest in me. Alice always played baseball at the gatherings, so I'll bet that's why they grew close and he chose her over me. A thickness formed in Rachel's throat as she held her arms against her stomach. *I need to move on from what David and I used to have. He doesn't love me, and I need to accept that, even if I don't want to believe it. Is it so wrong that I still have feelings for him, even after he betrayed me and broke my heart?*

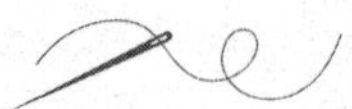

Except for the steady gait of King's hooves hitting the pavement, the ride back in the buggy was silent. Emma traced patterns on the upholstery as the moon shone brightly and the evening breeze cooled her skin. She thought about how withdrawn her sister had been during the young people's singing. Given that Rachel was usually regarded as the outgoing one, it was out of the ordinary for her to be unsocial the way she had been all evening.

When they approached the hitching rail near her grandparents' driveway, Emma raised her chin and realized she had been lost in thought.

Rachel was quick to climb out of the buggy as soon as the horse came to a stop, saying in a clipped voice that she needed to wash up and go to bed, leaving Emma and Ivan alone. Before she could say good night to him, Ivan nudged Emma's shoulder, his lips curving upward as he removed his straw hat and reached over to set it on the back seat.

"Rachel kept you pretty busy this evening, didn't she? You and I didn't get to spend much time together at all."

"I know, and I'm sorry. Rachel showed little interest in interacting with anyone there, despite my efforts to suggest that she should try. I didn't want to leave her alone by herself. I think she's still thinking about David and missing him, or. . ."

"Or what, Emma?"

"When my sister went with me to your home for my quilting lesson last week, she brought up how she couldn't date someone outside of our community since it would complicate things." Emma took in a deep breath. "Do you think we'd be able to make it work between us, even after I return home?"

He fiddled with the reins, dipping his chin slightly. "I can't pretend that I haven't been wondering the same thing, but I'm willing to make it work in any way I can."

"But how? I mean, I don't really know what could be done for that to happen."

"I'm sure we can figure it out. I could write you every day, or I can hire a driver so I can come visit you as often as I'm able to get away." Ivan slouched in his seat. "I truly hope you don't want our relationship to end before you go back home."

"You really want to continue courting me?" Emma questioned, as a feeling of warmth flourished in her face.

Ivan cocked his head to one side. "You're saying that as though you find it hard to believe."

"I'm not really the most suitable woman to be someone's girlfriend, and because of that, I've had little success garnering the attention of the young men in my community. So I have to wonder, Ivan, what do you see in me?"

"I'll tell you what, Emma. As much as you second-guess everything you do, you're driven more than you know, and you care about people. Emma, you always seem to prove yourself wrong, no matter how much you doubt, and I admire that about you." Ivan took hold of her hand. "I've grown quite fond of you over the time we've known each other, and I'm not going to let go of what we have so easily. So if you'll let me, I'll do whatever I can to make sure that we don't lose what we have together."

"I don't want to lose what we have either, Ivan," Emma admitted.

In response, Ivan rubbed his thumb against her knuckle, the pads of his fingers calloused yet still soothing enough that it brought Emma a sense of comfort despite the fluttering in her chest. Emma braced herself, breath half held as he inched closer, so close that she could feel the warmth of his breath. Then, as he lowered his head to hers, she prepared herself for what she was certain would transpire next. Although hesitant at first, Emma met him halfway, and Ivan pressed his lips to hers in a kiss so sweet, it nearly took her breath away.

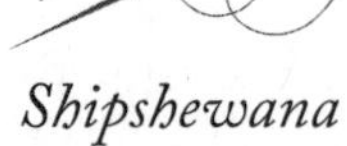

Shipshewana

Dianna had gone to the kitchen to fix a snack for herself and Philip when she heard a horse and buggy come into the yard. Shortly thereafter, a knock sounded on the front door. Dianna figured Philip would answer it, but when the knocking continued, she set the loaf of bread she'd taken out aside and stepped into the hall.

When she opened the door, Dianna was surprised to discover David on the porch. Before she could get a word out, he spoke.

"I didn't see Rachel in church this morning, and she wasn't at the singing tonight either." David's brows drew together. "Is she grank?"

Dianna shook her head. "Rachel isn't sick."

"Oh, that's good. Is she here? Can I talk to her for a few minutes?"

"Well, um. . . You see. . ."

"I really need to see Rachel. I have something important I need to tell her."

Dianna pressed her hands against her hips. "Rachel is not here, David."

"Where is she then?"

Dianna was tempted to say *"It's none of your business"* or something else that would most likely come across as rude, but she held herself in check and simply stated, "Rachel went to visit her grandparents."

"Oh, you mean the ones who live in Arthur, Illinois?"

"That's right." Dianna bit the inside of her cheek. *Now why did I admit that? David doesn't need to know where Rachel is right now.*

"How long will she be gone?" he questioned.

"Two weeks—not that it's any of your business, young man," Philip stated sternly as he approached them with his arms folded. "What are you doing here anyway, David? You broke up with our daughter, remember?"

"Of course I do, Philip, but. . ."

"But nothing." The cords on the sides of Philip's neck protruded. "Our daughter isn't here, and even if she was, we wouldn't let you in after what you did to her. In fact, I'd like you to leave, right now. Is that clear?"

Without another word, David turned on his heels and tromped down the stairs.

Dianna stood beside her husband, watching as the young man made his way out to his horse and buggy. She felt relief when a short time later he drove out of the yard. Many thoughts concerning their daughter flooded her mind as she watched David's horse and buggy disappear. Dianna found herself wondering what Rachel would do when she learned of his visit. How would Rachel have responded if she had been here and answered the door? Would she have listened to what he had to say?

Although Dianna wasn't sure what David wanted with her daughter, she had a feeling he might try to worm his way back into Rachel's life. Maybe he'd come to realize that the grass wasn't greener on the other side of the fence, and now he wanted back what he once had. Well, if Dianna had anything to say about it, a reunion between Rachel and David was not going to happen. The fact was, Rachel deserved better than that.

Dianna peered up at Philip, who still had a grim expression. "I can't believe that young man had the nerve to show up at our house," she said, "asking to talk to our daughter. I'm sure glad David doesn't know where my parents' house is in Arthur."

"Jah," Philip agreed. "I wouldn't put anything past that nervy fellow, including getting Rachel stirred up again."

Chapter 24

Arthur

LATE MONDAY AFTERNOON, EMMA HEADED outside to take the laundry off the line. Rachel had remained inside to make a blueberry cobbler for dessert and get started on supper. Grandpa had finally talked Grandma into going to a chiropractic clinic that had been established in 1948 in the town of Urbana. He'd hired a driver to take them there a few hours ago, saying he hoped the chiropractor could help her back. Emma hoped so too, and she'd been praying about the situation ever since her grandparents had left. It hurt to watch Grandma suffering the way she had been for a good many weeks, and probably longer, before Emma had even known about it.

Arriving at the clothesline, Emma set the wicker basket on the grass and reached up to take down a pair of her grandfather's trousers. She smiled, thinking about the way he sometimes rolled his pant legs up to his knees when he stretched out in his hammock for a summer nap. He always looked so peaceful with his eyes closed and face lifted toward the sun. Grandpa also liked to take off his shoes and walk around barefoot during the warm weather. Emma loved seeing the big grin on his face. He reminded her of a young boy who loved to be outside and explore.

Of course, I'm kind of like that too, she mused, plucking one of Grandpa's shirts off the line. *I've pretty much enjoyed spending time outdoors since I was a little girl. Being out in nature is a way to remember and reflect on*

God's beautiful creation, not to mention all that He has done for us. I truly need to be more grateful—especially when something negative happens and I feel like complaining.

Emma set her thoughts aside and removed the rest of the clothes from the line. When she picked up the basket, Emma spotted a car pulling into the yard. Although Emma didn't recognize the vehicle, she placed the basket back down and went to see who it was.

A few seconds later, the vehicle stopped in front of the house, the passenger-side door opened, and Rachel's ex-boyfriend stepped out.

A chill ran up Emma's spine, though that was quickly replaced with a flush of heat rushing to her face. *I can't believe David would be bold enough to come here. How'd he find out where Rachel is, and why has he come? I hope David has no plans of trying to win my sister back. Certainly not, if I have anything to say about it.*

With hands pressed against her hips, Emma walked right up to David and asked the question foremost on her mind. "What are you doing here?"

"I came to see Rachel." He glanced briefly at his driver, still waiting in his vehicle, then looked back at Emma. "I hope you don't have a problem with that."

"Who told you Rachel was here?" Emma asked without responding to David's comment.

"I went over to your folks' place last evening, and when I asked to speak to Rachel, your mamm told me she wasn't at home but was at her grandparents'." David shifted his weight from one leg to the other. "Then when I asked if it was the grandparents who lived in Arthur, she admitted that it was."

"Did my mother give you the address?"

He shook his head.

"How'd you find us then?"

"I asked around. It wasn't too hard to find the place, really."

The tightness that welled up in Emma's chest began to unravel, and she struggled to keep from shouting at him. Some nerve he had showing up here out of the blue. After what David did to Rachel, did he really think she would talk to him?

When Rachel heard voices outside, including Emma's, she left the kitchen and went to the front door to see who her sister was talking to. Shock spiraled through her body when she saw David standing next to a parked car, a short distance from where Emma stood with her hands pressed against her hips.

Rachel's heart pounded, and her mouth felt so dry she could barely swallow. She blinked a couple of times to be sure she wasn't seeing things and then slowly descended the porch stairs. *Why is David here?* Rachel asked herself as she approached the young man who had betrayed her. *I can't imagine he has anything to say that I'd want to hear.*

Before she was able to pose the question she was mulling over the most, David said, "Rachel, it's so good to see you." He took a step toward her. "I've missed you more than I can say."

She crossed her arms and stared at him. "Is that so?"

"Of course it is. I wouldn't have spoken those words if they weren't true."

"What about Alice? Does she know you're here?" Rachel's voice quavered as she spoke.

"No. I was planning to tell her after we go back to Shipshewana."

"We?" The single word came out as a squeak.

"Jah. You and me."

Rachel gave a vigorous shake of her head. "I'm not going anywhere with you, David."

"That's right," Emma interjected, turning to face him directly. "My sister is here, like me, visiting our grandparents, and you have no right to be here at all."

"I do have the right," he insisted. "I came here to ask Rachel's forgiveness and beg her to take me back."

"Don't listen to him, Sister," Emma whispered, moving closer to Rachel. "He can't be trusted. Not after what he did to you."

"I don't know why you should expect me to believe anything you say," Rachel said, staring straight into David's eyes. "You chose my best friend over me, while we were still together, and there's no way you can deny it."

"I—I did what you're accusing me of, but please give me a chance to explain."

Rachel remained silent, continuing to stare at him in disbelief.

"You need to understand something, Rachel," David continued. "The reason I broke things off with you and started seeing Alice is because I needed verification that the feelings I had for you were strong enough to propose marriage, which was what I'd been on the verge of doing a few weeks before I started going out with Alice." David dragged the toe of his left shoe in the dirt and stared down at it for a few seconds. When he finally looked up, Rachel saw tears in his eyes, which came to her as a surprise. Whatever the case, her guard did not waver, still uncertain of David's intentions.

"David, I'm not following you. If you really were about to ask me to marry you, then why did you drop me for Alice?"

"Because I got cold feet. You see, I wasn't sure if my feelings for you went deep enough. I needed some time apart to really know for sure that I wanted to spend the rest of my life with you, and now I know that I do. I made a horrible mistake breaking up with you, Rachel."

"That's a strange way of thinking," Emma cut in again. "You hurt my sister very much, and now you're here, trying to fill Rachel's head with promises I'm sure you don't plan to keep."

"Yes, I do." In addition to David's eyes appearing to be wet with tears, he'd begun to sweat profusely through the fabric of his shirt. "I'm truly sorry, and I am telling you the absolute truth. I hope you can find it in your heart to forgive me and believe what I'm saying." He extended his hand toward Rachel. "Please accept my apology and give me the opportunity to start over."

Rachel pulled back, knowing that if she allowed him to touch her, she might throw caution to the wind and agree to take him back. *You can't trust David,* an inner voice taunted. *But I still love him,* another side of Rachel argued. Why did she have to be put on the spot like that?

David must have sensed what she was thinking, because he inhaled through his nose and spoke in a steady, lower-pitched voice. "You've gotta believe me, Rachel—I've never loved anyone the way I love you."

Rachel deliberated on what he'd said, then drawing from her inner resources, she said, "Go back home, David. I'll be returning to Shipshewana on Monday of next week, and then we can talk about things. You hurt me deeply when you began seeing Alice, and what happened between us can't be fixed overnight."

"I realize that, but—"

He moved toward Rachel again, but Emma stepped between them. "You shouldn't have come here, David. Can't you see that you're upsetting my sister?"

"I didn't come here to do that. I just wanted to make her understand the reason I went out with Alice for a while."

Emma's cheeks turned bright pink as she shook her finger at David. "No man who supposedly loves a woman would hurt her like that, just to try and prove something to himself. It was dumm, David. You broke my sister's trust. Surely you must realize that."

"I do, and I'm truly sorry. If Rachel would just give me another chance, I would prove my love and devotion to her, once and for all."

Emma looked at Rachel with her hands turned palm-up. "So what are you gonna do, Sister?"

"I'm going to stay right here till my two weeks are up, and then I'll return home like I said I would do when I came here."

Emma gave a nod. "Good decision." She gestured to the man sitting in the driver's seat of the vehicle parked behind them. "Your driver's waiting, and it wouldn't be polite for you to hold him up."

Rachel held her breath, waiting to see how David would respond. She felt relief when he finally nodded and said, "Okay then." He looked at Rachel with a somber expression. "I'll come by your house soon after you get home, and hopefully we can work things out between us."

"We'll have to wait and see how it goes" was her only response.

Before David could comment, Rachel whirled around and ran back to the house. She turned the doorknob, fighting the need to glance over her shoulder at him. Once inside, Rachel leaned against the door and remained there long enough to catch her breath.

Soon, Rachel heard the roar of the car's engine, and she knew that David had left.

I can't believe I didn't crumble under the pressure and agree to take David back, Rachel told herself. *My hammering heart let me know that I do still care deeply for David. If only I could trust him not to break my heart with more lies and rejection.*

Rachel moved away from the door as another thought popped into her head. *What if David truly meant every word he said? Did I make a mistake by not going home with David today?* Seeing her ex-boyfriend again had given Rachel the assurance that she still really loved him.

A few minutes later, the front door opened, and Emma sauntered in with a basket of laundry she'd taken from the clothesline.

Rachel followed her sister into the dining room, and after Emma set the basket on the table, Rachel grabbed Emma in a hug and sobbed. "Oh, Emma, I can't believe David showed up like that without letting me know he was coming." She sniffed and swiped a hand across her damp cheeks. "I never expected him to declare his love for me again. I really thought he'd fallen in love with Alice. But as you heard, and according to David, he never loved her at all."

"I know what he said, Sister." Emma patted Rachel's trembling shoulder. "Listen, I understand that you want to believe him, but something's not sitting right with me about all of this, which is why I don't think you should take David's words at face value. Truth be told, I bet Alice broke up with David, and he came here looking for you because he wants to take a fraa."

Rachel's spine stiffened. "I don't believe for one minute that David came here looking for me so I would agree to become his wife. He came here to apologize, and—"

"And now you're defending him."

"No I'm not," Rachel insisted with a vigorous shake of her head. "I just think. . ."

Emma's lips compressed. "What exactly do you think, Rachel?"

"Well, there's a part of me that thinks David may have been sincere in what he said to me." Rachel paused a few seconds and then continued. "But another part of me doesn't trust him." Tears welled in her eyes again. "Oh, Emma, I know you probably don't understand this, but I still love David, and now after seeing him today, I'm more confused than ever."

Emma rolled her eyes. "Know what I think, Sister?"

Rachel shook her head.

"I think if Alice did break up with David, he can't stand the rejection, so he's coming back to you. And if the two of you get back together, David believes he will look good to all his friends."

"Do you really think that could be the case?" Rachel questioned.

"Jah. I wouldn't put anything past him." Emma's nose wrinkled, as though some foul odor had permeated the room. "This whole thing of him showing up here today stinks. Have you asked yourself why David didn't simply write you a letter of apology?"

"Well, no, but I guess that's a question I should ask him when I return home."

Emma opened her mouth like she was about to say something more, but her lips clamped together when the sound of a vehicle pulling into the yard could be heard outside.

Rachel's heart thumped in her chest. Had David asked his driver to come back? Maybe he had more to say to her. And if it was David's driver who had just pulled back in, it would give Rachel the chance to ask him some very pertinent questions.

While Marlin paid their driver, Luellen stepped cautiously out of the vehicle. They had paid good money for her chiropractor's adjustment, so she did not want to do anything that might disrupt it or cause unnecessary pain.

Luellen walked slowly toward the house, making sure to stay on the path while being careful not to step into any crevices or stumble on a rock. Even a small pebble could trip her up, so it was prudent to be careful.

Upon entering the house, she found both girls standing in the entryway near the door. Luellen wondered if they had heard the driver's car come into the yard and approached the door to wait for her.

"How are you, Grandma?" Emma and Rachel asked in unison.

"I'm okay. Or at least I will be after a few more trips to see the chiropractor," Luellen replied. "Of course, there are some things I'll need to do on my own in order to help my back heal." She gestured to the living room entrance. "Why don't the three of us take seats? Then I can tell you all about it."

"That's a good idea," Emma said. "We're definitely interested in how things went for you at the chiropractor's office."

Rachel bobbed her head, and they all filed into the living room. They'd barely taken seats when Marlin came into the house and joined them.

"Have you told the girls what the chiropractor said?" he asked as Luellen lowered herself into the rocking chair.

"Not yet, but I was about to do that." She leaned her head back and drew in a deep breath. "While there doesn't appear to be anything seriously wrong with my back, I do have some muscle spasms and misalignment." She readjusted her covering, which had slipped partway back on her head. Before she could continue, Rachel spoke up.

"What did the doctor do for you today, Grandma?"

"He started by taking X-rays of my back and neck, and then did a thorough exam of those places on my body as well. But of course, that was after I had told him what my symptoms were," Luellen explained.

"Tell them about your adjustment," Marlin put in. "And don't forget to mention how you felt afterward."

"Well, I laid face-down on a massage-like table, and he did a manual manipulation, using his hands to apply a gentle force to the area on my neck and spine where it's been hurting. This, the chiropractor said, was to stimulate the nervous system and restore my proper joint mobility."

Luellen shifted a bit on her chair, making sure she sat up straight and didn't slouch. "I was told by the chiropractic doctor that there are several common causes of back pain."

"What are they, Grandma?" Emma asked.

"Overexertion or improper lifting can lead to strained muscles in the back." Luellen grimaced. "Unfortunately, I've been guilty of both."

"He also mentioned that back pain can be caused by misalignments in the vertebrae, which can lead to nerve irritation and back pain," Marlin interjected.

"That's correct, and over time, poor posture can strain a person's muscles and ligaments. So that's another area I'll need to work on," Luellen commented.

"What about the adjustment the chiropractor did?" Rachel questioned. "Did it hurt?"

Luellen shook her head. "Not really. I heard a popping or cracking sound during the treatment, but it didn't hurt. In fact, it felt kind of good—like the tension in my back was being relieved."

"Will you see him again for more treatments?" Emma asked.

"Jah, and between appointments I am supposed to do certain exercises that will support my healing and strengthen my back." Luellen directed her gaze to the sofa, where her granddaughters sat. "Enough about me, now. I'd like to hear how your day went while your grandfather and I were gone."

Emma looked at her sister, and Rachel looked at Emma. Rachel began picking at her fingernails.

"Did something go wrong here today?" Luellen questioned.

"Whatever it is, you may as well tell her," Marlin said. "You know your grandmother will keep digging until she gets some answers."

"You make me seem like an old busybody," Luellen stated with a scowl. "I just want to know if something occurred that we should know about."

"I don't believe you're a busybody. I just think you worry too much about things that don't concern you." Marlin's forehead wrinkles deepened.

"Everything that involves any of my family members concerns me," she retaliated.

Marlin opened his mouth and leaned forward like he had something else to say, but Rachel spoke first.

"David came to see me today."

Luellen's lips quivered. "The used-to-be boyfriend who broke up with you so he could go out with your best friend?"

Rachel gave a slow nod. "He apologized, Grandma, and said he only did that so he could be sure what he felt for me was really love."

"Humph!" Marlin crossed his arms and muttered, "That's the dumbest thing I ever heard. If the young man truly loved you, then he should have proposed marriage, not started running around with some other woman, much less your best friend."

Luellen figured if she didn't nip this conversation in the bud, it would only get worse. So she quickly asked Rachel a question. "How did this David fellow know where we live?"

"I'm sure he probably asked around and someone blabbed." Marlin's upper lip curled like a dog snarling over a bone. "The nerve of that guy."

"Don't you worry, Grandpa," Emma said. "Rachel didn't take him back. In fact, she told David that he needed to return to Shipshewana."

"Does that mean you're not going to let him back into your life?" Luellen questioned.

Rachel lifted her shoulders in a brief shrug and said, "I–I'm not sure. I'll need to give it some thought and will make my decision after I return home."

Luellen's back muscles started to spasm, and she quickly reached around to rub them. She hoped with all of her heart that Rachel would not make a hasty decision and let David back into her life without truly knowing his intentions. It would be a shame if he broke her heart all over again.

Chapter 25

THE FOLLOWING MONDAY, SHORTLY AFTER the noon hour, Emma stood with Grandpa and Grandma beside the car her sister would soon be taking for her return trip to Shipshewana. She watched as Grandma gave Rachel a tearful hug, and Grandpa, in his usual good-natured way, said, "Have a good trip, and be sure to let us know that you got home okay."

"I definitely will," Rachel responded, and then she tapped an index finger against her bottom lip. "I'll ask our English neighbor to call your non-Amish neighbors who have a telephone, so you can receive a message from them."

"Yes, yes, please do." Grandma's words came out in a rush. "We'll be praying for you and your driver while you are on the road."

Rachel smiled. "Danki, I appreciate that." She turned to face Emma and gave her a hug. "I wish you all the best with Ivan and will look forward to you returning home at the end of the summer, which isn't too far off."

Don't remind me, Emma thought after releasing a sigh. *If I had my way, I'd stay right here with Grandma and Grandpa so Ivan and I could see each other often and continue our relationship. I want to have faith that Ivan and I could have a relationship that is miles apart, but if our courtship can even move forward to the point where we can eventually be married, one of us will have to relocate.* These thoughts had played in Emma's head before, but she couldn't keep them from returning, no matter how hard she tried.

While Rachel and Emma were still hugging, Emma whispered in her sister's ear, "I hope you take your time deciding what to do about David and don't make any hasty decisions."

"I won't," Rachel said quietly. "He needs to prove himself." When that had been said, Rachel told them all goodbye again, opened the car door, and climbed into the passenger's seat.

With a wave and a toot of her horn, Rachel's driver drove out of the yard and turned onto the road out front.

"It's hard to see her go." Grandma slipped her arm around Emma's waist. "And since you've been with us a lot longer than Rachel was, I'll feel even sadder when you go home. Your grandfather and I have loved having you here."

"That's right," Grandpa agreed. "We'll miss your smiling face, not to mention those great-tasting pancakes you've learned to make."

"You could stay another month or so past summer, if you like," Grandma said as the three of them began walking toward the house. "But then I guess your folks might not appreciate that. I'm sure they're missing you very much and are eager for both you and Rachel to return home."

"I miss Mom and Dad too," Emma acknowledged. "There's plenty that I miss from back home. Even so. . ."

"I bet you're gonna miss your old grandpa's teasing." Grandpa chuckled. "Right, Emma?"

She nodded. "Jah, I will."

Emma had a feeling that both of her grandparents knew she would also miss Ivan, but she kept quiet about that.

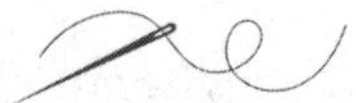

Rachel closed her eyes, hoping the bumps in the road would not keep her from sleeping. There were still a few hours until they would arrive in Shipshewana, and she'd quickly tired of trying to make conversation with her female driver. After all, there really wasn't much to talk about, other than the warm weather and the heavier-than-normal traffic.

Although Rachel felt tired, she couldn't sleep, as her mind was consumed with thoughts about David. She desperately wanted to believe that the things he'd said to her outside of her grandparents' house were true, but the nagging feeling she couldn't let go of was that David couldn't be trusted. Logic said he'd hurt her once and would be likely to do it again.

Woe is me, Rachel thought ruefully. *I want him back in my life, but I'm not sure it's possible for me to trust him again. Emma's told me several times that I shouldn't listen to David, and she's probably right.*

She opened her eyes and looked out the side window, trying to keep her focus on the passing scenery, but it was no use. All Rachel could think about was David's apology and promises, and all she could picture in her mind was the way he had looked at her last week, with sincerity in his voice and a softness in his expression that had left her feeling breathless and weak in the knees. Was David really missing her as much as she had missed him all this time that they had been apart?

There was no doubt about it—Rachel had some serious thinking and praying to do. She knew without a doubt that the next time she and David came face-to-face, she would have to give him an answer about whether he could start over and court her again.

Shipshewana

"For goodness' sake, Dianna, would you please sit down and relax?" Philip joined her at the living room window, where she'd been standing for the last several minutes. "Watching out the window will not bring Rachel here one minute faster."

"I know, but I'm excited that she's coming home today." Dianna's shoulders lifted as she drew in a deep breath. "And I'll admit, I'm also a bit concerned."

Philip leaned closer. "About her driver, or the fact that there might be more traffic on the road than usual, which could mean that Rachel will be late getting here?"

"Those are all concerns," Dianna admitted, "but my biggest worry is whether David will show up here again after Rachel gets home."

Philip's brows lifted. "If he does, I'll run him off."

Dianna gave a slow shake of her head. "Now, Philip, please don't get yourself worked up. I feel sure that if David does return to our house after Rachel comes home, she will refuse to see him."

"I certainly hope so." He frowned. "The last thing our daughter needs is a cheating ex-boyfriend trying to worm his way back into her life."

Dianna placed a hand on her husband's arm, hoping to calm him down. Philip had always been one to become riled easily—especially when it came to one of their daughters. She could still see the fire in his eyes when he'd argued with their eldest daughter the night before she'd left home. There were times when Dianna struggled not to feel bitterness toward Philip. It wasn't that he'd forced Betty to leave home, but he hadn't handled it well when she'd announced that she didn't want to join the Amish church and was striking out on her own. Philip had even told Betty that if she left home, she wouldn't be welcomed here again.

I'm sure he didn't mean it, though. Dianna clenched and unclenched her fingers into the palms of her hands. *Betty made her choice, and there's nothing Philip or I can do about it, so we've put all our effort into raising our two youngest daughters, and tried to do a good job. If Betty ever were to step foot on our porch, I would welcome her with open arms, and no doubt Philip would do the same, despite what he said to her.*

Dianna was thankful every waking moment that both Rachel and Emma had joined the Amish church and seemed content to be members and had never even mentioned leaving home permanently or walking away from the Amish life they'd been raised in since babyhood. It would have broken her heart if she'd lost another daughter to the English world.

"I'm going out to the kitchen to make a pot of *kaffi*," Philip said, scattering Dianna's thoughts like papers lost in a gust of wind. "Would you like a cup?"

She gave a gentle shake of her head. "No thanks. I've already had my share of coffee today, and too much caffeine makes me jittery."

"Okay, no problem. I can bring you a cup of tea or glass of milk if you like."

"I don't need anything to drink right now, but danki for asking," she replied.

Philip gave Dianna a quick peck on the cheek and strolled out of the living room.

Dianna's gaze remained fixed on the window she'd been looking out, the worry of her daughter lingering. She really hoped Rachel would get here soon so she could stop fretting.

Rachel had no more than stepped out of the driver's car when the front door opened and her mother rushed out. Rachel met her halfway as she hurried over to her, leaving her belongings along the walkway up to the house.

"Oh, it's so good to see you," Mom exclaimed, throwing her arms around Rachel and pulling her close. "I missed you so much."

"I missed you too, but you know, I was only gone two weeks," Rachel teased while returning her mother's embrace.

Mom pulled back slightly, and tears shone in her eyes. "I realize that, but with both you and Emma gone, it seemed a lot longer to me."

"I guess it would," Rachel acknowledged. "It won't be long, though, and Emma will be coming home too."

"That's how it's supposed to be, but what if she decides to stay in Arthur so she can remain close to her boyfriend?"

"I hadn't even thought about that," Rachel said. "She is quite smitten with Ivan, so I suppose it's possible that she might want to remain there at Grandma and Grandpa's."

Her mother's gaze dropped to the ground, and Rachel felt immediate regret. "Sorry, Mom. I shouldn't have said that. I'm sure there's nothing to worry about. It's quite possible that Ivan and Emma will be able to keep their relationship going even after she returns home."

"I hope you're right, Rachel." Lifting her head higher now, Mom pinched the skin at the base of her throat. "Even though you and your sister are adults now, I still find myself worrying about you and hoping the right decisions will be made."

Rachel managed a smile for her mother, but the comfort of her surroundings stood in stark contrast to the uneasiness of what had transpired in Arthur when David showed up unexpectedly. After listening to her mother's last words, Rachel decided it would be best not to say anything about David coming to see her at Grandma and Grandpa's house.

Being told what David said to me would only cause Mom to worry more, Rachel told herself. *And so, I shall keep quiet about it—at least for now. When Grandma writes a letter to Mom again, she's likely to mention David's visit, so I'll need to say something first, before that happens.*

Arthur

Ivan had seated himself at the worktable in his bedroom, when his mother hollered something up the stairs. Ivan couldn't make out the words, but since he was the only one upstairs, he figured whatever she'd said must be directed to him.

He left the room and yelled through cupped hands, "Were you calling to me, Mama?"

"Yes, I was," she responded. "There's a young woman on the front porch, waiting to see you."

Ivan's limbs tingled a bit. No doubt it was Emma, coming to surprise him, and he couldn't wait to see her. He had to wonder, though, why his mother didn't say Emma's name instead of referring to her merely as a young woman. It also seemed odd that Emma would wait for him on the porch and not come inside. Surely his mother would have invited his girlfriend into the house.

Wiping his sweaty hands on the sides of his trousers, Ivan hurried down the stairs and was quick to open the front door. The woman dressed in Amish clothes that he saw pacing from one end of the porch to the other was definitely not Emma. No, this young woman had dark hair and was much taller than Emma. Ivan pondered whether the unexpected guest had brought a message from someone he knew, or had possibly gotten lost and stopped for directions. If that was the case, then why had she asked for him specifically? This young woman had to have known Ivan from somewhere.

As Ivan approached, she whirled around to face him. At first, Ivan didn't recognize her, but then, when she spoke, he thought he recognized her high-pitched voice, although her face was not familiar.

"Hello, I'm Ivan Yoder," he said, reaching a hand out to her. Ivan was more than a bit surprised when she stepped forward and gave him a hug.

Ivan stepped back rather quickly. "I. . .uh. . .have we met before?" he asked in a voice that surely gave away his confusion.

"Of course we've met," she said, staring straight into his eyes. "It's me, Maggie Hertzler. Don't you remember the party you and I were invited to attend? It was held at your friend Toby Schrock's house in Arcola."

Ivan scratched his head. He didn't want to admit it, but he barely remembered attending a party at Toby's home. "How long ago was that?" he questioned.

"Nine months, plus a few weeks ago," she replied. "You were there, and we spent most of the evening together."

He gave a quick shake of his head. "Sorry, but I don't remember that."

"The party, or being with me?"

"Well, I do remember going to the party, and I may have seen you there, but I'd never met you before that evening, so I'm not sure why you're here." Ivan glanced back toward the house, hoping his mother wasn't watching out the window. He sure didn't want Mom to think there was something between him and this young woman, because the truth was, he only had eyes for Emma. It certainly wouldn't be good if his mother thought otherwise and passed the information along to Emma when she came for her next quilting lesson.

"I'll tell you why I'm here," Maggie said, tugging on Ivan's shirt-sleeve. "Our baby is in the back seat of my driver's station wagon, and I want you to accept responsibility for your son."

Shock spiraled through Ivan's body, leaving him feeling woozy. "Wh–what are you talking about?"

"Our son, Stephen. He's two weeks old today." She pointed at Ivan. "And you are Stephen's father."

Ivan shook his head vigorously. "No, I'm not. There's no way. You must have me mistaken for someone else."

"I'm telling you, Ivan, we were together that night." Maggie grabbed hold of his arm and held on tight. "Come with me out to the vehicle, and you can see for yourself that I'm telling the truth."

Ivan swallowed hard, and his gaze clouded as he stared at the station wagon parked in his parents' yard. He saw a female driver in the front seat but couldn't make out anything in the back seat. When he heard what sounded like a baby's cry through the open windows, his curiosity got the best of him and he moved slowly toward the vehicle.

As he approached the station wagon and peered into the back seat, Ivan couldn't deny that there was, indeed, a crying infant in a carrier. He turned to face Maggie, who had followed him there, and said, "Okay, I believe that you came here with a baby, but for me, seeing the child doesn't prove that I'm the father. In fact—"

"Don't you remember the time you and I spent together the night of Toby's party?" She tipped her head back and looked up at him with tears in her dark eyes. "How could you forget about that? Do you really not remember being with me?"

Ivan's mouth slackened as he absently rubbed his arms where goose bumps had erupted. He forced himself to relive the past and tried to focus on the happenings of that night.

Someone had brought a keg of beer; he remembered that much. Ivan had never been much of a drinker, unlike some of the kids he knew who had gone a little wild during their *rumspringa*. But Ivan also remembered how on that day at the harness shop, his dad had accused him of sloughing off. He'd stood up for himself and said he'd been working as hard as anyone else in his father's employment. Dad had shouted at Ivan and accused him of being disrespectful. He'd also stated that Ivan deserved to be fired.

Ivan remembered the anger he'd felt toward his father, and it had carried over into the evening and during Toby's planned get-together. Ivan had weakened and indulged in not one but several glasses of beer. As the evening wore on, everything had seemed fuzzy, and at one point,

Ivan had tripped over something and barely caught himself in time to keep from falling.

I was drunk, Ivan told himself. *It's no wonder I don't remember Maggie, or much of anything else from that night. Guess that means. . .*

Then, the reality of the situation hit him full in the face. Ivan glanced over at the station wagon again, his pulse hammering like an anvil in his ears. *Maggie must be telling the truth, and there's no way I can hide from my responsibility to her and the baby.*

A sharp pain hit Ivan right in the gut, and he wrapped an arm around his waist, hoping to subdue the anguish he felt. *I'm gonna have to tell my folks about this. And even though I wish it wasn't so, I need to do what's right for the baby and his mother.*

Ivan continued to hold his stomach as he became fully aware that this new, unexpected revelation would end his relationship with Emma, but the only thing he could do at this point was to marry this girl he didn't really know. Ivan couldn't deny that his life had been forever altered. He'd done wrong at the party that night and was paying the price for it now, which only proved the old saying "Your sin will find you out."

The infant wailed louder, jolting Ivan out of his contemplations. Feeling ashamed and flustered, he turned to Maggie and said, "You'd better get the baby and go inside with me to meet my parents. We both have some explaining to do."

Chapter 26

When Ida Mae heard the front door open, she stepped into the hall to greet her son and ask who he had been talking to out front. Her eyes opened wide, and she blinked a couple of times when Ivan entered the house with a dark-haired Amish woman who held a baby in her arms. Ida Mae figured from the size of the child it couldn't have been more than a few weeks old. She didn't recognize the young woman and wondered what she was doing here. She didn't have to wait long for an answer, because Ivan quickly made the introductions.

"Mom, this is Maggie." He paused, then turned to the young woman and said, "What's your last name?"

"It's Hertzler." She gave his arm a brief nudge. "Remember?"

"Oh yeah. Guess you did mention that earlier." With a somewhat dazed expression, Ivan pursed his lips, and then he gestured to the right, where the living room was located. "Mind if we sit down in there?" he asked, looking at Ida Mae. "There are some things we need to talk to you and Dad about."

Ida Mae held her index finger against her lips for a few seconds, and then she responded, "Your daed's in the kitchen. I'll go get him. Meanwhile, you two may as well get comfortable in the living room."

Something about the strange way her son was acting didn't seem right. And Ida Mae couldn't help but notice that the young woman with him seemed nervous, as she drew in some quick breaths and for the most part did not meet Ida Mae's gaze.

"Okay, Mama." Ivan's voice was barely above a whisper. "We'll take seats and wait for you and Papa there."

Just observing her son's pinched expression let Ida Mae know something was drastically wrong. While the young people shuffled off to the living room, she hurried her steps to the kitchen.

When Ida Mae entered the kitchen, she found her husband sitting at the table with a cup of coffee in one hand and a newspaper in the other. The lowering sunshine outside cast shadows over the flooring from the window above the sink, as if straining to reach them with its warming light.

"A young woman is in our living room with Ivan," she stated. "Our son made it clear that they want to talk to us about something."

His head shot up, and he pushed the paper aside. "I assume it must be Emma? If so, and they're wanting to talk to us, I certainly hope they're not thinking of marriage, because they haven't known each other long enough for that."

Ida Mae shook her head. "It's definitely not Emma in our living room. In fact, this young woman, whom I have never met before, has a baby with her."

Eldon's eyebrows rose above their normal position. "Now that's sure odd. Let's go find out who this woman is and what she wants."

Ivan had been sitting motionless on one end of the sofa, and Maggie sat beside him with the baby in her arms. He heard his parents murmuring in the other room but didn't bother to focus on that or try to make out their words. Ivan was aware that his parents didn't understand why a young woman was here, and he was concerned about how he would approach telling them about it.

As soon as Ivan saw his parents enter the room, he was on his feet. "Umm. . .Mama's met her already, but Papa, I'd like you to meet Maggie Hertzler and her baby, Stephen. Maggie's from Arcola." He gestured to both mother and child. "We met at my friend Toby's party, several months ago."

When his mother and father approached the sofa with hands

outstretched, Maggie stood and handed the baby to Ivan. "It's nice to meet you both." A pleasant smile formed on her face, and she shook their hands in turn with an eager expression. The apparent shyness that had appeared when she'd met Ivan's mother had disappeared.

Maggie pointed to her sleeping child and said, "I came here today to let Ivan know that Stephen is his son."

Ivan cringed when his mother's eyes widened. She let out a gasp.

Papa rubbed his forehead and took a step back. "Is this some kind of a joke?"

"No, it's not, Mr. Yoder. I'm telling you the truth." Maggie's high-pitched voice raised another notch. "My baby's conception took place the night of Toby's gathering, and your son Ivan is Stephen's father."

The room became deathly quiet, and Ivan's face grew hotter by the moment as the baby boy squirmed with his features contorting. In fact, Ivan was so warm it felt like he had a raging fever. In addition to the anguish of learning that he had fathered a child without any remembrance of the time spent with Maggie, it nearly broke his heart to assume that his parents must be thinking he was a terrible person to have fathered a child and never told them about it until this very moment. When Ivan thought he couldn't stand still another moment, his father looked directly at him and spoke.

"I'm really disappointed in you, Son. Why have you been courting one young woman, when you should have done the right thing and married another? You left her to raise that baby on her own?"

"I—I didn't. I mean—"

"What Ivan means, Mr. Yoder," Maggie cut in, "is that he didn't know about the baby until I showed up today."

"But how could he not have known?" Ivan's mother questioned. "Didn't you tell him that you were expecting a baby?"

She shook her head. "I knew Ivan didn't love me—at least not the way I wanted him to." Maggie lowered herself to the sofa and sagged against the cushion behind her back. "I asked my folks if they would help me raise the baby, but they flatly refused and said it was not their responsibility." Tears formed in Maggie's eyes and soon trickled down her sunken cheeks. "When it became obvious that I was in a family way, Dad said I should find the man who was responsible for my pregnancy and insist that he marry me." She paused and sniffed deeply. "My mamm talked Dad into letting me stay in their home until after the baby came, and when he asked me to leave a few days ago, I finally went looking for my baby's father."

Papa eyeballed Ivan with lips pressed into a tight grimace. Ivan wondered if he might be asked to leave his parents' house too. As he peered down at the little boy in his arms—the son to whom Ivan felt no attachment—the enormity of the situation pressed on him even harder.

Several minutes passed, and then Ivan's mother spoke up. "Ivan, if what this young woman has said is true, then you need to do right by her. Is that understood?"

Ivan swallowed against the bitter taste of bile rising in his throat. "Jah, Mama, but—"

"There are no buts, Son," his father was quick to say. "You'll need to join the church this fall so you can marry Stephen's mother." He looked at Maggie. "Are you a member of the Amish church district in Arcola?"

Ducking her chin, Maggie shook her head.

Papa's gaze went to Mama then. "I believe the two of us need to talk privately. Let's go back to the kitchen so we can discuss a few things."

"Yes, Eldon, I think that's a good idea." Mama turned to face Ivan, her eyebrows folding inward. "While we're gone, you two need to talk about what you feel needs to be done. Your daed and I will come back here again in thirty minutes or so and give our opinion on the best course of action for all involved."

All Ivan could manage was a brief nod as Maggie reached out to take back the little boy before settling on the sofa again.

Ivan's fists tightened as he gripped one wrist with the other hand behind his back. If he joined the church and married Maggie, whom he didn't even know, much less feel any love for, he would have to let Emma go. Was it possible that he could forget what he had with Emma and learn to love Maggie, as well as the baby boy she'd brought here to his parents' home?

Ivan lowered himself to the sofa, wishing he could sink farther in, and wondered, *Will anything ever be the same for me again?*

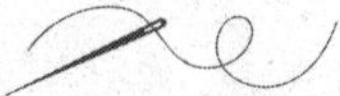

Ida Mae sat at the kitchen table, shaking her head. "I just can't believe our son fathered a child and did not tell us about it. Apparently, we didn't raise him as well as we thought."

"Probably not, I'm afraid. But remember, Maggie said he didn't know about the child." Eldon reached over and clasped her hand. "We did our best, Ida Mae, but you can't lead a horse to its stall and make it eat hay. We've taught all our kinner right from wrong, and as they've grown into adulthood, it's become their choice to pick which path to take—right or wrong."

"That is true, but it still hurts when we see one of our own take the wrong path." She reached for a napkin and dabbed the moisture beneath her eyes. "What do you think should be done now? Do we insist that Ivan marry the young woman and help raise their child?"

"I don't see any other solution," Eldon replied. "I mean, he can hardly turn her aside and expect to go on his merry way."

"You're right, but I can't help feeling sorry for sweet Emma. She's going to be devastated when Ivan tells her about Maggie and the baby. It's obvious to me how much she loves our son."

"I believe he loves her too, but it's clearly not meant to be." Eldon tapped the tabletop with the knuckles on his right hand. "Let's remain here a few more minutes and talk about what we think the plan of action should be for Ivan and Maggie. Once we agree on a solution that will benefit both of them and their infant son, we'll go back to the living room and tell the young couple what we've decided."

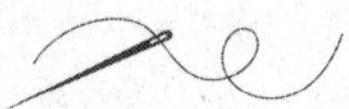

"Are you gonna marry me, or what?"

Maggie's unexpected question was so direct that Ivan nearly jumped off the sofa. His mother and father had been gone long enough to have come to some conclusion, but the whole time they'd been gone, all Ivan could do was sit quietly and watch the baby sleeping peacefully in his mother's arms.

It's not fair that this little guy should have to suffer because of my misdeed. Sweat poured off Ivan's forehead as he continued to ponder. *So as much as it pains me, guess I really have no choice but to marry the baby's mother. After all, that child is my son, and he needs me to be in his life. I can't abandon him just because I'm not prepared to accept responsibility for my actions.*

Ivan's contemplations halted when his parents entered the living room again. He clutched the armrest of the sofa, waiting to hear what his parents had to say to both him and Maggie.

"Your mamm and I talked things over, and we have a suggestion," Papa announced before taking a seat in his favorite chair. "We think the best thing right now is for Maggie to move in here and stay in the guest room with the baby." With a somber expression, he gestured to Ivan and then Maggie. "Come fall, when classes begin for joining the church, both of you should take those classes and then follow through by becoming church members. Within a few weeks after that, Ivan and Maggie, we believe that the only right thing to do is for the two of you to get married on a Sunday, following the main church service." Narrowing his eyes, Ivan's father glanced at Mama. "Would you like to tell them the rest?"

"Jah." Her smile appeared to be forced as she stated in a calm but firm voice, "As newlyweds, you will be invited to stay here in our home until you find a suitable place of your own to rent or purchase."

As much as Ivan didn't want to agree to his parents' plan, he knew deep within his heart that it was the right thing to do. "I'm okay with your suggestions," he said, before looking at Maggie. "How about you?"

Maggie bobbed her head. "I'm in favor of it too."

"All right then. It's settled." Papa rose to his feet. "Ivan, we'll leave you and Maggie alone now to work out the details." He clasped Mama's arm, and they silently walked out of the room.

A few minutes passed, and then Maggie looked over at Ivan and asked, "Would you mind going out to my driver's vehicle to get my suitcase? I've got my hands full right here, after all." She gestured to the baby.

"Okay," he responded, not knowing what else he could do or say.

"And while you're there, could you please pay the driver what I owe for the ride here?"

Ivan was tempted to ask Maggie if she hadn't brought her own money to pay the driver, but instead, he nodded and rushed out the front door.

I am living the worst nightmare of my life, he told himself. *Only this one I will never wake up from.*

Ivan felt almost numb as he headed with heavy feet toward the driver's vehicle. He just couldn't believe how his life had been turned upside down—and just when things were going really well between him and Emma. Now, thanks to his consuming too much beer at his friend's party over nine months ago, Ivan would spend the rest of his life paying the price for his foolishness.

After obtaining Maggie's luggage and shelling out the driver's payment, Ivan paused on the porch threshold, wishing he could avoid having to go inside. But facing the truth, Ivan knew he had no other choice.

Chapter 27

Ivan and Maggie did not attend church on Sunday morning. After getting her and the baby settled into the guest room six days ago and offering an explanation to his siblings who were old enough to understand, Ivan had been too exhausted to even get out of bed this morning, much less attend church, where he would have had to see Emma. There was no way he could do that yet. Besides, if Maggie had gone with him, he would have needed to offer some explanation to those who would have no doubt given them curious looks and probably plenty of questions concerning Maggie and the baby.

Fortunately, Maggie had also been willing to remain at the house this morning while the rest of the family went to church. Ivan could only hope that none of them would say anything to anyone in attendance about why he'd stayed home.

Mama had brought a tray up to Ivan's room before they'd all left for church. There was toast, cereal, and orange juice on the tray, but he hadn't touched a thing. The food still sat on top of his dresser, where his mother had placed it almost two hours ago. Ivan figured either Maggie had joined the family in the kitchen for breakfast or Mama had taken her a tray too.

All Ivan could manage this morning was to lie in his bed, staring at a string of cobwebs hanging from the ceiling. It wasn't like him to refuse to face his challenges head-on or to lounge around in bed all morning, but this new test had hit him harder than a runaway horse going at full speed.

Ivan reflected on how when Emma had come for her quilting lesson on Wednesday, his mother had met her at the door and said she wouldn't be able to teach her this week. Fortunately, Mama had offered no explanation, and thankfully Ivan had been at work when it had occurred. He was not up to speaking with Emma yet about Maggie and the baby. When he'd heard that Emma had been to the house and his mother had explained that there wouldn't be a quilting lesson this week, he'd been afraid that Emma may have met Maggie. But Mama had assured Ivan that Maggie and her baby were resting in the guest room when Emma came to the door. That was a relief, as Ivan needed to be the one to tell Emma the situation, and he knew it needed to be soon. He'd put it off long enough.

Ivan heard the baby crying from downstairs, filling the home with the reminder that his life before Maggie's arrival no longer existed. The infant's piercing wails traveled all the way up the steps and made Ivan want to plug his ears.

Some father I'll make, he thought while rolling onto his side. *I can't even stand to hear a baby's cry.*

Ivan wondered if Maggie had gotten any sleep last night and whether she felt as miserable as he did right now. He figured Maggie probably was more miserable since she had gone through the ordeal of giving birth to Stephen and had taken care of the boy all this time, while Ivan hadn't been the wiser. The poor girl had been forced to leave her parents' home, and now she was here, living with people she didn't know.

That includes me, Ivan told himself. *Just because we met at a party and did something we shouldn't have doesn't mean we know each other at all. We're just two people who made a mistake, and now we are both paying the price for it. Everyone in our lives has been affected by our mistake. Not Emma yet, though,* Ivan reminded himself.

Releasing a shallow breath, Ivan got out of bed and began pacing the floor. His bare feet led him toward the window, and then he flattened his palm against the cool glass as the child's wail overlapped with the other thoughts Ivan had rummaged through while lying on his bed.

I must let Emma know what's happened, before it's too late and someone else tells her. And I need to do it before this day is out. After my family returns from church, I'll take a drive over to Emma's grandparents' house and see if she's available to take a ride with me.

One thing Ivan knew for sure: He didn't want to tell Emma about Maggie and the baby in front of Marlin and Luellen. The two of them needed to talk about this in private, and Ivan knew that telling Emma why they couldn't be together would be the most agonizing thing he had ever done.

In the meantime, however, Ivan decided that he should get dressed, go downstairs, and see if he could do anything to help Maggie. She didn't deserve to be alone right now and might even need his assistance with the baby.

Chapter 28

As soon as supper was over Sunday evening, Ivan excused himself, saying he needed some fresh air and was going for a ride with his horse and open buggy. Ivan definitely needed some time away from the house, so it wasn't an exaggeration. Maybe the ride alone would clear his mind sufficiently for him to find the appropriate words to say to Emma.

Maggie was right behind him as he approached the back door. "Will you be gone very long?"

"Probably not. Do you need me to do something before I leave?"

"Not really," she responded. "I was just wondering if you're leaving for a while so you don't have to spend the rest of the evening with me and the baby."

Ivan shook his head. "It has nothing to do with you or the baby. I just need to take a ride somewhere." He wasn't about to tell Maggie that the reason he was leaving was to see his girlfriend so he could end his relationship with her. What good would that do anyway? Ivan figured Maggie probably wouldn't even care how hard it was for him to give up his relationship with Emma. Her motive for coming here was to find the baby's father and guilt him into marrying her. Well, Maggie need not worry. Ivan would keep true to his word and do what was right. If for no one else, he owed it to his son.

"Oh, okay," Maggie said. "I hope you enjoy your ride."

"If you should need anything while I'm gone, just ask my mamm or one of my sisters. I'm sure one of them will be available to help you."

Maggie took a step toward Ivan and reached out a hand, like she might touch him, but then she lowered her arm. "Jah, I'm sure one of them will help me. In fact, your mamm is holding Stephen right now." She paused a few seconds and added, "If you're not back before I go to the guest room with the baby for the night, I'll see you in the morning."

"You may not be up by the time I leave for work," Ivan said.

"What kind of work do you do at the harness shop?" Maggie asked. "You've never really explained it to me."

"I make and repair harnesses, but my daed owns the shop. I also repair clocks and pocket watches in my spare time."

She tipped her head to one side and blinked. "That's an unusual hobby. It is just a hobby, right?"

"For now, at least." Ivan paused and then turned and opened the back door. "I'm heading out now. Goodbye, Maggie." He went out and closed the door behind him, unaware of whether she'd responded or not.

As Ivan approached the Herschbergers' house, his throat thickened at the prospect of telling Emma that they had no future together. It wasn't fair that he would never have the opportunity of asking Emma to marry him. But then it wasn't fair that Maggie should be expected to raise her baby alone—especially when her parents had asked her to take the baby and leave.

How could anyone have abandoned their daughter and grandson? Ivan asked himself. Even though Ivan's parents didn't approve of what he and Maggie had done, they had been sensitive to their needs and had offered them a place to live, even after they were married.

What's it gonna be like, being married to someone I don't even know well, much less feel any love for? Ivan gripped his horse's reins even harder. *Dear Lord, is there even a chance that I can learn to love Maggie?* Ivan asked as his thoughts turned to a heartfelt prayer. *I'll have to rely on You to help me become a good father and husband, who will treat my wife and baby with love and understanding. Please help me now, as I speak with Emma. Give me the right words when I tell her the truth.*

After Ivan guided his rig up the driveway and to the hitching rail, he got out and secured his horse. With his neck bent forward and his shoulders curved, he trudged up the front steps and knocked on the door. If Emma was free to go for a ride with him, Ivan knew that it would be their last buggy ride together, and that thought turned his stomach.

In short order, the door opened, and Marlin poked his head out. "Well, if it isn't Ivan Yoder. Since you weren't at church today, we figured you must be sick."

Sick at heart, Ivan thought, but he didn't voice the words. Instead, he forced himself to stand up straight and said, "I wasn't feeling the best this morning, so I stayed home in bed." Ivan paused for a breath. "But now I'm here, and I need to see Emma. Is she available?"

"Yep." Marlin turned away from Ivan and hollered, "Emma, your boyfriend's come to pay a call on you."

If only it was as simple as that. Ivan wished he had some water to drink, for his throat felt extremely dry.

"I'll go check on Emma," Marlin said, glancing back at Ivan. "She might be in her room, or maybe she and her grandma are in the kitchen getting another helping of the blueberry cobbler the two of them made yesterday." He grinned and patted his belly. "That granddaughter of ours has turned out to be quite a good cook. Emma came here knowing little or nothing about cooking or sewing, but she'll return to her parents' home more than ready for marriage." He winked at Ivan and said, "Come on in and make yourself comfortable till Emma shows up. I'm sure she'll be glad to see you." With that, Marlin pivoted around once more and headed on down the hall in the direction of the kitchen.

Ivan's strides slowed as he walked into the house and leaned against the wall a few feet from the entrance. *I bet once Emma hears what I have to say, she won't be glad I came over at all.*

Ivan leaned away from the wall and was about to take a seat in the living room when Emma showed up, all smiles. "Ivan, it made me happy when Grandpa said you were here. With you not being in church today, I figured you might be grank, and I was worried about you."

"I didn't feel so great, but I wasn't actually sick," he responded. "I came over here this evening, hoping you could take a ride with me in my open carriage. There's something I want to talk to you about."

"That sounds nice, and I'm glad you're not ill. I'll go check with my grandparents to make sure they're okay with me being gone for a while." Emma gave Ivan another heart-melting smile and headed back to the kitchen.

Ivan clutched his arms to his chest. The shame he felt over the part he'd had in Maggie's pregnancy was nothing compared to the dread and pain he felt now about the confession he would soon be making to Emma. He hoped she would be able to forgive him and move on with her life once she found a more suitable boyfriend who could offer her the happiness she deserved.

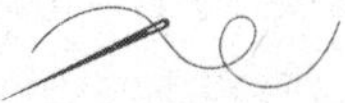

Emma settled herself on the buggy seat next to Ivan and grinned as he guided his horse and buggy out onto the road. The *clip-clop* of the horse's hooves, mixed with the soothing sound of crickets, could have lulled her to sleep if she hadn't been so excited to spend a few hours with the young man she'd come to love so much. She looked forward to more buggy rides like this before summer's end and hoped with all her heart that her parents would be okay with her remaining in Arthur into the fall, and perhaps even staying here permanently if Ivan should propose marriage.

I know Mom, Dad, and Rachel would miss me if I did end up staying in Arthur, but Shipshewana isn't really that far away. At least we could schedule visits and write letters to keep in touch. That's how it is when a person meets someone from outside their Amish community, or even in another state, she mused. *But those involved learn to accept it and schedule visits as often as possible.*

Aware that Ivan was unusually quiet, Emma glanced over at him, wondering if she should say something to get a conversation going.

When more time passed without Ivan speaking, Emma plunged ahead. "It's sure a lovely evening, don't you think?"

"Jah, weather-wise it's real nice."

Ivan lapsed into another period of silence, and Emma wondered why he wasn't as talkative as usual this evening. It wasn't like him to be so quiet. Ivan had said earlier that he wanted to talk to her about something. If that was still the case, then why hadn't he spoken right up?

Emma waited awhile, thinking surely Ivan would say something to her, but his silence continued. She shifted on her seat while fingering the ties on her head covering. Finally, when she could stand it no longer, Emma blurted, "I thought you had something to talk to me about, Ivan. If that's so, then why are you being so quiet?"

"I. . .uh. . .am looking for a good place to stop my horse and buggy so we can talk. I'm sorry, Emma." He scraped a hand through the back of his hair. "What I have to tell you is a serious matter, and I don't want to be concentrating on the road or my horse while I say it."

A serious matter? Emma couldn't imagine what that could be, but then a hopeful thought popped into her head. *Is it possible that Ivan might be planning to propose marriage to me? Could that be why he's acting so nervous?*

Emma's pulse quickened as she reflected on the possibility that he wanted her to be his wife. *But we haven't known each other very long,* she reminded herself. *Ivan doesn't seem like the kind of person who would rush into something as serious as marriage.*

She tapped a finger against her chin. *Unless he's worried that once I return to Shipshewana, I might forget about him. Maybe I should put Ivan's mind at ease by telling him that I plan to ask my parents if they would mind if I stayed here a few more months. That would certainly give Ivan and me more time to establish a stronger relationship.*

Emma decided to remain quiet until Ivan found a wide spot to pull off, and then she would tell him her plan. Even when no words were exchanged, Emma loved spending time with Ivan, although part of her was eager to hear what he planned to tell her.

They rode another mile or so before the perfect place to pull off emerged into view, and Emma was relieved when Ivan guided his horse in that direction. Once the horse and buggy were stopped, Ivan turned to Emma and said, "I'm ready to tell you what I need to say now."

Emma noticed that he was not looking at her. Instead, Ivan's focus seemed to be on his hands. She couldn't help but observe the way he gripped the reins so tight that the veins in his hands protruded.

Fussing with the sleeve of her dress, Emma held her breath. A tingling sensation swept along her shoulders as she waited to see what he would say next.

Ivan cleared his throat a few times, and without looking at her, he said, "I brought you here to tell you something I don't really want to say."

Emma clasped her hands tightly in her lap as worry and dread took over. If Ivan was going to propose, surely he wouldn't have said that he didn't really want to say what he was going to tell her.

I don't know why, but I have a horrible feeling that Ivan is about to break up with me.

Ivan reached over and clasped Emma's hand that was closest to him. "It pains me to say this, Emma, but our relationship has to end—now."

"How come?" Emma could barely get the words out.

"Because I have to marry another woman, and it will happen before the year is out."

Emma flinched and withdrew her hand. "You—you have another girlfriend? Is that it, Ivan? Have you been seeing her secretly all this time you and I have been courting?"

"No, it's not like that. You see. . ."

A knot formed in Emma's stomach, and a deep, heavy feeling settled in her limbs as she sat stiff as a board, listening to Ivan tell her about a young woman named Maggie, who he'd met at a friend's party nine and a half months ago. He'd gone on to say that he'd been drinking that night, and although he had no memory of much of anything that took place, he had apparently fathered a child. With every word Ivan continued to say, Emma cringed, and by the time he'd finished, she felt sick to her stomach and wanted to leap from the buggy and run as far away from him as she could possibly get. But where would she go? They'd driven several miles from her grandparents' house, and the sun was beginning to set. It wouldn't be safe for her to try walking that distance alone.

"I'm really sorry, Emma," Ivan said, his voice trembling. "I didn't want to tell you any of this, but there was no way I could keep it to myself or continue courting you under the circumstances. I wish things were so much different, but the choices I've made in my past can't be undone."

Emma didn't respond. What could she really say? Ivan was a father, and he had a responsibility to the baby—and to the child's mother. There would be no marriage proposal from the man she loved. Instead, before the year was out, Ivan and Maggie would be married.

They sat quietly for several moments, and then Ivan spoke again. "It's you I love, Emma. I have no feelings for Maggie, except compassion. But I know I must do the right thing and marry the mother of my child once Maggie and I have both joined the Amish church."

When Emma thought she could speak without choking up, she replied in a firm voice, "You're doing the right thing, of course." She paused to gain control of her swirling emotions. No way could she allow herself to break down in front of Ivan. That would only make their parting worse. "Would you please get the horse and buggy moving again? I need to get back to Grandma and Grandpa's house before the sky darkens and they begin to worry about me."

"I'm worried about you right now," Ivan said, his voice barely above a whisper.

"There's no need for you to worry. I'll be all right once I get back to Shipshewana, where I belong. I never should have left home. My place is there, and it always was. You and I should never have met."

Although Emma's heart was broken and tears had begun streaming down her face, she knew that Ivan must do what was right and become a church member so he could marry the mother of his child. Come morning, Emma would pack her bags and make plans for her trip home to her parents. Even though the summer wasn't over yet, she could not stay here now. Her place was in Indiana with her family and friends. Mama had been right when she'd told Emma at the beginning of summer that she would return home a different person. Although Emma had successfully learned new tasks while living with her grandparents, she couldn't feel good about any of it. Instead, it seemed that her whole world had been torn apart.

All the way back to her grandparents' house, stillness fell between them as the fields were enveloped in lengthy silhouettes from the waning sun. All Emma could think about was how she had foolishly given her heart to Ivan, only to have it torn asunder. At this moment, Emma doubted that she would ever trust another man or allow herself to fall in love again.

Emma's thoughts continued to race as she reflected on all the times she had spent with Ivan over the past few months. Clasping her quivering fingers to her lips in an attempt to squelch the sob that threatened to break forth, she held her teeth tightly together. In the back of her mind, even when she and Ivan began courting, she'd thought at times that it was all too good to be true.

Emma squeezed her eyes shut and swallowed multiple times. Now she knew fully how hurt her sister had been when David dropped her for another woman. The only difference was, David was not a father, and as far as Emma knew, he had no plans to marry Alice. In fact, from what David had said to Rachel when he'd come to see her while she was still at their grandparents' house, he had never stopped loving Rachel and wanted her back.

So she's the lucky one after all, Emma told herself. *There's a good chance my sister and her ex-boyfriend will get back together. But for me and Ivan, there is no possibility of that. He will move forward with a wife and baby, and I'll remain unmarried for the rest of my life.*

Chapter 29

"Are you sure you don't mind me going home earlier than originally planned?" Emma asked her grandmother the following morning.

Grandma slipped an arm around Emma's waist. "As your grandpa and I expressed to you last night when you told us what Ivan had said, we completely understand your reason for returning to your parents' home now. Of course, we will miss you, but we shall keep in touch through letters, and hopefully we can come to visit you and your family soon."

Emma heaved a lingering sigh. "I feel so bad leaving you—especially with your back issue and you not being able to do all of your chores."

"Now don't you worry about me. I'll be fine, and what I'm not able to do, your grandpa will take care of. So we'll get along okay, just like we did before you came to stay with us."

Emma sniffed as tears rolled down her cheeks. She would miss her grandparents very much, but the remembrance of time spent with Ivan would be even more painful. Emma was sure she would never love anyone the way she did him. It would probably be a long time before her strong feelings for Ivan would pass.

A horn tootled from outside, and Emma knew it must be her driver. It was time to say goodbye to her grandparents. It was time to head for home and somehow move on with her life. She gave Grandma and Grandpa a tight hug, and then Grandpa grabbed her suitcase and tote bag while Emma scooped up her dog before heading out to the vehicle.

She looked back and saw Grandma waving, and the sadness that came over Emma was unlike any she'd ever known.

Luellen stood on the front porch with Marlin, watching as Emma's driver, Holly, backed her vehicle out of the driveway and onto the road. A lump formed in Luellen's throat, and she swallowed hard, trying to push it down.

"We're gonna miss our precious granddaughter, that's for sure," she murmured. "I'll even miss that pesky mutt she ended up calling her own."

"Jah, and I'm glad she could take Fawn with her. I'm sure the dog will offer some needed comfort to Emma in the days ahead."

Marlin rested his hand on Luellen's shoulder and gave it a few tender pats. It was the comfort she sought in the moment while watching the car disappear from sight. She'd become used to Emma's company and would miss her so much.

"When things had become serious between Emma and Ivan, I'd begun to think there was a possibility that our granddaughter might stay here in Arthur permanently," Luellen said with a catch in her voice. "Wasn't it silly of me to hope for that?"

"Not at all. It would have been nice, and I'd hoped for that too, but I guess it was not meant to be," Marlin responded.

Luellen lifted a shaky hand to dab at the tears on her cheeks. "I can hardly believe how things turned out."

"Jah, well, it's all Ivan's fault. He brought this on by making a foolish decision during his rumspringa."

"You're right," Luellen agreed, "but at least he owned up to it and didn't run from the problem. I'm sure there are a lot of young men—even among the Amish—who would have denied their role in creating a baby and run from the situation, leaving the poor mother to raise the child."

"I suppose that's true. Even so, it's hard to see Emma hurting so badly over this ordeal." Marlin groaned. "Our sweet granddaughter deserves better than that."

"True, but life doesn't always give us what we want. And moving forward, we must learn to accept the bad with the good and try to make the best of whatever comes our way." The skirt of Luellen's dress swished as she turned away from the porch railing. "Well, we can't stand out here for the rest of the day feeling sorry for ourselves. I need to get busy with something, which I hope will take my mind off the sadness I feel right now."

"I agree," he said with a nod. "But my question now is do you have any idea what kind of busyness either of us should be doing today?"

"No, not really, but I'm sure we'll find something meaningful to do. After all, neither of us has ever been one to sit around all day and do nothing."

"That's true enough—even when your back is painful you still manage to do a few things around here." He lifted a finger. "And by the way—how do your back muscles feel today?"

"Not too bad. I think the chiropractor's adjustment really helped."

"I'm glad. We'll make sure that you get regular appointments with him."

Luellen appreciated Marlin's concern for her well-being. Not all husbands were as attentive as he was.

After heading into the house, with tears still trickling down her cheeks, Luellen plodded down the hall to her sewing room. She hoped that someday Emma would find a man as loving and caring as the man God had blessed her with. Luellen paused to whisper a silent prayer for her granddaughter. *Lord, please bless Emma and fill her life with joy again. If it be Your will, bring the right man into Emma's life.*

When the prayer ended, Luellen determined that she would pray for Emma every single day. Of course, she would be praying for Rachel too. Both of their granddaughters deserved to find good husbands, have children, and enjoy a happy, fulfilled life.

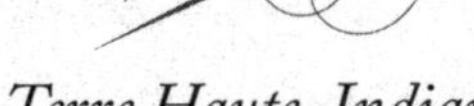

Terre Haute, Indiana

"Well, we've made it to the state line now, but we still have a good many hours left to go," Holly called over her shoulder. Emma had opted to sit in the back seat of the station wagon so she could be near her little dog, who'd been stuck in a cage.

"You're okay, little Fawn. Just lie down and relax," Emma said soothingly when the dog began to whine. "Once we get to my home, you'll be free to run and play in the yard." Although Emma knew her pet didn't understand her words, she felt sure that Fawn recognized the soothing tone of her voice.

"You really like your furry friend, don't you?" Holly asked as she looked at Emma through the reflection of the rearview mirror.

"Yes, I do." She stroked the dog's nose through the slats in the cage and was rewarded with a slurp from Fawn's pink tongue as she licked Emma's finger. Emma didn't mind, though. The dog's attention was a healing balm to her wounded soul.

As Emma rested her head against the side window, she observed the surrounding landscape of crops and pastures that blurred together. It still didn't seem real that she could be heading home several weeks earlier than planned, and the only thing she had to show for the time away from home was the ability to cook and quilt. She had never fully mastered the art of using her grandmother's treadle sewing machine, but at least she could get by with needle and thread. And it didn't really matter whether she was equipped to be some man's wife or not, because for Emma, the thought of marriage was impossible.

Once Fawn settled down and fell asleep, Emma leaned heavily against the seat back, hoping to drown out all her thoughts with much-needed sleep. She tried focusing on the whirring of the tires and the faint vibration of Holly's vehicle. *Sleep. . .sleep,* she told herself. *I just need to fall asleep and stay that way till I get home.*

Shipshewana

Emma's driver pulled onto her parents' property. With a hand around Fawn's carrier, Emma gazed at her parents' yard, which was dotted with bird feeders, spaced several feet apart.

"Are you awake, Emma?" Holly asked.

"Yes, I am. I've been awake for the last hour or so."

"You've been awfully quiet, so I wasn't sure."

Emma arched her back, and she reached up to make sure her head covering was in place. Her stomach growled, so she figured it must be close to suppertime. In fact, it was quite possible that her family had already eaten their evening meal, and she wouldn't have blamed them if they had. After all, they had no way of knowing the exact time she would arrive.

After Holly turned off the engine, Emma unlatched the dog carrier and took her faithful companion out. In one way, it was good to be home, but in another, sadness prevailed. Thanks to her grandparents' neighbor calling Mom and Dad's neighbor with a message that was to be given to Emma's parents, they knew she'd be coming home today, but they didn't know any of the details as to why. Telling them about her breakup with Ivan would be difficult, but Emma had no choice. They deserved an explanation as to why she'd decided to return to Shipshewana so abruptly. There was no way Emma could simply state that she'd missed her family and decided to come home earlier than originally planned. Mom and Dad were smart and would know something was up.

"Do you need help getting out?" Holly's question pushed Emma's thoughts aside.

"No, I was just thinking, is all. I'm getting out now with my dog." She stepped out of the vehicle and set Fawn on the ground. "Stay close by me now, you understand?"

As though she completely understood, the dog let out a couple of barks and ran circles around Emma's legs. There was no doubt that the pooch had plenty of pent-up energy from being cooped up in the carrier for so long.

Holly got out, and Emma had barely taken Fawn's cage out of the vehicle when Rachel came rushing up from the side yard with outstretched arms. "Oh, Sister, it's so good to see you." She hugged Emma tightly. "But I don't understand why you came home now. I thought you were staying in Arthur until summer was over."

"I was, but things changed," Emma replied. "You'll hear the whole story when I tell Mom and Dad about it."

Holly opened the back of the station wagon, and just as she got out Emma's suitcase, Mom and Dad showed up. After hugs were given and a few tears were shed, Dad paid Holly for bringing Emma home, while Rachel picked up Emma's suitcase and tote, quickly heading for the house.

Mom peered down at Fawn, then back at Emma and said, "You brought a dog with you?"

"Jah," Emma replied as she knelt to scratch her pet's chin. "Her name is Fawn, and I wrote you about her."

"I suppose you did, but I didn't realize you'd be bringing her home."

"Grandpa gave the dog to me, and I like her a lot, so. . ."

"It's okay." Mom sighed, slipping her arm around Emma's waist. "I've never been one to allow a hund in the house, but I guess we can come up with some place for the dog to sleep."

Emma didn't like the sound of that, but she decided it was best to keep quiet about her mother's comment. Maybe once Mom saw what a good dog Fawn was, she'd change her mind about allowing Emma's pet to come into the house.

During supper, many questions were asked of Emma. It pained her to tell her parents and sister why she'd come home early. Yet it had to be done, and she'd managed to get the words out without falling apart.

"Oh, Emma, dear, I am so sorry." Mom spoke in a gentle tone as she patted Emma's arm. "I can't imagine how heartbroken you must be."

Emma heaved a weighted sigh and slouched in her chair. If she wasn't careful, she'd end up sobbing and wouldn't be able to say another word.

Rachel clasped Emma's hand under the table and squeezed it gently. "I'm sorry too, Sister. I know from the things you've said that you loved Ivan so much."

Again, Emma couldn't find the words to respond. She blinked rapidly, trying to prevent the tears blurring her vision from spilling over.

Dad, with flaring nostrils, spoke up. "That young fellow oughta be horsewhipped, leading you on all that time." He looked at Rachel for a few seconds. "He's no better than David, except that Rachel's ex-boyfriend didn't father a child out of wedlock."

Emma's mother gave a slow shake of her head. "No, Philip, you shouldn't talk that way. Ivan did not intentionally hurt Emma, and he's only doing what's right by the mother of his child. Young people, and even those who are older, can be prone to making mistakes. It's what we do about the error of our ways that's important."

"I guess you're right," he acknowledged, "but I can't feel good about the way both of our girls have been hurt by the young men who had once proclaimed their love for them."

"I don't feel good about it either," Mom stated. "However, it's not my place to judge others. The Lord deals with each of us individually, and the Bible tells us that we must forgive those who trespass against us."

Emma sat in silence as she reflected on her mother's words. Although she had not admitted it to herself until now, part of her had been angry at Ivan for having been with the girl he'd met at his friend's party and creating a baby when they were not married. She'd also been struggling with bitterness because Ivan's actions from the past had made it so that he could no longer court Emma and would soon be getting married to some other woman. Emma reminded herself that even though she was devastated by the situation at hand, Ivan was the one bearing the consequences of his mistake. Emma could, if she wanted, always start over with someone new, but that was no longer an option for Ivan. She remembered Matthew 6:14–15, which read: "For if ye forgive men their trespasses, your heavenly Father will also forgive you: But if ye forgive not men their trespasses, neither will your Father forgive your trespasses." Holding onto bitterness would only prevent Emma from undergoing the healing she needed to carry on. In order to do as the Bible said, she would have to find it in her heart to forgive Ivan.

Arthur

"Supper is really good, Mrs. Yoder," Maggie said, reaching for another piece of fried chicken. "You obviously know your way around the kitchen."

"I'm glad you're enjoying it, but I can't take all the credit, because my three daughters helped with the meal," Ivan's mother responded. "Oh, and Maggie, please call me Ida Mae. After all, it won't be too many months, and I'll be your mother-in-law."

Before Maggie could respond, Ivan's dad chimed in. "There's no need to refer to me as Mr. Yoder, either. My first name is Eldon."

"Okay." Maggie glanced Ivan's way and smiled. Then, with a drumstick in hand, she gestured to Ivan's sisters, sitting across the table. "Which of you is Jane, and who is Norma? I'm not very good with remembering names."

"I'm Jane." Ivan's oldest sister pointed to Norma. "This is Norma, and our younger sister is Bertha."

"All right then," Maggie said. "Jane, Norma, and Bertha. Think I've got it."

"The sisters aren't my only siblings," Ivan interjected. "I also have three married brothers. Their names are Amos, Peter, and Delbert."

Maggie's dark eyebrows lifted. "Wow! You have a big family. Seven kids in all, huh?"

"That's right," Ivan's mother said, "but we lost one at birth, and if she'd lived, we would have been blessed with eight kinner."

"How many children are in your family, Maggie?" Jane questioned.

"I have two older sisters, but none of them ever got kicked out of the house." Maggie's cheeks colored. "Then again, they didn't do anything to disgrace my parents. Guess I'm the black sheep in the family, so I got what they thought I deserved."

Ivan heard the bitterness in Maggie's tone. She'd obviously not had the best relationship with her parents, and he felt sorry for her. Even though Ivan had no love for this young woman who sat beside him at the supper table, he did feel compassion and would try to be as kind to Maggie as possible. Right now, and possibly for the rest of his life, that might be all he was capable of feeling for the mother of his child, who lay sleeping in the guest room down the hall.

Chapter 30

Shipshewana

EMMA HAD BEEN HOME FOR two weeks, and she still didn't feel settled in, nor was she content. How could she be when she'd left so much behind? Emma had managed to keep busy by helping her mother with various chores during the day while Rachel was at her job. Busyness helped, but it didn't fill the void in her life. What she needed was something truly meaningful to do.

After a trip to the mailbox, Emma discovered a letter from her grandmother. She was excited to read it but at the same time filled with regret. Emma missed Grandpa's wisecracks and carefree demeanor. She also longed to be with Grandma, guided by her gentle teaching. And most of all, she missed seeing Ivan.

Now don't start focusing on that again, Emma reminded herself. *Ivan is out of my life, and he's moving on, so I need to do the same.*

Emma stopped walking toward the house and bent down to pet Fawn, who'd dropped a rubber ball by her feet. "Oh, so you wanna play, do ya?" Emma leaned over, picked up the ball, and gave it a good toss. When the dog chased after it, Emma hurried her steps until she was on the porch, where she could sit on the glider and sort through the mail. Other than a few envelopes she figured must be bills, the only other piece of mail was the letter from Grandma, addressed to Emma.

Tearing open the flap, Emma inhaled deeply. She couldn't miss the distinctive smell of lilac on her grandmother's stationery. Her eyes fluttered shut for a few seconds, visualizing her grandmother sitting at the kitchen table, pen in hand. Grandma had stated many times that she enjoyed writing letters, and her lovely penmanship proved it.

"I wish my cursive writing was even half that beautiful," Emma murmured.

"Who are you talking to, Daughter?"

Emma's head jerked at the sound of her mother's voice. She hadn't heard Mom come out of the house, which was unusual, since the screen door always squeaked.

"I was talking to myself." Emma scooted over on the glider so her mother could sit down.

Mom chuckled. "I catch myself doing that sometimes too." She pushed her feet against the porch floor, which got the glider moving. "Did we get anything interesting in today's mail?"

Emma handed her mother all the envelopes, except the one from Grandma. "This letter is for me, from Grandma."

"How nice. I'm sure you're eager to find out what she has to say." Mom patted Emma's arm. "Would you like me to go back inside while you read it?"

"No, that's okay. I'll just read it silently, if that's all right with you. When I'm finished, I'll pass the letter over to you."

"That's fine, Emma, but if there's anything in the letter you don't want to share with me, I won't read it at all."

"I have nothing to hide from you, Mom," Emma responded. "And I'm sure that your mamm doesn't either."

"You're probably right, but she may have written something about. . ." Mom's voice trailed off.

"Ivan? Is that who you meant?"

"Jah."

Emma scratched an itch behind her right ear before speaking again. "I doubt that Grandma would have anything to say about Ivan, but if she did, I'm sure it wouldn't be anything I wouldn't want you to know."

"Okay, well. . .you go ahead and read your letter while I look through the rest of the mail."

"Danki, Mom." Emma picked up the piece of paper and began to read:

Dearest Emma,

Your grandfather and I are doing well, but we surely do miss you. I hope we'll be able to make a trip there to see you and the family before the cold winter weather sets in.

How are you? Have you found plenty of things to keep busy? Are you doing any quilting at all?

There's not much here to report. It's basically the same old thing. I sew and bake, and your grandfather does a lot of reading and putting puzzles together. He's working on a one-thousand-piece puzzle right now. The picture on the box shows a beautiful eagle soaring through the sky above a mountain covered in snow.

I haven't done much with any of my friends lately, but there's a hen party scheduled for one day next week, so I'll probably try to attend that. It will be nice to get together with friends and chat.

Oh, and I'm seeing the chiropractor, with good results.

Please write soon and let me know what you've been up to. Tell the rest of the family I said hello, and let your mamm know I'll be dropping her a note soon too.

All my love and prayers,
Grandma

Emma's shoulders lifted as she folded the letter, struggling not to cry.

"Is everything all right with my folks, Emma?" Mom questioned.

"They're both fine. I do miss them, though."

"Are you sure it's only them you're missing?"

Emma didn't want to admit it to Mom, or herself, but she missed Ivan terribly. She forced a smile and said, "Well, I can't say I miss my hund, 'cause she came home with me." Emma glanced into the yard and focused on Fawn nudging the ball around with her nose. It was necessary for Emma to keep her attention on other things, because it helped her not to think about Ivan and wonder how he was doing.

Arthur

Ida Mae had been busy setting out some bolts of material that had arrived at the store, and she was pleased to take a break when Luellen entered the store.

"Well, hello! I haven't seen you in here for a while." Ida Mae set aside the bolt of fabric that she'd been holding and gave Luellen a hug.

"That's true," her friend admitted. "I've done a lot of mending lately but haven't created anything new for a while. Now that I'm caught up, I decided to make a new frack, which is what brought me into the store here today."

"I'm glad you came in." Ida Mae smiled. "Do you know what color material you'd like for the dress?"

"I'm not sure. Maybe gray or dark brown."

"You're in luck then, because I have both colors in stock." Ida Mae pointed to a bolt of brown material, and then one in gray.

Luellen nodded. "I'll consider those, but I might choose some other color if it catches my eye."

"Feel free to look around."

Ida Mae went back to her task until Luellen brought her material up to the counter to be cut. "How are things going with you these days?" Luellen asked.

"Pretty well. We're all keeping busy, and Ivan and Maggie will be taking classes soon to be baptized and join the church so they can get married." Ida Mae paused to spread the material out in front of her in preparation to cut the right length. "You met Maggie and the baby last Sunday, right?"

"Jah, I did. She seemed friendly enough, and the baby is cute."

"We think so too." Ida Mae smiled. "It's kind of nice having a baby in the house again. It certainly keeps us entertained and plenty busy helping Maggie when she needs a break."

"I can imagine."

Ida Mae cut the material and folded it neatly before placing it in a paper sack. "Have you heard anything from Emma recently?"

"Just once since she returned home. I miss that sweet girl so much. The house seems awfully quiet without Emma." Luellen laid a hand against her chest. "I even miss that yappy dog she inherited after Marlin found it."

"I miss seeing Emma too," Ida Mae admitted. "We had so much fun during her quilting lessons, and it was a pleasure for me to get to know her better." She dropped her gaze to the floor. "I feel bad about what happened between Emma and Ivan. They seemed to be moving forward in their relationship until. . ." Her voice trailed off. This was a touchy subject for her to discuss, and Ida Mae figured it was for Luellen as well. She looked up and handed Luellen her purchase. "Is Emma still quilting?"

"I don't know. She didn't mention anything about quilting in her letter, but of course, that doesn't mean she quit doing it." Luellen handed Ida Mae the money she owed.

"I hope she will stick with it," Ida Mae said. "From the very first day I taught her about quilting, the interest she showed let me know that she would have a knack for it. I hope you'll encourage her to continue quilting."

"I shall try, but you know how the young people can be. Some do as you suggest, and others have a mind of their own."

"So true." Ida Mae squinted as she pinched the bridge of her nose. *If Ivan had listened to what my husband and I told him about the dangers of drinking alcohol, he wouldn't be in the fix he's in now, and it might be his and Emma's wedding he'd be planning now, instead of with Maggie—a young woman we know so little about.*

Shipshewana

"Emma, I think you need to take a look at this." Dianna held a piece of cardstock out to her daughter. It had been inside one of the envelopes Emma brought in from the mailbox earlier that morning.

Emma looked up from the cookbook she'd been studying. "What is it, Mom?"

"This is a notification about a quilting contest that will take place in Middlebury in two months. Do you think you could make a quilt in that time frame?"

"You want me to make a quilt and enter it in a contest?" Emma's eyes widened.

"You are correct."

"But, Mom, quilts take time to make—especially full-size bed coverings." Emma shook her head. "I could never get one made in two months. It would take me at least four to six months to complete a quilt—even a twin-size covering."

A desire to see her daughter doing something meaningful set in, and Dianna decided to say a few more things, which she hoped would encourage Emma to at least try.

"Do you have any quilting projects that you started during your time in Arthur and haven't finished? If so, I was thinking you could finish it for the contest."

Emma tapped her forehead a couple of times. "I did start a twin-size quilt top during the time I was taking lessons from Ivan's mother. Maybe if I work really hard, I could finish it in time for the quilting contest."

Dianna clapped her hands. "That's wunderbaar, Emma. What's the name of the pattern? Is it a beginner's patchwork quilt?"

"No, Mom. It's a very unusual pattern called the Tree of Life."

"Really? I've not heard of that one before. Can you show me what it looks like?"

"It's upstairs in my room, in the bottom of my suitcase. It's only partially finished, and I haven't even taken it out yet."

"You haven't emptied your suitcase since you've been home?"

"I took out my clothes, but decided to leave the quilt in there to keep it safe."

"Well, let's go see—should we, Emma?"

Emma set the cookbook aside and followed her mother out of the kitchen.

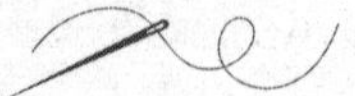

When Rachel got off work, she walked to the small café on the other side of town, where she'd promised to meet David today. She hadn't told her parents yet, or even Emma, but she and David had gotten back together a week ago. It hadn't been easy at first, but David managed to convince Rachel that he truly loved her and wanted them to spend the rest of their lives together. After declaring his love once again, David had said, "Why should we have to wait? I love you, and you love me, and there's no point in us waiting till next year to get married."

It was true—Rachel did love David with all her heart. They'd both agreed that their wedding should take place on the second Thursday of November. That was only two months away, so there was a lot to do in a very short time. Rachel could only hope that when David came to her house this evening to tell her parents about their plans, they would agree, and everything would go well.

Of course, she told herself as she picked up speed, *there's a good chance my parents won't be happy about it. I can only hope David and I can make them understand how much we love each other and want to be married as soon as possible.*

That evening after supper, a knock sounded on the front door. Rachel's heartbeat picked up speed. She felt sure it was David, so she raced to the door before anyone else could and pulled it open. Seeing that it was indeed David, Rachel invited him in.

"You didn't say anything to your parents yet, did you?" he whispered, leaning close to Rachel's ear.

"No, of course not. We said we were going to tell them together, and I kept true to my word."

David stole a kiss, which Rachel was perfectly fine with, since no one but the two of them were in the entryway right now.

When the kiss ended, Rachel clasped David's hand and said, "Let's go in the living room now. My parents are there, and so is Emma."

Rachel had to admit she was more than a little nervous, but having her husband-to-be by her side gave her the courage she needed. She found Mom and Dad in their favorite chairs. They were both reading a book, and Emma sat on the sofa with a piece of material and a good-sized quilting hoop in her lap. It was quiet enough in the room to hear a hairpin drop, and Rachel felt bad about disturbing them. But they needed to hear what she and David had to say.

Rachel was glad when David was the first to speak. "Mr. and Mrs. Bontrager, Rachel and I have something we want to tell you."

Dad's head jerked, and his book nearly tumbled out of his hands. "What are you doing here, David? The last time you were here looking for Rachel, I thought I told you—"

"I know what you said," David interrupted. "But I would appreciate it if you and Rachel's mother would at least hear what I have to say."

Dad leaned forward with both elbows on his knees. "I'm really not interested in anything you might want to say."

Rachel was pleased when Mom touched Dad's shoulder and said, "Philip, I think it would be good if we listened."

He shrugged his shoulder and grunted before saying, "Okay, but please be short about it because I had been enjoying the book I was reading, and I'd like to get back to it soon."

"This shouldn't take more than a few minutes," David stated.

Dad swatted the air with his hand and muttered, "Go ahead."

David looked at Rachel. "Do you want to tell them or should I?"

"You go ahead." Rachel glanced at her sister and noticed that Emma appeared to be absorbed in her project, because she never even looked their way. *Maybe it's for the best,* Rachel decided. *After all, what David has to say will be spoken to Mom and Dad and not Emma, who doesn't need to give her blessing.*

David cleared his throat a couple of times before he spoke. After wiping the sweat off his forehead, he blurted out, "I love Rachel, and she loves me."

Dad's lips moved, as if to say something, but David rushed on.

"As I said, Rachel and I love each other. And the thing is, we want to get married, and we'd like it to be on the second Thursday of November."

Rachel held her breath a few seconds, until Dad hollered, "You must be kidding, young man. In case you've forgotten—you hurt Rachel deeply when you dropped her and starting courting her best friend. Have you forgotten that?"

"No, sir, and I've apologized to Rachel and explained my reasons."

"Humph! I can think of no good reason for doing what you did!"

"Philip, please calm down," Mom said in a pleading voice. "Let's give David the benefit of the doubt and hear what else he has to say."

"Fine then. I'm listening." With brows lowered like a drawbridge, Dad folded his arms across his chest.

Rachel felt it might be her turn to speak up, and coming from her, she hoped Dad might be more understanding. "The thing is," she began slowly, "David and I have known each other since we were in school, and he courted me for two full years."

"Yeah, till he started seeing Alice." Dad's face reddened. "Admit it, Rachel. You were deeply hurt."

She nodded while clasping her hands. "I was, but David apologized, and I chose to forgive him. We've talked everything out, and we don't want to wait till next year to get married. We're both church members, and I really feel that—"

"We need to give them our blessing, Philip. No one stood in the way of us getting married. Remember?"

Rachel was ever so glad when Mom cut in. She inhaled more air into her lungs, hoping Dad would listen to what her mother had said. Fortunately, she didn't have to wait long.

"All right then, so be it," Dad said. "I think the two of you are making a mistake, but I won't stand in your way if you want to get married."

"Danki." David reached his hand out to Dad, and all tension in Rachel's body was released when her father clasped David's hand and gave it a shake.

"Treat her right," Dad said in a most serious tone.

David nodded. "I will. You can count on it."

Rachel studied Emma's pursed lips and noticed that there were tears in her sister's eyes. Were they happy tears or ones of envy because poor Emma had lost the love of her life? Rachel wished she could do or say something that would make her sister feel better, but that healing would take time, and perhaps even finding a new boyfriend who would treat Emma the way she deserved to be treated. Rachel hoped that would happen soon, because it broke her heart to know that her younger sister was pining for a love she could never have.

Chapter 31

"WHAT MADE YOU DECIDE ON the Tree of Life pattern?" Emma's mother asked as she looked over Emma's shoulder at the quilt she'd been working on for a good portion of the day in the sewing room.

"It's a vintage pattern," Emma stated, "and I'm attracted to old things. Plus, I think it's an unusual design with a very special name."

"Do you know the origin of the pattern or its name?" Mom questioned, pulling up an empty chair and taking a seat beside Emma.

"Jah, I do know. Ida Mae, my quilt teacher, said the pattern could be traced back as far as the early 1700s. Its symbolism and name dates all the way to the beginning of recorded history, based on the Tree of the Knowledge of Good and Evil in the Bible."

"So in some ways it has a biblical reference."

"It sure seems that way," Emma responded.

Emma's mother picked up one edge of the bed covering where no design was present. "This cotton material makes a nice lightweight bed covering for warmer weather and isn't so heavy like most traditional quilts."

"That's true," Emma agreed.

"Do you think you'll have it done in time to enter the quilting contest next month?"

Emma pursed her lips before responding. "I hope so, but if I don't finish in time to, I'll just hold on to it till next year."

"That would be an option, but if I were you, I'd work extra hard and try to finish it for this year's quilt contest." Mom eyed the quilt once more. "It's over halfway done, Emma, and I believe you could do it."

Emma paused her stitching for a bit, resting her needle on the sewing table and allowing her thoughts to stray to the upcoming contest. She hadn't felt at ease since returning home until she began stitching again, and now that the contest was motivating her to finish this project, she had something hopeful to strive for.

"I'll do my best, Mom," Emma said, "but if I spend too much time working on the quilt, I won't be available to help you around the house or in the yard as much."

Her mother waved a hand, as if in dismissal. "Don't worry about that, Emma. During the time you were at your grandparents' house and Rachel was at her job, I got along pretty well on my own. But if there are certain things I really need help with, I'll be sure to let you know."

"All right then," Emma said with gratitude, "I'll keep pushing and try extra hard to get the quilt done on time."

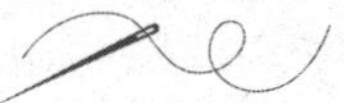

Dianna went outside to check on the bird feeders, feeling better about things where her youngest daughter was concerned. Sending Emma to her grandparents, even for a short time, had been a good decision because Emma had learned to quilt. It was good to see Emma immersed in something that would take her mind off the broken relationship with Ivan Yoder. Dianna saw this as the first step in Emma's emotional healing, and perhaps it would open the door for Emma to begin a new relationship with some other man when the time was right. Dianna certainly wanted that for her daughter. It would be a shame to see Emma pining indefinitely for a love she could never have.

Philip has always said I worry too much about our children, but ever since Betty left home, I've been overly protective with Rachel, and then again when Emma came along. Dianna paused her contemplations to open the first feeder and pour the birdseed in. *I can't help feeling that it was somehow my fault Betty moved away and didn't want to live near her friends and family anymore. Maybe I pushed too hard, trying to convince her that the Amish way of life was best for her—even pleading with Betty not to leave home or lose contact with her family.*

A bird flew in toward the feeder, nearly landing on Dianna's head. She gasped and jumped back, lifting her arms high in the air. "Whew! That was too close for comfort." She'd always enjoyed feeding the birds, but she didn't like it when they got too close or became aggressive. No doubt her fear was from some childhood trauma concerning a bird, but she refused to allow her mind to figure it out. After all, Dianna had better things to do today than worry about irrational fears—especially those that might stem from the past.

Turning from the feeder, which now had plenty of seeds, Dianna moved on to another one, closer to the house, and took care of filling that. Once all the feeders were filled, she headed back to the house.

When Dianna stepped onto the porch, she stood by the railing and inhaled the fragrant aroma of fall. The days were still warm enough to be outside, but the cool nights often brought frost come morning. Dianna chuckled as she enjoyed observing the flock of finches darting from feeder to feeder as if this might be their last meal.

When Dianna had seen enough, she reentered the house and made her way down the basement stairs to do some laundry. Seeing one of Rachel's dresses among the other clothes in the basket, her heart clenched. After Rachel married David, there would be an empty chair at the table during meals. Dianna would miss Rachel, but it looked like her and Philip's youngest daughter would continue living with them for a while yet—maybe even several more years—since she had no steady boyfriend and might never find one she would open her heart to. Dianna feared that the hurt of losing her first love might stick with Emma for the rest of her life, and then she would never consider marriage.

Arthur

Marlin took a spoonful of the bean-with-bacon soup Luellen had made. She didn't know what to think when he looked across the kitchen table at her and wrinkled his nose.

"What's wrong?" Luellen asked. "Is there something you don't like about your supp? Is it missing some ingredient?"

He gave a vigorous bob of his head. "I'll say! I can't taste any salt in this soup at all."

"Sorry about that. Ever since Emma went home, my mind hasn't been on cooking." She heaved a sigh. "Or much of anything else, for that matter. All I can think about is how sad she looked the day the driver came and picked her up for the trip to Shipshewana." Luellen placed a hand against her breastbone. "It nearly broke my heart to see her sadness."

"Mine as well." Marlin grabbed the salt shaker from the center of the table, shook some on his soup, and stirred it around. After taking another spoonful, he smiled and said, "That's much better. Maybe I should take over the cooking from now on."

Luellen rolled her eyes. "I think not, Husband. I know my way around the kitchen far better than you do."

"That's true," he admitted. "Even so, I'm thinkin' it might be a good idea if I do a taste test of everything while you're cooking. How's that sound?"

She shrugged. "It's up to you, but after a while, you'll likely get tired of following me around the kitchen while I prepare breakfast, lunch, and supper meals. If you did manage that, you'd most likely be worn out by the end of the day and need a nap after every meal."

"So what's wrong with that? At least then I'd know ahead of time if the food was up to my standards or not." Marlin patted his stomach and let loose with a belly laugh before going back to work on his bowl of soup.

Luellen smiled. From the first day she'd met him at a work frolic, she had enjoyed Marlin's good humor. He was also very direct and almost always said exactly how he felt about things, which wasn't a bad trait, unless it was stated harshly. Fortunately, that was normally not the case.

Luellen hadn't tried her bowl of soup yet, but she figured this might be the opportune moment to do so. After the first bite, she knew Marlin had been right—it did lack flavor and was in need of some salt. So she reached for the shaker and added a bit to her soup, and then they both sat quietly throughout the rest of their meal. Luellen had no idea what thoughts were in her husband's head while he finished eating, but her own contemplations were mostly focused on Emma and Rachel. She couldn't help wondering how they were both doing.

The smell of the bean soup still permeated the house as Luellen scrubbed the table after clearing their dishes and setting them in the sink. She glanced at the calendar while tidying up the kitchen. The days were growing shorter as fall weather set in, accompanied by cool gusts of wind and the change of the leaf colors. This was especially noticeable because nightfall was already so close. The gas lamps were almost ready to be lit so she and Marlin could spend the remainder of the evening together drinking steaming cups of tea and doing their devotions before bed.

Luellen looked forward to hiring a driver and making the trip to Shipshewana in November for Rachel's wedding. It would be good to see Dianna, Philip, and their two daughters again. And maybe—just maybe—Emma would make Luellen happy by saying that she had a new suitor.

"What are you up to?" Maggie asked when she wandered into Ivan's bedroom without knocking. As though Maggie had lived in this house her entire life, she stood near the threshold, leaning a hand against the doorframe. Lately, she'd been quite bold, and it had begun to unnerve Ivan. Especially today when he wanted—and needed—to be alone to get the job done that was set before him on his workbench.

"I'm working on a clock that needs to be repaired," he replied through tight lips. "That's why my door was closed." They weren't married yet, and even if they had been, Ivan thought it would have been nice if she'd knocked instead of just barging in. Apparently, since Ivan had agreed to marry Maggie, she thought she had the right to interrupt him whenever she felt like it. Would he have any privacy in the days following their wedding?

"Oh, sorry," she mumbled, coming fully into the room. "Guess I should have knocked first, huh?"

"Jah, that would have been appreciated. But you're here now, so is there something you need?"

Maggie shrugged her slim shoulders. "Not really, but Stephen's sleeping right now, so I thought the two of us could sit outside and enjoy the crisp air of fall while we get better acquainted." She moved closer to Ivan's worktable. "If we don't get to know each other more personally, we'll be like two strangers when we get married. That wouldn't be a good way to start our lives together as husband and wife."

Although his room wasn't overly warm, Ivan's forehead broke out in a sweat. The thought of becoming Maggie's husband filled him with dread. Yet it was a fact—he had agreed to marry her, and he couldn't take it back now. But how could he live the rest of his life with a woman he didn't love? There were times when Maggie spoke too loudly and more often than he liked, and that got on his nerves. It was especially irritating when Ivan tried to work on a clock and all he wanted was some peace and quiet so he could concentrate on the job at hand. It would be one thing if she sat in silence while he labored over his project, or perhaps showed some curiosity about his craft, but it was quite apparent that Maggie had no interest whatsoever.

"Did you hear what I said?" Maggie's high-pitched tone seemed even more shrill than usual. It was enough to put his teeth on edge.

"Yes, I heard you," Ivan responded, struggling not to let his irritation show.

"Then don't you agree that we need to spend more time together?"

"I suppose, but right now I'm busy, as you can certainly see." Ivan gestured to the clock he needed to work on. "This is a gift for someone's birthday, which is next week, so if I don't keep working, it won't get done on time."

Maggie's shoulders slumped, and her head lowered a bit. "Okay. Guess I'll find something else to do till Stephen wakes up." She turned and started for the door, but then paused and whirled around. "If you don't want to marry me, you may as well say it right now, so we don't have to take those boring classes to join the church. I'm sure you're dreading it as much as I am."

Ivan's mouth opened slightly, and at first, he couldn't get the proper words out. Then, as she stood staring at him with a blank expression, he finally spoke. "I'm not dreading the classes. I'm looking forward to joining the church."

"Really?" Maggie's eyes widened.

"Jah, and as a matter of fact, for the last year or so, I've been thinking about joining. Just never got around to it till now."

"I see." Maggie's lips pressed into a tight-looking grimace, but then her facial muscles relaxed and she said, "I really don't mind the thought of becoming a church member. It's just taking the classes I'm dreading."

He tipped his head. "Why is that?"

"As you know, our instruction classes will take place in a separate room during our Sunday church services."

Ivan merely gave a brief nod in response.

"And also," Maggie continued, "we'll have nine weeks of instructional classes to sit through."

"That's correct."

"What am I supposed to do with the baby during the time we're taking the classes?" she asked.

"I'm sure my mamm will hold him," Ivan replied while he twisted another tiny gear within the mechanism of the clock. "If not, then maybe one of my sisters will be happy to do it."

"Thanks for the suggestion." Maggie placed her hand on Ivan's shoulder and gave it a squeeze. "Your family has been so nice. I really appreciate the way they've opened this home to me and Stephen, welcoming us like we are one of the family."

Ivan's only response was a slow nod. He wished Maggie would leave the room so he could keep working on the clock. Didn't she realize how important getting this job done was to him?

In some ways Ivan felt sorry for Maggie. She seemed so needy, which could be because her mother and father had asked her to leave their home soon after the baby was born. It saddened Ivan to think that any parent would do that to their own flesh and blood. One would think they would have been willing to help Maggie raise their grandson.

Maggie gave his shoulder another squeeze and said, "I can take a hint, Ivan. I'll leave you alone to your clock repair. It's obviously more important to you than talking to me."

"Talking to you is important," he replied. Still crouched over his work desk, Ivan stretched his fingers, trying not to be too harsh with his choice of words. "Just not when I'm trying to work. Please try to understand that it's even more important to the person who will be getting it as a birthday present."

"Guess that makes sense. Sorry I bothered you," Maggie murmured, lowering her head and speaking more softly. "I'll leave you alone now and find something constructive to do." Before Ivan could form a response, she left, closing the door behind her, but it hadn't clicked, so it was still open a crack.

As Maggie's footsteps receded down the hallway, Ivan returned his focus to the clock between his palms. His aching fingers were smeared with oil from all the work he had done thus far. A part of Ivan wanted to exhale with relief that she had finally left him alone, but another part felt sorry for her, to the point that he almost set the clock aside to spend some time with her. The determination and need to get it done on time won over, however. After supper, Ivan would set some time aside and give Maggie and Stephen the attention they both needed. After all, it was the right thing to do.

Chapter 32

Emma could hardly sit still as she sat between her mother and sister, waiting to see whose name would be announced as the winner in each category of the quilting contest. She had worked so hard to get the quilt done on time, and at her mother's insistence, she'd spent eight to ten hours per day to finish the quilt. And the amazing thing was, Emma had submitted her entry in the nick of time.

She watched breathlessly as the three judges walked slowly around the area where each of the contestants' quilts had been displayed. There was a tangible sense of suspense in the air as the crowd and other competitors waited to hear the outcome soon to be announced. Emma couldn't make out what any of the judges were saying, but she saw their lips move and knew they were talking among themselves. There were numerous quilts for the judges to view, and Emma was convinced that most of them were more colorful and stitched better than hers. She felt sure that her Tree of Life quilt didn't stand a chance of winning in any category—not when it was up against so many lovely quilts that had been made in a variety of patterns and colors. She especially liked the Lone Star quilt pattern because she could relate to the feeling of being alone. Of course, she had her family around her, but Dad worked every day, and so did Rachel. Emma's mother kept busy as well. What really caused Emma to feel lonely was not being able to see Grandpa and Grandma every day.

Who am I kidding? Emma asked herself while taking in a shaky breath. *The biggest reason I can relate to the Lone Star pattern is because I have no promise of marriage, and probably never will.* She blinked, trying to keep tears from falling. This was no time to feel sorry for herself. Emma remembered the guidance that Ida Mae had offered during their quilting lessons. The kindly woman had once expressed to Emma that she'd come a long way in her quilting journey, and Emma knew it was true. But was it enough to earn a ribbon?

Emma closed her eyes and prayed silently. *Heavenly Father, I thank You for the opportunity to be part of this contest where there are so many beautiful, well-made quilts. Whether my Tree of Life quilt wins or not, I'm thankful for the joy of being able to lose myself in quilting.*

Emma's prayer ended when she heard her name called. Her eyes snapped open, and she pinned her focus back on the judges.

"They called your name, Emma," Mom said with a gentle nudge. "They want you to go up front to receive your award."

"Award? I won an award?"

"Jah, Emma," Rachel whispered in Emma's ear. "The judges are waiting for you."

Emma gave a small intake of breath and stood. On shaky legs, she made her way to the front of the room, where the three women judges stood. One of them handed Emma a blue ribbon along with a twenty-dollar bill. "This is for you, Emma Bontrager. You're the top winner in our vintage quilt pattern division." She shook Emma's free hand. "Congratulations on a job well done."

Emma was so surprised and nervous that she could barely get the words out. "Th–thank you."

A round of applause went up around the room, and Emma's cheeks warmed. This was the first time she'd ever won anything, and the fact that she'd received a prize for a quilt she'd worked so hard to finish made every stitch worthwhile.

I need to write Grandma and Grandpa about this. I'm sure they'll be pleased, Emma thought as she returned to her seat, clutching her well-earned ribbon and cash. *I'll ask Grandma to let Ida Mae know too. After all, it's her I have to thank for teaching me how to quilt.*

Thoughts of Ida Mae caused Emma to think about Ivan. *I hope he's happy and doing okay. I know it's not right to think this way, but I wonder if he ever misses me.* A lump formed in her throat, and she swallowed against it. *Try as I may not to, I still miss him.* Emma glanced at the blue ribbon and bill in her hand. As happy as it made her to have won this prize, in no way did it compare to the joy Emma used to feel when Ivan held her hand.

Once again, Emma reminded herself that she needed to stop thinking about Ivan and what they'd once had. She folded the prize money and tucked it and the ribbon into her handbag. Today should be a day of celebration, and Emma realized that in order to appreciate her achievement, she needed to move on with her life. By now, or at least soon, Ivan would be a married man, and his wife would become the recipient of his love.

Arthur

Since there were fewer customers at this time of day, Ida Mae decided it would be a good idea to leave the front counter of the fabric store and browse through her inventory. As she halted her steps near a shelf lined with bolts of fabric, Ida Mae's hand hovered over them. Somehow, it reminded her of Emma in her sewing room, learning how to piece together a quilt. She wondered if Emma had continued to work on the quilt she had begun while she was in Arthur. Ida Mae hoped so, and perhaps someday, Emma would show her the finished quilt with the Tree of Life pattern.

Emma had initially known very little about quilting, but this wasn't due to a lack of interest in the craft, and Ida Mae had sensed that the young woman lacked confidence in her ability to quilt. Ida Mae had made sure to teach Emma everything she needed to know to branch off on her own someday. Emma was almost like another daughter to Ida Mae, and although Emma was reserved, she'd opened up and shown what a truly sweet person she was.

Maggie, on the other hand, didn't seem to show much interest in the quilts Ida Mae had made. She'd turned down Ida Mae's repeated attempts to establish a relationship with her future daughter-in-law, including invitations to lunch and sipping iced tea on the porch. Ida Mae figured it was because Maggie needed to concentrate on caring for her son.

Hopefully with time, Maggie will feel more comfortable around our family. Regardless, I'm worried about Ivan, Ida Mae thought as she walked along the aisles of fabric. *He's so quiet most of the time—not the fun-loving young man he used to be.*

Everything was in order after sorting the fabrics and filling empty shelves with stock from the back of the store, so Ida Mae made her way back to the counter and settled on the stool, craning her neck toward the window. The afternoon sunlight seeped in, revealing a layer of dust on the windowsill. Despite her desire to get up and wipe it away, Ida Mae remained seated, allowing herself to think about her son and his relationship with a young woman he hardly connected with at all.

Ida Mae was certain that Ivan had no love for Maggie and was only marrying her to do the right thing and provide for the baby. But what kind of life would this couple have together when there was no love? Would it be a marriage of convenience only, or might Ivan eventually develop strong feelings for his wife? Oh, she hoped that would be the case, because a loveless marriage would be difficult for both her son and his wife. Even their child could be affected by the lack of love between the parents. She wished there was something she could do to make things better, but at this point, she could think of nothing except continuing to be supportive, help with the baby, and pray for the young couple.

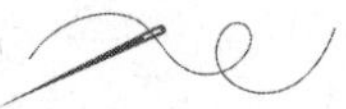

"Ivan, are you coming or not?" Papa shouted from the front entrance of the harness shop. "John Lapp's here waiting for the harness he brought in for repairs two weeks ago."

"I'll be right out with it," Ivan hollered in return. He scrambled to locate the harness in question, not sure which shelf it had been placed upon. If Ivan didn't locate John's harness soon, his father would probably come back here and get the item himself. Of course, once John left the shop, Ivan would no doubt receive a lecture from Papa.

Ivan kept looking, while thinking how bored he was with this job. He was eager to get off work for the day so he could go home and relax a few minutes before supper was served. Oh, how Ivan wished he had more customers bringing him clocks to repair so he could quit working for his dad here in the harness shop. If he could strike out on his own, he wouldn't have a boss looking over his shoulder all the time, telling him what to do, the way Papa often did. Ivan would also be doing work that he enjoyed.

"Ivan, we're still waiting!"

"And I'm still looking," Ivan muttered under his breath.

After getting down on his knees, he finally stumbled on John's harness, which had been on the bottom shelf. Ivan grabbed the finished harness and stood, just as Papa opened the door separating the workshop from the front part of the shop. "Did ya find it or not?" he questioned, poking his head in past the open door.

"Jah." Ivan held up the refurbished harness. "Do you want me to bring it out?"

"Of course," Papa responded. "That's what I'd asked you to do, right?"

Ivan gave a nod and quickly carried the harness into the other room, placing it on the front counter.

"Danki." John Lapp looked over at Ivan's father when he spoke. "It looks real good—like brand new, in fact. You did a fine job."

"You're welcome. I'm glad you're satisfied with it," Papa said.

Ivan figured since his father had done part of the work on the harness, he was entitled to take the credit for it. Ivan didn't need any praise for his part of the work. Besides, being boastful or proud was considered hochmut. Ivan always tried to be humble, and today was no exception. Even so, Ivan wished his father would give him a little credit once in a while. It would be nice to be appreciated for the work he did here.

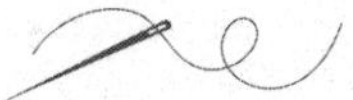

When Ivan arrived home that afternoon, the sound that greeted him was a baby's piercing wail. Apparently, something was going on that little Stephen didn't like.

He probably has a wet diaper, Ivan decided. *Either that, or it's time for the little fellow to eat.*

Ivan approached the living room, where Maggie sat thumbing through the pages of a magazine. Stephen wasn't with her, so Ivan assumed the baby was in the guest room, in the crib that used to be Ivan's when he was a baby. Mama had seemed pleased when Papa brought it out of the basement shortly after Maggie and Stephen moved into their home. For a moment, Ivan wondered why Maggie didn't seem to be bothered about the commotion coming from the guest room, but he opted not to dwell on that for too long. He couldn't allow the baby's crying to continue, however.

Without saying anything to Maggie, Ivan headed for the guest room. He found the red-faced, squalling baby kicking his arms and feet.

"Poor little guy." Ivan leaned over and gingerly picked the infant up, hoping it might quell the infant's cries. "What seems to be the problem? Are you hungerich, or do you need your *windel* changed?"

"Our son doesn't need to be fed or have his diaper changed. Those were both done thirty minutes ago."

Ivan looked over his shoulder where Maggie now stood. "Then why is he crying?"

"He wants to be held."

"How come you're not holding him?"

"I wanted some time to myself." Maggie's shoulders pushed back, displaying a firm posture. "Besides, it's good for a baby to cry once in a while. Stephen gets too much attention, and he will expect to be held all the time if you rush in and pick him up when he becomes fussy."

"I'd say he's a little more than fussy." Ivan gently patted the baby's back and smiled when the little guy calmed down and stopped crying.

"See what I mean?" With her eyes squinted, Maggie pointed at

Ivan. "You picked him up. He quit crying."

"Exactly. And I don't see anything wrong with me holding him right now." Ivan didn't know a lot about babies, but one thing he did know was that they needed plenty of love and attention. No child wanted to feel abandoned.

"Okay, do whatever you like, but if Stephen becomes spoiled, we'll both have to deal with it."

"I'll take my chances," Ivan said. "Why don't you go back to the living room and relax? I'll stay here with the baby for a while."

"Okay."

After Maggie left the room, Ivan took a seat in the rocking chair and cradled the baby in his arms. He figured if his mother wasn't working at the fabric store today, she'd probably be here right now, trying to settle her grandson down. But since Mama wasn't available and Maggie didn't seem to care, Ivan would take on the responsibility, like any good father should.

When Ivan got the rocking chair moving slowly, Stephen's body relaxed, and he soon fell asleep.

Ivan studied his son's features. Except for having the same color eyes as Ivan's, the infant's face looked more like his mother's. Ivan leaned forward and nuzzled the baby's nose. "That's okay, little Stephen," he whispered. "It doesn't matter who you resemble. Someday you'll grow up to be a big boy, and later a man. Then, you could very well grow tall like me and maybe even carry more of my physical traits than you do your mother's."

As Ivan continued to rock, he began to feel drowsy, but when he closed his eyes, instead of sleep, troubling thoughts about his bride-to-be took over. For the last four weeks, he and Maggie had been taking classes, along with six other young people in their church district who planned to join the church. Everyone else seemed attentive, but not Maggie. She yawned and looked around a lot like she was bored with the things being taught. Ivan, on the other hand, was interested in everything they were told. He was excited about getting baptized and joining the church. He only wished the wedding that would follow a few weeks after their last class could be with Emma and not Maggie.

Just stop it! Ivan told himself. *I should not continue to think about Emma—especially with me on the brink of marrying another woman—the mother of my child.*

Ivan had made every effort to bond with the baby, which had been difficult because he hadn't been there when Stephen was born and didn't even know of his son's existence until a few months ago.

Ivan opened his eyes and stared at the sleeping baby. *I believe I'm doing a fairly good job of bonding with my child right now, but unfortunately, I have yet to make a strong connection with Maggie, and maybe I never will.*

Ivan grimaced. *If I never fall in love with my wife, then what? If I were to back out of this marriage, Maggie and Stephen would have no place to go, and I'd be avoiding my responsibility as Stephen's father.*

Ivan set his jaw with determination. *I must come to terms with the fact that this is my future and it is the best way for me to rectify the wrong I committed that night at Toby's party. I will marry Maggie and fulfill the duty I owe to my wife and our son.*

Chapter 33

Arthur

While Emma sat beside Rachel, as one of her witnesses, her scattered thoughts went everyplace except where they should be. This was her sister's wedding day, but all Emma could think about was Ivan and how she wished it was her getting married to him today. If Maggie hadn't shown up when she had, Ivan and Emma might be the ones sitting here listening to the bishop quote scriptures about marriage and preach on the importance and duties of husbands and wives.

But that's never going to happen, Emma told herself. *I need to accept that fact and move on with my life, just as Ivan is doing.*

Emma pulled her thoughts aside and focused on the groom and his two witnesses sitting in chairs across from the bride and her witnesses. David kept rubbing his hands down the sides of his pant legs. Emma figured he must be nervous. Rachel was too. Earlier this morning before the service began, she had expressed her feelings to her sister. Emma felt sure that the bride's and groom's nervousness wasn't because they had second thoughts about getting married. Instead, they were both apprehensive about sitting here so long with all eyes upon them.

That would make me naerfich too, Emma thought. *I'd be a nervous wreck.*

Her mind wandered some more, and she reflected on the young people's singing that had taken place in their church district last week. It was Rachel and David's last night to attend the event as an unmarried couple. Rachel had tried to get Emma to join them. But Emma had stubbornly refused to go. At least that's what their mother had called it. Emma thought it was just plain good sense, since she wasn't comfortable socializing with so many already-paired couples. And none of the single fellows appealed to her at all, so there was no point in going to a singing with the hope of finding a young man she might actually like well enough to begin courting. Maybe one of these days she would attend a singing, just to keep the peace at home, so Mom and Rachel would stop pestering her about it. And if by some chance she found someone in attendance appealing, and if he offered to give her a ride home in his courting buggy, Emma might be glad that she'd agreed to go. Although it was doubtful that anyone would affect her the way Ivan had in the short time she'd known him. Even so, what harm would there be in at least giving some nice-looking young fellow a chance?

Emma chanced a peek at the woman's side of the room and spotted her grandmother. How thankful she was that Grandma and Grandpa had hired a driver to bring them here to attend Rachel and David's wedding. The wonder of today wouldn't seem the same without them here, celebrating with the rest of the family. They had arrived last evening, and Emma had presented her grandmother with not one but four lovely pot holders that she'd quilted. Grandma had said she appreciated the time it took for Emma to make the hot pads. Emma appreciated the praise she'd received. However, she would not allow herself to feel pride regarding the talent God had given her.

When the bishop called David and Rachel to leave their chairs and stand before him to respond to his questions, Emma's private thoughts ended, and she gave her full attention to this important part of the ceremony.

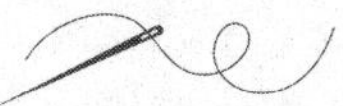

Rachel was so excited to become David's wife, she could hardly contain herself. Yet, filled with anticipation, she forced herself to stand straight and tall, ignoring her sweaty palms and racing heart. At the conclusion of the wedding ceremony and dinner that would follow, she and David would begin establishing their own life, with their own home and future family to look forward to.

Rachel's attention was drawn to the bishop's strong words as he looked at her and David and spoke with the presence of authority. "Can you both confess and believe that God has ordained marriage to be a union between one man and one wife, and do you also have the confidence that you are approaching marriage in accordance with the way you have been taught?"

David and Rachel each replied affirmatively.

The bishop turned to David then, and he asked, "Do you also have confidence, brother, that the Lord has provided this, our sister, as a marriage partner for you?"

David's head bobbed as he said, "Yes."

Next, Rachel was asked, "Do you have confidence, sister, that the Lord has provided this, our brother, as a marriage partner for you?"

With no hesitation, she responded, "Yes."

The bishop then asked David another question. "Do you also promise your wife that if she should, in bodily weakness, sickness, or any similar circumstances, need your help, that you will care for her as is fitting for a Christian husband?"

David, glancing briefly at Rachel, said, "Yes."

The bishop turned to Rachel again. "Do you promise your husband the same thing, that if he should, in bodily weakness, sickness, or any similar circumstances, need your help, that you will care for him as is fitting for a Christian wife?"

"Yes," she responded.

The next question he asked both of them. "Do you promise together that you will, with love, forbearance, and patience, live with each other and not part from each other until God will separate you in death?"

In unison, David and Rachel replied together, "Yes."

The bishop bowed his head and prayed, and following the prayer, he took the bride's hand and placed it in her husband's hand. As he did so, and while clasping both of their hands in his, he said, "The God of Abraham, and the God of Isaac, and the God of Jacob be with you and help you together and give His blessings richly unto you, and this through Jesus Christ, Amen."

As David and Rachel returned to their seats, now officially husband and wife, Rachel thanked the Lord silently for David, the only man she'd ever wanted to marry. She marveled at the fact that they were now one in God's sight.

During the evening meal served especially for the young people, Nathan Byler, one of David's witnesses, who was also his cousin, left his seat and came straight up to Emma. With a light tap to her shoulder, he asked an unexpected question. "I was wondering if it would be okay if I could come to your parents' house one night next week. Would that be all right with you, Emma?"

"Wh–what for?" Emma stammered, blushing and feeling rather foolish for almost choking on her water.

"I would like very much to pay a call on you." The charming young man grinned at her. "That is, unless you're already seeing some other fellow."

Taken aback, Emma shifted on the chair with her mouth agape, unable to form a reply. She certainly hadn't expected this tall, blond-haired Amish man to pose such a question—especially here in front of all these people. She hoped most of those sitting at the tables in this room were too busy eating and talking to have heard what Nathan said to her. The fact that David's cousin, visiting here from Paradise, Pennsylvania, wanted to pay a call on Emma made it even more surprising. If Nathan planned to return to his home in Pennsylvania, why was he asking to call on an Indiana girl? Could Nathan be looking for a wife, and did he hope to find one here who'd be willing to leave her home state and move to Paradise, Pennsylvania? Was that what Nathan had on his mind? If so, then he could forget about Emma, for she was content to live right here in Shipshewana and didn't have any plans to move.

Of course, Emma thought, *if things had worked out well for Ivan and me, and he'd asked me to move to Arthur, Illinois, to be his wife, I'd have said yes with no hesitation. I'm sure Ivan would've done the same for me, wouldn't he?*

Nathan remained near Emma's chair with his head tipped slightly to one side. No doubt he was waiting for her response, which she simply wasn't able to give at the moment.

Suddenly, Rachel got up from her chair at the corner table, called the *eck*, walked straight over to where Emma sat, and whispered in Emma's ear, "Say yes, Sister. Tell Nathan that you'd be happy to have him pay a call on you one evening next week."

Emma's face radiated with heat. Rachel's words were an embarrassment to her, and she hoped her sister had spoken quietly enough that Nathan, or anyone else, hadn't heard what was said.

The bold young man didn't appear to have heard, as he continued to stand quietly with his arms folded, a few feet from where Emma sat with the other witnesses. Emma's mind raced with a slew of questions as she attempted to take in everything, while her eyes darted back and forth between the other young people chatting among themselves. What would her parents think of this young man arriving at their doorstep? Would they be thrilled for Emma, or would Mom and Dad agree that this was all too soon for her? Her sister surely wasn't opposed to the idea of Nathan taking an interest in Emma.

At least he seems to be a patient person, Emma told herself. *That's a good virtue. I suppose it wouldn't hurt to let him come calling. At least we could get to know each other, and it would give me a chance to find out why he chose me to call upon. And maybe, if I ask the right questions, I can learn whether he is looking for a future wife who'd be willing to move to his home state.*

Drawing from her inner strength, Emma looked up at him, smiled, and said, "One night next week would be fine for you to visit me, Nathan. Which evening would be best for you?"

"I was thinking Friday. Would that work okay for you, Emma?" he asked as a grin spread across his clean-shaven face.

"Jah, Friday would be fine."

"Good. I'll get your address from David and come around seven. See you then, Emma." With that, Nathan went on back to his seat.

Emma sat staring at her unfinished plate of food. There was no point in finishing off the morsels she'd left behind since they were now cold and her nerves stifled her appetite. Although she did not feel ready to begin a new relationship, the fact that someone wanted to court her was a pleasant thought. It didn't have to be a serious relationship either. A few casual dates with the young man might be refreshing. It could even be the first step Emma needed to take to fully move forward with her life.

And who knows? Emma mused. *Even though I can't see into the future, Nathan might be the man God has in mind for me.* She inhaled deeply. *At least it's worth finding out.*

Arthur

"You doin' okay, Son?" Ivan's father questioned as he and Ivan did their evening chores in the barn after supper.

Ivan rubbed the bridge of his nose while slowly shaking his head. "I'm all right, Papa. Just mied is all."

"Are you sure? Your furrowed brows and rounded shoulders make me think it's more than just feeling tired. Seems like you've got a lot on your mind."

Ivan dragged the toe of his boot through the straw beneath his feet. "Jah, I guess so. Why do you ask?"

"You haven't been yourself here lately, and with your wedding coming up in a few weeks, I figured you'd be more joyous." Papa dumped some oats into his horse's feeding trough. "I was pretty excited when your mamm's and my wedding day was getting close."

Ivan swallowed hard, but the wad of phlegm in his throat wouldn't ease up. He wasn't sure how to respond. Ivan tried not to look on his and Maggie's upcoming wedding event with dread, but he couldn't find it within himself to get excited about marrying her. Ivan always tried to be kind to Maggie, but she often got on his nerves.

He stopped what he'd been doing here in the barn and wondered if he should tell his father that he dreaded the thought of marrying Maggie. Or would it be better if he simply remained quiet about it?

Truthfully, it surprised Ivan that Papa had even noticed something was wrong. Normally, he was preoccupied with work at the harness shop and other things here at home, and he didn't seem to pay any mind to what else was going on around him.

"Guess I am a little naerfich," Ivan finally admitted, after clearing his throat. "Nervous and concerned that I won't be a good husband and father."

"You mean because you're not in love with the woman you're on the verge of marrying?"

That question caught Ivan off guard. Apparently, Papa was more perceptive than he'd ever realized. "Jah," Ivan said with a nod.

"So you're going to follow through with it because you believe it's the right thing to do?"

Ivan nodded again. "Don't you?"

His father squinted as he tugged on his lower lip. "I suppose, but it's not fair to you."

"Life isn't fair sometimes, is it?"

"No, Son, it's not. But here's some food for thought." Papa paused a few seconds, pulling his fingers through the ends of his full beard. "There's always time for you to reconsider what's the best for you. Maybe you oughta think about it a little more before you jump into a loveless marriage."

"I have thought about it," Ivan said. "If only Maggie and I were involved, that would be one thing, but I have to think about our son, and what kind of a life he would have if I turned my back on him. Does that make sense?"

Papa draped his arm around Ivan's shoulder. "Jah, and I see your point, but maybe there's some other way."

Ivan gave a vigorous shake of his head. "There is no other way, and I've made up my mind. I'm gonna marry Maggie on the last Sunday of November, following our regular church service, just like we've planned."

"Okay then, if you're sure, but remember, Ivan, I'm here for you if ever you need a listening ear."

"Danki, Papa. I'm gonna make the best of the situation I caused by my lack of good sense the night of Toby's party, but knowing that you're here for me really helps. And I'll also need a lot of prayer," Ivan added. "I already know it won't get much easier once we're married."

His father pointed upward where the remainder of the outside light filtered through the gaps in the barn's roof. "You've got it, and I'm sure your mamm will be praying too."

"Are you feeling naerfich about your upcoming wedding?" Ida Mae asked as she and Maggie did the supper dishes.

Maggie gave a quick shake of her head. "No, I'm not nervous."

"Not even a little? Marriage is a big step, you know," Ida Mae commented. "And most brides and grooms usually feel a bit of apprehension as their wedding day approaches."

"I can't speak for Ivan," Maggie said, "but I'm filled with excitement about becoming his fraa."

Ida Mae reached for a dish and placed it in the sudsy tub of water to wash. "Will your parents or any other family members be coming to the wedding?"

"It's not likely, since I didn't invite them." Maggie grabbed a glass to dry.

"Why not?"

"Because they kicked me and Stephen out of their house."

"I'm aware of that, Maggie, but perhaps if they knew that you're settling down and getting married, it might make a difference in your relationship with them."

Maggie's lips pressed together as she gave a firm shake of her head. The silence hung between them as the young woman's concentration seemed to be on using a clean towel to dry off another plate. Then, with a voice above a whisper, Maggie said, "I don't think I could ever thank you enough for taking me and my son in. I want to do what's best for Stephen, and—well, from what I've seen from Ivan, I know he'll be a good father to him."

Glancing over at Maggie, Ida Mae couldn't even begin to fathom what it must be like to be completely cut off from one's own family. Ida Mae's heart went out to this young woman, who obviously felt unloved by her parents. On the other hand, maybe Maggie had done or said some things to someone in her family that put a big wedge between them. Given how much this girl had previously gone through, was it improper of Ida Mae to consider that as a possibility?

Ida Mae remembered the day Maggie, with babe in arms, had arrived on their doorstep. The young woman's shoulders drooped, and her eyes held no sparkle. It had been obvious that Maggie needed someone to care for both her and the baby. Ida Mae and the rest of their family had done just that. Ivan had obviously been in a state of shock, learning that he'd fathered a child he'd previously known nothing about. But he'd set his feelings for Emma aside and done the right thing by Maggie and Stephen. Ida Mae felt bad that her son had been forced to give up the woman he truly loved to do the right thing, but at the same time, she was pleased that he had stepped up and taken responsibility.

Her only concern now was how things would turn out once Ivan and Maggie were married. She asked herself once again if Ivan could learn to love and cherish his wife and if there would be more children down the road. Or would her son simply go through the motions of being a husband and father, and never truly know the beautiful love between a husband and wife?

Chapter 34

Shipshewana

Friday evening, although there was a bit of a chill in the house, Emma broke out in a sweat when she looked at the clock and saw that it was a quarter to seven. In just fifteen minutes, if he was true to his word, Nathan would most likely show up. In some ways, Emma hoped he wouldn't come, but in another way, the idea of being courted again was kind of exciting. It meant that a good-looking young man was interested in her.

But for what reason? she asked herself. *Is this just a social call, or is Nathan looking for the possibility of choosing a wife? If so, why did he choose me to call upon?* Emma continued to stare at the clock. *Maybe David's cousin has a list of potential prospects, and he plans to make calls on each of those young women until he finds the right one.*

Emma didn't know why she was thinking such thoughts. It was ridiculous to speculate on something she had no knowledge of at all. Wouldn't it be better to wait and see how things went with Nathan this evening?

"Why are you staring at the clock?"

Emma turned at the sound of her mother's voice. "I wanted to see what time it was."

"It's getting close to seven," Mom said, slipping an arm around Emma's waist. "I imagine your suitor will be showing up soon."

"Nathan's not really a suitor, Mom. He's just coming to make a call on me."

"There must be an interest on his part, or he wouldn't have asked you if he could come here this evening," Mom stated.

Emma sighed. "I still don't understand why he wants to spend time with me. Nathan lives in Pennsylvania, and I'm sure he plans to go back there soon. As far as I know, the only reason he came to Indiana was to be David's witness."

"Maybe Nathan is thinking about moving here," Mom suggested. "Or he might be staying awhile to visit with David or some of his family members."

"I suppose that's possible, but. . ." Emma stopped talking when she heard the *clippity-clop* of a horse's hooves coming up the driveway. She clung to her mother's arm. "Oh no. He's here."

"Settle down and try to relax." Mom patted Emma's hand. "Would you like to answer the door, or would you prefer that either I or your father does it?"

Emma didn't think it would be a good idea if Dad answered the door. He'd probably ply Nathan with all sorts of questions. On the other hand, if Emma's mother greeted Nathan at the door, she might be apt to invite him right into the kitchen, where Emma stood, trembling inwardly, like a willow tree during a brisk windstorm.

Emma drew in a quick breath and held her head high. Surely it couldn't be that difficult to greet the young man that would soon be at their door.

"I'll greet Nathan at the door," Emma told her mother. "After all, it's me he came to see, and I don't want to disappoint him by hiding out here in the kitchen."

Mom offered Emma a broad smile. "Good for you, Emma dear. That's the polite thing to do."

Emma left the kitchen and waited in the hall until she heard footsteps on the porch stairs. When Nathan's knock came a few seconds later, she opened the door.

There stood Nathan, wearing a pleasant smile and holding a box of chocolates. "Good evening, Emma." He held the candy out to her. "These are for you."

"Danki." Emma clasped the box tightly and offered him a smile that she hoped looked sincere. "Please come in, Nathan."

When he stepped inside and closed the door, she offered to take his coat. After hanging it on a wall peg, Emma suggested they go to the living room to visit with her parents, and she led the way.

Mom and Dad were seated in their favorite chairs, which left the sofa for Emma and Nathan. Emma took a seat there while Nathan greeted her parents with a handshake.

"It's nice to see you both again," he said. "We didn't get to visit much at the wedding, so I'm glad for the opportunity to be here this evening and have the chance to get to know you both better."

Emma felt a sense of relief knowing that Nathan hadn't come here just to spend time with her but that he wanted to get to know her parents too. Maybe he didn't have marriage on his mind. Perhaps he'd gotten bored staying at David's parents' house this week and wanted to visit with David's in-laws.

But then at the evening wedding meal, Nathan did say he wanted to pay a call on me, Emma reminded herself.

After Nathan greeted Emma's parents, he wandered over to the sofa and plunked down next to her. In fact, he was so close, his hand brushed Emma's arm when he reached up to pull his fingers through the back of his thick hair.

Emma was glad when Nathan directed a fair amount of his conversation to her father. Dad seemed eager to talk to the young man, so Emma mostly sat, fooling with the ties on her head covering. She made an effort to calm herself by affirming that this was just a casual visit and nothing more.

When the conversation lulled, Mom rose from her chair and asked Emma if she would join her in the kitchen to prepare some refreshments. Emma didn't have to be asked twice, and she was immediately on her feet and heading down the hall to the kitchen.

"Nathan seems like a nice young man," Mom said quietly. "I'm glad he came over tonight so we could get to know him."

Emma's only reply was a brief nod as she opened the box of chocolates and placed some on the platter beside the pumpkin cookies she and her mother had made earlier today.

"You were pretty quiet in the living room, Emma."

"I couldn't think of much to contribute to the conversation," Emma replied. "Besides, the things Dad and Nathan talked about didn't really interest me."

"Maybe we will eat our refreshments and play a game. Nathan might have more to say to you then."

Emma shrugged. "We'll see how it goes."

"It sounded like Nathan enjoys his job at the shoe store his father owns."

Once more, Emma only nodded in response to her mother's statement. While Nathan seemed nice enough, Emma wasn't sure she could ever have deep feelings for him—at least not the way she felt about Ivan. But Emma decided that it would only be right to give Nathan a chance. After all, Emma wasn't too sure about Ivan either when they'd first met.

Arthur

When Ivan entered the kitchen Saturday morning, he was surprised to see his mother making breakfast by herself. Normally, Maggie would be here with her, either holding the fussy baby or, if Stephen was still asleep, helping his mother with breakfast.

"Where's Maggie?" Ivan asked, approaching the stove, where Mama stood stirring a pot of oatmeal.

"She's in bed with a koppweh, and the baby's still asleep." Mama offered Ivan a weary-looking smile. "If Maggie's headache doesn't improve, someone will need to care for Stephen."

"Would you like me to ask Papa if I can have the day off so I can stay here and help out?" Ivan offered.

She shook her head. "You're needed at the harness shop. Maybe

Maggie will feel better soon and be out of bed. If not, I'll see if one of your sisters might be free to take care of the baby, since I'm supposed to work at the fabric store today. If neither of them is available, then I'll stay home."

Ivan put his hand on his mother's shoulder. "I'm sorry for bringing all this extra work on you, Mama. Between your work at the fabric store and everything you do around here, you're busy enough, but now, with Maggie and the baby living here, there are even more things taking up your time."

"It's all right, Son. You're dealing with a lot right now, and I want to help however I can."

Ivan gave her a hug. "Danki, Mama. I'm pretty stressed out right now, and it helps to know that I have your support."

Ivan let his mind wander as he poured himself a cup of coffee. He pulled his fingers down the side of his face as the anxiety about the upcoming wedding took over yet again. Despite Ivan's best efforts to remain optimistic, he couldn't get rid of the weight he felt in his chest, always questioning whether he was doing the right thing going through with the plan to marry Maggie.

"Is there something more you would like to say?" his mother asked.

"I was just thinking about the wedding, is all, and hoping everything goes okay for me and Maggie."

"You mean the day of the ceremony, or afterward?"

"I'm not too concerned about the wedding itself, since it will be a smaller gathering than most." Ivan swished a sip of coffee around in his mouth before swallowing it.

"That's true," Mama acknowledged. "Maggie doesn't know many people from our church district, and her parents and other family members aren't likely to come, so it will only be those you have invited from among your friends and people you know well who will stay for the wedding ceremony after the main church service. And don't forget," she added, "there will only be one meal after the wedding service, which will make things a little less stressful for everyone involved."

For everyone but me. Ivan kept his thoughts to himself. There was no point discussing his lack of love for a woman he barely knew. Mama already knew, but that didn't change a thing. The fact was, and Ivan had come to grips with it, there was a price to pay for everything a person did that was wrong in God's eyes. Ivan was prepared to make the best of the hand he'd dealt for himself that night at Toby's party.

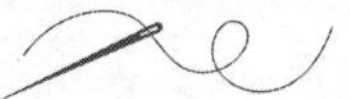

"Say, Ivan, I have a favor to ask of you," Papa said when Ivan entered the harness shop that morning.

"What do you need?"

"Could you please hire a driver and take a harness to one of my customers in Arcola, since he hasn't been by yet to pick it up? Oh, and while you're there, feel free to go someplace for your noon meal before heading back to the shop."

"Okay, sure. I can do that. I'll go over to the non-Amish family down the road a piece and ask if I can borrow their phone to make the call."

"Thanks, Ivan. I appreciate it. I'd do it myself, but there's a lot of work stacked up in my shop, and I'd like to try and get caught up if possible."

"No problem, Papa. I'll go now and see about getting a ride to Arcola." With no hesitation, Ivan grabbed his jacket and headed out the front door.

One good thing that had come from his unexpected relationship with Maggie was that his father had recently begun treating him with kindness and a lot more patience and understanding. At least Ivan had that in his favor.

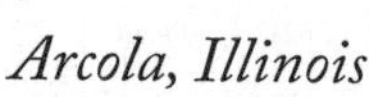

Arcola, Illinois

After Ivan delivered the harness, he stopped at the Hen House Restaurant for something to eat while waiting for his driver, Sam, to pick him up. Sam had some errands of his own to run and said he'd meet up with Ivan here at the restaurant.

Ivan had barely taken a seat when he spotted someone coming

through the front door whom he hadn't seen for nearly a year. It was his old friend, Toby Schrock.

When Toby spotted Ivan, he waved and sauntered over to his table. "Well, well, I haven't seen you in a while. Not since the night of my party." He took the chair beside Ivan and thumped his back. "I'll bet you don't remember much about that party, though, do ya? You were pretty wasted."

Ivan lifted his gaze to the ceiling. "Don't remind me. I was a fool and did something I never had before."

"You mean drinking too much alcohol?"

"Jah, that was wrong, and so was sleeping with a young woman I didn't even know." Ivan kept his voice down, in case anyone in the restaurant might be listening to their conversation.

Toby bobbed his head. "A lot of that goes on at some of the wild parties."

"Well, I'm paying for my sins now."

"How so?"

In a tone just above a whisper, Ivan told his friend how Maggie had showed up at his house a few months ago with a baby and announced that Ivan was the child's father.

Toby blinked in succession. "Are you serious?"

"Absolutely. So I did the only thing I thought was right and agreed to marry Maggie. Our wedding's just a few weeks away."

Toby took hold of Ivan's arm and gave it a shake. "Hold on a minute. Are you talking about Maggie Hertzler?"

"That's right."

"That's sure odd, Ivan. I never saw you and Maggie together that evening."

"You didn't?"

"No way! She hung around Oba Miller all night. And as I recall—they left the party early—together."

Ivan's mouth went dry, and he picked up his glass of water and took a hefty drink. "I've gotta go, Toby. It was nice seeing you again." He got up and rushed out the door, nearly bumping into his driver. "Sorry, Sam, but I don't have time to eat lunch. I need to get home right away."

Arthur

Sam had barely pulled into Ivan's parents' yard when Ivan stuck his hand in his pocket, withdrew the money he owed for the ride, and handed it to Sam. Then, forgetting to say "thanks for the ride" or "goodbye," Ivan opened the car door, hopped out, and made a beeline for the house. He hoped Maggie's headache was better and she was out of bed, because what he had to say to her couldn't wait.

"Where's Maggie?" Ivan asked his mother when he spotted her washing the front windows in the living room. She'd obviously stayed home from the fabric store today. "I need to see Maggie right now!"

Mama turned to face him, her brows nearly squished together. "What's wrong, Ivan? Why are you home in the middle of the day? Did something happen at the harness shop?"

"No, nothing like that. Something happened at the restaurant in Arcola, though, and I need to speak with Maggie immediately."

"She's still in the guest room, awake but resting." She pointed at him. "Your face is red, Son, and there's sweat on your skin. Whatever is going on, I think you should calm down before going in to see Maggie."

"This can't wait, Mama. I have to see her now!" Ivan darted out of the room and ran down the hall. He paused a few seconds outside the guest room to catch his breath and think about the exact words he needed to say. The door was closed, and he thought about barging in without knocking, the way she had done to him on more than one occasion. Instead, he decided Mama was right—he did need to calm down. Ivan stood there, breathing in and out and telling himself to use the right choice of words while speaking to Maggie. He didn't want to shout, which would likely wake the baby if the little guy was sleeping.

Stephen's not my son, Ivan reminded himself. *But I've become attached to him nonetheless. If I call off the wedding, how would it affect the baby's future?*

When Ivan's brain felt like it was going to explode, he closed his fist and rapped lightly on the guest room door.

"Who's there?" Maggie called.

"It's Ivan."

"Oh, you're home early. Come on in."

Ivan took in one more breath and opened the door. When he entered the room, Ivan saw Maggie on the bed, atop the covers, with the baby cradled in her arms. It was a touching sight, but Ivan had come here on a mission, and he had to see it through.

"How come you're home so early?" Maggie questioned.

"I went to Arcola to deliver a harness, and while I was there, I learned something new about you."

"What did you learn?"

"I found out that the father of your child is Oba Miller, not me." Ivan was amazed at how steady he spoke, without a trace of anger in his voice.

Maggie's mouth opened wide. "Who told you that?"

"Does it matter?"

"Yes it does, because how do you know they weren't lying?"

Ivan's nails dug into his clenched palms. "Because it was my friend Toby who told me that you weren't with me the night of his party. It was Oba you hung out with that evening. It was Oba you left the party with too. Toby saw it with his own eyes, and he had no reason to lie about it, Maggie."

She averted her gaze, and then her chin began to quiver, like she might be about to cry.

"It's true, isn't it? Oba is Stephen's true father, not me. Right?"

She gave a slow nod; then tears poured forth.

Ivan stood patiently, waiting for Maggie's tears to subside. "Did Oba know you were expecting his baby?"

"Jah, I told him."

"Then why aren't you married to him?"

"Because," she answered, dabbing at the wetness beneath her eyes, "he refused to be responsible for me and the baby. He even denied it at first and said he wasn't with me the evening of the party."

"What did you do then?"

"I begged Oba to marry me, but he refused." She looked directly at

Ivan and pointed. "So I turned to you."

"Why me, Maggie? Why not some other fellow who was at the party?"

"I knew you were a nice guy. Someone had said that evening that they were surprised you were even at Toby's party."

"Yeah, me too," Ivan muttered. His gaze came to rest on the baby, and something stirred in his heart. With him and Maggie being on the threshold of marriage, Ivan did not know what to do. For the sake of the baby, should he marry Maggie anyway, even though he hadn't fathered her child? Under the circumstances, and to give little Stephen a home and a father's last name, wouldn't marrying the baby's mother be the right thing to do?

Chapter 35

"Would it be okay if I took a few days off from work?" Ivan asked his father Sunday morning as they were getting the horse and buggy ready to leave for church after breakfast.

Papa quirked an eyebrow. "How come?"

"I want to get away for a while, and I'd like to leave today, because I need time to be alone so I can think and pray about something important."

"Is it about you and Maggie?"

"Jah." Ivan hadn't told either of his parents what he'd found out yesterday, or that he'd confronted Maggie about it. This mess was his problem, and he needed to deal with it somehow. Even though Ivan had come to that conclusion, he was torn up inside and had only slept a few hours last night.

Papa put his hand on Ivan's shoulder. "Want to talk about it?"

Ivan gave a slow shake of his head. "I can't right now. Something came up yesterday, and I haven't fully decided what to do."

"Sounds serious." Papa lowered his hand and reached for the horse's bridle. "Maybe I can help with whatever it is."

"I appreciate the offer," Ivan said, "but this is a problem I need to deal with myself."

"All right, Son. I respect your wishes. Feel free to take Monday and Tuesday off, but I really do need you back in the harness shop by Wednesday."

"Okay, thanks, Papa. Hopefully by then, I'll have some sense of direction."

Arcola

Ivan had attended church service with his family, but as soon as the noon meal was over, he'd gone to one of their neighbors and called for a driver, because he was on a mission. Ivan could only hope that the person he wanted to talk to would listen. If not, then he would have a second stop to make.

When Ivan's driver, Sam, pulled up in front of the large two-story home, Ivan spotted Oba leading a horse into the barn.

"I'll be back," Ivan told Sam. "Hopefully, this won't take long." He opened the door and stepped out of the vehicle, then sprinted for the barn and popped in a few feet behind Oba.

"Hey, Oba, can I talk to you a few minutes?" Ivan called.

The young Amish man whirled around, squinting at Ivan. "You obviously know me, but I'm not sure I know you."

"I'm Ivan Yoder. We both attended a party here in Arcola almost a year ago."

Oba shrugged. "What of it? I've attended a lot of events in the last few years."

"The one that was put on by my friend Toby Schrock."

Oba reached under his black felt Sunday hat and scratched his head with his long fingers. "Jah, well—what about it?"

"You were there with Maggie Hertzler, right?"

Oba shrugged his broad shoulders. "Yeah, okay. So what?"

"She became pregnant that night—with your child."

Oba's face contorted as it turned a bright red color. "Did Maggie send you over here to plead her case? Is that what this visit is all about?"

"She has no idea I came to see you." Ivan shook his head.

"Then what are you here for?"

"I came to hopefully convince you to do what's right by Maggie and her baby boy. Have you even seen the child you fathered?"

Oba shook his head. "That's ridiculous. And what proof do you have that it's my child anyhow?"

"Maggie admitted it, and Toby said he'd seen you with Maggie the whole evening at his party. He also saw the two of you leave together."

Oba said nothing in response as he walked toward the back of the barn, leading his horse.

Ivan followed, matching the young man's strides to keep up. "You need to marry Maggie and make things right."

Still no reply.

When Oba entered the stall with his horse, Ivan went in with him. "I understand that your daed is one of the ministers in this church district."

"So what?"

"I have to wonder what he'd have to say if he knew you fathered a child and have refused to take responsibility for it." Ivan couldn't believe he was being so bold, but he was desperate to get through to this selfish, stubborn man.

Oba tapped his fingers along a bucket of feed. "My dad would make me marry the girl, that's for sure."

That's what I was prepared to do, Ivan thought. *Even though I had no recollection of having been with Maggie.*

"What then? Are you plannin' to tell my dad on me?" Oba stood quietly for several minutes, and then he exclaimed, "All right! I'll go over to Maggie's house and admit that I'm the baby's father. Then I'll ask her to marry me." He looked right at Ivan and held up one hand. "Does that satisfy you now?"

"Yes, it does, but there's something you should know."

"What's that?"

"Maggie doesn't live with her parents anymore. They kicked her out soon after she had the baby."

Oba's eyes widened. "Would they accept her back if she was married?"

"I don't know. Maybe."

"If I marry Maggie, we wouldn't have a place to stay till I could afford to buy or rent a house. We'd have to move in with one of our parents for a while."

"You'd better go talk to her then and make some decisions. Agreed?"

"Yeah, but if she's not livin' with her folks, where is she?"

"At my parents' house."

"What's she doin' there?" Oba questioned.

"It's a long story, and I don't have time to explain it all to you right now." Ivan pulled a stubby pencil and a small notepad from the pocket of his trousers. "I'll write down my parents' address, and if I were you, I'd head over there right now, before your folks get home from church. I assume that's where you and your family have been. Am I right?"

"Jah, but I left as soon as the service was over. Mom and Dad will probably be back shortly, though." He reached under his hat again and then lowered his hand. "A soon as you write down the address, I'll saddle my horse and ride over to your folks' place. I can get there faster that way." In a surprising gesture, Oba held his hand out toward Ivan.

Ivan gave it a hearty shake. A mixture of relief and apprehension flooded through Ivan, as he hadn't anticipated Oba's cooperation. He was ever so glad that Stephen's real father had listened to him and was ready to do the right thing.

Ivan wrote down his folks' address, told Oba goodbye, and got back into his driver's vehicle. "Sam, would you please take me one more place?"

Sam nodded. "That is what you hired me for, right?"

"Yes. I just wasn't sure things would work out the way I'd hoped here today."

Ivan felt the throb of his heartbeat. He sent up a quick prayer, hoping Oba would follow through and everything would work out for Maggie and her son. Now that things were settled with Oba, Ivan had one more important thing to do.

Shipshewana

It was getting close to bedtime, and Nathan had recently brought Emma home from a singing. This was the second time Emma had seen him socially, and she knew now that he wanted more than a casual relationship. He'd openly admitted to her this evening on the ride home that he was seriously thinking about moving to Shipshewana if he were to find a suitable wife. He'd even hinted that it might be her.

"Talk about a bold statement to make to a woman he barely knows," Emma murmured as she hung her outer garments on a wall peg near the front entrance. "That wife he's looking for won't be me," she determined. "Nathan would be better off going back to Pennsylvania and seeking someone there."

Emma could tell from the dimly lit house that her parents had already gone to bed. *Sure hope I didn't wake them. When I see Rachel later this week, I can't wait to tell her about the interesting date I had tonight. I bet she'll agree with me about Nathan being too bold.*

Emma was on the verge of turning out the gas lamp in the living room when she heard a car pull into the yard. *I wonder who that could be at this hour.* She rushed over to the window and peered out, but the moon wasn't bright enough to allow her a full view of the vehicle.

A few minutes later, there was a knock on the front door. *What should I do? Do I wake Mom and Dad?*

When the knocking persisted, Emma cautiously opened the front door, just a crack.

"Emma, it's me. I know it's late, but I need to talk to you right away, and it can't wait till tomorrow."

"Ivan?" Emma thought she must be hearing things. Surely Ivan would not be on her front porch at this hour. For that matter, she couldn't imagine why he'd be here at all.

"Please, Emma. Will you allow me to come inside?"

"It's late, and my parents are sleeping." Emma parted the door a little more. Oh, she wished it was still light outside so she could see his face more clearly. It didn't seem possible that he was even here right now, and she didn't understand the reason for it.

It was a chilly night, so Emma grabbed a jacket, slipped it on, and went out on the porch. Under the light of the moon, and standing closer to him now, she could see Ivan's face better, and her heart skipped a beat. "What are you doing here, Ivan?"

"I came to see you. There's something important I need to say." Ivan stood so close to Emma, she could feel his breath on her face.

"What could you possibly have to say that brought you all this way, and so late at night?" Emma's voice sounded strained, even to her own ears. "Does your wife know you're here? Surely you must have married Maggie by now."

Ivan clasped Emma's trembling hands. "Maggie and I are not married, Emma, and we're not planning to be."

Emma pulled away. "Why would you not marry the mother of your child? What kind of man are you, Ivan?"

"Emma, please listen. I'm not Stephen's father. When I questioned Maggie about it, she broke down and admitted that she was with some other fellow, not me, the night of my friend's party."

In disbelief, Emma backed away from Ivan, whirled around, and clasped the porch railing. "But you told me before that. . ."

"I said that I'd been drinking heavily that night and didn't remember being with Maggie." He moved to stand beside her. "You have to believe me, Emma. I would never walk away from Maggie and Stephen if I believed I was the baby's father. But I know now that I'm not, because I spoke to the man who owned up to having been with Maggie. His name is Oba, and he's agreed to accept responsibility for Maggie and the baby." Ivan leaned closer and said, "Don't you see, Emma—Maggie tricked me into believing that I had been with her at the party."

"Why would she do such a terrible thing?" Emma still wasn't fully convinced, although she wanted desperately to believe everything Ivan had said.

"Because soon after the baby was born, Maggie's parents had told her to leave their house. When Maggie first approached Oba, he turned his back on her. She would've had to raise Stephen on her own, and Maggie was desperate. So she convinced me that I was the one responsible for getting her pregnant. But now, all that has changed."

Emma stood in stunned silence, trying to process all that Ivan had said and wondering how to respond. She wanted desperately to express to Ivan that she had secretly hoped to see him again, but the words wouldn't come.

"I just needed to tell you. I don't expect you to take me back, but you deserved to hear the truth." Ivan took hold of Emma's hand again, gently squeezing her fingers. "I'm here now, asking forgiveness for all that I put you through. And for no good reason," he added.

"There was a good reason," Emma assured him. "You believed what Maggie said was true, and you did what you knew was right by agreeing to marry her and help raise the baby. You felt that you had no choice, which is why you broke up with me." She paused to gain control of her swirling emotions. "As much as it hurt when our relationship ended, I had to accept it and move on with my life."

"Have you moved on, Emma? Were you able to forget about the feelings we had for each other?"

"I tried to," she admitted. "But the memory of the times we spent together was never far from my mind."

"I thought about you a lot too, even though I knew that I shouldn't." Ivan released Emma's hand and pulled her close to his side. "I'm sorry for everything, Emma. Will you forgive me for all that I put you through?"

Emma leaned her head on Ivan's shoulder. "You only did what you thought was right, and that's an admirable quality. Maggie was the one in the wrong, Ivan. She should not have lied about who the baby's father was. I'm sure she felt desperate, but what she did was dishonest."

"You're right," he agreed, "but I was also at fault, because I should not have been at my friend's party that night where there was drinking. And most definitely, I shouldn't have been under the influence of alcohol." Ivan groaned. "I wish there was a way to let all Amish young people know that their time of rumspringa should not have to include alcohol or taking part in wild parties."

"I agree, Ivan, but unfortunately, some people have to learn things the hard way."

"Jah, and I guess I was one of them," Ivan responded. "Anyway, I have chosen to forgive Maggie for lying to me. I hope you will too. What she did was terrible, but I understand why she did it, and I don't hold it against her. It'd be frightening for any young woman to raise a child on her own, especially when they've lost the support of their family."

Emma thought about the words of Luke 6:37, and she quoted them to Ivan: "Judge not, and ye shall not be judged: condemn not, and ye shall not be condemned: forgive, and ye shall be forgiven."

"Exactly, Emma. It is not our place to judge Maggie, or Oba, or even Maggie's parents. Each of them must ask God's forgiveness for what they've done and make it right with the ones they have hurt."

They stood quietly for a few minutes, until Ivan spoke again. "If you're okay with it, I would really like for us to start over, Emma."

"I'd like that too, Ivan, but you live in Arthur, and your family does as well. Also, you have a job at your father's harness shop," Emma stated. "And as you know, my family lives here. We both are aware that a long-distance courtship would be difficult for us to manage."

"It wouldn't have to be long-distance," Ivan stated. "I could move here to Shipshewana and find another job. Then we could see each other often and make plans for our future together." He turned to face Emma and brought her close. "It might seem like it's too soon to ask this question, but when the time is right, would you do me the honor of becoming my wife?"

"Oh yes, Ivan, I would be more than willing to marry you, after we've courted a bit longer." She smiled. "Otherwise, our parents might object."

"I have to admit that my folks may not be thrilled about the prospect of me leaving Arthur and moving here, but they know how much I love you, and I feel sure that they will give us their blessing."

"Same with my parents," Emma said, struggling not to give in to the tears pushing the back of her eyes. She'd never dreamed that things would turn out this way. She'd been convinced that she had lost Ivan forever and didn't think she could ever love any other man the way she did him.

Emma closed her eyes and silently prayed: *Thank You, God, for this unexpected turn of events. I look forward to seeing what plans You have for me and Ivan in the days ahead. And please, Lord, help us to remember to seek Your will in all things.*

When Emma's prayer ended and she opened her eyes, Ivan lifted her chin, lowered his head, and kissed her tenderly on the lips. "I will love you with every ounce of my being, Emma, right up until the day I die."

Leaning into Ivan's loving embrace, Emma hoped that day would not come for a long, long time. But she would not waste precious time worrying about it. The uncertainty of where her future would lead faded away, leaving nothing but Ivan's comfort and assurance that he'd forever hold Emma in his heart. However many days God gave them to be together, she would cherish each and every one.

Epilogue

Two years later

EMMA SAT AT HER TREADLE sewing machine, thinking about Ivan and how the Lord had blessed them since their marriage a year ago. She felt thankful for a loving husband who didn't mind if supper was late sometimes because she'd been busy making a new quilted item or teaching a friend or family member how to quilt.

Emma paused from her sewing and tipped her head to one side, believing that she'd heard her baby girl fussing in the next room.

A few seconds passed, and Emma identified the noise she'd heard when her dog, Fawn, plodded into the room, panting and whimpering pathetically.

"What do you want, Fawn? Is your water dish empty?"

Fawn let out a few barks, and Emma put a finger to her lips. "Shh. . .you'll wake the baby."

Emma rose from her chair and headed for the kitchen, with Fawn right at her heels. After filling the dish with water, Emma left the room and went to check on her sweet baby girl. Seeing that the infant was still asleep, Emma quietly left the room and headed back to the sewing machine.

When the lovely clock on the mantel chimed, Emma looked up and smiled. It was not a clock that Ivan had repaired—this was one he'd created from scratch, and it kept perfect time. In fact, Ivan had become so good at making and repairing clocks, he'd been able to open his own business. Between what he made in his new venture and what Emma made teaching and selling quilts, they were able to manage financially, both doing what they loved in the process.

As she glanced around the room, Emma's gaze fell upon the blue ribbon attached to the first quilt she had completed that had won a first-place prize in a quilting contest. Emma found it hard to imagine that just a few years ago, she believed she would never be able to stitch together her own quilt, but Emma had since made several quilts with different patterns. She recalled the moment Ivan's mother had laid eyes on her finished quilt for the first time, and how pleased her dear mother-in-law had been with Emma's quilting talents. Emma was thankful for everything she had learned from Ida Mae, and she could now teach others who were new to quilting.

It was a beginner's quilt that made me want to stick with quilting, Emma mused. *But the Tree of Life pattern was more than that to me. It represented the Tree of Knowledge of Good and Evil mentioned in the Bible, and it was also a reminder that I always need to put God first in everything and trust Him no matter what the future holds for me, Ivan, and our daughter.*

Emma sighed with contentment and thanked God for all He had given them, and she promised to be faithful and trust Him all the days of her life.

Emma's Speedy Brownies

Ingredients:

2 cups sugar
½ cup cocoa powder
5 eggs
1 teaspoon vanilla
1¾ cups flour
1 teaspoon salt
1 cup vegetable oil of choice
1 cup semisweet chocolate chips

Instructions:

Preheat oven to 350 degrees. In mixing bowl, combine all ingredients except chocolate chips. Beat until smooth. Pour batter into greased 9"x13" pan. Sprinkle with chocolate chips. Bake 30 minutes or until toothpick inserted near center comes out clean. Cool on wire rack.

Author's Note

I hope you enjoyed Emma Bontrager's story in *The Beginner's Quilt*. This novel is a prequel to my *Half-Stitched Amish Quilting Club* book, which later became a musical play. Following that novel, I wrote two more books about Emma and her quilting adventures—*The Tattered Quilt* and *The Healing Quilt*. After writing those three books, while Emma was in her sixties, I began to wonder what she was like when she was a young woman and how she became a quilter, capable of teaching others the art of quilting. In Book 1, Emma was a widow, filled with fond memories of her first husband. I was also curious about how Emma met Ivan, and what had made him so special. I eventually concluded that Emma and Ivan's story needed to be told. And if you haven't read the series where Emma is older and teaches others to quilt, then I hope you will find and enjoy those three books as well.

Many Blessings,
Wanda Brunstetter

New York Times bestselling and award-winning author Wanda E. Brunstetter is one of the founders of the Amish fiction genre. She has written more than one hundred books, with several translated in other languages. With over twelve million copies sold, Wanda's stories consistently earn spots on the nation's most prestigious bestseller lists and have received numerous awards.

Wanda's ancestors were part of the Anabaptist faith, and her novels are based on personal research intended to accurately portray the Amish way of life. Her books are read and trusted by many Amish people, who credit her for giving readers a deeper understanding of the people and their customs.

When Wanda visits her Amish friends, she finds herself drawn to their peaceful lifestyle, sincerity, and close family ties. Wanda enjoys photography, ventriloquism, gardening, bird-watching, beachcombing, and spending time with her family. She has been blessed with two grown children, six grandchildren, and four great-grandchildren.

To learn more about Wanda, visit her website at www.wandabrunstetter.com.